NEPHILIM'S HEX

TIMELESSNESS
BOOK 3

SUSANA IMAGINÁRIO

ISBN: 978-1-9161402-8-8 (hardback)
ISBN: 978-1-9161402-7-1 (paperback)
ISBN: 978-1-9161402-6-4 (ebook)

For the Wyrd

Some gods rule over their worlds. Others are part of the fabric of the Universe where those worlds exist.

Chronos – God of Time – was the first, or so he claims; Kali – Goddess of Death – disagrees, whilst Gaea – Goddess of Life – appeared much later.

Where the Three came from, who knows? Perhaps forces more ancient and powerful than these primordial Gods exist out there.

Some things are not worth considering, for sanity's sake…

Only when sanity is no longer a concern will we finally understand the Universe and its Gods.

INTERLUDE 0

The Voices in Your Head

The night is dark – as all nights are on worlds with no moons. I wonder why that is. After all, moons, when compared with worlds, are easy to create, and moonlight can be a powerful asset for both gods and mortals. But what do I care? Niflheim is not my world. I have no interest in witchcraft, and I can see just fine in the dark.

I lean against the door frame of Ulcan's cabin, gazing at the stars while Aedan laconically explains our current situation to a reluctant audience. It's a wasted effort, really. The hunter, sat precariously on a rickety chair, stares at the bottle in his hand, too drunk to appreciate the significance of Aedan's words; Ulla, curled up on the bed, is too consumed with grief and horror to even hear a word he says; and Pan, the one who convinced us to come here in the first place, only pretends to listen. I can hear him humming to himself, thinking about his favourite nymph. As for me… Well, I suppose I'm not paying much attention to what the Dharkan is saying either, but it's only because I already know the story and I'd rather stare at my beloved stars, or more precisely at their light, shining across the vast Universe millennia after their deaths.

Like me, I think mournfully, then summon my temper to push the thought away. This is not the time for melancholia or regret. Besides, I'm more alive now than I've ever been. I am a goddess. I must start thinking like one. Damnation! I only did what I had to do. If I can will away the dirt, blood and seed from my skin, why can't I erase their memory as well? Hephaestus is dead, and yet it's as if he still lives inside my mind.

Memories are like starlight; they too take a long time to fade, it seems.

I curse them and their goddess. Where is Mnemosyne when I need her? Fucking bitch. She took away memories I probably cherished and left my mind filled with the corrupted memories of another. The least she could do now is take away these as well since it's because of her I'm in this mess. Her and Prometheus and Zeus and –

It's a long list of culprits…

I bite the inside of my cheek and curse at the absurdity of this habit. Developed back when I was a mortal out of frustration for being forced to remain passive – smiling, even! – while others dictated my fate, it should have been abandoned the moment I became a deity, and yet here I am, still hurting myself in private, leaving marks where others can't see them, all for the sake of propriety. At least now my cheeks heal almost immediately. The faint taste of blood lingers on my tongue, but not the pain. If only the mind healed as quickly!

A moth enters the cabin. It flies straight to the darkest corner, ignoring the lantern on the table. A chill runs down my spine. Stars, I need to pull myself together.

'*Psyche…*' A voice echoes timidly through my Reach, jolting memories, emotions, grievances. Too many of them.

I can't deal with this right now on top of everything else, so I pretend not to listen.

'*I know you can hear me,*' the voice says.

I remain silent, staring at the night sky.

'*You can't ignore me forever.*'

Yes, I can, I growl to myself.

'*You did well.*'

I bite my cheek again. *I swear, I'll take his soul. I'll find a way. I'll shred it to bits. Even if it's the last thing I do!*

'*Thank you…*' the voice whispers.

I take a deep breath, then stop breathing altogether. After all, it's not like I need to. I'm not mortal anymore. Gods only breathe when they are angry or afraid. Fear is useless; there's no point in fearing the inevitable, and anger gets you in trouble every –

"Psyche, would you mind?" Pan asks, pointing at the empty bottle in Ulcan's hand.

You've got to be kidding me. The nerve of him to ask me to indulge the hunter's habit! Sure, most gods can conjure potations at will, but I'm the goddess of the soul. I create ideas and inspiration, not spirits, for fuck's sake. *I'll teach him to respect my talents.* I'm about to fill the bottle with piss when another fills it with mead.

'*You're welcome,*' the voice says.

Get out of my head! I shout telepathically.

'*Ah, so you can hear me.*' The tone implies both relief and amusement.

Fuck...

As I was saying, anger gets you in trouble every fucking time.

I look at the night sky, cursing all emotions, and notice one star shines brighter and closer than the others. *That's odd.*

'*They're coming,*' the voice says.

It's too soon. We're not ready yet.

'*Will we ever be?*'

I suppose not...

I close my eyes, unable to sustain the anger for much longer. *Leave me alone...*

'*As you will, Butterfly.*'

CHAPTER 1

Iva

Iva stood by the caustic shore of the Boiling Lake, staring in disbelief as Aedan walked away from her. He didn't even look back.

She'd offered him everything: power, leadership, revenge… herself. And he'd simply walked away. In his wake, surrounded by dozens of Dharkan faithful to her cause, she'd never felt so humiliated and alone.

Coward. Traitor. How could he!

'*I warned you,*' her goddess said inside her mind. '*Aedan is weak. He lost his way long ago.*'

Gods, always so keen to offer righteous wisdom instead of comfort.

You were the one who encouraged me to bring him back into the fold, Iva said to the soul she resentfully hosted.

Annoyance radiated through their bond. '*And things would be much easier had you succeeded. It's no wonder you failed. You've lost touch with your femininity, Iva. You should have seduced him as I suggested, instead of trying to persuade him with the truth. Seduction always works best on men.*'

Not with him, Iva thought grudgingly. At least, not until recently. What could the dryad have had that she didn't?

'*Not what, whom,*' the goddess replied. Annoyance turned to something dangerously close to envy.

"He always was an honourable prick, wasn't he?" Emil asked rhetorically.

Inhale… "That's not honour. That's…" *Exhale.* "I don't know what it is," Iva admitted. "It's like he's under a spell or something. Perhaps he's hosting as well? I mean, you saw the lightning…" Her body still stung with the memory of it. "Such power has to come from somewhere. Could he be hosting Zeus without realising?"

Emil scoffed. "If anything of Zeus' will remained in Aedan, he would have taken you and the Dharkan in a heartbeat. Nah, if I didn't know better, I'd say he's in love." He laughed at his own words.

"In lust, you mean," Iva sneered.

Emil shrugged. "Love, lust… just two sides of the same curse, really."

Iva frowned at him. "Oh, are they? And what do you know about it?"

Emil was just a boy, or had been when this campaign started. He still hadn't taken any of the captives to her knowledge. And no Dharkan had claimed him either. She'd made sure of that.

"Everything," he said with a predatory smile. Her legs trembled at the sight. Then again, they hadn't been particularly stable since the lightning strike. "Love is the most powerful force in the Universe. The only thing able to alter fate and bring both gods and mortals to their knees. Always remember that." The reminder was uttered as a threat.

"Tsk," Iva said, pretending to dismiss it. To listen to him or any Dharkan talk about love was ludicrous. They were creatures of passion, not sentiment.

"So what now?" Emil asked casually. He kept throwing Persephone's box up in the air and catching it. The motion, along with the clapping sound it made every time he caught it, did nothing to improve Iva's nerves.

"Be careful with that thing," she hissed.

"I am," he said smugly, throwing the box higher in defiance of her mood.

Iva forced herself to breathe, sucking air in and out of her chest the way her goddess often instructed. She failed to understand the benefits of the activity for a Dharkan, for whom breathing was futile. At most, the effort kept her mind engaged on something besides the need to express her urges. Burning sun, Emil resembled his older brother so much it hurt Iva to even look at the boy. She wanted to do to him all the things she yearned to do to Aedan, starting with ripping off his clothes and lashing him with a whip until he begged for her mercy.

"If only looks could fuck." He smirked, obviously guessing her thoughts. "You should do something about all that pent-up passion, Iva."

"What are you suggesting?"

"Put it to good use." He winked.

Her eyes widened at the prospect.

"Er... Mistress?"

With some effort, Iva peeled her gaze from Emil to

focus on Asher, one of her followers with ambitions to take her leadership for himself. "Yes, what is it?"

"What do we do now?"

The question offended her. Still, she mustn't forget herself in front of her faithful. Not now, not after she'd been so thoroughly humiliated by her rival. She cleared her throat. "The plan remains the same. We march to Portum."

Asher made a face. She'd seen it too often lately.

"Is there a problem?"

"Pardon, mistress, but... considering recent events, we can assume our arrival will be expected there. Shouldn't we go straight to Relicum instead?"

"Portum has fewer guards."

"Portum has fewer lives," Asher said meaningfully.

"Portum's been badly affected by the storm. It has no defences. Most of its inhabitants are women sheltering at the temple, which should be full since the Tribute didn't happen. They are easy prey." She spoke in a similar meaningful tone, then raised her voice to the rest of her followers, who were listening expectantly.

"You may all feel invincible right now with a god's Prana running through your veins, but you must get accustomed to your new power before you can use it, and I need to know exactly what's burning down in Relicum before facing that fire. I want no more surprises. The Suzerain may be gone, but don't expect the living to make things easy for us. We take Portum, we take away their primary route of escape to the forest. They'll be caught between us and the Shadow."

"Good plan," Emil said, throwing the box up in the air again. Asher nodded dutifully, clearly unconvinced.

She scowled at them both. "If that thing breaks, Emil –"

"It won't." Emil threw it one more time before putting it away somewhere inside his cloak. He wore nothing underneath it, and Iva had to refrain from biting her lip at the glimpse of exquisitely well-defined muscles around his navel.

Why does he get to keep it? she asked her goddess.

'It was his bargain; it's his responsibility.'

It's my prize.

'You don't want that prize. Trust me.'

Iva had tried to trust Freya. It wasn't easy. The relationship between the Dharkan and their guests was a complicated one – as most relationships involving two minds sharing one body are. Honesty and mutual respect were crucial to making them work, and Freya had too many secrets for Iva's liking. For example, she'd struck a bargain with some foreign god without consulting her and wouldn't even tell her who he was. He had to be a powerful god indeed to make Emil mature so fast. She worried that the boy was not entirely in control of his guest either.

"Very well, I'll meet you in Portum," Emil said, hoisting a bag to his shoulder.

"Where do you think you're going?" she asked, taken aback.

"I need to run an errand for my guest," he said, as if it were the most obvious thing in the land.

"Who is the god hiding inside you, brother?" If the goddess wouldn't tell her, well, she'd ask him straight, burn it.

He tutted. "Come now, *sister*. You know it's not polite to ask such things to one of our kind. You keep your goddess's secrets, I keep mine."

Burn the gods and their secrets, Iva thought resentfully. This would be the last time she hosted. She had Ambrosia now, so she had no need for gods or their souls. Just like she had no need for Aedan or followers either.

"Goodbye, gorgeous." Emil grabbed the back of Iva's neck, pulled her face to his and kissed her on the lips. This caught her by surprise, even more so as she kissed him back passionately.

"Er… What about *her*?" Asher asked, interrupting the kiss and pointing at Persephone's shrivelled form defrosting at their feet.

"Throw her in the lake. Let her body return to the Underworld, where it belongs," Emil suggested spitefully before he took off, whistling cheerfully to himself.

Iva watched, mouth slightly agape, as the young Dharkan swayed his way down the hill, more stricken by that kiss than she'd been by Aedan's lightning.

Goddess, who is this creature haunting Emil? Goddess? Freya!

The goddess had retreated from her awareness, feeling – for lack of a better term – breathless.

"Asher," Iva called.

He turned around slowly. "Yes, mistress?"

"Come with me."

CHAPTER 2

Loki

Loki left Hephaestus' smithy with something dangerously close to a heavy conscience. Not because he'd
killed the Olympian; Loki would never feel guilty for
any action which ensured his survival. Besides, the
Blacksmith had it coming. Clearly, he had not been the
only god to commission Hephaestus' work. There were
enough weapons piled against the smithy's volcanic
walls to supply an army. Which one, and for what purpose? The Blacksmith's charred remains still burned
on the forge, but it was too late to ask him now. Once
again Loki had let his anger interfere with his genius.

*Hel, don't let the bastard get too comfortable; he still has
a lot to answer for. Hel?*

There was no reply, nor even a sign that his message got through to her. He cursed. Hel should really
work on her communication skills. Maybe it was for
the best. She had a lot on her plate at the moment. Loki
winced at the memory of Apollo and Artemis held
powerless inside the vault.

'You'll get what you deserve,' the oracle had prophesied. If true, Loki would be the first to receive such

treatment, for fairness was not a tenet the Universe had been built on.

The prophecy was vague – as all prophecies are – conveniently open to interpretation until *after* the prophesied events took place. He understood why mortals believed in such nonsense. After all, Prometheus made them predisposed to believe the improbable and the magical, so they could easily believe in the gods and obey them. Gods, on the other hand, were not particularly inclined to believe in anything, especially other gods. Oracles, though... those were another matter entirely. Their talents were connected to fate, and the Fates to the fabric of the Universe. Their messages were not to be taken lightly.

Loki strode across the pitch-black forest, slapping the long blade of the dagger repeatedly against his thigh as his mind reeled.

And what did he deserve, exactly? Ask ten creatures, they'd have ten different answers. Still, all would agree it would have to be something terrible. He glanced at the dagger in his hand again and had to fight the urge to cut himself with it. Well, he'd gotten what he wanted, at least. He regretted what it had cost but took comfort in the fact he would put it to good use, and hopefully by the time he was done, there would be no one left with a grudge to give him what he deserved.

Loki froze in his tracks when he noticed the building ahead. He'd absent-mindedly half walked, half teleported to a cabin in the forest, guided by the inexorable pull of an ancient curse. *What he deserved, indeed.*

He'd endured much in his long existence: torture,

grief, hate, loneliness, anger. So much anger! And still the worst punishments he ever received were the ones he inflicted on himself. Let the oracle try to topple that. He gripped the dagger harder. *Bring it on.*

There was quite the gathering inside the hunter's cabin: two deities – well, one deity and one Wyrd – a dryad, a Narrum and a Dharkan with barely an arm span between them. They were all exhausted, on edge, and annoyed with each other. Something was bound to go wrong soon.

Surprisingly, Aedan was the only one talking. The Dharkan rarely talked, not even in his thoughts, which was why Loki chose him as a host in the first place. Now he almost sounded like Odin, reiterating events and laying down plans with clever words. As if taking Zeus' ability to control lightning had not been troublesome enough. The truth was, Loki was becoming increasingly concerned with Hel and her creations. Their talents, so useful to the gods, could easily be used as weapons against them. As a father and one of the most despised gods outside the Underworlds, Loki could only hope Hel handled her mistakes better than he had.

Loki turned into a moth and fluttered inside – he just could not help himself.

The goddess of the soul stiffened, aware of his presence, but kept her eyes on the sky, her mind a fortress designed specifically to keep the likes of him out.

What I deserve, he thought bitterly. *What if what I deserve doesn't deserve me?*

CHAPTER 3

Iva / Freya

Iva had just taught a lesson in leadership to Asher when she heard the loud crash. Commotion followed.

"What now," she groaned. Between Freya constantly interrupting her thoughts, the demands of leadership, and the restless living of Aegea, she rarely had a moment to herself these days.

"Sounds important," Asher said, not particularly disturbed himself.

Burn it. It really did. Another crash followed. She stood up and tied the remnants of her clothes around herself as best she could. After being scorched by Aedan's lightning, then torn to shreds during the vigorous humping, her attire resembled something a tree hugger would wear. She'd have to find more suitable raiments soon, or come daylight, not even Ambrosia would spare her the sunburn.

"Stay here. We're not done yet," she ordered. There was plenty of time before dawn, and Iva still had a lot left to teach him.

Asher nodded obediently, all notions of leadership drained out of him.

She strode up to the hill above the lake, her sight set on the clear sky, searching for the source of the thunder. No, not thunder, she realised – timber. Her gaze shifted to the forest below. Someone, or something, was knocking down the trees, too fast to be using an axe and too neatly to be the result of a cataclysm.

"What in the flaming light is doing *that*?" she wondered aloud.

"Some god trying to intimidate us, you think?" one of her followers suggested. He was wearing a daisy behind his ear.

"Or a monstrous beast showing off," another replied. This one had a crown of daffodils on his head.

Iva blinked at them. "What's this?" She ripped off the flower arrangement from the latter and shoved it in his face.

"Flowers," he said meekly.

Iva inhaled deeply. "I can see that. Why are they on your head?"

Both Dharkan exchanged confused glances, then looked back at the others. To Iva's aggravation, almost all her followers had flowers on them.

"I don't know, mistress…" the one with the daisy behind his ear said in an apologetic tone. "It seemed like a good idea. We never noticed how pretty they were before."

Far away, another tree fell. Iva barely noticed it. Her attention was on the Dharkan and their newly found absurd obsession.

"It's what you get for feeding on a goddess of spring," said a cold, familiar voice.

The Dharkan turned in the speaker's direction, gasped, then abased themselves.

"Stand up, fools," Iva hissed.

"But –" one fool protested.

Iva slapped him.

"I said stand. Hel's not your goddess. Not anymore," Iva stated defiantly to the goddess in question.

Hel showed her teeth in a disgusted snarl, then stopped a few inches away from Iva, looking her up and down, the snarl deepening. "The state of you," she chided, shaking her head to emphasise her disapproval. "And to think I once considered you as a host."

Iva spat a bitter laugh. "Your loss – goddess. It's too late now. I already host a god's soul. A better soul."

"I figured as much." Hel turned to their audience. "Leave us. All of you. This is between your leader and me."

The Dharkan lowered their heads and began to retreat.

"You take orders from me, not her," Iva protested.

The Dharkan halted, their spirits withering as fast as the flowers on them with the sudden drop in temperature.

Hel stepped closer to Iva. "Do not push me, creature. Causing havoc in my world is one thing. Killing gods and conspiring with rival deities against your creator, quite another. This little rebellion ends now."

The words were ice shards in her ears. Still, Iva didn't flinch. "You don't scare me, and you can't harm me, either," she said proudly.

"Are you certain?"

"I am." Iva stared into Hel's freezing gaze levelly. An arctic silence followed. The Dharkan shuffled away.

Hel narrowed her eyes. "I see. In that case, I demand to talk to the one behind this farce."

Iva smiled smugly. "Come now, you know that's against the rules."

Hel shifted to her true form: half her face icy perfection, the other death incarnate. Behind them, the Boiling Lake stopped bubbling. Instead of mist, frost now crept over the volcanic shingle around its shore. "I made the rules. I can break them," Hel said. "Now show yourself!"

Instead of telling the goddess of the dead to go burn in Tartarus, as she intended, Iva felt herself faint. She remained conscious but was seemingly locked out of her own body. She couldn't move or speak of her own free will.

Freya, you can't! This shouldn't be possible. Dharkan were vessels for gods' souls, not their puppets like the living or cursed like the Wyrd.

The goddess didn't reply to her. She addressed Hel instead.

"You shouldn't have sent a man to do a goddess's work, girl."

Hel scowled. "Freya." She spat the name. "I should have known."

"Yes, you should have. But you didn't. Your creations are perfect to hide in, I'll give you that." Iva heard herself speak the words she did not intend to say in a voice not her own. Fear wormed inside her, along with a sense of revulsion – hers or Freya's, she really couldn't tell the difference at this point.

"You just earned yourself a place by Odin's side in Helheim," Hel said.

"Is that where the idiot is now?" Freya laughed. "It was just a matter of time, I suppose. Like father, like son. If only he'd followed my advice."

"Oh, but he did. Odin constantly engaged in breathing exercises to calm himself. He breathed better than most mortals. His temper, however, remained unchanged."

"That's unfortunate," Freya said cynically. "Still, to take me to him, you'll need to get hold of my soul first. Good luck with that."

"And why would I need luck when I can simply ask the goddess of the soul to rip it out of your host and throw it in the Underworld as she did to Odin?"

"Ah, yes. I heard you have Psyche under your thumb. Or is it the other way around?" Iva's head tilted petulantly.

Ice cracked at their feet. "Do not test my patience, Freya. I really don't have time to indulge you in this fancy. I have an entire world and the souls of two Underworlds to attend to. Can you grasp how much responsibility that is?"

The question brought Freya's emotions to a boiling point. Iva actually felt her blood burn as if she were under the light of the banished blue sun.

Goddess, calm. Remember: Inhale –

A sharp pain bloomed behind Iva's eyes. She couldn't see, couldn't think, all she could do was scream inwardly.

"What do you expect to gain from this, hmm?" Hel asked.

"What is rightfully mine," Freya said.

"Is this about Baldur again? For what it's worth, Loki had nothing to do with –"

Freya's composure cracked under her emotions. "This is about *me* and what you've stolen from me!"

Hel grew very still. The intensity of the rage and power coming from her was such that had Iva any control over herself, she'd be running for the hills.

"Niflheim is mine." Hel said coldly, and the entire world rumbled in agreement.

Freya scoffed. "You can keep your frozen husk of a world. I don't want it. Especially now that it's contaminated with Olympian scum."

"So why burn my patience with this?"

"You know exactly why! The souls."

Hel rolled her eyes. "Flaming light… Still?"

"Always!" Freya shrieked.

"Poor Freya, not getting enough adoration lately?" Hel shook her head and began counting on her fingers. "You already claim the titles of goddess of beauty, sex, gold, war, magic – am I missing something? – and you want to be goddess of the dead as well? Is there no end to your greed? Look at yourself! Look at what you've done to your host. You have no talent for the dead, never mind their souls!"

"I have the right," Freya insisted.

"Oh, shut up. I've had enough of this ash." Hel turned her back to her and started to walk away.

Freya's outrage was like shards of the blue sun piercing Iva's mind. She followed, cutting in front of the icy goddess. "I *do* have the right! I earned it when I married Odin. Warriors who die gloriously in battle go to Valhalla and the rest to Folkvangr. You've been stealing souls from me for millennia, keeping them on ice, for whatever twisted purpose. You've even kept my favourite son! I'm tired of waiting for justice, and since Odin got himself cursed, I'm taking matters into my own hands."

"Baldur's soul came to me freely! It was his choice. Same as the others."

Freya bristled. "And it was your choice to keep him from me. How can a sun god be happier in the dark than in the company of his own mother? How can any soul prefer your realm of ice and shadow to my sunny meadow? Only the souls of those who don't know any better. For *I am* better!" Freya bashed Iva's chest painfully as she spoke. "You tricked them somehow. You and your perverted father. I know you did."

"You dare to accuse me of deceiving the souls under my care?" Hel enunciated each word slowly between clenched teeth.

"I certainly do."

"I am not my father!" Hel's eyes turned blue as she shouted the words, making her look and sound very much like him.

Freya inhaled deeply. "I guess not, for even Loki has more sense than you. You've stretched yourself too thin, goddess of the dead. One foot in this realm, the other on the other side. You said it yourself, an entire world and two Underworlds is too much for one god to handle. Look around: Aegea is in shambles, and the souls in the Underworld are suffering. I can feel their misery from up here."

"Aegea was not my doing. But it's still my responsibility, and I will not give up a single soul to you, dead or otherwise."

"This land and your affiliation with Hades will destroy Niflheim along with every soul in it," Freya said ruefully, then feigned enlightenment. "On second thought, you two are perfect for each other, since he too has no talent to rule a realm. Now, give back my souls and I'll return the Dharkan to you. No one else needs to get hurt. You can even keep the flimsy spirits of the dryads and other inferior Olympian creatures for company in your lover's Underworld."

Hel crossed her arms. "And if I refuse?"

Freya faked a smile. "One of my talents is war, remember?"

Hel snorted. "You arrogant bitch. I'm not your enemy. Not yet. And you do not want me as such."

"You sure act like my enemy."

"You're making a huge mistake," Hel said.

"Time will tell," Freya replied righteously.

"Time already has." Hel leaned closer. "Listen to me very carefully, Freya. This is *my* world. Loki and I created it together, for us, for *our* family. The family you and Odin scorned. I don't pick the souls who live here or in Helheim. They pick me. They found their way to me because they know I protect my souls, not smother them. Many gods prefer to be at peace rather than surrounded by nagging worshippers, scrabbling for attention, believe it or not. Unlike you, they've had enough of that during their existence. I will never – ever! – give up my souls to you or any other god. Chronos himself cannot take them away from me. Are we clear?"

Freya lifted her chin. "We will see."

Hel's lips parted in disbelief. Then she shook her head. "You know what: fine! You want my souls, you'll have to convince them to leave my realm. Good luck with that," she sneered in imitation of Freya's tone previously. "I'm done with you." Hel rubbed her hands together and gave Iva an imaginary shove. The rude gesture was meant as a curse cast on those unworthy of a god's attention.

Iva was familiar with rage. The gods knew she'd felt it often enough. What she felt now barely compared. Freya screeched at the insult and launched herself at Hel's face, clawing it in ways to put a cat to shame. Caught off guard, Hel retaliated in kind. She scratched Iva's face and saw the deep gashes heal before her eyes. The healing too slow and natural to have been induced by a god's will.

"Flames! Freya, what have you done?" Hel gasped, the fury draining out of her.

"What you were too selfish to do," Freya said proudly. "Iva found out about the Ambrosia. She figured there had to be a good reason for you to allow the Goddess of Life into Niflheim so often. You should have picked her as your host. Imagine her disappointment when she realised you had no intention of giving the resin to the Dharkan. That's when she prayed to me. And if not for the incident with those loggers, I would have given immortality to the dead long ago. Because I, unlike you, am a fair goddess. You, *Hela*, don't even deserve your own creations," Freya said spitefully.

Hel smiled, a genuine, self-content smile. "And you

should have chosen a less ambitious host, Freya. Ambrosia was never meant for the Dharkan, and it's certainly not meant for gods."

Freya frowned. "What do you mean?"

"You'll find out soon enough." Hel laughed. The surrounding ice melted away.

Both Freya and Iva shared a moment of apprehension. To a god, ignorance was not bliss but a threat to their very existence.

"Oh, and by the way, you heard that, right?" Hel pointed in the direction the trees had been falling. They weren't falling anymore, and Iva had no idea when or why they had stopped. The entire forest was silent now. Too silent.

"Your little ploy with Persephone caused a breach in Tartarus. There's a primordial beast loose in Aegea," Hel said.

"Which one?" Freya tried and failed to hide the alarm in Iva's voice. If there was one thing they both knew about the creatures imprisoned in Tartarus, it was that each and every one of them had been sent there because they had the potential to harm gods.

"A big bad one." Hel spoke in spooky childish tones. "It's probably after what you've stolen. Now, if you'll excuse me, I need to take care of important matters. I'll make sure to send the beast your way before putting it back in its cage. Then we'll see just how well Ambrosia works on the Dharkan." Hel faded away, her laughter echoing after her.

Flaming sun, Freya, Iva thought, *Persephone was supposed to bring a sample of the blood, not the whole creature! Is this your doing or that of the god in Emil?*

Freya cursed, but she didn't answer. Her focus was still on Hel. In Iva's body, she couldn't follow the goddess. Flesh had its disadvantages, after all, the lack of translocation being one of the most inconvenient. A soulless Dharkan was able to travel the bridge between realms, but her own soul couldn't will its host to translocate even across the land. Had Hel made it so intentionally? Probably, the bitch. There was no way around it. Freya would have to abandon her host to confront the goddess of the dead on even ground and settle their differences once and for all. She'd had enough of the hiding and subterfuge. Hel had been right about one thing: they had no time for this; the Nephilim's ship was about to land. She had to take control of the situation now.

Freya willed herself free of Iva's body. Nothing happened.

She tried to leave again, and again she failed.

'*Iva! Stop being stubborn. Let me go.*'

I'm not! Ash, I want you gone after what you just did to me. I won't tolerate being used like this. Go, and never ask me to host you again. You're not welcome!

But Freya couldn't leave Iva's body, no matter how hard she willed it.

You'll find out soon enough. Hel's mocking words echoed in both Iva's and Freya's minds.

They screamed.

∞

Iva stumbled her way back to Asher on unstable legs. He was still lying down, holding a tulip to his nose. Upon seeing her, he smiled foolishly, lifted himself up on his elbows and offered the flower to her. She took it from his hand and crushed it beneath her heel, for all the good it would do.

"Get up! Gather the others and the remaining prey. We're leaving for Portum. Now!" she commanded.

"And fetch me a damned cloak," Freya said.

"A cloak, mistress?" Asher asked absently while standing buck naked, picking up crushed petals.

"Yes, strip it from the dead if you must."

"Don't you dare. I won't be wearing any cloaks. Shirt and trousers only," Iva said.

Asher spared a confused glance in her direction. "Mistress?"

Iva held her head in both hands. "Just go. Get out of my sight," she said exasperatedly, then slid her hands down from her temples to cover her face, and she couldn't tell if the gesture had been prompted by herself or Freya. Then she did something she hadn't done since she was a girl. She cried.

CHAPTER 4

Ulcan

Ulcan peered into the empty bottle in his hand. There was a sweet spot between sober and drunk where the mind worked at its finest. He was not quite there yet. "I need more drink," he said wistfully.

Aedan fell silent. Frost crept over the Dharkan's forearm to the palm resting on the table, then down to the floor and up the walls. The cabin's temperature dropped alarmingly. "Are you paying attention to my words?" he asked.

"Yes, yes. I'm just thirsty. By all means, keep talking." Ulcan sat up straight and signalled for him to continue.

In all the years they'd known each other, Ulcan had never heard the terse Dharkan string so many sentences together. He had to admit, Aedan had a wonderful voice for speeches: modulated and pleasant to the ear, even with his accent. It was worth listening to him blather away just for the novelty of it. The trouble was, Ulcan refused to believe half of what the man said and liked none of it: An incursion of faithless Dharkan in Aegea feeding on the living. The Underworld in flames. Fake gods? It was all too much, too strange. And what did any of it have to do with him, anyway? If there was one thing Ulcan did well, besides drinking and hunting snakes, of course, it was staying the fuck away from gods and the world's dramas. A curse on Pan for bringing Aedan and that foul-tongued goddess to his shelter, another on Jonas for telling Ulla where he sheltered in the first place. Ulcan hadn't had a visitor in years! Now his small cabin was as crowded as Relicum's market at sundown. He detested crowds and visitors alike.

"No," Aedan said, crossing his arms. "It's your turn to speak now. I'd like to hear your thoughts on the matter."

A moth fluttered past Ulcan's nose and the silence inside the cabin stretched on as every eye in the room settled on him. Were they actually expecting him to have an opinion on any of this shit? He was a hunter, not a thinker! There had been too much speculation in Aedan's speech to comment on, and if Psyche thought healing the wounds from the gryphon's attack and pulling his ass out of the fire back at the sanctuary would put him in their debt, she had grossly miscalculated. Ulcan was not a man who paid for gifts.

He sighed at the empty bottle again.

"Psyche, would you mind?" Pan asked sheepishly, as if reading his thoughts. "I'd do it myself, but sadly I'm not much of a brewer these days…"

The goddess, brooding by the cabin's door and looking far less divine than she had earlier in Jonas' sanctuary, had the haunted mien of a cornered prey who'd just been targeted by its predator. She narrowed her dark eyes at the satyr. Moments later, the bottle in Ulcan's hand was full again.

"Hmm. Er… thank you." Ulcan eyed the yellow liquid suspiciously. It looked like piss. From the little he knew of gods, he would not be surprised if it was. She scowled at him, clearly reading his mind. Fucking gods and their complete lack of respect for the privacy of one's thoughts. Ulcan tilted the bottle to his lips, took a swig and grimaced. It tasted awfully sweet.

"What the fuck is this shit?"

The goddess hit the back of her head against the door frame in what looked like the overtures of a tantrum but quickly composed herself.

"Mead," she replied dryly.

"Mead? What do you think I am, a bard?"

She eyed him balefully. "I think you're a drunk who wants to get drunker. That will do the trick."

"I thought Olympians drank wine," Aedan said dubiously.

Psyche bit her cheek, shooting daggers at the Dharkan. "I'm not Olympian, and I don't like wine," she sneered.

"I do," Ulcan declared.

"Tough. Mead is all you'll get."

"Why aren't you drinking it?" he asked, genuinely curious. She'd downed two pints of cider earlier and was now obviously distraught. Ulcan figured if he were a god, able to create his own alcohol at will, he'd be drunk all the time. He chuckled at the notion. That actually explained many of the gods' behaviours.

"I'm not thirsty," she replied waspishly.

He glared at her. How Ulcan hated hot-tempered, opinionated women. The fact that one such as this was a deity proved the Universe was fucked.

"You have something to say to me, hunter?"

As a matter of fact, he did. "You're a snake."

She cocked an eyebrow at him. "Well, thank you."

"It's not a compliment. You know what I do to snakes."

"Huh. I always thought snakes were highly misunderstood creatures. So much hate towards them, and yet they never attack unless hungry or provoked. Constrictors in particular take great care not to swallow their prey while they still breathe," she said meaningfully.

"True," he conceded. "Except their reasons are selfish. They don't do it for the prey's benefit, but to avoid it ripping out their entrails."

Psyche smiled sardonically. "All killing is selfish, hunter. Anyone who claims otherwise is lying."

He spat, disgruntled with the conversation, lifted the bottle to his lips and took another swig. The sweet flavour sickened him, but it certainly had a fire to it. He shrugged, then drank until the taste, the goddess, and the plummeting temperature inside the cabin no longer bothered him.

Ulla cursed and curled herself tighter on the bed, scowling at the group. To say she'd reacted poorly to the news of her pregnancy was an understatement. She kept clutching her stomach during the entire exchange. Ulcan couldn't tell if it was in an attempt to cradle the unborn baby or to claw it out.

"I can't stay here with these… these…" She stood up suddenly and ran from the cabin, leaving the sentence unfinished.

"Ulla, come back here!" Ulcan shouted after her. "Dramatic bitch," he murmured when she was too far away to hear him.

"It's pitch black outside. She'll get lost. Or worse," Pan said.

"Thanks for pointing out the obvious." Ulcan took another long swig of the sickening beverage, took down a lantern hanging from the wall, and walked to the door on wobbly legs.

Psyche sighed, blocking his way. "Stay. I'll go after her."

Aedan gripped her arm. "You can Reach her whereabouts well enough from here."

"I too need fresh air." She jerked away from him and strode into the night.

"Let her go," Pan said, unfazed by the Dharkan's icy gaze.

"Since when do I take orders from you, *Wyrd*?"

"I thought you were used to being ordered about by Wyrds." Pan grinned sinisterly.

Sparks crackled between Aedan's fingers.

Pan tutted. "Very impressive. Save it for the nymphs. I don't swoon at the sight of lightning." The temperature dropped to freezing. "Oh, get a grip on yourself. She won't go far."

"How do you know?" Aedan growled.

"There's nowhere to go." Pan sighed miserably, then stood up. "So, now that the women are absent, can we please focus on the problem at hand and be sensible about it?"

Ulcan liked the sound of that. "You want to be sensible, do you? Here's a sensible option: leave!"

Aedan took the bottle from him. "Enough of this. Haven't you heard a thing I've said?"

"I have. And I don't understand what you want from me. I'm not a fighter, Aedan. I'm a hunter. If Iva were a snake, I'd be thrilled with the prospect of hunting her, but as it is…" He shrugged.

"Iva is not your problem. I need you to lead the Narrum out of the forest to safety."

Ulcan laughed. "I'm certainly not a leader, either."

"You know where to find the forest folk. Where they live. Where they hunt. Where they hide," Pan said.

"So do you!" Ulcan spat back at him.

Pan waved a dismissive hand. "They won't listen to me. Stars, they are more afraid of me than of the Dharkan."

"And whose fault is that?"

"Mine," he said with an impish smile. "Ah, I won't even pretend to be sorry, for I enjoyed every moment of every scare. It's what I do, Ulcan. I'm fated, not tamed. Believe me, had I the full use of my talents, I would gladly terrify them away from the forest. Sadly, I don't, and we're running out of options. You must do it. I'll gather the nymphs and the remaining tree huggers."

"And then what?"

"We take them to the Gharb."

Ulcan laughed again, glad for the mead's ability to

help him find humour in the situation. "Not a chance. The Suzerain himself couldn't convince them to leave the forest for the Gharb. They'd rather deal with the Dharkan. I say let them. It's not the first time the Wraiths have come for our lives. We'll kick them back to the shadow, same as we did before." Ulcan shrugged at Aedan. "No offence, but we are used to monsters worse than you around these parts."

Aedan gritted his teeth. "You have not paid attention to my words. For the last time, breather, the Dharkan are not why your kind must leave Aegea."

Ulcan scratched his beard pensively. "Oh, right. The fake gods are the enemy. These… Nephilim, is it? They're coming for us. And? What's new? They've been culling our children since I was a boy. That is the reason people ran to the forest in the first place!"

Ulcan might have skipped some of Aedan's speech, but the Wraith seemed to have skipped an entire generation hidden in his cave. It was far too late to pretend to care about the fate of the living in Aegea, and Ulcan reckoned the real reason behind his sudden concern had yet to be disclosed.

"Thank the Suzerain for his selective Tributes," Pan said. "When the Nephilim come this time, they'll cull more than children from the settlements. They'll take every creature in the land."

"Good!" Ulcan said, exasperated. "Maybe these fake gods will do what the actual gods failed to and finally take us to a better world. They fucked this one up."

Aedan snatched the bottle from Ulcan's hand and tossed it across the room. It hit the wall and fell to the wooden floor intact. He picked it up, staring at it, confused, then slammed it hard against the table. It remained unbroken. In a fit of fury and frustration, the Dharkan proceeded to bang the bottle repeatedly on the furniture, shouting what Ulcan assumed to be curses in his native tongue.

"It's one of the Blacksmith's crafts. It won't break," Ulcan said patiently. For creatures of cold, the Dharkan could be extremely hot tempered sometimes.

Aedan kept slamming the bottle against every conceivable surface as if its inability to break was a personal affront, until he hit Ulcan's trophy shelf.

The glass shattered to sand; the shelf fell from the wall, along with everything on it.

"Oh, for fuck's sake, are you happy now –" Ulcan fell silent, horrified.

Aedan's eyes were fixed on the shelf's contents, now scattered at his feet.

Pan gave out a long-suffering whimper. "I'll be outside."

Aedan peeled his stare from the floor and pinned it on Ulcan.

Fuck, was all Ulcan thought as the furious Dharkan bent slowly to pick up Cornus' horn.

"Aedan, it's not what you think. I found it! Ah!"

The Wraith's hand seized Ulcan's throat. He tried to push it away, but Aedan was strong. Stronger than him. "I can expla–"

An agonising jolt of energy hit Ulcan, and he bit his tongue. Aedan's eyes turned a deep blue and sparkled with lightning. Ulcan couldn't speak. The air left his lungs as life drained from his body. He was freezing.

Not just cold, but actually freezing. Ice crystals formed on his beard and around his nose. His free hand frantically searched for something – anything! – to fight the Wraith off. It found a fork. He wrapped his numb fingers around it and stabbed it into Aedan's chest to no effect. His vision blurred. Beyond the fear, Ulcan, who until recently had been defending the Dharkan from Ulla's accusations, felt pretty stupid for having done so. She'd been right. This was not how he expected to die: feeling cold and stupid, thinking Ulla had been right. After everything he'd been through in the last couple of days, better if that gryphon had ended him.

He closed his fist and smashed it into the Wraith's nose with purpose. A satisfying crunch followed. Aedan howled and staggered off balance, nearly tearing Ulcan's windpipe loose in the process. Blood poured from his nostrils. The reminder that Dharkan were still flesh and blood invigorated Ulcan. He threw another punch. Aedan loosened his grip long enough for the hunter to shake his neck free and recover his breath. Teeth rattling, dizzy and lacking any better ideas, he ran to the door.

"Help!" The plea cost him a good chunk of pride, but what good is pride when you're dead?

On the way out, Ulcan grabbed the only thing at hand: Bertho's crossbow. Unfortunately, it was pretty much useless without arrows, and he certainly wouldn't have time to nock any with Aedan closing on him. The truth was, Ulcan had long crossed the sweet spot where the mind worked its best, and fear was ever an enemy of thought. He threw the crossbow at Aedan. The Dharkan tossed it aside without breaking stride, then lunged, falling down upon him with all his weight.

The two men collapsed over the woodpile outside the cabin. During the fall, Aedan snatched at Ulcan's neck again, missed it, his grip covering Ulcan's mouth, and the hunter bit his hand as hard as he could. Wraith blood tasted the same as wolf, which was pretty tasty, Ulcan thought. The idea of hunting Dharkan for their meat had never crossed his mind before, and in that moment, it seemed a pretty good one. He bit harder, rabidly. The Wraith roared in pain and pried his hand free from Ulcan's teeth.

Ulcan tried to explain himself again, plead, bargain, beg. All to no avail. Aedan wasn't listening. Lightning spread from his hands and ran through Ulcan's body. His jaw clenched painfully. Aedan picked up a log and bashed it against his head. Stars filled Ulcan's senses; consciousness faltered. Aedan clutched his neck again. Ulcan couldn't fight back, couldn't breathe or think. He was cold. So cold. Life, strength, will, it was all draining from him. Aedan lifted him up with unnatural strength, his eyes burning brighter than the missing blue sun amidst the lightning storm.

I'm dead, Ulcan thought just before darkness took him.

Chapter 5

Hades

Hades sneaked through the Underworld, making sure he remained invisible within his cloak of shadows.

This is ridiculous, he thought, furious with himself. The Underworld was his realm. He should not have to scuttle about it, hiding in the shadows like some dead hero, afraid of facing the creatures he'd slain in life for wealth and glory. Persephone no longer had the power to interfere in his affairs. She was just another condemned soul amongst millions of others.

Still, he'd rather not have to deal with her again just yet.

Far from his proudest moment, it was a necessary one. His late wife wasn't the only disgruntled shade he was trying to avoid. Tartarus had been breached, and Hades had no reasonable explanation to offer the souls in his realm. He had to find out how Persephone had managed to get through the barrier, why she had done it, and more importantly, what had come out of that forsaken pit with her. His reputation, his very existence, depended on it.

And he knew exactly who to ask.

Medusa had been gorgeous once, a devout priestess of the goddess Athena. As with so many young and beautiful women back in ancient Midgard, she'd caught the attention of a god, none other than Zeus' favourite brother, Poseidon – and nothing good ever came from a god's fixation with a mortal, not even for the gods themselves. After her subsequent misfortune, there was no place left for Medusa on the side of the living, so Hades had offered her sanctuary in his realm and freedom to roam wherever she liked there.

The Lord of the Underworld was ever gracious to guests who harboured a grudge against Olympians.

Over the years, Medusa became the closest thing he'd had to a friend. More than that, he considered her family, the sister he never had (certainly the Olympian ones he did have didn't count). He'd sheltered her, cared for her, confided in her. More importantly, he'd trusted her. And now she had betrayed him. So he'd taken up Hel's suggestion to leave her with Cerberus for a while. His hound may not be as impressive a monster as Fenrir, but even so, Hades reckoned Medusa should be ready to talk by now.

Still wrapped in shadow, he held up a mirror to ascertain if Medusa had her goggles on before he entered the dungeon – one could never be too careful with gorgons, after all – and winced when he saw the state of her: sat naked and bloody in the cell's corner, her flesh ripped and torn in dozens of places. The snakes on her head lay limp to her shoulders, but they slithered to attention as the hound barked a greeting, then flicked the tips of their tongues in Hades' direction. Medusa's gaze followed, glaring at him from behind the thick lenses. A gift from Hephaestus to prevent her from accidentally using her talent on anyone.

Hades let go of his invisibility and walked in, patting each of Cerberus' heads in turn. "Good boy." The hound's muzzles were stained red, and his self-satisfied panting grins grew wider at the praise.

Medusa tried to speak, but only a muffled, gurgling sound came from between her teeth. Her lips were missing. Half her cheek was missing too, the gaping hole exposing the bloodied tongue behind it. Hades eyed his hound again.

"Someone got a bit carried away, hmm, boy?"

The hound lowered one head in shame, tilted another slightly sideways as if he didn't quite understand what his master meant, whilst the middle head remained high, ears and muzzle pointing straight at him with indignation.

Hades sighed. "Yeah, you're right. It's not your fault."

If anything, Cerberus had showed restraint. Any other hound wouldn't have stopped chewing on such a fleshy treat. Sadly, it appeared Medusa wasn't healing. She no longer had the perks of an immortal, and yet, being alive in the Underworld, she was not exactly mortal either. Hades wasn't sure what she was now, if she could die or not, but he did not want to risk losing track of her soul. He was not like Hel. Finding specific souls in the Underworld took some effort, and he had no time to play hide-and-seek with her anymore. He sighed again, remembering the good times they had together, and willed her flesh to heal so she could at least speak properly. It seemed Reach was beyond her abilities as well, and he'd rather not have to violate her mind without giving her a chance to come clean by her own free will.

"Medusa, I'm so disappointed in you," he said, pacing the room in what he hoped was an intimidating manner. Loki and Hel always marched about while they made threats. It seemed to work well for them.

Her brown eyes shone with tears behind the thick glass.

"The disappointment goes both ways, Hades."

"How have I disappointed you?"

"You brought the cold goddess to this realm."

Hades halted his march in disbelief. Was she jealous? He'd never considered the possibility she might be interested in him, or any man for that matter. The best thing about his relationship with Medusa was the complete lack of romantic notions between them. Not that Medusa wasn't attractive. She was, snakes and all! Being attractive was what got her into trouble in the first place. But she also had an immature, almost childlike disposition and was too prudish for Hades' tastes. Had she been less pious and less priggish as a mortal, she might even have used the situation to her advantage and become a goddess, as Psyche had. Instead, she'd become a gorgon, hiding in the Underworld. The stars knew Poseidon had been smitten with her – literally. Eros had shot him as payback for some petty offence, and the crazed god could not find rest until he possessed the object of his... *affection*. Hades knew how he must have felt. He suspected a similar curse had been responsible for his relationship with Persephone. Come to think of it, Eros was responsible for many Olympian dramas. From Zeus' infidelities to Apollo's obsession with bay trees and countless demigods in between.

"Don't flatter yourself, Hades. It's not jealousy," she said, as if reading his thoughts.

Well, that was a relief. However, considering her devotion to Athena, perhaps it was the relationship with Persephone that went beyond friendship. "What is it then?"

"You betrayed us."

"Us?"

"Olympians."

Hades' flaming features turned darker. "I'm not Olympian!" he shouted at her. "I can't believe you, of all creatures, would lecture me about turning my back on Olympus. After what they did to you, to us!"

"Yes, they deserve to suffer. But not at the cost of the suffering of the souls in the Underworld. Have you noticed there's more Aesir souls wandering about than Olympian ones? And what's worse, I can barely tell them apart these days."

No, Hades had not noticed, and frankly, he didn't care either. The souls of dead mortals all looked alike to him.

"I'm not the one who merged the worlds," he said defensively.

"No. But you all but gave Hel your realm along with your heart. Neither your guests nor Persephone deserved to be treated in such a way. *I* did not deserve it."

"So it is about jealousy," Hades said.

"It's about loyalty!" The snakes in her hair hissed as she spoke. One actually struck at him. "Persephone was never my friend. She was mean, false and vain, and she used me. I know that. I've never chastised you for how you treated her, either. I always defended you, in fact. For you at least married her before you raped her," she scoffed.

"Hey! I raped no one." Persephone was quite willing, at first anyway. Thrilled by the opportunity to escape her overprotective mother and misbehave like Aphrodite. The passion only dwindled when she realised she was stuck with him in the Underworld. And as for the lack of romance and unfair treatment, well, over the years it went both ways. It's a common problem in marriages, with or without curses.

Medusa shrugged. "Whatever."

Hades nearly burst into flames with anger. "Not 'whatever'. You need to explain to me why you helped her steal the blood of the Hydra. And don't you dare lecture me about loyalty! I gave you access to Tartarus so you could visit the other gorgons as you asked. I didn't even question why, because I *trusted* you. Cerberus breath!" The hound turned his heads quizzically. "Do you know what Persephone did with the Hydra's blood? She gave it to the Dharkan! And you lecture *me* about betrayal?!"

"I bet you were heartbroken when they murdered her."

Hades pulled at his hair. It hurt. Horns were much better for this sort of thing. *Why did women have to be so difficult?* he asked himself while trying to soothe his temper as well as his scalp.

"I am heartbroken. Not for her. But for you, Medusa." Hades knelt by her side, held her hand, looked into those deadly eyes of hers hidden behind the glass, so full of hate and sorrow, and he sighed. "After everything we've been through together, if you were so upset with me, why didn't you say something earlier?"

Her lip trembled. "I was afraid."

"Of me?!"

She gave him a condescending smirk. "No, you idiot. Of Hel."

Hades was about to ask why, but there was no need. Hel could be intimidating even without trying. It was one of her best features.

"Hel wouldn't harm you," he said. Then he remembered it was she who suggested giving Medusa to Cerberus, and suddenly he wasn't so sure anymore.

Medusa laughed mirthlessly. "You don't know her."

"I love her," he heard himself say. It was true. It had been true for quite some time, he realised. "And she loves me."

"Pfff," Medusa said. "Poor Hades. From one curse to another."

"Our love is real. Not a 'gift' from a god's arrow." Of that he was sure. One had to have been shot by Eros to know the difference.

"Love is a curse, with or without the arrow," Medusa said bitterly.

Hades' anger dwindled, sensing her misery. He sat down next to her; his mind reeling for understanding. "Did you let yourself get bitten by the Hydra so you could die?"

Medusa blinked. "Wow. Men are so stupid. They just can't see past their own egos."

"Medusa," Hades warned. His ego was not up to dealing with insults. Cerberus, sensing his mood, took a step closer, growling low.

"I was bitten trying to stop Persephone from taking its blood!"

"Then why did you let her get near the Hydra in the first place?"

She slumped on her chains again. "Because I've been waiting for her to ask me to break into Tartarus. It's the reason I came here. But I didn't know she'd be crazy enough to go for the Hydra. I only did what I had to do." Medusa began sobbing, and Hades was more confused than ever. Perhaps leaving her with Cerberus had been a terrible idea.

"What are you talking about?" he demanded.

"Chronos! He told me to do it." Medusa sobbed in earnest now. Snot streaked with blood poured from her swollen nose.

Hades fire went out at the mention of the God of Time. Despite what He'd done to his realm, Chronos could not have entered it. Could he?

"When?" Hades asked, straining to remain calm.

"Oh, long before the Merge," Medusa explained. "He told me the time would come when Persephone would ask me to gain access to Tartarus, and I should help her. You can imagine my puzzlement. Back then, you weren't even married to her!"

Hades massaged his forehead, trying to come to terms with the idea that Medusa, who he'd considered his best friend, had intended to betray him for millennia.

"Explain," he grated, putting an end to her sobs.

"Long before the Merge, before the gods fell from grace with the humans, when I was still hiding amongst the living, filled with hatred and despair, I found a Chronodéndron, and I prayed for another chance."

Hades' heart sank. "A chance for what?"

"I wanted to go back, to avoid or even… submit to Poseidon if I had to. Back then, I believed it would be a better option to my fate, so I prayed for a chance to do things differently and not end up like this. I prayed to be mortal again and have a normal life. I prayed for a chance to be happy." She hung her head in misery. "Of course, what was done to me was done by gods, and not even Chronos could undo Athena's curse. But he offered me an alternative."

"What alternative?" Hades muttered the words slowly, anxious about what he might learn next.

"Revenge on Athena for turning me away." Medusa gritted her teeth with suppressed rage. "For punishing me instead of Poseidon. Chronos offered me revenge on all gods who abuse their powers. Any who disrespected him. How could I refuse?"

Hades froze. That applied to pretty much every god in the Universe. Including him.

"Medusa…" Hades whispered, almost afraid to ask. "Who did you free?"

The Hydra was still there, its heads growing back nicely. Prometheus too, unfortunately. He'd checked. Hades had to give it to Zeus, his curses were strong indeed. The great monsters of old were also accounted for, including the Typhon, thank the stars. But someone had gotten out. He had to know whom.

"Hecate," Medusa said in a small voice.

Hades sighed in relief, then held his breath again. "How does freeing that crazy sorceress bring revenge on Athena?"

"I don't know. But he promised me it would. So… It is done. I'm sorry, Hades."

"Yes… well, me too, Medusa." He stood up, relief replacing dread along with the pain of betrayal. Hecate was a goddess of peculiar talents, but fortunately for him, she would be powerless in Niflheim, a world with no moons.

"Hades?" Medusa's tone was soft, almost pleading.

He looked down at her. She was calm now; the sort of calmness that comes from resignation or catharsis. Her snakes were intent on him, their tongues still. "The irony of it is: I've been happy. All these years, here, with you, I was happy. And for that, I thank you."

The words cut him deep. "Cerberus!" Hades called louder than was necessary, trying not to tear up.

The hound perked his six ears towards him, tail wagging expectantly.

"Keep an eye on her. But no more biting."

Cerberus' enthusiasm deflated, but he nodded in synchronised obedience.

Hades left the Underworld dungeon wrapped in flames so all could see him clearly. He was their lord, their god, and he would tolerate no one interfering with his realm. (Except for Hel, of course.) Whatever Chronos' scheme was, he had no power in their world.

Hecate would soon be back where she belonged.

CHAPTER 6

Hel

Hel savoured her victory over Freya while she waited. The conceited goddess had been right about one thing, though. Hel shouldn't have sent Aedan to do a god's work. He might have the power of a god, even the temper to match one, but he lacked the will, and more importantly the knowledge, necessary to get things done. He couldn't have known Iva was hosting Freya, and even if he had, it took a god as cunning as Odin to deal with the likes of her. The hubris of the goddess to assume she could just take what was Hel's by merit! She'd worked hard to be the sort of deity the dead needed, and now they were bound to her. Freya, who always had everything handed to her on a golden platter, would never understand that. And Iva… Oh well, Hel supposed dissidents were useful in their own way, for they served as an example to the others of what *not* to do to survive. Bottom line, the best way to make sure things were done properly was to do them yourself, as her father had taught her.

"Finally!" she said when Hades left the Underworld blazing like a torch. She couldn't tell if he was showing off in an attempt to bring attention to himself or to keep everyone away from him. Perhaps he was just in the mood for flames. They looked good on him, Hel had to admit (if only to herself). She really liked his new look; the combination of flame and shadow had always excited her. She rolled her eyes. Flaming sun, it was almost as if she liked getting burned.

Hades would be looking for her now, so she had to do this quickly. Without the option of invisibility, she strode proudly along the Olympian Underworld, for this was as much her realm as Hades'. A suspicious crowd gathered to watch her go by. She smiled at her audience and got nothing but resentful scowls in return. *Ungrateful creatures*, she thought with disgust. They would get used to her presence. Without her, they'd all be burned to oblivion, so a little gratitude wouldn't go amiss. Except gratitude was in short supply amongst these dead. To them, their existence couldn't get any worse; after all, they'd already died. If only they knew how wrong they were... No matter, she'd freeze the prejudice out of them soon enough, starting with the one who'd caused the most dissent amongst the Olympian: Hades' special friend, Medusa.

Hel didn't slow down when she entered the foul dungeon. Cerberus stood on guard, as she'd suggested. Upon seeing her, the hound raised his hackles and bared his teeth menacingly. She almost laughed at the three-headed daemon: an impressive sight indeed – to anyone who hadn't seen Fenrir angry.

"Get out of my way," Hel barked.

Cerberus barked back. She froze him. He didn't even have a chance to whimper, poor thing. Each head fixed in varying facets of surprised horror. Hel loved how all Olympian creatures were vulnerable to her power, Hades included.

Medusa herself sat in the far corner of a small cell carved from the obsidian rock by a god's will, hands tied high above her head. The poor creature was a pitiful sight. Hel clicked her tongue, wishing things hadn't come to this. She abhorred torture, dungeons and interrogations, but her good-natured side had been unsuccessful in persuading, let alone defeating, her enemies, so perhaps her unpleasant side would.

"I wondered when you would come," Medusa said defiantly, dark eyes glaring from behind the thick glass held by a contrivance of exquisite craftsmanship. It moulded itself to her cheeks, brows and head almost seamlessly. She doubted the gorgon ever felt the need to take it off, unless she intended to use her talent.

Hel didn't slow her stride. She crossed the cell and grabbed the cursed woman by the neck. Her hair coiled to strike, and Hel froze each snake with an icy glare, leaving Medusa wide-eyed with a crown of startled, open-mouthed vipers.

"Have you come to kill me properly?" Medusa asked, a glint of hope in her bitter tone.

"Perhaps. If you cooperate."

"I already told Hades everything."

"You lie."

Hel touched the tip of a fang of the closest snake. A drop of frozen venom broke from it. She pretended to inspect it, then put the drop in her mouth, shivered and smiled at Medusa, who blinked back at her in disgust.

During the time Hel had spent in Hades' Underworld, she'd become friends with many of its most prominent residents, especially Kharon. Such a charming fellow, grossly misunderstood, like herself. But Medusa had always avoided her, scorned her, even. At first Hel thought she was jealous of her relationship with Hades, but now, she didn't know what to think except that she'd certainly underestimated the creature and her influence in Hades' realm.

"You've never liked me, Medusa. Why not?"

"You're a cold and ambitious whore. Like father, like daughter."

Hel feigned offence. If she had a world for every time someone blamed her for Loki's deeds, she'd own an entire galaxy by now.

"How morally righteous of you to judge me on my parentage. What did my father ever do to you, anyway?"

"He was here, in this very dungeon. For centuries I heard his screams, his dreams – his thoughts."

And you never told me about it, Hel thought, resentful of the fact that she'd spent nearly two decades stuck in the Underworld without ever knowing her father was being tortured only a few levels below. It was unforgivable, especially for her, who was supposed to be able to track every soul in her realm. Then again, the Olympian Underworld wasn't exactly part of her realm, not yet. And Hades was too good at keeping secrets.

Hel poured her resentfulness into her words. "So you spied on him. Watched his pain, did you? Did you enjoy it?"

Medusa smirked. "I enjoyed what I learnt from it."

"Ahh. I see. And still you think you're the only one the gods treated unfairly. It's my turn to teach you something, then."

Medusa's eyes grew wider behind her lenses as Hel straddled her, pinning her arms and back to the obsidian with ice so she couldn't move an inch. Then she reached for her goggles.

"How does the curse go, again?" Hel mused. "One look from you will turn living flesh to stone, is that it?"

Medusa flinched. "What are you doing? I'll petrify you."

Without hesitation, Hel lifted the apparatus to Medusa's forehead. "Isn't that what you want? Open your eyes!"

"Hades will never forgive me!" Medusa shrieked, keeping them shut.

"Look at me!" Hel demanded.

Slowly, fearfully, Medusa did. She had large brown eyes, almost as dark as Psyche's. After a brief hesitation, they looked straight into Hel's.

The goddess of the dead laughed at Medusa's startled expression when she showed her her true form: half skeletal corpse, half Dharkan.

"Why so surprised, gorgon? After all, I *am* the goddess of the dead." Hel moved her head from side to side. "Do you like what you see? Do you think I chose to be like this?"

Medusa tried to look away, but Hel held her chin straight to her face and said, "You and I could have been friends."

Medusa closed her eyes. Hel couldn't tell if in shame or fear. It didn't matter.

"Well, now that we understand each other, you will tell me what I want to know."

"Poor Hades," Medusa murmured.

"There's nothing poor about Hades, trust me."

Medusa's eyes glittered with tears.

The sight only made Hel angrier, for crying was something she, with one dead eye and the other only able to shed ice, could never do properly no matter what form she assumed. "Talk!" she demanded.

"I hate you," Medusa said.

Hel clicked her tongue. "That's fine. Many do. I stopped caring about their opinions a long time ago. I too dislike those who dislike me. But do you know what I hate the most? Being misunderstood. I bet the reasons you hate me are not even based on truth. And yet you go about spreading them like a disease to every weak mind who likes the sound of them."

Medusa shook her head. "I know what you're doing. To Hades, to this world. It takes a snake to spot a snake," she hissed.

One of Medusa's snakes stirred. Hel poured more cold into it until it froze again. "Is that so? What about what you did, huh? Hades is too good to creatures like you. You might still convince him of your innocence but, between us girls, I know you helped Persephone. You were holding the Hydra when it bit you, not fighting it. Why would you fight it? You could have turned it to stone with a glance, but then you'd turn its blood to stone too, rendering it useless. You may not have known what Persephone was up to, but once you found out, you hoped she'd use the blood on me, didn't you?"

"You're crazy."

"No, gorgon. I'm well informed. You see, Persephone herself told me everything. After some persuasion, of course."

This seemed to disarm Medusa. "She's in your realm?"

"Yes. Didn't you find it strange she didn't come visit you after her misfortune with the Dharkan? With the Merge, the realms of the dead became so… blurred. It's hard to tell where one ends and the other begins. A nuisance for the most part, especially since Hades is so careless with his guests. I, myself, prefer to keep things organised. To that effect, I have a special place reserved just for traitors, tailored to lure those who died engaging in betrayal. I don't tolerate treason in my realms, you see. Funnily enough, Persephone's soul went straight there with no extra effort on my part."

Medusa cursed.

"The good news is," Hel continued matter-of-factly, "the goddess of spring wasn't cunning enough to carry out my demise directly. She gave the blood to my enemies instead, who seem to have subsequently lost it. And now every god in Aegea is in danger. Any weapon held by a Narrum or a Dharkan might be tainted with the poison. And that's bad news for everyone. For you, specifically, once the truth comes out."

"So what will you do to me?" Medusa asked, resigned. At least she didn't insult Hel further by denying it – a good sign.

"I think I'll take you to your vain friend," Hel said.

"Maybe set up a cosy little ice cavern for the both of you deep beneath Helheim, where you can be bitter together for eternity. I hope you don't mind the cold. I've heard reptiles really struggle with it. As do flowers. Do you know what happens to spring when it's plunged into eternal winter?"

"No…"

"Neither do I. But I look forward to finding out. Don't you?"

Hel could tell the idea of being stuck with Persephone in an ice cavern for the rest of her existence did not appeal to Medusa one bit.

"I'll tell you what I told Hades," Medusa bargained.

"Not good enough. If I wanted to learn that, I'd just ask him. No, no. You'll tell me what you told him, plus everything else you didn't. And I want to know all there is to know about this Hecate character wandering free in my forest."

Medusa frowned. "How do you –"

"It's a talent," Hel sneered. "Now, you have until Cerberus defrosts. It's quite hot in here, so I suggest you talk fast. Go."

Medusa locked her deadly eyes on Hel's. "On one condition."

"Burn it, creature. Is avoiding a slow and painfully cold eternity not condition enough?"

"I want what was promised to me long ago," Medusa declared. The glare in her eyes turned into a gleam.

"Not by me. All promises I've made were made right here, right now, and they are expiring along with my patience."

Medusa straightened herself, as much as was possible while pinned to the wall behind her. The snakes, now slithering lethargically on her head, flicked their tongues at Hel with malicious interest.

"I will tell you all I know about Chronos, Hecate, Tartarus, and Olympus." She hesitated, then smiled wickedly. "Plus what I've learnt from your father's delirious rambles, if you give me another chance. Take me out of this realm. I don't belong here anymore. I want to be up there, with the living in Aegea. Keep me alive *and* well," she added emphatically, "and I'll help you rid this world of both Olympians and the Nephilim."

"Oh, is that so? That's quite the substantial offer. Does this mean you and I are friends now?"

"Oh," Medusa mimicked Hel's mocking tone perfectly. "I like you even less now than I did before. We will *never* be friends, goddess of the dead, but that doesn't mean we can't be allies."

Hel grinned.

CHAPTER 7

Iosh

Iosh was praying – again. Ever since he'd taken control of Relicum, he'd done little else, for what else was there to do? He never thought he'd become bored with the endeavour; after all, he was a shrine. The most handsome, most virile man in Aegea. One could say he was made for praying, and yet, it felt like such a one-sided activity these days, like talking to himself or masturbating. The women he prayed with didn't really pray with him either. They prayed for themselves, for what they would get from him. And he was tired of giving it to them. He gazed into the eyes of the girl he was with, searching for some sort of connection, a vestige of devotion even, but she wasn't looking back.

"Oh, Galeus," she moaned in Iosh's ear when she came. Who was he? A god, her husband, the name she'd chosen for her conceptualised son, perhaps? Whoever Galeus was, it certainly wasn't Iosh, nor even Judoc. He wasn't being worshipped, he was being used. How had this happened? *When* had it happened? Had it always been so?

Iosh rolled off the girl, walked to the basin, filled it with water and began washing himself.

"Are we done?" she asked, lifting her hips to improve fertilisation.

"Yes. Get your clothes and leave."

He had no need to repeat himself. She was up and out of the room in moments. His worshippers might not care for his pleasure, but they sure did their best to avoid his displeasure.

Ileana's mother had once warned him to stay away from Ileana and all women. Had he listened to her, how different might his life have been, he wondered, then immediately cursed the idea. He knew exactly how his life would have been: short, lonely and miserable. No, Iosh did not regret his choices. He was simply tired of their consequences. Being the most important man in the land was hard work.

You're not the most important man yet, he reminded himself – or something did. Ever since he'd been gifted, Iosh had been able to hear his own thoughts. He figured that was what enlightened people meant when they claimed to be following their consciences. Lately, though, his thoughts and his conscience had been slightly at odds with each other, and more annoyingly, at odds with his own feelings too. The truth was, he was drained of lust and had found little ecstasy in prayers these days. His mind was occupied by other pursuits. He was hungry for something more than flesh or pleasure. He wanted power, control, dominion over the world and those in it. Adoration alone wouldn't give him that, especially coming from those beneath him; he needed respect – the respect due to a god. And as far as he knew, there was only one place in Aegea where mortals became gods.

"Sire." Toman's head peeked through the curtain. "Should I let the next one in?"

"No. I'm done for the day."

Toman looked up as if he could see the sun through the roof. "But, sire, it's only –"

"I said I'm done. Take the women to the other room. Isko can take over when he's ready."

The Wyrd was ever ready to help with the shrine's duties, and as long as they were performed in complete darkness, the women didn't seem to notice the difference. That offended Iosh, for it spoke volumes about how much they paid attention to him or his performance. He told himself Isko was a god, or had been one once, so aesthetic features aside, maybe there wasn't much difference between their performances under the sheets.

"Where is Seshat?" he asked.

Toman flinched at the name. He was terrified of the goddess, who he believed to be a daemon, especially after he'd seen the things she could do with a quill. Writing was considered nefarious to the Narrum and strictly forbidden under the Suzerain's rule. Toman feared she would bind his life with words on a page, denying him agency over his fate. Alek himself suspected the written word, but unlike his subjects, he spent most of his time studying old texts.

"The goddess Seshat is on the roof again, sire," his assistant said reproachfully.

"Right…" Iosh sighed. For someone who hated cats, Seshat sure acted like one often enough. Funny how one tends to hate the things they should relate to. "Thank you, Toman, that will be all."

Iosh put on his best garment along with his new bracelet, then went up to the balcony, and sure enough, there she was, perched atop the temple's dome like a statue. The chronicler had done little to no writing in the last few days. She just sat there, scowling at the world. Gods have too much leisure on their hands, Iosh decided.

Her eyes shone like the sun when she fixed them on him. He winced at the glare. She was wearing her true form, and what a fine form it was. And to think he'd known her for years as a tiresome middle-aged man. They'd sat next to each other during endless meetings, travelled together, even slept together in the same room on occasion, and never once had she revealed herself to him. Now Seshat pretended not to like him, but he knew better. She might have been indifferent to him before, as gods are to most mortals, but once she saw what he could do, how gifted he truly was, her indifference shattered. He was sure that deep down she secretly wanted him. All women did. It was just her nature to pretend she didn't, just like she pretended she didn't like cats.

Oric and Isko were playing a game with black and white stones on the balcony's floor. Iosh had tried to make sense of it a few times, with little success, but judging by the number of white stones left on the board, he reckoned Isko was the one losing for a change.

"You're out early," Oric said without taking his eyes from the game.

"It's your turn," Iosh said to Isko, who grinned lopsidedly, still intent on his next move.

"So soon? Feeling a bit low on stamina today, are we?" Oric teased.

Iosh did not indulge him with a reply.

"You lose," Isko said, scattering the pieces.

"Hey! I was winning, you piece of slush. You could at least have finished the game."

"I could, but I have more interesting things to do than lose." The Wyrd spared a glance at Seshat before dashing inside. Iosh hadn't yet been able to figure out the nature of their relationship. He was fairly sure they weren't praying. Most relationships between gods seemed odd to mortals. This one was no exception.

"How come that mistake of nature is allowed to cover for you while I'm not?" Oric said while reluctantly gathering the scattered pieces into their pouch.

"Because he has two arms and gave me his bracelet," Iosh replied waspishly, not for the first time.

Oric scoffed. "Wait until the Suzerain finds out how you've compromised the lineage of the Tributes with his seed."

"I'm tired of waiting!" Iosh snapped.

Oric had claimed the Suzerain would resurrect soon. A prospect that both worried and annoyed Iosh, for he was doing just fine without his master. Still, in many ways it was as if Alek had never died in the first place. Everyone still talked about him and obeyed his rules. They worshipped him. Seshat even had to impersonate the man to appease the masses when they suspected he might not be looking over them anymore. Immortality was not connected to life or flesh, Iosh decided, but to the memory of those who fear you.

"I'm going to the Stump, to bring Arianh back," Iosh declared.

"By force?" Seshat said in her detached, slightly mocking tone.

"If I have to."

She chuckled. "Yes. That will surely win you her devotion."

"I can't just stay here waiting." *Waiting for her to come to me*, Iosh almost said. The goddess gave him a pitiful look. He cursed. Gods: you not only had to be careful around them with words but with thoughts too. There was no need to be mean just because she was jealous.

"You're the most important man in Relicum," she said derisively. "You can't go anywhere. People will miss you."

"Like they missed Guilho?" Iosh could still hardly believe no one had enquired about the governor's absence apart from his elderly mother. Had he known how easy it was to dispose of the man, he'd have done it years ago.

"He wasn't favoured by the people, you are. Only cats know why," Seshat grumbled.

Favoured, maybe, but not adored, he thought.

"You can cover for me," he told her. Another proof of her undisclosed attraction to him was the fact she was able and willing to impersonate him flawlessly.

She guffawed. "I can. But why would I? I've done too much for you and your kind already."

"You'll do it because you're bored." It was the usual lame excuse. Iosh almost felt sorry for the goddess.

"I'm not nearly bored enough to play your character, *Shrine*," she said with derision. There was hope.

"Come on, Seshat," he said, using his gift. "Just for the day. One praying session, that's it. Isko and Toman will do the rest. I'll return tomorrow by nightfall. I promise."

"Promises are for gods," she hissed. "What makes you think Hel and the others will even let you inside the Stump?"

"I don't need their permission. I have this." He showed her the bracelet. Isko had made modifications to the device, so it was now linked to him. And if for some reason it didn't work, Arianh would let him in. He was sure she would. He could already picture the queen's delight when she saw him materialise over the ring, her astonishment and admiration when he told her what he'd done and how much he'd achieved in the last few days. She would finally come to her senses and realise he was the best, no, the *only* man for her.

Seshat chuckled. "Yes, I'm sure Fenrir will be glad to see you too."

Iosh felt the hairs on the back of his neck rise at the mention of the wolf. He'd rather face the Suzerain again than *it*. Still...

"I have to go. I can't leave her there, wasting away under the gods' influences. She needs help. Someone to guide her." Iosh disagreed with the Suzerain in many subjects. Even before, when he was only Alek Dveer, leader of the Anann, his ideas and theories were too outlandish for Iosh, but they did agree on one thing: no woman should rule, especially not alone.

Seshat sighed, then slid down the roof, landing gracefully on her feet. "All right. One day, for Arianh's sake. The Stump is no place for a dryad. Besides, I can hear her people's discontentment from here. If she remains absent for much longer, she won't have a realm to rule when she returns."

"Yes, of course. For Arianh's sake." Iosh smiled boyishly.

"I'll go with you," Oric said, standing up.

"Are you sunstroked? Aedan will ice you," Seshat said. "After the lengths I went through to stir everyone's attention from you back at the caves so you could escape, you'd go there? What happened to 'let them freeze in their own graves'?"

Oric scowled at her. "I have no intention of stepping foot inside the Stump until Alek returns, I'm just tired of being stuck here playing with stones. I'll accompany him as far as the Grove, all right? See if I can find a tree hugger who's not too fussy about limbs. I'll be back before you even miss me."

Seshat rolled her eyes. "Sure." She pointed her quill at Iosh. "Judoc, you better be back before sunset tomorrow. One praying session is all I'll endure," she said.

To Iosh's ears it sounded more like "One day without you is all I'll endure." The smile widened.

"Now, go. Both of you. Out of my sight."

They promptly obeyed before she changed her mind. Seshat's moods, like those of most females, could change quite suddenly.

The moment Iosh left the temple, his own mood improved considerably. This was the right thing to do. Both his mind and his gut agreed. He would rescue Arianh, marry her, take her kingdom, and with it, he would be the one accomplishing what not even Alek had managed to accomplish. He would unite all the living in Aegea under one rule: his rule. Only then would he truly be the most important man in the land. And he would finally be able to claim his prize.

CHAPTER 8

Loki

That went well, Loki lied to himself as he flew away from the cabin where Aedan was about to kill the hunter. Perhaps he shouldn't have filled the bottle with such strong mead, or loosened the trophy shelf. Then again, he was Loki. Causing chaos was what he did best. Things just took too long to happen otherwise.

He could still get no reply from Hel or Hades. Loki figured they were probably in the Underworld busy with each other in one last *argument* before the Nephilim arrived. Loki considered paying a visit to Seshat but immediately abandoned the idea. It would be centuries before she forgave him this time. Besides, he had no time for arguments, and she definitely deserved better than him. So instead he translocated to Gaea's domain, hidden deep in the mountains, and found her taking the life of her youngest tree.

"Happy now, Trickster?" She too had always been able to sense his arrival.

Happy? No. He wasn't. Far from it. "What have you done?! *Why* have you done it? Have you lost your mind? They are coming as we speak!" The sapling was supposed to be their way out if things went wrong – as they often did – a backup plan to an unlikely to be successful plan; a desperate plan, but a solid plan nonetheless.

"I know." Gaea caressed the last leaf on her now dead tree and watched as it fell onto the snow. "That's why it had to be done. I cannot protect her, and I can't risk this one falling into the hands of the Nephilim as well."

"What do you mean you can't protect her? You're the Mother of Life! You can do anything," he said, only half convinced it was true. He'd known Gaea since before he knew himself, and there was a lot he still did not understand about her. Her motivations, for one, but mainly her powers and how she used them. Unlike most deities to whom their talents came naturally, effortlessly even, and with little or no cost, Gaea always had to pay dearly for them. It was almost as if Life wasn't her talent at all, merely a consequence of something else.

She gave him a sour glance.

"What about our plan?" he insisted.

"It's still in place, if it comes to that," she said. "And it's another reason why I had to let go of this tree. I cannot afford both..." Her face was careworn, aged beyond what any deity should be. This was no illusion, nor a mere reflection of her mood.

"Gaea?" he whispered. "This isn't just about the Nephilim, is it?"

She shook her head, looked him in the eyes and said, "It's Chronos. He's here."

There was silence. Then laughter. "Nonsense! I helped Hel build Niflheim, remember? Chronos won't get in. He already did all he could do to this world. Your trees are safe here." Loki glanced at the withered sapling. "From him, anyway."

She shook her head and looked so sad when she spoke, Loki actually felt for her. "I was wrong about him, Loki. Chronos doesn't care about Ambrosia. He never did. He just let me believe he did so I wouldn't see what he was really up to until it was too late." Gaea fixed her gaze on Loki's. "He *is* here."

Loki wasn't laughing anymore. "Fuck, how?"

"How do you think?"

He looked at the sky. The Nephilim's ship was already in orbit. "No, they couldn't. He would never allow himself to be captured by them. He's too strong, too proud, his soul is too..." Loki trailed off, unable to describe it with words.

"He wasn't captured," Gaea said. "He's here willingly. The Suzerain found a way to create a host for his soul."

Loki frowned and paced, shaking his head, thinking furiously. "No. No, even if the Suzerain had somehow built a body strong enough to host Chronos' soul, he would still need to overcome the curses keeping him out of Niflheim."

"He has Hecate."

Loki covered his face. "Hades, you fucking idiot," he growled between his teeth, then shook his head again. "He would also need to have the soul transferred into the host. Hecate is not strong enough to do it. Only one deity can do that, and *she* wouldn't do it."

"She would if she didn't know she was doing it. Or if she didn't know it was *his* soul," Gaea said darkly.

He chuckled. "How could she not know?"

"She was a Wyrd when she arrived, claiming to have no memory of how or why she was here, cut off from her talent, powerless."

"Precisely," he said.

"But her host was conscious. What if *she* knew?"

"Nonsense," Loki said. "Conscious or not, the Wyrds' hosts are as helpless as their gods."

"Not Ileana. She was the Suzerain's daughter – his creation. I believe he built her for this very purpose."

Loki felt lightheaded with the implications.

"Why would Chronos want to come to Niflheim, anyway. To go to all this trouble because of one tree?" Loki shook his head. "I knew he hated you but never imagined how much."

"It's not hate, it's fear."

"Chronos fears nothing," Loki said, feeling more than a bit apprehensive himself. If what Gaea said was true, then all his plans could fall apart. The words *what you deserve* echoed again in his mind.

"Oh, but he does," Gaea said ruefully. "Thinking he hated my creations because of me was my ego's mistake. He cares not for life. Don't you see? It's the *after*life that concerns him."

"What can he possibly…" He trailed off, realisation dawning on him. "Fuck… the souls."

"Yes. You understand now."

Loki couldn't breathe, couldn't think. This revelation burned through his mind, his pride, even his anger, straight to his heart.

Gaea stepped closer to him. "Why is the goddess of the soul here, Loki?" she asked, searching his face. "You thought it was because of you, didn't you?"

He did.

Gaea puffed out a breath. "So did I, at first. Then I had the *pleasure* to meet her. And now I think you are the reason she did not want to be here in the first place, the reason she wants to leave so badly. Probably the reason she hid all these years." Gaea tutted. "Someone sure went through a lot of trouble and great risk to lure her here despite her reluctance."

"Who?" Loki whispered, floored by Gaea's deductions.

Gaea sighed. "Zeus would be my first guess, but he's out of the picture. So the Suzerain is my next choice. Maybe Chronos himself. Of course, it would have helped if Psyche shared what she knows, but she gave me nothing, Loki. I hoped she would talk to you, at least. But you were never around. Now… it's too late."

How foolish he felt. Gaea was right. Curse or no curse, Psyche would never come for him. Not willingly.

Fuck…

"But the Nephilim –" he insisted.

"Are his minions. Chronos' own faithful pantheon of apotheosised mortals and enslaved gods. You helped create them; she let Him through. They will be our end, and it's both your faults."

What Gaea said made sense, but it did not feel right. And if it was indeed the case, there was still something he could do. "I'll free Prometheus. I owe him that much, and once he's free, this whole mess can be undone."

A mocking sound escaped Gaea's throat. "Undo humans?"

"Yes," he snapped. "He created them, he can destroy them."

Gaea gaped at him. "Was that part of your plan, Loki?" The answer was obvious, and it was her turn to laugh. "It doesn't work like that, Trickster. Perhaps when there was only a handful of humans, sure, but now? Prometheus can no more undo humanity than I can undo life. Besides, the Nephilim are no longer human. They haven't been in a long time. We are, as you like to say, fucked."

Loki refused to believe her, to believe *this*. "Kali, then," he suggested.

There was something in the way Gaea looked at him: not pity, not exactly sorrow either. It was the sort of anguished look one gets when holding a secret they can't share. "Kali won't do anything about it," she said. It sounded like the truth, but there was something in the way she said it that told Loki there was a lot left unsaid.

Loki had never met this great Goddess of Death. If not for the fact that death happened constantly, one would think she did not exist. Maybe she was just too busy or too unaware to care. He'd met a few deities like that. The gods of old were forces ill-equipped for socialisation. But Gaea, she had to know how to Reach Kali. After all, she was one of the damned Three.

"Can't *you* do something about it, Gaea?" he asked humbly.

She chuckled bitterly. "Yes, Trickster. There is one thing I can do. Kali and I are anathema to each other, after all. But I was hoping you had a better idea."

Loki had many ideas, all rubbish, except one so dangerous, so improbable and insane that it might just work.

"Come on, Loki. Don't hold out on me. What do you have in mind?"

"You said Chronos' soul is trapped in flesh, in this realm? That makes him vulnerable."

"Not his whole soul, just enough to animate the host, and the host is not entirely made of flesh. Oh, and technically he's not in this realm either. So if your plan was to stab him with that shiny new dagger of yours, forget about it."

"Damn it!" Loki didn't know what upset him the most: Gaea's uncanny ability to not only be immune to his illusions but also read his mind, or that she so blatantly dismissed his idea.

Gaea clicked her tongue. "Slaughtering gods in cold blood, Loki? That's bold, even for you. Sooner or later, you'll have to answer for it."

"Don't I always?" he said glibly. Gaea was powerful, all right. Loki made a note to himself to never underestimate her again. Fortunately for him, his misdeeds were not the Goddess's main concern at the moment.

She frowned slightly as if pondering something distasteful. "However, that does give *me* an idea," she said.

"I'm opened to suggestions," Loki replied, pinching the bridge of his nose, unable to come up with anything likely to succeed in solving their predicament.

"You're not going to like it," Gaea warned almost blithely.

And she was right. He didn't.

CHAPTER 9

Hades

It was dark by the time Hades translocated back to the Stump, eager to share with Hel what he'd learnt from Medusa. Except Hel wasn't there. No one was except Gaea, curled up by the ring, rocking back and forth with her eyes aflutter. Her mind was shielded. That was weird. Usually it was him who had to shield his mind from hers.

"Er…" he said, then pursed his lips. Gaea was a strange one, getting stranger each age. Better to not interrupt whatever she had going on at the moment.

After they'd sensed Persephone's demise, Hel had gone to the Boiling Lake to deal with the faithless Dharkan while Hades put Medusa in chains. Hel had been adamant she didn't need or want his help with the Dharkan, and he'd agreed, since he didn't want her interfering with Medusa either. Still, she should have been back by now.

Hel, where are you? he asked telepathically. There was no reply. When Hel didn't want to be found, she succeeded. How he wished he had her ability to just vanish from everyone's Reach, and try as he might, he'd never been able to see into the depths of her do-main. Which was where she probably was, avoiding him. Either there or inside the cursed Stump. Hel spent a lot of time inside the thing. He could not fathom why, considering how uncomfortable it was for their kind. In that regard, as in so many others, Hel was much stronger than him, for she didn't let the discomfort get to her. Well, maybe he should be uncomfortable too, for her sake.

Hades made a move towards the ramp and stopped, reluctant to go in. He'd rather go into Tartarus again first.

"Is Hel back yet?" he risked asking the Mother of Life.

She didn't answer and began chanting nonsensi-cally to herself instead. He figured this had something to do with the trance she'd shared earlier with Ideth and the eerie Xylo, who despite having an unreach-able mind could now speak. Of course, it was only a matter of time before the Mother of Life gave sentience to the hybrid creature. She loved to waste her talents on trees. Honestly, what use had trees for intellect or speech? Then again, Xylo was not entirely tree, and he'd been the Suzerain's pet. Maybe now they could interrogate him about the Nephilim. Hades frowned. Could Hel already be interrogating Xylo without him? He would not put it past her. No. She wouldn't do that, surely.

Hades grabbed a handful of hair in frustration. Oh, who was he kidding? Hel would interrogate Xylo behind his back and much more. He had to kidnap her to get her attention in the first place, of course he would have to stalk her to know what she was up to. He considered going inside again, and again his instinct decided against it. He waited. The longer he waited, the worse the scenarios his mind came up with. Maybe something had happened at the lake? Maybe the Dharkan had used the Hydra's blood on her? No, he would know immediately if they had. Maybe she didn't love him anymore. Maybe she never did. No, she was probably still angry about Persephone and needed some time for herself. She would return soon, then they would put Hecate in her rightful place and interrogate Xylo together.

Cerberus breath! This was maddening. More than not knowing things, Hades hated having to wait to learn them.

Gaea uttered a heart-wrenching howl and curled herself tighter before collapsing on her side.

"Gaea? Gaea!" He ran to her.

Hades was an anxious god. Living in an Underworld with nothing but a curse separating you from the worst monsters ever spawned into existence would do that to you. But he'd rarely been afraid. His anger always kept fear at bay, yet in that moment he felt great fear – Gaea's fear. Which made it much worse.

"Mother of Life!" He tried to shake her out of her state. Gods aren't known to faint, especially primordial ones like her.

She gripped his arm and opened her eyes wide. Unfocused at first, they settled on him with fierce intensity. Hades had never put much stock in the superior hierarchy of the Three. To him, Gaea was just a glorified Titan. She had significant power, true, but the difference between the Titans' powers and those of the younger gods was one of range, not degree. In that moment, however, as her fevered gaze pierced his mind, blocking his Reach, and her grip crushed his arm, paralysing him, he considered the possibility he might have underestimated her greatly.

"Take her away. To the Underworld. Take them all! It's the only way to save them," she said feverishly.

Hades tried to free himself from Gaea's clutches to translocate, move even, but found himself helpless, completely at her mercy.

"*He*'s here!" she cried out, releasing him, then seemingly folding in on herself. When she lifted her head again, her face was that of an old woman, lined and wasted. "And they're almost here, toooo!" she howled dramatically, and pushed him away before he could stammer a reply.

Hades scrambled backwards to put some distance between them in case she changed her mind and grabbed him again. Gaea vanished even before he got to his feet, leaving him there, alone and aghast, his heart racing and his mind reeling, trying hard to make sense of what had just happened.

I need to find Hel.

He was about to translocate to the Boiling Lake when something Reached him: a prayer. That was odd. Hades rarely received prayers. Odder still was the voice of the one praying.

Chiron, is that you? he asked, knowing it couldn't be. It just couldn't. Gods don't pray.

'*Yes. Hades, I need… I need your help – please hurry.*'

Hades fumed. Gods don't plead for help either,

especially Titans. It was the damned Trickster meddling with his mind again. Had to be. He was probably the one who put Gaea into such a state, too.

Damn you, Loki! I'm in no mood for your games. What do you want?

'It's not Loki. It is I, Chiron. I need you at the Chronodéndron.'

Hades pulled at his hair again. This had to be a trap. Why would Chiron try to lure him to Yewlow if not for some wicked purpose? He sounded so desperate, though. No, it could not be him, but whoever it was, he was good. Too good to ignore. Hades spared a glance at the ring. Hel would be even more angry with him if the Nephilim came through because he left it unguarded. But something nefarious was definitely afoot. Perhaps Hecate was not as powerless as he'd hoped in Hel's moonless world. He had to be careful and play along with this impostor to figure it out. If he succeeded, perhaps Hel would not be too upset with him for leaving the Stump. He shook his head. Optimism didn't suit him. How come even his smallest choices always had to be between bad and dire? He sighed.

Yeah, sure, man. I'll be there in a moment, Hades replied casually to the prayer. He suspected someone had arrived through the Chronodéndron. Someone important. But it still did not explain why the horse was praying instead of Reaching to him.

It can't be Chiron, Hades reminded himself one last time before he vanished.

∞

Hades materialised some distance away from the Chronodéndron. He kept to his true form, for whoever was baiting him probably knew his old disguise well. He used to come here every dawn pretending to be a satyr to check for new arrivals, always taking great pains to avoid the centaur. How ironic that he now came purposely to meet him. He moved silently, invisible amidst the shadows, determined to ambush whoever was trying to ambush him.

Two mortals appeared in his Reach. One he recognised, the other... couldn't be right. He moved closer, not trusting his godly senses. He had to see this with his eyes.

Chiron lay against the Chronodéndron. Agnar sat by his side, a bowl of water in one hand, a handful of lavender in the other keeping flies away from the centaur's wounds.

Hades abandoned his invisibility along with his caution.

"Oh, you stupid horse." He tried to sound mocking, condescending even, but all he managed was disbelieving sympathy. "What has happened to you?" The answer to his question was obvious. After ages dealing with the dead, Hades knew well the look of a soon-to-be corpse. He should be dancing with joy. Instead, he dropped to his knees in front of the Titan, laden with sorrow.

"*How* did you let this happen?" Hades touched the gaping wound in the centaur's leg, confirming with horror the state of his mortal flesh. He didn't understand. How had Persephone or the Dharkan managed to ambush the Titan? Reach, never mind normal senses, should have been enough to warn him of danger. Sure, translocating wasn't Chiron's forte, but he could literally run like a horse; he could fly, for crying out loud!

"I figured you'd know," Chiron said morosely.

Hades' heart sank deeper. The Hydra had been his responsibility. Of course he would be blamed for this.

"It wasn't me! I had nothing to do with it, I swear. Persephone arrived unannounced. She took a ride with Apollo, apparently, and made an alliance with the rebel Dharkan behind my back. For what reason, I haven't a clue. I didn't know what she was doing. I'm sorry. I still don't, and I certainly didn't agree to any of it. You have to believe me!" The words came out rushed, unthought, almost desperate. Why did he need the Titan to know it hadn't been his fault? Hades should be taking credit for his mortality, not apologising for his wife's deeds. After all, this was what he'd wanted, wasn't it?

"Hel had nothing to do with it, either." *Had she?* Stars, he hoped not. And even if she had, why should he care what the dying horse thought? Cerberus breath, he wanted to punch something and stopped himself just short of punching the tree.

Chiron dismissed his concerns with a weary wave. "I know, I know. It was a child," he said, as if it explained the whole affair. "We were playing. I let my guard down."

Hades blinked. "A *child*? You were *playing* with a child?!" Brilliant. Hades threw his hands in the air in exasperation. Well, ain't that just the sort of stupid behaviour to expect from the horse. If he wasn't already dying, Hades would have killed him for his stupidity. Every god knows that of all the stages in a mortal's life, childhood is the most dangerous to mess with. Narrum children can be as vicious as adults. If not more so, because they either can't tell their actions are harmful to others or they know they have a good chance of getting away with their crimes unpunished.

"Do not blame the child, Hades. Nor me. We've both paid a dire price already. Blame the one who gave the weapon to the child." Chiron tried to talk further and coughed. Agnar offered the water bowl to his lips. He waved it away. "The funny thing is. I knew this would happen. I've known it for ages. It is the reason I came here. Ideth even told me how it would happen. And still I could not avoid it." He smiled bitterly. "We are far less powerful than we think, my friend."

Hades frowned. "You knew Persephone would come for the Hydra too?" Had every god in Olympus been plotting with Chronos behind his back all these aeons? He wouldn't put it past them. It would at least explain why he so often felt left out, caught off guard. Unwelcome and unappreciated. Hades pressed his lips and focused back on Chiron, a lot less sympathetic to his condition than he'd been before.

"No. Persephone was a surprise." Chiron tutted. "I always figured she'd find a way to harm you. But not like this. Not through me."

"Indeed." Hades agreed. It didn't make sense. "She's dead now, by the way."

The centaur raised his eyebrows. "Was she stupid enough to accidentally poison herself?" he asked in all seriousness.

Hades almost laughed. "She probably would have, had the poison been mixed with one of her rouges."

"Ah, missed opportunities, huh?" Chiron said as if reading his thoughts. They both chuckled, momentarily ignoring the mirthlessness of the situation.

Agnar murmured a criticism under his breath. Whenever Hades looked at the man, he saw Odin, so he didn't look at him very often. Still, the dryad's judgemental gaze, bouncing between him and Chiron while he absently waved insects away, was grating on Hades.

"The Dharkan turned on her, so I guess whatever her scheme was, it failed." Hades shrugged, doing his best to ignore the dryad's thoughts. "I just don't understand why she came after you, never mind how she got herself involved with the Dharkan in the first place. They despise Olympians."

Chiron nodded thoughtfully. "I have a theory. Persephone was impulsive, and she definitely wanted you dead, but she wasn't stupid enough to trust the Dharkan. She wouldn't just give them the Hydra's blood in good faith. She must have made some sort of bargain with one of the Aesir in exchange for her safety. Perhaps the Faithless Dharkan aren't so faithless after all. As to why me… maybe it was a test to see how fast the poison would act or a demonstration of what would it actually do to gods. After all, no one remembers the last time it was used on one. I believe the poison was meant to disable me, not kill. The Dharkan intended to feed on me, but I escaped before they had a chance to."

"Feed on you?" Hades asked, appalled at the idea.

"They probably learnt of Aedan's powers and how he'd gotten them," Chiron said gravely.

"Cerberus breath!" If Chiron was right, the situation was worse than Hades thought. Dharkan wanting to kill gods was one thing; Dharkan wanting to be gods themselves, something else entirely. Could Hel handle them if this was the case? Damnation, he should never have let her out of his sight.

Chiron gripped Hades' shoulder. *'There is more,'* he prayed, glancing at Agnar, obviously wanting to keep the dryad ignorant of whatever he said next. *'Before I... before this happened, I sensed something disturbing. I think one of the rebel Dharkan was hosting not an Aesir but an Olympian. Persephone might not have been the only one striking a deal with them.'*

That's preposterous. Who would dare? Hades thought. He certainly wouldn't. Taking a Dharkan as host was not much different from being a Wyrd, in his opinion, no matter what Hel said. Hades would never be a guest in anyone else's body. Then again, he was not Olympian.

'I suspect Hephaestus. He made the weapon for the child, after all,' Chiron prayed.

Hades shook his head. *Unlikely. He'd dead too.* And since Zeus was also dead and Apollo and Artemis were under Hel's 'care', or so she claimed, there weren't many other options left. Demeter, perhaps? No, Persephone would never agree with her mother long enough to work with her. Poseidon would not leave his precious ocean, and Hera would not leave Olympus, not even for Zeus or her children, especially after all this mess.

Chiron seemed taken aback for a moment, likely following a similar train of thought. He moved his front hoof to scratch the ground as he often did when angry, then laughed bitterly. '*Hephaestus is dead... That's two Olympians gone in one day. Soon to be three.*' He looked at himself and laughed some more, a mirthless laugh. Agnar stopped tending the wounds and sat back, silently cursing all deities.

'*Hades, I know how you feel about Hel,*' Chiron prayed once his feverish mirth faded. '*Even without Reach, I can see the way your eyes shine every time you think of her, how you smile when she looks at you. But you have to consider the possibility that she might be the one responsible for this, old friend.*'

Hades shook his head.

Chiron persisted. '*The Dharkan are hers. If she lures enough Olympian gods into them and imprisons the ones she can't ice directly like she did Artemis, she'll eventually rule both pantheons and their Underworlds.*'

Hades shook his head again. *No. Hel wouldn't do that to me or you, and she holds no grudge against Olympians. Everything she does is to defend herself, her world and those in it.* Hades realised the moment he thought the words that this fact fit well within Chiron's hypothesis. After all, Chiron's ambition had been to rule the forest, Zeus had tried to rule Aegea through the Suzerain, and Hades had crashed her domain uninvited. Not intentionally, mind, but still. His realm had caused a lot of trouble to hers.

'*Then do me a favour: Find Hephaestus. Ask him why he did it. For me,*' Chiron insisted.

Hephaestus is not in the Underworld. Not in my Underworld, that is, Hades admitted, pulling at his hair.

'Ah… It's worse than I thought, then.'

Hades disliked the accusation in the Titan's tone, yet he could neither deny it nor allow himself to consider it further. *That's mortality making you paranoid, horse. You helped us defeat the Suzerain. Why would Hel want to kill you?*

Chiron took a moment to answer, as if he was hoping he didn't have to. *'Because I'm no longer useful.'* He sighed. *'And because she knows I'm your friend, Hades. That I've always been. Our arguments kept me sane, especially while Ideth was away. There's only so much a god can share with mortals, no matter how special they are.'* He paused. *'But mostly because Loki wants to free Prometheus. Doesn't he? A Titan for a Titan.'*

Hades winced. How did Chiron know of his deal with Loki? Apparently mortality had finally made the Titan wise. Hades never intended to go ahead with it. Not permanently, anyway. Stars, it was all he could do not to translocate away in shame.

'It's all right. I should have died a long time ago, Hades. Apollo foresaw it. That was why Zeus brought me here. We created the forest as a sort of back garden of the Underworld for those retired from life but not quite dead yet. We hoped that by living alongside the dead I could be counted as one of them by the fates. We even told everyone I had died, gone to the stars. I became a myth amongst mortals. But no one cheats fate, not even us…'

"I don't want to hear it," Hades said out loud. He'd often wondered why Zeus had invested so much of his power to create this haunted version of Elysium. Like everything the king of Olympus did, he figured it was to annoy him, even if he had to admit he quite enjoyed having somewhere to go open to the sky.

Chiron sighed and remained silent.

Hades, unable to meet his friend's gaze, focused on Agnar. Stars, the frail creature looked more dejected than the dying Titan and twice as annoyed.

"Agnar, what in the shadow are you doing here with him?" the Underworld lord demanded angrily, changing the subject and hoping for a good reason to unleash his frustration on the dryad.

"I came with Arianh," Agnar replied in a deadpan tone, not taken aback in the slightest by the flames in Hades' eyes.

"And where is she?"

Agnar stared at the Chronodéndron morosely.

"Oh, Cerberus breath." *Women… They are every man's and god's curse*, Hades thought, pulling at his hair again. He'd better go back to horns before he made himself bald.

"Can you take me to Ideth?" Chiron asked. "She's the other reason I called you here. I need to see her, before…"

Hades refused to hear any more of the Titan's dying talk. "I can do better. I'll take you to Gaea. She'll fix you." She had to. Of course, he had to find her first and hope whatever had gotten into her had passed.

Chiron shook his head. "No. I don't want to be fixed. I want Ideth. Take me to Ideth."

"She's with Gaea at the Stump," Hades lied. The

truth was, he had no idea where Ideth was, but he expected she hadn't strayed far from her obtuse son.

"You're wrong. She's here, in the forest. About a half a day's walk in that direction," Chiron said.

"How can you possibly know that?"

Chiron pointed at the tree by his side. "Yewlow told me."

Hades eyed the Chronodéndron suspiciously. Chronodéndrons didn't lie, it was known. They also didn't speak unless their God had something to say. And for Chronos to have something so specific to say meant he had his attention focused on this world. Time did not exist in the Underworld, but in Aegea… *Oh stars, could it be?* Hades expanded his senses as far as they would go, almost expecting to see the God of Time jumping out from behind a bush. Nothing. A presence like Chronos would be sensed even from the depths of his realm. Hades allowed himself to relax a fraction.

"Fine. We'll find Ideth, then I'll still take you to Gaea. Agreed?"

Chiron nodded dutifully.

Hades stood up, pondering how he was ever going to translocate with the mortally wounded Titan.

"Take the glider," Agnar said, pointing somewhere beyond the rocks as if he'd read his mind. "I won't need it."

"All right, bring it over here," Hades said to him.

"You're a god, can't you will it closer by yourself?" Agnar asked rhetorically.

Hades glared at him. There was definitely too much of Odin left in the dryad for his taste.

"There's no need," Chiron said, struggling to stand up, then limping his way on three legs towards the Suzerain's mount. He covered about three-quarters of the distance before falling over, stood up again and made it the rest of the way. Hades had to admit, even if only to himself, Titans were indeed tougher than Olympians. Or just far more stubborn.

"What about you?" Hades asked Agnar before he left to join the centaur.

"I won't go anywhere until Arianh returns," he said, sitting cross-legged by the tree.

"Suit yourself." Hades really couldn't care less about him or Arianh at the moment. He translocated to Chiron before the mulish creature, bracing precariously against the glider, fell over again.

"Give me a hand," Chiron said, trying to get himself on the mount. His back legs were not complying.

"Hold on…" Hades almost said "friend," but his nature demanded he say "horse" instead. Chiron tutted.

Hades used his will to lift the centaur up on it. Under different circumstances this would be an affront even to a minor deity, but the effort of walking had cost the Titan almost all his remaining strength along with his pride, so he made no protest.

Hades sat himself in the driver's space, unsure of what to do with the controls in front of him. If they were going anywhere in the forest, they'd have to drive there. Moving an object to him was simple; moving an object with him on it was not.

He was about to try a button at random when Hel summoned him to her presence. She sounded both furious and terrified. He pulled on his hair again. "Women," he muttered under his breath. When you need them, you can't find them, but if they need you, you better translocate to their aid immediately or else. And they always needed you at the most inconvenient moments.

"It's all right, I can drive it by myself," Chiron said, guessing his thoughts.

"Are you sure?" Hades was already climbing off the damn thing.

"Yes. Go to her." Chiron sighed, holding the wheel. "Just remember what I said. Hel might be innocent, she might even love you, however… she is her father's daughter. No love stands a chance against a god's selfishness."

"Are you seriously giving me relationship advice?"

Chiron leaned closer. "I'm asking you to be the selfish, distrustful prick I know you can be, hmm?"

Hades nodded reluctantly.

"Good. On this side or the other, we'll see each other again soon – friend." With that, Chiron departed, gliding over the ferns.

Hades mulled over his friend's words while he watched him zigzagging through the trees, wondering when the Titan had learnt to drive one of those so well.

Then the sky exploded.

INTERLUDE 1

The Arrival

I find Ulla sobbing by a creek behind Ulcan's cabin. After what she witnessed inside it, I'm amazed she was sensible enough not to stray too far away. The poor woman looks more wretched than I feel, and to be fair, her appearance does little justice to her own state of mind either. Fabrian's death left quite a dent in her thought process, and whatever she's been through since that fated night in Relicum's temple has only made it worse. To now come face to face with the man responsible for her lover's death and be utterly powerless against him is pushing her spirit to a breaking point.

"Ulla…" I say, placing a hand on her shoulder.

She slaps it away. "Don't touch me!"

Stars, give me patience.

"May I sit by your side?"

"Why?"

"Because I want to speak to you, and I would rather not talk to the back of your head."

"Pfff. I don't know you, and we have nothing to talk about, *goddess*. I hate gods almost as much as I do

Wraiths." She glowers at me. "Freezing gods… always meddling in our affairs, messing with our minds. You don't get to *talk* to me, to tell me what to think or how to feel. Leave me alone!"

When I don't, she unsheathes her sword, its runes glowing a bright red. I recognise it as Hephaestus' work, embedded with rune magic borrowed from the Aesir. A protection spell, maybe? Whatever it is, I keep my distance from the blade.

"Actually, you do know me," I say, sitting down out of Ulla's reach. "We've met before. A few days ago, in Relicum. I was wearing a different body."

Ulla clears the tears from her eyes to stare at me intently. I doubt she can see much in the dark, so I create a tiny amount of starlight in the palm of my hand. This seems to simultaneously amaze and aggravate her.

"You were the Wyrd in Ileana's body," she murmurs.

I smile. "Yes. Thanks to me, the Suzerain is gone. So you see, I'm on your side."

Ulla stands up in a fury. "It's because of *you* the Dharkan escaped!" She lunges her sword at me. I realise the runes are not part of a protection spell, but some sort of curse to curb the dryad's aversion to kill. I close my hand and extinguish the light just in time to dodge the blow aimed at my throat and move further away from the irate dryad.

"You're the one to blame for all this!" Ulla screams in the darkness.

For fuck's sake… From plagues of locusts and poor harvests back when I was mortal, to the war of the pantheons after I became a goddess, whenever there's blame to be assigned, sure enough it will be to Psyche. I have no patience for this. I flick my hand and will Ulla's fingers to go numb. The sword drops on the rocks at her feet. She whimpers, standing defenceless in the dark, terrified though still furious.

"Freezing coward! What would you gods be without your tricks, huh? Come on, show yourself and fight me as a mortal. I dare you!"

I sigh, fully aware that it's this sort of reaction that reinforces the blame. But I have no desire to elaborate on the current situation or to apologise for something I didn't do. Sometimes taking the blame is easier than explaining your innocence.

I glance up at the fast-approaching ship, take a deep breath, then release a long-suffering exhalation. *Sometimes yes; not this time.*

"I'm not fighting you, Ulla. And you are mistaken. Aedan wasn't there for me, or Ileana. He was doing Odin's bidding, meeting with Arianh to discuss their union."

"But you didn't –"

"You're right. I did nothing. I could have raised the alarm sooner. Perhaps even stopped him. I didn't. I am truly sorry for what happened to Fabrian. I liked him, believe it or not. At the time, I wasn't sure what was happening. I felt reluctant to interfere, for I admit, I was curious to know what the Dharkan would do next." I shake my head at the memory of Aedan's touch, pressing Ileana's body against the wall, his bite on her neck, and I have to clear my throat before continuing. "You have to let go of this hate, Ulla.

Looking for something or someone to blame won't bring Fabrian back. It just takes him away, again and again. Believe me, I know a few things about blame and hatred. Channel your grief into something more constructive, for there are bigger things happening in this world right now than your grief."

"Of course the gods' petty skirmishes always take precedence over the suffering of mortals," she sneers.

Breathe. "The gods' petty skirmishes often are the cause of suffering to mortals, so yes, they should take precedence. And Fabrian's death was an accident, Ulla. Aedan never meant him, you, or any of the living harm."

"Liar. He just admitted that the Dharkan are about to invade our settlements!"

"And he came here to *warn* you. To seek an alliance with the living, for their sake, not his. Aedan is not like the other Dharkan. Every rule has exceptions, and those exceptions are worth paying attention to, so hopefully one day they'll become the rule. And to be fair, this was *their* world long before the gods brought your kind here. Give him a chance. Please, for your baby's sake?" I'd rather not use her pregnancy like this, but most women are more susceptible to a change of opinion when pregnant, and I have no time to reason with her with fairer arguments.

Ulla clutches her stomach for a long, silent moment.

"Then it's true what he said..." The words are inaudible without Reach.

"Yes. Surely, you must have known."

She shakes her head. "No. I didn't think I could. I

shouldn't be. I took the tea… I –" Her expression hardens. "Give him a chance? If what he says is true – if *anything* he said is true, now more than ever, we must eliminate their race."

"They will destroy themselves under Iva's command," I say hopefully.

"After taking how many lives?"

I press my lips together. Dent or no, her mind is sharper than most. I'm about to say something profound and deceitful, but she has no interest in listening to any of it. Her focus is not on the lives of others, only on the one growing inside her.

"I should be happy. And yet I feel worse," she whispers.

I move closer, realising I've completely misread her apprehension and despair. "Ah… Because you don't want it. I'm sorry…"

"Don't listen to my thoughts," she hissed. "I'm thinking all sorts of bad things at the moment. It doesn't mean I mean them!"

"Fair enough."

I move to sit on a rock nearby and soak my feet in the water. A few moments pass.

"Oh goddess. What is wrong with me?" Ulla asks.

"Er… are you talking to me, or –?" By the way mortals so often invoke the gods, sometimes it's hard to tell if we're being prayed to or cursed at.

Ulla looks in my general direction. "This baby is all I have of Fabrian, and I resent it. What sort of creature am I to feel this way? Maybe something broke in me when that monster hit my head."

There's almost too much anguish and guilt in her

statement for any woman to bear. I bring forth the tiny star again so she can see my face when I speak.

"Did you want children before?" I ask solemnly.

"No. No, I never did."

"Then there's nothing wrong with you or your head. You remain the same. The only thing that has changed is your circumstance, so stop punishing yourself for being who you are."

"It's easy for you to say."

"Yes, it is. Not every woman is cut out to be a mother. Gaea only gives the ability to create life, not the talent to nourish it, nor even the desire to do so. Most manage to at least adapt to the role. Others never do. And no, I don't know which type you are. You'll have to figure it out for yourself. But once again, blame and hate won't solve a thing."

Ulla blinks. "You speak from experience."

"Sort of… it was a long time ago."

"What did you do?"

Cold water splashes my face. I realise I am hitting the stream with my feet a little too vigorously and force myself to stop. "Nothing. Things just sorted themselves out."

Lightning cracks above us. Not a good sign.

"Help!" someone shouts. Sounds like Ulcan.

"Stay here," I urge Ulla and run back to the cabin, glad for the distraction. Stars, the conversation really wasn't going the way I planned.

I find Pan pacing by the rear window, bushy ears hanging low. "Aedan found Cornus' horn," he explains.

Fuck…

The two bulky men roll on a pile of firewood, intent on killing each other. Except the hunter doesn't stand a chance against the Dharkan.

"Aedan, stop!" I shout with as much authority as I can put into a word. It's of no use. Aedan's wrath would put many gods to shame. As does his power. Power and rage are seldom a healthy combination. The trees burning around us can testify to that.

I curse again. My talents are practically useless against forces of nature. Still, I have to do something.

∞

"Aedan, stop!" Psyche commands in her aristocratic tone.

I'm done taking orders from you, little princess. Done with being the good Wraith. Done with being kept in the dark, used, overruled, underestimated, blamed, shouted at, slapped. Just done with it all! They want a monster? Well, they have one. The hunter is not an honourable man. Why should I refrain from taking his life? He has taken many lives, more than most Dharkan. If we are murderers, then so is he. He doesn't even care that much for his own life, judging by the way he treats his body, and he's too selfish to help his own people. In all the years we've known each other, he has never shown me any friendship, kindness or respect. All he ever did was show up at my cave unannounced asking for favours: 'Aedan, can you freeze this snake?' or 'Aedan, will you help me carry that deer?' And in return he'd give me a half-hearted 'Thanks.' Burn his thanks! Thanks don't buy leather to keep the sunlight from burning me to a crisp. I couldn't pay for Cornus' shoes with 'thanks'. And now, not only does he blatantly mock my plea for help, not even for myself but for the sake of his miserable race, I find the greedy bastard had the nerve to mutilate my friend's corpse as well? And he bit me to boot! No, Psyche. I won't stop. I'll enjoy freezing this piece of ash even while his Prana, rancid with the many lives he's consumed, makes me sick. The world will not mourn his loss.

'*I said, stop!*' Psyche shouts directly into my mind. My knees weaken, and my hands lose their grip on the hunter's throat. I stare at them, momentarily unable to stand or move properly. She did this to me before when I tried to take her Prana. Back then, I did not understand how. Now I realise her power is sheer force of will.

"We need him," she says, panting.

"What for?"

She hesitates. "The horn. He knows something important about the horn. I... I never got a chance to figure out what back at the tavern," she says sheepishly. "Please, can I..."

"Don't!" I push her hand away from the hunter's forehead. As if I'll ever let Psyche touch my prey after what she did to Odin. She purses her lips, radiating annoyance.

I give the hunter a vigorous shake to force him back to consciousness. "What does the horn do?" I ask him, glaring at her.

"Er... what?" he croaks, eyes unfocused on the canopies above.

"I know you weren't the one who killed Cornus, and that's the only reason you're still breathing, but I want to know why you took his horn. What does it do?"

"I don't know…" he mumbles.

"You lie." I shake him again. Harder this time.

"The Blacksmith wants it! Every hunter and his cousin knows about it. He's promised a reward and everything. I never expected to find one, and I would never hunt Cornus to get it, but…" He shivers with cold. "I'd just been attacked. My catch was ruined. Cornus was dead, and the horn was right there for the taking. I did what I had to."

Burn me, this creature really can't see past his own greed.

"What did the Blacksmith want it for?" I ask, striving to remain reasonable lest I accidentally ice him.

"You'll have to ask him."

"He's dead," Psyche says a bit too emphatically.

Ulcan sneers at her suspiciously, then turns his bloodshot gaze back to me again. "Well, fuck me, Aedan. If only there was a god around whom you could ask about these things. I bet my beard your lovely companion knows why he wanted it."

I blink back at Psyche. "Do you?"

She shakes her head vehemently.

The hunter points a finger at her. "She knew I had the horn, and she didn't tell you. I bet my beard –"

Psyche pulls his beard hard enough to shut him up. "You ungrateful piece of shit! I didn't tell him because I knew he would kill you. As he nearly bloody did now!"

"So neither of you can tell me why the horn was important to the Blacksmith?" I ask, straining patience.

Hunter and goddess exchange bewildered glances in silence.

"Then he dies."

"Noooo!" Psyche shrills.

Flaming sun, I've heard banshees make less agonising cries. The hunter can't possibly mean that much to her, can he? Psyche's writhing on the ground, eyes rolling back, drool spilling over her chin. There's no way she cared this much for the man, or anyone else for that matter.

Something's wrong.

∞

I've just braced myself to separate Aedan from his prey – and be shocked again in the process, I'm sure – when an acute, almost unbearable howl pierces my Reach.

Mika? I recognise his voice immediately. What comes next makes no sense, though.

There are no words to describe his anguish. I feel it as if it's my own. It burns and tears me from within. Unlike any pain of the flesh, this is the pain of a soul being ripped from its true self, like mine was when I travelled through the Chronodéndron in Ileana's body.

An image forms in my minds' eye: A puppy writhing amongst mangled corpses. Bloody foam pours from his mouth; his lips move in a silent plea, but neither I nor anyone can help him now. He uses his last vestiges of willpower in this realm to send me a message – a warning.

Mika, no. No. "Noooo!"

∞

"Psyche?"

"Noooo," she howls. Actually *howls*! Pan is at her side now, trying to ease her distress, a strong and genuine concern on his fiendish features.

I reluctantly let go of the hunter's neck to join him. "What is wrong with her?"

"I don't know," the satyr says, shaking his head, ears flat along his skull.

"She was fine a moment ago," I say.

"Are you blind or plain stupid?" Pan asks rhetorically. "She was one drop away from bursting the dam."

I stare at him. "What in the shadow does that mean?"

The satyr shakes his head while Psyche mutters her distress, using words I don't understand.

"What is she saying?" I ask.

"Nonsense."

"What sort of nonsense?"

Pan's bushy ears move restlessly as he glares at me. "She's saying 'no, don't, no' and 'Mika, no'. What the frost is a Mika?"

"The wolf," I say, now actually concerned.

"Wolf? As in Fenrir wolf?" Pan's expression turns feral. "He's attacking her from another realm. Leave her be!" he shouts to the trees. "She's suffered enough because of you monsters!"

I gape incomprehensibly at the satyr. "What are you talkin–"

The sky comes alight in a multitude of colours, each piercing my eyes like hot needles, frustrating all attempts to reopen them properly. The night turns to day – except no day in Aegea is ever this bright. A deafening roar follows, and the entire world seems to warp. A force washes over me, similar to when a god's soul takes over my body. Only worse.

I roar with distress, unable to speak.

"Ice spikes! What the frost are you gods doing now?" Ulla asks accusingly. Flaming sun, she sounds as if she's right on top of me. I chastise myself for letting my guard down and immediately put some distance between us, for I have not forgotten her murderous hatred, and I'd rather not experience the sting of her blade on top of everything else.

"Not *we*! No god I know can do *that*," Pan says.

"Do what?" I ask, as blind and almost as helpless as a cub. The light is not only painfully bright, it's unnatural. It has no heat. Something this bright ought to result from a conflagration.

"The Stump. It's like a thousand suns shine above it," Pan explains.

"You can't possibly see the Stump from here."

"I said above it!"

Sound waves crash over the land repeatedly. The ground quakes. The air itself seems to shimmer.

"It's happening again," Ulla whimpers. "It's the Fell all over again!"

"Nephilim," Psyche croaks.

"Burn it!" I curse in frustration, still prostrated on the ground, unable to act.

They got through. Somehow they got through the portal, I pray to Hel and get no answer. Fear creeps into my mind. I search for Psyche's hand and find one of Pan's already holding it. I have to fight the urge to take back the life force I gave him earlier. I don't know why. I couldn't care less about her hand, and this is no time to be jealous or petty. I just wish I could see properly so I could at least aim a lightning bolt at whatever is causing this nightmare.

The light goes out as suddenly as it appeared, leaving the world in complete darkness. A cacophony of screams, howls, coos, cries, bleats and squeaks echo across the land.

Nearby, the hunter coughs.

"Not. Dead," he says right before he loses consciousness again.

Ulla goes to him. Apparently taking her revenge on me is not a priority. A good thing, since the rage that fuelled me just moments ago has drained. Replacing it is a deep sense of disquiet. I turn to Psyche. If someone knows what's happened, it's her, and I'll be burned if I let her keep me in the dark once again.

∞

"Psyche? Psyche!" The Dharkan's voice scrapes through my sore senses like a chalk stick scratching on a schist board. I want to tell him to be quiet and let me think, but the words lose their way somewhere between my mind and my tongue. I struggle to reconnect with my body. Aedan slapping me hard across the cheek to snap me to attention only makes the task harder. I wonder how long he's been waiting for an excuse to do that and curse at the man. This time the words come out loud and clear. For some reason, cursing always came easy for me.

"That's my girl," Pan says. He's squeezing my hand so hard, it hurts. I ask him to let it go.

"What did she say?" Aedan asks. I must have spoken in my native tongue. My mind is not quite right yet.

"It's not important," Pan says, releasing the hand.

I open my eyes with difficulty. The sky is dark again. Stars shine above us, the ground is steady, and the water in the brook runs down its course as usual. The forest is intact, more or less; its inhabitants, I'm not so sure. Their fear reeks to the heavens, and their cries fill my senses. Even Pan, of all creatures, oozes apprehension. And with reason. Every plane of existence, every realm, every reality rippled over each other during the event. And at its centre…

"What just happened?" Aedan demands to know.

I don't know how to explain it. "Help me up. I think it's better if you see it for yourself."

I get on my feet with the Dharkan's help and make my way up the hill to find a better vantage point. Pan leads the way, eager to contemplate the thing able to frighten even him. Ulla stays with the hunter, which is just as well.

"Aedan…" I say, still holding on to his arm, and I pull him close for a private word while we walk. "What happened back there, with Ulcan… I mean, your power. You're struggling to control it."

"I'm learning to control it."

"It's corrupting you," I say bluntly. "Gods' power requires souls. It was not meant to be wielded by mortals. I believe it turned the Suzerain insane and will turn you too."

"Says the apotheosised human princess."

I bite my cheek. "So perhaps you should listen to her."

He stares me down in that cold, suspicious way of his. "What do you care?"

"Someone has to."

He sneers. "No. This is not about my well-being or sanity. This is about me hosting you again. You're wasting your breath. As I told you before, I will never host you, goddess of the soul. Ever."

I'm so angry I want to hit him. Too late I realise I sank my nails into his arm instead.

He gives me a quizzical look. "You are afraid," he says. "Not of me. And not of whatever just happened. Not really." He tilts his head as if he can see through me better from that angle. "Who is it you want to hide from and why?"

I shake my head. It's uncanny how perceptive Aedan can be sometimes. But perception is nothing without context. "It's better if you don't know."

"I disagree, little princess. And who were you talking to back at the cabin?"

I skip a step. "How could you tell?" He doesn't reply. "Was someone talking to you as well?"

He shakes his head, amused.

"You know the way Hel closes her eyes when she's Reaching for souls?" he says. "You do that too. But when you actually communicate with them, you just stare into nothing and you forget to breathe."

"Stars, I didn't realise I was that transparent." I try to sound sarcastic, but the truth is, I feel dizzy and more than a bit foolish for not realising that. It seems I put so much effort into hiding my thoughts that I forget to disguise my behaviour. *Damnation…*

"All gods are transparent when you really pay them attention," Aedan says casually.

I'm still awed by his insight when we reach the top of the hill. It's dark, so I close my eyes and Reach across the land, directly at the Stump. It is as I feared.

"Stars. We are so fucked," I say.

"What in the shadow…" Aedan murmurs, squinting in confusion. "Is that…?" He massages his eyelids and then takes another look, as if to be sure his eyes are not playing tricks on him.

"What do you see?" Pan asks impatiently. As a Wyrd, he has no Reach nor the Dharkan's ability to see in the dark. As frustrating as the condition is, in this particular case, he's the fortunate one.

"It's a spaceship, er… a stellar chariot," I explain to him.

"It's obscene," Aedan adds.

"Huh?" Pan asks.

My battered mind struggles to find the appropriate words to describe the sight. If these Nephilim based their technology on the old gods' magic, the ship's design was probably intentional, for the stars know the gods have a lot to answer for humankind's obsession with their genitals. But to call it a giant phallus, as fairly accurate as it is, wouldn't do justice to the severity of the monstrosity looming over the land.

"A giant cock just landed on the Stump," Hades says as he materialises right in front of us, sparing me the explanation. He's wearing his actual form: a handsome daemon with skin black as coal, smouldering eyes and long shadowy hair falling over a cloak of darkness.

"You just can't help yourself, can you?" Hel says, appearing at his side, glacial and acerbic as ever.

Hades shrugs. "It's what you were all thinking."

"Hades? You have quite the nerve to show your face up here. Your real face, no less," Pan says belligerently.

The dark lord grins. "Pan! You're alive. And still fated, I see."

The two gods glower at each other.

"No thanks to you," Pan mutters between gritted teeth. "Are you done playing the satyr?"

"Yeah… My disguise was blown. Blame this one." He points at me, then lifts to his tippy toes. "And I could never get the hang of the hoofs. I don't know how you manage."

"I was born with them," Pan says dryly.

"Oh well, we all bear our curses."

"Indeed," Hel says pointedly to Hades.

"What are you two doing here?" I ask the Underworldly couple. The forest is hardly their element, with or without disguises.

"Better than over there," Hades sneers at the World Tree, then spreads his arms wide. "Hey, big guy, it's good to see you're all right." Hades hugs a very confused Aedan before he can react. I raise a suspicious eyebrow at him. Gods don't touch mortals unless there's a good reason. He grins at me from behind Aedan's shoulder.

"How did you find us?" the Dharkan asks, putting some distance between him and the overly affectionate Hades.

"I followed your prayers. So you can stop praying now," Hel replies to him.

"Apologies, goddess. It's been a tough night."

"Tell me about it." Despite her usual coldness, there's genuine weariness behind Hel's words.

"I followed her," Hades says a little too defensively, pointing at Hel.

From where, I wonder when I see the mixed look of surprise and suspicious sheepishness they give each other.

"Where are the others?" I ask.

Hades and Hel exchange cagey glances again. Stars, they are perfect for each other. They claim to have no idea what happened to the others, which means whatever shady machinations these two were up to, they did not take place in this realm.

Hel closes her eyes to better see her world as only she can. "Arianh and Agnar left earlier today on one of the Suzerain's mounts. Last I checked they were on their merry way to the Gharb, which is probably where they are now. I guess ruling Aegea turned out to be too much for the Aossi queen." Hel frowns. "No, wait." She opens her mouth to speak, then hesitates, tilting her head as if straining to hear something. "Agnar is still in the forest. He's at the Chronodéndron! What does he think he's doing?" She grimaces. "That's strange." The grimace deepens. "There's some sort of anomaly in the forest. I can't quite pin it down to a specific location. It's constantly shifting. No… transposing." Hel opens her eyes wide. I see a fleeting concern in them, quickly banished under layers of emotionless ice. "Do you know anything about this, Hades?"

Dark as he is now, Hades almost disappears into the gloom when she asks, the fire momentarily fading within him. "I believe it's Hecate. She has a talent for barriers, my lady," he replies almost apologetically.

"What about Ideth? Is she still in *there*?" Aedan spares an anguished glance across the land. In his strange honourable way, he considers Ideth his responsibility, and the thought of the nymph at the Nephilim's mercy clearly disturbs him. And then there's Ileana, of course, or what was left of her, locked inside the vault.

"I don't know, Aedan," Hel says tiredly, "but I can't find her anywhere, so it is likely…" She turns to me. "I was hoping you could help us find out more, goddess of the soul."

"You can't Reach any of the others?" I ask, puzzled. "It's your world."

Hel's jaw tenses. "Psyche, my world is under attack. And in case you haven't noticed, we've also suffered a major temporal and spatial distortion. I can barely find my bearings, let alone anyone else's. So can you, for once, just answer the burning question."

Beneath her icy demeanour, Hel appears beyond weary, worried on the verge of anguish. What I have to say will only make things worse. I have to tell her about Fenrir, but there's an awful lot in my Reach I don't understand. I need to be extra mindful of anything I say.

"I can Reach Chiron. He's alive but not well. And you're right, there is an anomaly in the forest: a hex. He's heading towards it at great speed," I say to her meaningfully, avoiding Hades' gaze then take a deep breath and begin pacing in a circle, eyes tightly shut, making sure I don't miss anything or say the wrong thing. "I can't Reach Gaea's soul anywhere. The soul of the Goddess of Life is pretty hard to miss, so she's either not in this realm or she's inside the Stump."

"She's fine," Hel grumbles. "She went to check on her precious little tree again." Ice spreads over her skin with barely contained rage. "Burn her! She was supposed to protect *that* tree."

I glance at the Stump and back at Hel. "Is there another?"

"She has many trees," Hades interjects dismissively.

"Forget about Gaea. She can take care of herself. We have larger issues at hand," Hel says.

"Larger than Gaea?"

"Hades!"

"Give me a break, Hel! Believe it or not, I am quite anxious with the turn of events. This is how I cope."

He's more than anxious; he's afraid. But not of the thing standing over the dead Tree. There's something else; something worse haunting his thoughts that I can't quite Reach. And a sadness unlike any I've ever experienced from the Underworld lord. There one moment, then banished the next.

"Fenrir…" I begin, but lose my nerve. Stars, it's one thing to think something, quite another to put it in words.

"You can Reach him?" Relief washes over Hel. "Flaming pup. Where is he?"

"He was in the vault with the others," I say pointedly.

A thin layer of ice appears over Hel's face. Her version of a blanch.

Yes, I know what you did, I say to her telepathically.

"What others?" Hades asks, eyes darting between Hel and me. He doesn't know. It doesn't surprise me, really. For every secret a god shares with another, there are three or four they keep to themselves.

"Burn it! We need to get him out," the Niflheim goddess says, recovering fast. She's a better liar than I gave her credit for. Well, she is Loki's daughter, after all.

"We can't," I say.

"Why not?"

I think about what I saw, what I felt, what Mika told me, and share the information with her. The goddess falters, leaning on Hades for support. Her lips struggle to remain pressed together; her eyes glaze behind a thin sheet of sleet. There's no pretence there.

"Why would he Reach you instead of me?"

I bite my lip. "Maybe because it was easier for his soul?" It is the truth, just not the whole truth. The amount of willpower required to break through the Stump, never mind the vault itself, would tear most gods apart, but souls that share a certain affinity are able to communicate on a level beyond Reach.

Hel pins me with her glacial stare, reading me as well as I read her.

"Girls, care to share?" Hades prompts.

"Fenrir's dead," I say. Stars, I'm starting to sound like a broken herald.

"He can't be! He's not in my realm," Hel says adamantly.

"Are you sure?" Hades asks.

"I think I'd recognise my brother's soul!"

"So he's probably still trapped inside the vault. Either that, or…" I realise what I'm about to say and stop talking, unwilling to admit the possibility.

"Spell it out," Hel demands.

My cheeks are raw at this point. "Or it's destroyed," I whisper.

"Did you destroy it?" Aedan asks. "Is that why you were in a state back there?"

I scowl at him and his opinion of me. "No," I say scornfully. "I was *in a state* because I felt his pain as the poison burned through his body after he –" I stop myself again, pinching the bridge of my nose whilst surreptitiously drying a stubborn tear.

"After he what?" Pan asks, eyes open wide, ears pointed with interest in our conversation.

I moan. *There's really no proper way to say this.* "After he… ate the Suzerain."

Hel's eyes flash a deep blue. Trees freeze and crack all around us. "The Suzerain is gone. His body and spirit obliterated. I personally saw to it!"

I throw up my arms in surrender. "As best I can tell, he built himself a new body in your absence. His flesh was tainted by a similar substance he injected Ileana's body with. I believe he did it on purpose. He must have known who Mika is… somehow. Either that or he's even more paranoid than a god."

"Cerberus breath, woman! How can you possibly know all this?"

"Fenrir told me. Right before the Nephilim arrived. I felt his soul sundering from his body… I Reached it. He showed me what happened… He urged us to run to the other side, to save ourselves. He was so scared…" I'm crying now. I really didn't want to cry again, for fuck's sake.

"Oh pup…" Hel turns away, ice gathering at the corner of her eyes.

"And the evening started so well," Hades says ruefully. "Two Olympians dead. I was about to throw a party."

I frown at him. Sometimes I think Hades is colder than Hel. Whatever the cause for his deep sadness, it's not Fenrir, nor Persephone.

"One of those Olympians was your wife," Aedan accuses him, as if reading my thoughts.

"So?" Hades asks menacingly.

"So you finally found a way to break the curse. Well done," I say sarcastically.

Without his satyr features, he can't hide the spitefulness behind those flaming eyes. *'She broke it herself. I didn't care enough to stop her,'* Hades says directly to my mind, so as not to further distress Hel or to not expose himself to the others as the devious creature he is, it's hard to tell.

Why did you do it? I have to ask him.

'Why? For love, dear Butterfly. The most powerful force in the Universe. You should know that.'

Eros' love is not real.

'No. But my love for Hel is. And I won't let past mistakes get between us.'

And I meant why did you send me to Hephaestus, knowing what he would do to me.

Hades' flaming eyes narrow to slits. To his credit, he doesn't deny it. *'Ah, careful with those accusations, Butterfly. Yes, I knew what he wanted, not what he would do to get it. I don't have the talent for foresight. And sure, I have a reputation to maintain, but it's not fair to always blame the dark lord for your misfortunes. Especially when you know very well there are other, darker lords to blame.'*

I swallow. "You lie," I say out loud.

"Do I?" He grins. "And yet, I'm not the one hiding the truth. Really, Psyche, when will you learn to shield your thoughts properly? Come on, will you tell Aedan or shall I?" The way Hades is able to read my mind disconcerts me. I'm sure it has something to do with when he accessed it through Ileana. And although he's got the best of me now, he should have known better.

"Tell me what?" Aedan demands.

"Nothing," I say, taking a purposeful step towards Hades. He steps back cautiously. Good, at least he still fears what I can do to him, even if his fear is not strong enough to stop him antagonising me. He must fear something or someone more, then.

Hel turns around, curiosity making her forget her grief for a moment. "There's more?"

"Oh yes. Go on, tell them, Butterfly."

I glare at Hades, wondering what he can possibly gain from this.

"Tell me what?" Aedan repeats, sparks cracking between his fingers.

Now here's a stellar opportunity to lie, for I know the truth will only make things worse. Not to mention it will be a nightmare to explain it. I pinch the bridge of my nose again, considering how much to reveal to appease their curiosities, then glance up at Aedan. *Stars, he's going to blame me for this too.* The thing is, if I don't tell him now and he finds out later, he'll never trust me. And if he does believe me now, then the stars know what he might do next. I take a deep breath and address him directly.

"It's Ileana."

His expression doesn't change. "What about her?"

"She's alive."

CHAPTER 10

Ileana

Ileana ambled her way up the Stump, partially because the teleportation rings freaked her out, but mostly because she was in no hurry to meet the Nephilim.

They too freaked her out.

She had yet to come up with a good explanation for her father's absence. To say the Suzerain's been eaten by a giant wolf was bad enough; to say that wolf had been a god from a rival pantheon who disguised himself as a boy to successfully gain access to the Stump and that he then got close enough to her father to eat him was the sort of thing the Nephilim executed their subjects for. Psyche, the goddess who had temporarily haunted Ileana's body and mind, believed the truth to be disappointing. She obviously never had to deal with the truths in Ileana's life. A good thing, for if Psyche ever found out the truth about how she became a Wyrd, she'd probably kill her – again.

Ileana still wasn't sure what happened on that fated evening by the Chronodéndron, not exactly. She could hardly tell the difference between the memories of events she experienced while sharing her mind with Psyche and what had been transferred into her new body from her life before. She knew she had successfully lured the goddess of the soul from whatever corner of the Universe she was hiding in, trapped her and brought her to her father in order to be reborn as a goddess herself. It'd taken her years of prayers and curses to get the goddess's attention, but she'd done it. She'd become her host, then travelled through time only to find out her father had already found a better, more efficient way to own a god.

He'd also lied about the Dharkan and his role in their extinction.

Oh, Ileana was not surprised her father had used her as another expendable pawn to achieve his goals, then left her to wither at the end of the world, nor that he'd kept her in the dark regarding the part he'd played in bringing about the end of said world. He always liked to withhold information from others so he would appear cleverer than them. As he used to say: 'The easiest way to get ahead is to hold everyone else back.' But what he did to Aedan was unforgivable. One thing Ileana knew for certain: She would not shed tears for the man. Even if for no other reason than the fact death would never truly claim him.

Still… had he known about the wolf all along? Was that why he'd made his flesh poisonous? Ileana wouldn't put it past him. Could he also have known how she would feel about Aedan? Could that have been the reason he'd been so intent on destroying his entire race? No, she refused to believe it. Alek Dveer was a heartless piece of slush, paranoid beyond reason, and he certainly had a knack for crippling others with paranoia and self-doubt, but he was not omniscient. And neither was she. Falling in love was definitely not part of *her* plan.

Ileana groaned in frustration. What a mess this situation turned out to be for her. Couldn't the wolf boy have waited until *after* the Nephilim arrived to eat her father? That would have been more useful. True, the wolf saved her the trouble of having to kill him herself, which she eventually would, of course. But not just yet. Dealing with the Nephilim was his job. She wasn't prepared for the task. He hadn't had the chance to educate her about the Stump, its machines, or the details of his agreement with the Nephilim gods. She hadn't even had time to adjust to her new body, to say nothing of the mess Psyche left behind in her mind.

Ileana felt a pang of shame at the thought of killing her father. How strange. She'd fantasised about his death often enough. And yet when she saw him being brutally devoured, she felt nothing. It wasn't shock, nor pity. A life spent in the harsh Gharb would cure anyone of such weaknesses. So where did this alien emotion come from? It was as if her brain was at odds with her mind. Even worse than the conflict with Psyche's mind. A chilling thought occurred to her. Can a mind remain the same in a different brain? Psyche had struggled to hold on to her identity. Then again, Ileana's spirit hadn't made it easy for the goddess of the soul. The truth was, in a weird way, she felt more herself now than she had in a long time. She was her old self. The girl she used to be before everyone left her behind. No, she'd wanted to stay. That was the plan. It was her choice. Wasn't it?

Ileana had just begun pondering if her new body had a spirit when she noticed she'd stopped walking and had been standing in the middle of the corridor like a dumb tree. *Gods, I really need to sort myself out.*

The surrounding walls shook, creaked and cracked, putting an end to her musings and bringing her attention back to more immediate and substantial matters. For example, how much more pressure could the dead World Tree take? The Stump didn't exist in her time, of that she was sure. And something as large as it could not simply disappear from the land unless it was purposely and thoroughly destroyed. This could be it. Slush, she had not come all this way to perish again!

Determined to not let that happen, she shook herself and her suspicions away, confident she just needed time to adjust, then ran the rest of the way down the corridor and up the ramp leading to the top to find... nothing.

What a...?

There was no one there. Nothing. No sky, no stars, no light, just a pitch-black void.

Had she taken a wrong turn somewhere? Her sense of direction was appalling, true, and her memory still foggy, but up was up. How wrong could she have gone? She took a few more steps. Underfoot, wood became metal. The large teleportation portal was still there, at least. What had happened to the sky, then?

Light, much brighter than the sun, exploded above her. She cursed, covering her eyes. A deafening sound boomed overhead, a gush of stale air and foul fumes followed. She squinted upwards. Something moved towards her, a sort of platform with two figures standing on it, descending slowly from the domed sky of glaring light.

Frost. She was definitely not prepared for this.

"They're here!" Oreth said, suddenly at her side, further fraying her nerves. By the way he was panting, he must have run all the way there, eager to greet them. "Where is Father?"

"He's not coming," she replied.

"What? Why?"

She didn't answer. Having to deal with the Nephilim alone was one thing, having to deal with this boy, quite another.

Oreth claimed to have been adopted by the Suzerain. He even had the nerve to call her 'little sister'! She had made it clear to the creature that she had no brothers, least of all weak-minded, foul-smelling brats like him, and that had been enough to set matters straight. Or so she thought. Apparently one can never be too nice to idiots.

She hated the way he kept staring at her. His eyes reminded her of Ideth, the forest nymph who'd trapped Aedan inside the cave, and Ileana hated her even more than she hated him.

"Is that blood?" he finally asked, making no attempt to conceal his disgust as he put some distance between them so as not to compromise the immaculateness of his formal attire.

Ileana looked down at her dress, all splattered with gore. Her hair was too, she was sure. She felt sick. Why had Father not got rid of the dryad's aversion to blood? After all, weren't these bodies supposed to be an improvement on the real ones? And frost Oreth for making her feel self-conscious on top of everything else!

"Sister, what happened? Where is our father?" the boy insisted.

"Mika ate him." She really didn't know how else to put it. It wasn't like she could hide what happened in the vault covered head to toe in the event's aftermath. The vault door wouldn't even close with all the bits and pieces of bodies strewn about on the floor.

"No..." Oreth whimpered.

"Yes," she hissed.

His face turned red, cheeks puffing in outrage. "It's your fault! How could you let this happen?"

"Me?! I didn't know what Mika was! You knew, apparently. Why didn't you warn us?"

"Father knew about him too!" Oreth hesitated. "Didn't he?"

Goddess, but the boy was thick. She wondered what her father had seen in him. "Apparently not."

"Frost. Occa didn't tell you either?"

"She tried to a bit too late." Another brief acquaintance for Ileana. Occa had been a clever one though, and she seemed to have been aiming to call her daughter rather than sister. Ileana would not miss her either.

Oreth cursed again, this time in approbation. "Where's the wolf now?"

"Dead too, I think. At least I doubt he'll eat anyone again."

The platform stopped its descent, floating slightly above the floor some distance away from them. The two figures stepped down from it and walked in their direction. Well, one walked, the other, Ileana was at a loss for words to describe its motion.

"Frost, what do I do?" Ileana asked herself out loud.

"Er… smile," Oreth said, taking his own suggestion and waving at the pair with a forced display of teeth.

"Do you recognise them?" Ileana asked him through her own exaggerated grin.

"No. I haven't seen these two before. Then again, the Nephilim change bodies as often as we change dresses."

"Great…"

"Whatever you do, don't lie. They can always tell," Oreth said.

Well, that narrowed her options.

"In that case, go wake the rest of the faithful. Have them clear the corpses in the vault. Apollo and Artemis are the only thing we have to show for ourselves, so let's make the room presentable, at least. I'll stall these two as long as I can," Ileana said.

"But I thought –"

"Go on, make Father proud," she added by means of encouragement. There were no more faithful available in the labs, but Oreth didn't need to know that. He just needed to be out of her sight.

He hesitated, torn between curiosity and obedience.

"I can't believe I washed for nothing," the boy grumbled, then sparing another wave to the newcomers, dashed down the ramp. Ileana sighed with relief. At least now she only had to worry about what *she* might say.

The Nephilim stopped a few paces from her, their expressions unreadable.

The woman – or so Ileana thought the svelte figure was even if her body had no distinct female features to speak of – was unnaturally tall and thin, with a long, oval-shaped head and no hair on it at all, not even eyebrows. Yet somehow the baldness suited her flawless features to perfection. She wore a gilded dress of a fabric Ileana couldn't identify. Not that she was an expert on fabrics, mind, but it didn't look like anything she'd ever come across: a thick mixture of silk and something resembling wool, giving it a soft, furry shine of its own. The woman herself looked like she'd come out of a jewellery box. Her skin gleamed with gold and precious gemstones. Except she didn't just wear them dangling from every appendage and limb, some were actually embedded in her flesh. Ileana cringed at the sight.

The man – for only men walked with such arrogance in their stride – was shorter than his companion with skin the colour of sun-dried almonds. He had a strip of short, spiky hair running along the top of his head. One eye was copper, the other a disturbing shade of burgundy. He wore a long black robe streaked with silver threads in that same strange fabric and no jewellery that she could see. He was handsome for a Narrum, Ileana had to admit. Not in the way Iosh was handsome, with his soft features and boyish looks. This was a more mature sort of beauty, born of power and intelligence.

The woman pointedly looked down at her. Up close she resembled a naiad with her cerulean skin tone and black, diamond-shaped eyes over high cheekbones. Ileana felt the urge to flee when those eyes fixed on her, analysing every inch of her face. They were not completely black, she noticed. There was a greyish glint where the iris should be. It flickered.

"Where is Alek Dveer?" the man asked in a deep nasal voice.

Ileana swallowed and turned her attention to him. "He had a… hmm, an accident. I am his daughter, Ileana Dveer," she said, squaring her shoulders, chin held high as her mother had taught her.

She'd taken posture very seriously.

The couple remained inscrutable for a long nerve-wracking moment assessing the veracity of her statement. Or was she supposed to do something? Bow, shake their hands, hug them? Somehow none of those options seemed right, so Ileana forced herself to remain still while waiting for their reaction.

"What is your purpose here?" the woman asked. She had a silvery voice, with a steel timbre and a strange cadence to it.

"To welcome you," she said.

They exchanged glances. A hint of annoyance crossed the woman's lips.

"We do not feel welcome. Take us to your father, girl," the man said.

Ileana bristled at that, but before she could respond, the woman spoke. "I refuse to be greeted by a child."

"I'm not a child!" Ileana protested childishly.

The woman looked down at her with such scorn it was almost unbearable. Ileana bet she could have withered even Ideth's spirits with that stare.

"Where are the Tributes?" the man asked. He sounded bored now.

"The gods have probably taken them," Ileana answered in a small voice.

"And where are these gods you speak of?"

Ileana bit her lip. "I'm not sure. They were already gone when I woke up. But we hold two of them prisoner!" Surely the Olympian twins would make up for some of their loses.

"Whose blood is that on you?" the man asked.

"Er… several people." Ileana sighed, deflating. "It's better if you come with me and see it for yourself."

"Anubis!" The familiar voice came from behind her, triggering instant hostility. She spun around, not wanting to believe what she saw.

"You!" she cursed under her breath.

The man was thinner and was missing an arm, but it was him all right: Oric. The one who had stabbed Aedan at the temple, the one who'd nearly killed him in fact. He was alive, and greeting the Nephilim as if they were old friends. Frost, they probably were!

Her eyes widened, her nostrils flared. She clenched her hands into fists. He was all dressed up, long hair washed and combed to perfection, a wide arrogant smirk on his lips. His step faltered when their eyes met, as if he'd not recognised her at first, and she had to sink her nails into her palms to keep herself still.

"My friends. Apologies for the delay and the er… the reception." Oric stared openly at her then, shaking his head reproachfully, seemingly as disgruntled and disbelieving of both her presence and appearance as she was of his, but doing a much better job at hiding it. He was all verve and confidence. Gods, how she hated the man.

"I cannot express how happy I am to finally have you both here," he said, sounding sincere.

"Apparently not, since happy is not how you feel," the hairless woman replied matter-of-factly.

Oric laughed. "Ah… Namrive, always so perceptive. I've had a rough few days, as you can see." He showed her his stump. "I guess, under the circumstances, *pleased* is a more accurate term for my feelings. Yes, I am pleased and, dare I say, relieved by your arrival." His smile was a beacon of sincerity.

Namrive nodded. "You are also apprehensive, annoyed, disgusted, hungry, sleep deprived and in need of sexual release."

Oric wasn't taken aback by her insights. If anything, he seemed to take them as compliments. "Yes, all those things! We mortals are never content with just one emotion at a time, as you well know. But enough about my feelings. We have a situation that needs your immediate attention."

"So we gather. Something about an incursion led by a god?" Anubis said.

"Gods, plural. There were several of the bastards. But fear not, everything is well under control now."

"Fear of the gods is not something we concern ourselves with," Namrive said.

"How fortunate – ow!" Ileana had spent so long thinking out loud inside her head, unable to speak freely while Psyche controlled her body, that she hadn't realised she'd actually spoken aloud this time until Oric elbowed her into silence.

Namrive focused her onyx eyes on her. "Insolence from mortals, however, is far more grievous."

Ileana recoiled from that gaze. They say eyes are the windows to the soul. Namrive's eyes were more like windows to an abyss. The only thing Ileana found there was her mortified reflection.

"I sense hardly any life forms inside this structure. Have these gods stolen our Tribute?" Anubis asked.

"No, no. Rest assured, the Tributes are waiting in Relicum for your cull." Oric gestured behind him. "We thought it better to keep them there until we were sure the Stump was safe."

Namrive nodded, then looked past Ileana. "And who are you?" she asked.

"Judoc of Relicum – a pleasure to finally make your acquaintance."

Ileana's throat constricted. She wanted to glance behind her but dared not. She kept her eyes on Namrive instead.

The strange woman looked Iosh up and down. "You're one of the Suzerain's shrines."

"Indeed, I am. And much more," he teased.

Anubis stepped forward, pushing Namrive aside, pulled Iosh closer and sniffed him. *What is it with gods and sniffing?* Ileana wondered. Odin had done the same thing to her when they met. As he did so, a spectral snout appeared in front of Anubis' face, resembling a fox. Ileana blinked. Not a fox, a jackal.

"Gifted." Anubis drawled the word with scorn.

"The best of us are," Iosh said brightly.

The god grunted. In the heavy silence that followed, she finally gathered enough courage to glance sideways. Iosh's eyes were set on her, unblinking. His mouth twisted unflatteringly in a sceptical and yet slightly amused expression.

"Shouldn't you be at the temple with the Tributes, *Shrine*?" Anubis asked dryly.

Iosh glanced at Oric as if looking for support. He found none. "A reliable lookalike has taken my place. I figured I'd be more useful here."

"Did you now?" Anubis said with disdain.

Iosh lifted his left arm. "Oric lost his bracelet. He needed mine, and my bracelet can't work without me, therefore…" He left the sentence unfinished, crossing both arms and smiling smugly. Ileana nearly gaped. Iosh had always thought a lot of himself, but he'd never been this confident, let alone insolent to authority figures.

Anubis narrowed his kohl-lined eyes to slits.

"Did you become incomplete during the incursion?" Namrive asked Oric, preventing Anubis from speaking whatever he'd been about to.

"Not exactly. I had an altercation with one of the natives. Also resolved now," he added with a pointed glare at Ileana.

Her nails dug deeper into her palms. He was lying. She'd seen Aedan riding a winged horse just before she'd lost consciousness. He'd survived the ambush at the cave, so Oric had to be lying. Except Aedan wasn't there anymore – *he* was. And she had no idea what had happened between then and now.

Namrive nodded, apparently satisfied. Either he'd lied to her successfully, or it wasn't a lie. Ileana wanted to scream.

"Very well, show us this 'situation'," Namrive said, bidding Oric to lead the way.

"I'd rather interrogate these prisoners the girl mentioned first," Anubis said, looking at Ileana, still trying to stop herself from spiralling out of control.

Oric hesitated. He clearly didn't know what the Nephilim were talking about.

"They are in the same place," Ileana said, forcing a smile. She'd not make it easy for the despicable man.

"The soul source, of course!" Oric said triumphantly, as if he'd known it all along. "Girl, you look like a Narrum swine slaughterer. Why don't you go make yourself more presentable while I escort our guests there?" He started down the ramp with the two Nephilim in tow, leaving her behind, apoplectic with indignation.

"Illy," Iosh whispered when the others were some distance away.

"Do not speak to me," she hissed, recovering from the insult and prompting herself to follow them. He took her hand, holding her back. She jerked it away, determined to catch up with the group. "Do not touch me either!"

"I'm just so glad to see you alive," he said in his charming tone, chasing after her.

"Gods! I can't have this conversation again. Not here, not now," she said, exasperated. It was all too much, all at once. She needed a moment to collect her thoughts, and that left no room for dealing with discarded ones.

"Don't you remember me? I know I look older but –"

"Oh, I remember you all right. Very clearly. You used me to get to my father and then left me behind, just as he did."

Iosh put on a martyr's expression. "I had no choice."

"Lies! You weren't exiled, you were chosen. You and Father were in it together from the very start!"

Oric and the Nephilim arrived at the teleportation ring, and she could swear she saw the man's smug smile just before the light took them, not waiting for her to join the party. Ileana screeched with frustrated rage.

"Your father made me promise not to tell you," Iosh persisted. "He feared you might try to follow us before the right time, if you knew. He needed you desperate and a few years older for the task. Not so many years older, mind. I almost didn't recognise you at the temple, and truth be told, I never expected to ever see you again. And then, there you were, right in front of me. In a room crowded with women, and I could see only you."

She glared at him, offended by his presence and the fact he was still talking to her. Then he touched her face, and she shuddered.

"I never had a chance to ask. What took you so long, Illy? I missed you so much."

She felt herself warm to his plea as well as his touch. He was using his gift on her again. How dare he!

She furiously brushed his hand away. "You made me care for you; claimed to love me. Then you not only humped every girl in Aegea, you fell in love with another. You even had the nerve to seduce my Wyrd! I wish I'd not come at all." It was a lie, of course. She was exceedingly happy to be there, for she'd met Aedan. And that had made the wait and the entire ordeal in the Gharb worth it.

"You remember my conversations with Psyche?" Iosh seemed surprised.

"I was there, you fool! Conscious the whole time. You actually succeeded, you know. For a brief moment, she was quite taken with you." Ileana shook her head. A goddess should know better. Then again, Psyche did. She just didn't care. That one was far more comfortable with lust than affection.

"She was?" The pride in his voice revolted her.

Ileana gave Iosh a long, hard look. He was indeed breathtakingly handsome. Older, yes, but age had only improved him – or so her senses told her. Her brain insisted otherwise. If this contradiction was due to his gift, her new body, Aedan, or common sense, it made no difference. She stepped closer to him so he could see the contempt in her eyes clearly as she spoke. "You were really not worth it, Iosh."

To her surprise, he smiled, seemingly pleased with himself. Only his vanity matched his beauty, after all. The pleading lovesick gaze dissipated, replaced by something much sicker. "You were," he said plainly. "Thanks to you, I got everything I ever wanted as a child. So thank you, Illy. I pray you always remember that." He kissed her forehead as her uncle used to do, then stepped inside the ring, whistling to himself. "Are you coming?"

She shook her head and watched him go with a

grimace, mouth slightly open, heart and mind disconcerted. Neither her memories nor Psyche's matched this creature. The Iosh of her childhood was dead. She ran to her father's quarters.

CHAPTER 11

Apollo & Artemis

The vault door began to shut in Ileana's wake, threatening to leave Apollo and Artemis locked in a void of sensory deprivation and hopelessness once again. Except it didn't. There were too many body parts in its path.

"Brother mine," Artemis urged in a whisper: a trapped prey sensing an opportunity to escape its cage.

Apollo moaned in response, barely conscious and unable to decide which agony was greater: the pain from the wounds in his flesh or the emptiness in his Reach.

"Brother!"

"I'm here, sister," he mumbled. Even this close to each other, their telepathy didn't work. They had to talk. He really didn't feel like talking. Fenrir had done a number on his throat, and willing it as he might, he was not healing properly inside that cursed room.

Never had the Olympian sun god been so powerless, but fortunately he still had his talents to take his mind off the pain. While the Suzerain and his daughter had talked about his and his sister's fate as if they were not even there in the room with them, he'd closed his eyes and dreamed the wolf had died at his feet. Or had it been a vision? He couldn't tell sometimes. Regardless, it had been a good one. He smiled, opened his eyes and confirmed that his dream had indeed come true.

"What just happened?" he asked. The Stump shook, an awful grinding noise running through its walls. He corrected himself. "What is happening?"

"They're here," Artemis said. "Can you free yourself?"

He shook his head. Whatever light imprisoned them, it wasn't one he could control.

"Is he really dead?" Apollo asked, gazing at Mika's corpse. The whole thing had happened so fast, so unexpectedly. To his diminished senses, it almost hadn't seemed real.

"Yes," Artemis said angrily. She had the talent to detect life. "I've been hunting the wolf for years. And now the Suzerain got him."

"Looks like they got each other," Apollo said.

"It's not fair, brother."

He smiled, despite the pain. Only his sister would think fairness had any place in the Universe. He was just glad that for once one of his visions had come to pass in a timely fashion.

During his torture, Apollo had entertained himself by imagining all the things he would do to Fenrir once he was free. Still, he would not let disappointment get in the way of the relief he felt upon seeing him dead, as short-lived as it might be, for he suspected they might join the wolf in the Underworld soon enough.

"I always thought the wolf was his true form," Apollo mused.

Artemis snorted. "He's the son of a trickster."

"Right," Apollo said, trying not to think about Loki and all that he deserved.

"Brother, we need to get out of here," Artemis said feverishly.

"Agree," Apollo replied tiredly.

"I won't be a mortal's puppet like Zeus was," she insisted.

"I'll do everything I can to spare you that fate, sister."

"And yet instead of saving me from the dead goddess, you fell right into her trap! Stars, brother, I can't believe you gave yourself to her as easily as a nymph gives herself to you."

"Chastity is your talent, sister, not mine!" he snapped, well aware he'd been a fool to get involved with Hel and let her lure him here, but the last thing he needed at the moment was to be berated for his mistakes.

"But *her*?"

He sighed, too tired to argue. "After Daphne, I needed a challenge, I suppose. Some reassurance of my qualities as a man and a god. I was not thinking straight." That was an understatement; he'd not been thinking at all. In order to avoid being consumed by unrequited love, he'd given himself over to lust and jealousy instead. Hard to tell which one was worse. Fortunately, he'd long lost the ability to feel shame or remorse for his actions.

"And that is why I choose to remain chaste," Artemis stated.

"Careful sister. Do I need to remind you of the amount of trouble your chastity caused us?"

Her chameleon skin changed colour to match her mood. "You didn't need to turn Orion into a sun," she grumbled.

"He volunteered. You'd have hunted down anything else!"

She cursed, then agreed, and Apollo hoped the subject would die there. It didn't. "Do you know where Orion is now?"

"No," he said curtly. "The Trickster put some sort of illusion on him. I can sense him but can't find him. Eos must still be with him, though, as that is her curse. And I doubt Loki can keep her, a Titan, hidden for long."

"Good," Artemis said.

They fell silent, listening to the ominous sounds coming from above.

"What did you mean about the Trickster? That he would get what he deserved?" Artemis asked, likely to disturb the uncomfortable stillness that followed the sounds.

Apollo wasn't sure what he had meant, to be honest. His prophecies were always open to interpretation, but he had seen Loki on his knees with tears in his eyes, utterly broken. As visions go, that one had seemed pretty clear to him. And whatever had caused the god of mischief such grief had to be deserved.

"It's bad luck to reveal a prophecy to those whom it does not concern," he reminded his sister. Also, it resembled a memory he'd rather not talk about.

She grunted in resignation.

Apollo glanced sideways. "The girl who was just here and the woman hanging over there are the same at different ages." His vision was a bit blurry since Fenrir had nibbled on his right eye, but still, he was sure of it. "How can this be? Chronos forbids any creature to exist in the same reality with another self."

Artemis' expression hardened. "They are not the same, brother. When last I saw that one, she was a Wyrd. And the younger one… she smells funny."

"Funny how?"

"Like a rock drenched in spirits. Her flesh is not right. Neither is the Suzerain's." Artemis' skin rippled, trying to match the surrounding gloom. "Brother, he was supposed to be dead. That's how Hel took over the Stump in the first place. Her pet Dharkan sucked his Prana and froze him to pieces."

"You survived the Dharkan's feeding," Apollo pointed out.

Her skin rippled again before settling on a dull grey. "He let me live," she admitted in a whisper. "He could have killed me, had he wished to. I felt weaker during his attack than I do now."

Apollo groaned. Hel had crossed a line. Once he was free, he'd have to personally burn every single one of her creations. A shame, for he'd quite enjoyed being in one of them. They allowed gods all the perks of a Wyrd without the inconvenient curse associated with them. And thanks to Aecius' hospitality, he'd been able to enter Asgard and extinguish his greatest rival, Baldur. Absently, he wondered what had become of the old Dharkan.

"Brother?"

"I heard you," he said. "I do not believe he would have killed you, sister. Even if he froze your body to pieces, you'd still have your soul. Death is relative to gods, after all."

Artemis dismissed his deduction. "Tell that to Zeus. As to the Suzerain, he can't be killed, not even by a Dharkan, because he's not alive to begin with. My guess is that he died long ago. The Nephilim can build bodies like those of gods, but they have no pith, no spirit. That's why they need our souls. When we're free, you need to burn them, brother. Burn every Nephilim and every Dharkan. Only then will we be safe."

"Oh, I intend to, sister."

A sound came from outside the room. They fell silent again, listening to footsteps sounding closer and closer. Moments later, a young male dryad dressed in finery appeared at the door. He cursed a few times, then began kicking the corpses away from the entrance so the door would close properly.

"Hey, boy," Apollo called. He'd much rather it stayed open. "Help us down and we'll reward you. I promise."

"Sure you do," the boy replied without even looking up at him.

Gods deserved more respect than that! "Do you know who we are?"

"Yes."

"So you know the value of a god's promise."

The boy was about to kick the Suzerain's legs and stopped, visibly upset. "Shut up, stupid god," he said, covering his mouth to stifle a gag.

Apollo bristled. On top of everything, must he also be insulted by a nymph!

"Hush, brother," Artemis said before he had a chance to spell out the curses running through his mind. "Let me speak to him."

Apollo nodded to his sister, making a mental note to include the boy amongst the first to burn upon his release from this prison.

"What is your name?" she asked in a tone he'd rarely heard coming from her. She sounded feminine, almost motherly.

"Oreth," the boy replied, teary-eyed.

Her skin rippled again, assuming a pattern Apollo recognised as shock, followed by anger. "What is it?"

"Nothing," she hissed. "He's useless to us."

All further attempts to engage the young dryad yielded only curses and scorn until the door was properly closed and he was gone.

"You should have warned Zeus," Artemis said in all seriousness once they were alone again. "He never would have let things get this far had he known."

The twins eyed the dead god between them.

"You warned him. He didn't listen," Apollo said, a vision forming in his mind.

"No one ever listens to me," his sister said bitterly. "Everyone thinks I'm crazy."

"But you are crazy, dear sister," he said lovingly.

She half smiled. "Perhaps. But crazy is not the same as stupid, and a chaotic mind sometimes understands the world better than a sane one, for it can pierce the veil and see the Universe for what it is." She shook her head. "He would have believed you, had you been more convincing."

"You didn't think I was?"

"I know you too well, brother."

Apollo didn't lie. He could lie to any god, but not to her. "True. I had… other plans at the time." He rolled his eyes; the vision became clear.

"You still had frost on your mind, you mean. Stars, brother. Hel really turned your brain to slush," Artemis said, shaking her head.

"She was a means to an end." Apollo smiled, recovered from the vision.

"This end, apparently," she huffed.

"No, sister. This is not our end. Be patient. We have only just begun our journey."

CHAPTER 12

Anubis

Anubis cringed as he prepared to enter the soul source.

Three gods – one dead and two more or less still alive – stared out at him from their luminous cages, reminding Anubis how easily he could end up there with them. It was one reason to keep the interrogation brief; another was the state of the room itself, littered with dismembered bodies. Their presence did not perturb him. After all, his talent involved embalming the dead. It was their general state of disarray that left him restless. He felt compelled to put the pieces together in the proper order, and he had no time for that. He blinked, recognising the corpse of the boy lying amongst several nondescript faithful. Cats! Now he really wanted to be brief.

"Come on in, don't be shy. You're far from the only god with a tail," Artemis said. There was something disturbingly predatory in her tone. She had a reputation for being insane, but Anubis thought the word *mad* did her better justice.

"We are all ourselves in here," Apollo agreed. His

mangled chin trembled as he strained to utter each word.

Anubis had been in several of these cursed rooms before, and they never got any easier to endure. He still didn't understand many of the details behind the Nephilim's technology, but he had learnt enough over the years to at least rig the door so it would remain open, for he feared he might actually suffocate otherwise. Quite the irrational thought for a god, but in there, he felt like anything but one.

"Do you know who I am?" Anubis asked the restrained Olympians as he walked in, displaying his true form. One would think being free to express his true self would be empowering, and perhaps it was to handsome gods like Apollo, yet he'd always struggled to be taken seriously when he had a snout instead of a face. Then again, the Olympian sun god was anything but handsome at the moment.

"Everyone knows you, Anubis, former god of the Underworld. Or should I say, *an Underworld*; there are so many of those." Apollo smirked. "I heard you gave up your rule of the dead to Osiris upon his misfortune with his brother, Seth. How altruistic of you," he added sarcastically. "You managed to trick both your uncle – a god of chaos – as well as your father *and* still came out as the most righteous of the three, bright and free as sunlight. I'd bow, but as you can see, I can barely blink."

"Indeed." Anubis felt pretty uncomfortable and powerless himself. But at least he could move and he still had all his senses. It seemed excessive to add that extra layer of powerlessness inside the cursed chamber. It only showed how much the Nephilim feared their captives.

He bent over to touch the forehead of the dead boy at his feet while weighing the implications of how much Apollo knew about him. Was his history common knowledge in the pantheons, or did the sun god know it because he was an oracle? Anubis had been away from his kind for so long, he hoped he'd been forgotten by now. He should have known better.

"What no one knows is where you've been for the past millennia," Apollo continued in the same condescending tone. "I guess the answer just presented itself. Zeus wondered what became of you after you left Osiris in charge of the Underworld. He even searched for you."

Anubis looked up at Zeus' corpse. He didn't need to touch the Olympian king to know there was only an empty shell hovering there. Next to it was what looked like an older version of the girl who'd greeted him earlier. Her mother, perhaps? No. It was the same woman. He snarled, wondering what could have warranted this mortal such special treatment, then turned his attention back to his brethren.

"It surprises me I featured so prominently in Zeus' mind," he said.

Apollo snorted. "He was always concerned with the Underworlds and their gods."

"Is that so?"

Apollo gave him a bloodied smile. "I rather wondered what became of Seth. He's probably trapped in a room similar to this one. Am I wrong?"

Anubis did not answer. He had no need to. Apollo knew too much already. Cats, how he hated oracles. Prophet gods always made him uneasy with their uncanny deductions. No god should have the talent to know, let alone dictate, one's fate. Too much foresight in one god was bad for the others. Then again, what was power and knowledge without good sense?

"It seems the Nephilim have been hunting our kind for longer than we realised, brother," Artemis said.

"No, sister. Just longer than we cared to notice. After all, they were doing us a favour… at first."

"How does someone with your gifts end up in here?" Anubis asked, pointedly ignoring Apollo's implications.

Apollo glanced at his twin sister, who returned the glance with fathomless devotion. "Love and duty."

"It must be excruciating to know everyone's fate but your own," Anubis said.

"Who says I don't know my own fate?" Apollo teased.

Anubis frowned. "You are here. You got caught and tortured. And now you and your sister are the Nephilim's property."

"Knowing one's fate and avoiding it are two very different things. Ra could have told you that, had you given him a chance."

"I don't understand your meaning," Anubis lied.

"Sure you do – scion of Ra."

"In my pantheon, we are all scions of Ra."

"And where is he?"

"You are the oracle."

Apollo chuckled. "I don't need prophecy to know

when a sun god returns to the fabric of the Universe. These friends of yours, they really don't like sun gods. Why is that?"

There was no point in denying it. Yet he couldn't tell the whole truth either. "You travel faster than them," Anubis admitted.

"Ah… well, not in this state. I assume you are here to put an end to my travels, god of the dead."

"Unless you have something to offer. A reason to keep you suffering, perhaps?"

"What about a prophecy?" Apollo suggested.

"I hate those."

"Me too." Apollo tried to laugh but coughed instead. "Yet everyone else seems to love them, don't they?"

Anubis crossed his hands behind his back. *Brief,* he reminded himself. *Don't let the Olympian lull you into a conversation where you might say more than you want. Keep it brief.*

"Yes, the Nephilim are interested in your gifts, Apollo. Enough to overlook your other talents. I won't make any promises, but if you can provide them with enough accurate prophecies, maybe they'll consider some sort of arrangement. Not for your sake, mind, but your sister might still see the stars again."

"Do not insult me," Apollo scorned. "I'll make no deals with the Nephilim. I only deal with real gods. And prophecies can't be forced. They either happen or they don't, and trust me, they never happen when I want them to. I can, however, offer *you* an educated guess."

"I'm all ears." His ears perked up, and Anubis cursed at his poor choice of words.

Apollo smiled, then his eyes rolled. He convulsed, writhed and shivered until finally, he babbled in a disembodied voice. "She'll come for the wolf."

"Hel?" Anubis asked, unimpressed with the act.

Apollo's answer was a stream of bloody drool down his chin.

"When?"

"I don't know. But when she does. You'd better not be here." He laughed, a grating sound due to the fluids filling up his lungs.

"Is that a threat?" Anubis said.

"Call it advice. A courtesy between gods in exchange for a favour – when the time comes." Apollo glanced at his sister again.

Artemis remained silent. Her skin, now matching the featureless grey of the walls, made her presence all too easy to dismiss.

Anubis glanced over his shoulder, where he knew Namrive would be watching through the room's crystal eye, then turned slightly, keeping his back to it.

"Beware, sun god. The walls have eyes, and I'm just a prisoner, same as you," he said, moving his lips but not making a sound.

"Not the same as us," Artemis whispered. Camouflaged as she was, Anubis couldn't see her lips move, which meant, hopefully, neither could Namrive. "Our allegiances never changed."

"Neither have mine," Anubis replied in the same fashion.

"Prove it," she said.

"Can you still control fire?" he asked Apollo.

"Give him a flame and he'll burn this place down," Artemis replied.

Anubis shook his head several times, then spoke loud and clear. "Your offer is not good enough, Apollo."

He turned around and left, desperate for a breath. Behind his back, his hands signalled hope.

CHAPTER 13

Ileana

Should have taken the freezing portal, Ileana chastised herself.

When she – at last! – arrived at the Suzerain's chambers, after having taken the wrong turn at a major intersection, she found Namrive standing in the middle of the room inspecting a black leather coat. She'd hoped Oric, if not the carnage, would keep the Nephilim occupied a while longer.

"What are you doing here?" Ileana asked without thinking.

"I'm waiting for you," Namrive said with a hint of a smile. Ileana couldn't tell if it was amusement or smugness. Namrive's face and manner were harder to interpret than Aedan's.

A horrible thought occurred to her then. Could the captive Olympians have escaped? She did leave the door open. "Didn't Oric take you to the prisoners?" she asked tactfully.

Namrive's eyes flickered behind the rim of the coat's fabric. "He did. Anubis is with them now."

Why aren't you? she almost asked but thankfully restrained herself.

"I have no patience for gods and their riddles," Namrive said with what sounded like resentment.

Ileana frowned. "Aren't you a goddess?"

Namrive's eyes flashed deep within their sockets. "Do I look like one?" Her tone was dry, more a dare than a question. The sort of question her father would pose as a trap for an honest answer.

"Gods can assume many aspects," Ileana replied vaguely.

Namrive grunted with what sounded like agreement, then returned her attention to the coat. "Such a strange garment for a dryad," she said, turning it over.

Ileana nearly gasped. It was Aedan's.

"I don't think it belongs to my father," she said, clearing her throat. "May I see it?" She stepped inside the room, tentatively holding her hand out to take it from Namrive without looking too eager.

The Nephilim woman handed it to her, scrutinising her every action.

Ileana lifted the coat to her nose to inhale its heady scent. A surge of emotions ran through her, stronger than any prompted by Iosh's touch. She forced herself to remain calm and glanced around the room. "Someone else must have been using his quarters during the incursion."

"Another god, perhaps," Namrive suggested casually.

"How can I know?" Ileana said, avoiding the trap while trying to sound reasonable. "I've been stuck in the lab the whole time they were here."

Reluctantly, Ileana discarded the coat on the floor. Aedan *was* alive. He had been there recently. That was all she needed to know for now.

Namrive displayed her teeth in something stuck between a sneer and a leer. "You should keep it. Since you like it so much. I've already learnt everything I need to from it."

Ileana blushed with anger rather than embarrassment.

Namrive pointed to the bed. "Sit." Not a suggestion.

"Can I change first?"

"No, you cannot."

"Very well." Ileana sighed, then sat reluctantly on the bed, bracing herself for the lecture she was sure was about to happen.

To say Namrive had been displeased with the state of the Stump in general and the soul source room in particular was an understatement. The woman had an extensive vocabulary to express her displeasure and make you feel like slush. It was quite pointless, really. Namrive should have known any subordinate of her father would be impervious to verbal abuse.

Still, the reprimand was not a complete waste of Ileana's time. She learnt a lot about the Stump, the Nephilim and their relationship with Father. And while Namrive pontificated about respect, duty and responsibility, Ileana's mind worked on an escape plan. She had to find Aedan. Every moment she stayed there was a moment she could have spent with him. It took all her self-restraint not to dash out of the room, leaving the hairless creature talking to herself.

"And you will not leave this structure until I say so. Are we clear?" Namrive's unnatural eyes flashed red, almost daring Ileana to disagree.

"Yes," Ileana replied automatically in the contrite tone she'd developed over years of enduring her father's sermons. She'd expected this, of course. These sorts of conversations always ended up with her grounded. Regardless, she still wanted to sink her nails into the woman's shiny eyes.

Namrive nodded, blissfully unaware of her thoughts, stood up and left the room, apparently pleased with herself. Ileana made a rude gesture upon her departure and uttered a few choice words she'd learnt from Psyche. Finally alone in her father's room, she spared a moment to caress Aedan's coat again, then washed, donned a new dress and was about to make her way to the soul source through the portal when she noticed something on the bedside table – a deathwand. It hadn't been there before; she was certain. Someone had been in the room while she changed and left it there for her to find. Another trap? Or a test, more likely. But who was doing the testing and to what end?

Ileana had seen one of these wands before, back when her father first returned from Yewlow. When she asked him what it was, he put it away and ordered her to never, ever touch one. She picked it up cautiously and turned it over. There was a note with instructions on how to use it, but nothing about on whom or why it had been left there in the first place.

She took it, obviously, then activated the teleportation ring.

∞

Ileana materialised in the room between the soul source and the labs. Both doors were wide open. Oreth and Oric stood amongst a pile of corpses, arguing with each other in front of the Olympian twins. Ileana stifled a gag. No matter how many times she saw blood, her body's reaction to it never changed.

"There she is." Oric sounded far from pleased. He had a translucent tube edged with tiny blinking lights around the stump of his arm, and to Ileana's eyes there seemed to be more arm there than previously. "The strangest thing happened while you were away," he said, ambling in her direction. "I was in the lab, stretching my legs and waiting for my arm to grow back, when I received a communication from Namrive ordering me to clean this mess." He pressed a finger against her chest. "Your idea, I assume."

Ileana smiled. Yes, she had suggested that Oric should do it, and it pleased her no end that Namrive took her advice. It was all she could do to him, really. For now.

"I merely pointed out to Namrive that you were far better suited for the task with your manly strength, your supernatural ability to kill without remorse and total indifference to bodily fluids," she said with sarcastic innocence. "While I'm just a witless young dryad girl with a weak stomach and a fragile mind, so poorly equipped for such tasks."

"You thorny weed! You're more aggravating than nettles. My life has been one muddy slush hole after another since you came along! If not for the respect

I owe your father… Argh! I have one hand, creature. How do you expect me to carry all of these to the incinerator?"

"Where's Iosh?" she asked. He had been her second suggestion. "He can help you."

"Summoned," Oric said curtly.

"In that case, Oreth will help you, surely," she said innocently.

"No, I won't," Oreth protested, but he changed his mind when she assured him she would acknowledge him as her older brother and put in a good word with Father once he was revived again – which would be never, if she had her way. And so the foolish boy grudgingly helped the outraged Oric drag the corpses down a shaft to the incinerator room while she pretended to supervise their work. In truth, she was working out how many eyes the walls had and how far they could see. She spotted one staring at every teleportation ring and another inside the soul source, fixed on its prisoners still held in their bright prisons, two along the corridors and countless in the labs. However, there was none inside the incinerator room that she could see. *Excellent.*

Ileana pulled out her father's clever ring.

CHAPTER XIV

Nexus

Light flickered through Namrive's onyx eyes as she assimilated the computer's reports into her matrix.

"You cunning bug," she murmured to herself, hairless brows knitted tight with the effort of processing so much senseless information. "What were you hiding?"

"Am I interrupting?" Anubis asked rhetorically. He'd made sure his presence in the control room went unnoticed until he was close enough to startle her with the question.

"Of course not," Namrive lied. She pretended to continue with her task unperturbed, for she knew this would annoy the god as much as his surreptitiousness annoyed her.

Anubis paced around the room nonchalantly, hands clasped behind his back, eyeing its many screens with scornful suspicion. Some showed images taken from other rooms inside the Stump and their unaware occupants, others displayed what was only gibberish to his eyes. He scorned those the most.

"Can we talk?" he asked patiently.

"Yes. I'm perfectly capable of multitasking," she replied in the same tone.

"Humph. Are you sure? Looks like you're having a seizure."

"Seizures are an ailment of the biological mind."

"Right..."

Namrive waited for him to settle his nerves. Anubis was always skittish around the network of screens, buttons, and crystals. The old god found the idea of thoughts stored in gems disturbing, for gems had no consciousness, no soul. Despite all their power, or maybe because of it, gods still relied on things like flesh and telepathy. They claimed information could only be judged correctly when taking into consideration the emotions corrupting it. To Namrive, gods were nothing more than glorified mortals, slaves to their feelings, purposely misleading each other for personal gain. They were less than mortals, in fact, since the humans who created her kind had overcome emotions to achieve immortality, which made them better than gods in her eyes. Suffice it to say, the relationship between the Nephilim and their creator's creators was a strained one.

"So what do the records show?" Anubis asked, annoyed at his inability to access them himself. This almost complete reliance on the Nephilim's constructs frustrated him more each time he had to ask Namrive to translate the information.

"There are gaps in the records," she said vaguely.

"A glitch?" He almost stuttered the word.

Pathetic, she thought. The god couldn't even attempt to understand the meaning of the words related to their technology, let alone consider other reasons for their failure.

"No," she replied tersely. "The information has been carefully and methodically erased by a user."

Anubis sucked his teeth, looking both pensive and peeved while he considered the implications behind her statement. "The girl claims the gods controlled the Stump for several days. We've seen the damage they did to the soul source and the main portal. Who knows what else they might have interfered with. We need to be thorough in our efforts to find out," he stated.

Namrive laughed, and Anubis cringed at the staccato sound. The Nephilim had managed to replicate and even improve on many human traits; laughter had not been one of them. Their understanding of emotions and their expression was as good as Anubis' understanding of their technology.

"The gods weren't even able to turn the computer on, let alone access the information stored within its drive. If they'd accessed the network, we would not be here," she said.

Neither would they, Anubis thought. And in fact, they weren't. Why go to the trouble of taking over the World Tree only to abandon it shortly after? Namrive loved to underestimate gods. Just because their talents defied every law and equation created by her kind didn't mean they were ignorant of how the Universe worked. Quite the contrary. Gods had been running the Universe long before the Nephilim decided to define it.

"Well, something disabled the portal," Anubis said instead.

"The mechanical failure occurred due to extreme temperature, not a faulty command," she said.

When Anubis did not reply, Namrive stopped scrolling through the records to check his expression again. Had he a screen on his forehead, it would read 'I told you so' in flashing red letters. She sighed. "Yes, perhaps we underestimated the control gods can wield over the elements. Regardless, the structure, once defrosted, remains operational, and the damage to the memory core was not caused by cold."

"It was a mistake to trust a god to build a cage for their own kind," Anubis said angrily. *Especially when said god had been an Olympian under threat of blackmail,* he thought.

"Well, you should know," she replied pointedly.

Anubis' patience dwindled. "Yes, I do. The Stump shouldn't have been affected by the elements at all. Can you even sense what's wrong with it?"

"This structure is 83% functional. Repairs have –"

"Pfff," he spat, dismissing her report with a curt gesture. "Spare me the statistics. The Universe is composed of more than just numbers. All your instruments and data banks and technology, and you still can only grasp one reality."

She bristled at that. "One is enough. The realms of dreams or spirits are of no consequence to our purposes."

"Well, they should be!"

Namrive short-fused at the god's insolence. All gods were tempered with arrogance and pride, as if part of the fabric of their precious souls. They were a nuisance to deal with because of it. Fortunately, the

Nephilim had long learnt to harness the will of a soul, not be subject to it.

She put all her tasks on hold and smiled as one does to a petulant child. "And that is exactly why you're here, remember? To offer your 'expertise' on such realms when and if needed. So, pray tell, in your *expert* opinion, could the damage to the Stump's structure or the computer memory be caused by dreams or forces from the Underworld?"

Anubis brooded for a long moment. "I don't know." It wasn't his Underworld, he could have added, but the truth was he really had no idea how one realm could interfere with the other in this way. He knew one thing though: This Underworld was not like his or any other he'd been to before. This one had layers upon layers of realms and an unmatched population density. In fact, the entire world defied the god's comprehension, even before the Merge, so it was no wonder Namrive's instruments were having so much trouble measuring it.

"You don't know," she echoed reproachfully. "Then I recommend you refrain from conclusions until you figure it out. We should stick to our areas of expertise."

"Agreed," he said resentfully.

"Speaking of, there are two different Underworlds in this world as I understand it. What is your assessment of them?"

He waved his hand again, this time deliberately in dismissal, for he'd be damned if she ever found out how he truly felt about them. "Hades' realm is barely skin deep," he said in a reasonable tone. "Well warded, yes, but unstable, on the brink of collapse. Hel's another story. Her realm is well hidden, protected by geography, monsters and curses I'm ignorant of. I suggest we leave it alone for now."

Few gods ever admitted to such a thing as ignorance. Not Anubis, though. Namrive liked that about him. It was pretty much the only thing she liked, mind. She plugged herself back into the computer, this time to analyse the recorded images of the incursion in the main hall. Even Seth would have been impressed with the level of brutality on display. "Very well," she said. "Tell me about the wolf boy."

Anubis grimaced. He'd rather not, so he kept it brief. "His name is Fenrir. He is the brother of Hel."

"What is his talent?" Namrive knew talents, more than power or appearances, were the true measure of a god's significance in the Universe. She'd written about it at length in her treatise on pantheons and status amongst the deities.

"He's little more than a beast; a faithful hound left behind to guard the place," Anubis said a bit too succinctly.

"I see. And where does he stand in your hierarchy of existence?" she asked. As best as she was able to understand, to gods, life and death were not mutually exclusive states but more of a spectrum along their perceived realities constantly overlapping each other. Her kind had trouble processing such a convoluted way of experiencing the Universe. Convoluted and obsolete, since for 99.3% of the creatures in it, life and death were mutually exclusive and one reality was enough.

"He's dead. His body is corrupted beyond repair, so is his ability to form a new one," Anubis said truthfully.

"Isn't that what happens when you die, anyway?"

Anubis shook his head, eyeing the walls as if they were eyeing him, which of course, they were. "Not to gods," he sighed. "By all rights he should be in the Underworld, but his soul remains trapped in the vault."

"The door was left wide open," Namrive pointed out. "Why didn't he leave?"

Anubis had no suitable answer to give her, so he just told the truth. "I guess he didn't want to."

Namrive frowned. Every god trapped in a soul source wanted to leave. Why not this one? "Are you able to communicate with him – with his soul, I mean?" She really wasn't sure how best to phrase it.

"Yes." The question was an insult, and Anubis had to refrain from adding, *I am a god of the dead, aren't I?* Namrive would pay for her insolence soon enough. "However, he's refusing to cooperate with me. He claims he'll only speak to the goddess of the soul."

Namrive blinked. "The goddess of what now?" It never ceased to amaze her the variety of talents gods attributed themselves. But soul? What next: a god of ghosts? She chuckled to herself, then remembered she was talking to a god whose talent was to look after the departed spirits of sentient beings and mummify their bodies for future use, making sure no one else possessed them. Really, who would want to return to a heartless, brainless husk? *Sooo obsolete!* Or he would be soon enough. The gods' days were numbered. And they knew it.

"Can't you use your talent to force him to talk?" she asked.

"No," he said, offended. Namrive obviously had no idea how his talent worked.

She sighed. "We could link his soul to a new body – a very sensitive one. Pain always improves communication."

You wouldn't know, would you, Anubis thought bitterly. The Nephilim built their bodies with no pain receptors to avoid such inconveniences. No creature should claim to be alive without having experienced the pain of living. Even the dead felt more than she did.

"It doesn't work like that. Fenrir's soul is not free as much as it's untethered from this realm. Without a body, the only thing keeping him here is the curse on those walls. And no, I can't force him into a new body, and I can't make him leave either. That is why we have a goddess of the soul," he said pointedly.

Namrive's patience was dropping to alarmingly low levels. "Will he cause trouble?"

"No. He's harmless, completely powerless in his state."

"Good. What about the other two?"

"The twins, Apollo and Artemis, are very talkative and willing to cooperate, with a couple of minor conditions, of course."

Namrive smacked her lips in annoyance. "Sun gods cause us too much trouble. We can't let him go, no matter what he offers," she said adamantly. According to protocol, Apollo should have been eliminated already. The only reason she'd relented into keeping him suspended was because Apollo had the talent for prophecy as well. It was frowned upon amongst her kind to put stock in such talents, but she believed that with enough data and the right equation, the future could be predicted. And if Apollo's talent could help write such an equation, it was worth putting up with the rest of his attributes. For the time being.

"He's not asking for his freedom. Only his sister's and Zeus'," Anubis said.

Namrive tapped the console while considering the proposal. "Artemis can go. Her mind is useless, as are her talents. Hunting and chastity." She tutted. No Nephilim would ever want to hunt beasts or be chaste. They had eliminated all the mortal urges and weaknesses of the flesh as they evolved to express their passions in more abstract and less messy ways. "And Zeus' body is an empty shell," she said. "What is he still doing in the vault, anyway? What a waste."

Without further thought, Namrive deactivated his power source. Through the screen, Anubis saw the alarmed expressions of the Olympian twins as their eyes darted around the room, certainly wondering what had just happened and what would happen to them next. Gods shouldn't have to feel this powerless.

"I don't suppose you know what happened to *his* soul?" Namrive asked, unaware of Anubis' indignation.

"No. Once again, that would be the department of –"

"I swear if you say 'goddess of the souls' again!"

"Soul, not souls," he corrected her smugly.

Namrive closed her eyes and paused all her major functions for a moment before she overloaded. "Why am I only learning of this type of deity now?"

"We don't have one of those in our pantheon," Anubis said. "Nor in any other pantheon besides the Olympian, that I know of."

"Why is that?" she asked patiently.

Anubis debated if he should reveal what he knew. He'd heard the story of the apotheosized human back when it happened, and even before that, like most gods, he'd frowned upon Zeus' and Gaea's experimentation with Ambrosia. Turning mortals into godlike creatures could never end well. If anything, the Nephilim were proof of that. Then again, giving Namrive a new foe, a worthy foe to focus her analytical mind on, would be beneficial for him.

"She used to be a mortal," he said, as if the information was of no consequence.

Namrive unplugged herself again. "All right. Tell me everything you know." It was not a request.

He had to stop himself from grinning. If he had a screen on his forehead – as she often liked to point out he did in response to his remarks about the advantages of Reach – she would see him doing cartwheels right now. "You've heard of Ambrosia, correct?"

"It's what we use to sunder souls from their gods," she said, as if he needed a reminder.

He almost laughed at the irony. "Yes. But why do you call it that?"

Her eyes flickered. She had to dig through pretty old files to answer this one. "It's named after an ancient myth from the time of the Maker. It means 'god's bane'."

It seems the meaning got somewhat lost in translation during the ages, Anubis mused. "Ah, well, I guess it's one name for it. Ambrosia was originally created by Gaea with the purpose of giving mortals immortality. Of course, there's no such thing as immortality for mortals, only a longer life if they're careful and lucky enough to live it. No one really paid much attention to the substance until Zeus decided to try it on his demigod children and they turned into proper gods. Not very powerful ones, mind, but still, gods. This caused some consternation. There were too many of us back then. The last thing we needed was more deities claiming a stake in the Universe. And Zeus, he had many children. Most were headstrong warriors and heroes during their lifetime, so imagine the size of their egos after apotheosis. Anyway, the Titans were most unhappy. Still rankled by their recent war with the Olympians, they feared this was another ploy to annihilate their kind completely. That's when Prometheus, a Titan and a trickster, decided to create a new type of mortal to even out the scales. One immune to Ambrosia and loyal to the old gods. A race intelligent and driven enough to eventually find godhood themselves by their own means." He smiled smugly. "Does any of this sound familiar to you, Namrive?"

Namrive's eyes narrowed to slits. "How do you know his name?" He couldn't have accessed the computer, and even if he had, that information wasn't there. The name of the Maker as well as the Mentor had never been recorded outside of the mainframe on the Nephilim's home world, and it would only be spoken aloud upon his return to them.

Anubis moved closer to her – uncomfortably close – and grinned. "Because I was there, Namrive. Your mythology is my history."

Time, she cursed to herself. It was the only thing gods still had more of than the Nephilim. Well, they might have lived longer. But they would die sooner. She remained collected when she spoke. "What does it all have to do with Ambrosia and this goddess of the soul?"

Anubis backed away, inspecting the screens as if he'd just noticed them. The dryads had disposed of the faithful but were all still gathered in the incinerator room. This didn't surprise him. It was the warmest room, after all. *And the one with the least noticeable eye.* He smiled, running a finger casually over the console before he answered Namrive's question.

"Humans eventually became a sensation in every pantheon. They replaced all other races as the gods' favourites, for never before was there a creature more willing to please them. They were so eager to understand us, to worship us, to make us happy. And they did. Personally, they made me very happy." He smiled and winked at her before continuing. She blinked back in annoyance.

"Most creatures, when they die, they stop caring about things. Their minds become dazed, and they go through eternity in a blissful haze of fragmented memories and bland emotions. Not humans. They have souls, you see. Through them, their will remains, along with their need for purpose and feeling. They serve us, even in death. It was amazing to watch them evolve, really. Finally, a creature who could make us proud with their architecture, art and devotion. And we doted on them too. Many gods went as far as to fall in love with humans. It was madness." He chuckled fondly at the memory. Namrive's eyes flickered with impatience, so he continued.

"The god of love himself kept a human lover for years. When his mother, Aphrodite, found out about it, she went berserk. Of all humans, she hated this one the most, especially because many believed this mortal to be more beautiful than she was. But Eros refused to let his pet human go, and so his mother, incapable of denying him anything, demanded Zeus give the girl immortality so at least his son would not further demean himself with the union. This way the girl would become a proper goddess and they would be together, forever."

"How romantic," Namrive said sarcastically. "You just said Ambrosia didn't work on humans."

"Correct. Not unless they already had god's blood in them. But the besotted god didn't know that back then. It was all part of Aphrodite's plan to break the girl, you see. Together with Zeus, she devised a convincing ordeal for the transition. Gods do nothing for free, after all. First, they made the poor girl do the most appalling and impossible of tasks – impossible for a mortal, that is. And yet, somehow, she accomplished them. The power of love, I suppose." He laughed in earnest, then. "Undeterred, and using her amazing success as an excuse for celebration, Eros demanded her status to be made official in Olympus, in front of the entire pantheon. The wedding ceremony took place in the presence of almost every god in the pantheon, and at the end, they presented the bride with Ambrosia as a gift. They told her it was the nourishment of the gods, their best kept secret. Overwhelmed and trusting as only a mortal can be, she took it from Zeus' hand with full-hearted gratitude, and she ate it. Everyone cheered. Moments later, she clutched her stomach and screamed. In her agony, she unconsciously pulled on all their souls. She didn't know what she was doing. How could she? She was like a blind child who'd found something to hold on to so she wouldn't fall down the abyss. Zeus understood, of course. He immediately brought the sky down on her. No one dared to stop him. Not even Eros. For they felt her power too, and they knew what it meant. But when the dust settled, she still stood there, not a scratch on her. Instead of dying, her own soul had transformed. She had become a true goddess, more powerful than most. Aphrodite told me once that it was as if she had grown wings, like a butterfly coming out of her cocoon. No one spoke, and no one else dared to move against her. The whole pantheon just stood there, terrified, including her husband, whose capricious love immediately turned to hatred. Not that they'd ever admit having been afraid, of course. No god would ever admit to such a thing. But she knew. Through her newfound Reach she could see their souls, their true selves. I suppose she did not like what she saw, for she immediately vanished without a trace, and the whole incident was, if not entirely forgotten, put out of their minds. I hadn't even heard of the creature again until Fenrir mentioned her today."

Namrive stared at him as if he'd bored her. That was disappointing.

"Your *history* is ridiculous," she said.

"How so?" he asked, slightly offended.

"She had to have god's blood in her," Namrive said. Gods were so prone to believe in stories, they did not think to consider facts.

"Both her parents were mortal," he stated.

"Then she obviously had it in her womb."

Anubis blinked. Then burst out laughing. Cats, Namrive was probably right.

"That is how we use our Ambrosia," she continued. "Every woman and Tribute is tested with it to avoid what you call demigods from being born."

Anubis found that piece of information far less amusing, but one of the most useful he'd learnt since allying himself with the Nephilim.

"Still," Namrive continued, "it doesn't explain why she became the goddess of the soul."

"No, I guess it does not. No one knows what determines a god's talents."

"Magic," Namrive scoffed inaudibly to anyone but a god. Then her eyes widened, and she began inputting commands on the computer. "Of course! That is what he was trying to hide. She must have been here all along."

"Who, Psyche?"

"Alek probably learnt about her and her talent through Zeus. A god's power is linked to their soul, correct? If her control over souls is as you say, we wouldn't need to keep the gods alive in servitude inside the source. We could just take their souls, permanently. The masters wouldn't need to be bound to the source of their power. They could go anywhere. Rule any world!"

The gems on Namrive's temples came alight, a sign she was really excited about the information being processed in her brain.

"I suppose…" Anubis said, not liking where her deductions were going.

"I found endless fragments of deleted reports of experiments done with a substance made of god's blood and tree sap," Namrive continued. "Ambrosia, the one gods used, came from a tree, correct?"

He nodded reluctantly. Namrive was manic now. He'd never seen her so animated, and it scared him. Her fingers moved too fast over the keyboard for his eyes to follow.

"I also found entries about there being a Wyrd in his daughter, Ileana. That's why the girl needed a new body. She was hosting the goddess."

"Psyche was here?" Anubis repeated, still considering the implications. Could she have been in Niflheim this whole time? It made sense. No Olympian would think to look for her there, of all places.

Anubis remembered the first time he'd heard of this world, a gloomy prison for Loki's children and other outcasts. As worlds went, it was a joke. Filled with ice and death and monsters, with only one tiny patch of land able to support normal life. It held no appeal to the Nephilim, especially after the Merge made it so unstable, and yet Alek claimed to know how to make it profitable. The only reason he, a dryad, even got to rule it was because no one else wanted the job. And, against all odds, he delivered. For over twenty years his Tributes, few as they were compared with other worlds, were amongst the most resilient and genetically diverse. The Suzerain had never asked for support when dealing with the people under his rule or reported a glitch in the systems. He'd never missed a report and they were always glowing. Never gave the Nephilim any reason to warrant an inspection. And so he'd conducted his own experiments in peace. Behind their backs, using their technology. Anubis smiled. Seshat had been right to stay with the man.

"Cunning bastard," Namrive growled, reaching a similar conclusion. Alek Dveer's success had always intrigued her. According to her research, the thing that distinguished most humans from Narrum, apart from negligible biological traits regarding digestion and bone structure, was that Narrum didn't have leaders. It was against their culture, their very nature. Instead, they possessed an unstoppable, unyielding herd mentality, driven by numbers and greed, not laws or lords. The way the Suzerain had managed to control the world's primitive population was uncanny. Especially since he was a dryad, which many Narrum still considered an exotic meal. She hit the console with a closed fist. "I want him brought back to consciousness. Now!"

Anubis watched her frantically input commands; however, flesh would not be rushed. 'Now' would take a couple of days at least, and there was a lot a god could do in that time.

"How did Alek know the whereabouts of the goddess of the soul?" Anubis asked, almost to himself.

"The same way he knew about us, I assume," Namrive said.

Anubis waited for more.

"The gods told him!"

"Which gods?" He certainly didn't.

She straightened herself away from the screen to stare down at him. "I don't know. Gods are your department. That's why we keep you around. You find out who."

And how had the gods found out about Alek? Anubis thought. "How did the Nephilim first meet Alek?" he asked, instead.

"He arrived in Heaven through the World Tree. It was quite the surprise. We didn't even know this world existed until he showed up. Huh, we didn't even know how World Trees worked until then, to be fair. And they never worked for us until the reconfiguration."

Felling, you mean, Anubis thought bitterly but remained silent. There was no denying the Nephilim ingenuity in retrofitting the old World Trees with their portals to enable them to travel across galaxies in moments, but they were incapable of creating anything without destroying something first.

"In any case," Namrive continued, "we thought dryads were long extinct, so naturally we were intrigued by him, and upon testing the Anann's genetic code, we deemed them worthy of the investment. Any people who submit to our rule without a fuss is worthy of investment. Obviously we didn't just give him control of this world. Alek was thoroughly tested first, and he passed every test! He was just another ambitious mortal with no conscience who genuinely hated the gods. No mortal can fake that sort of hate. We had no reason to suspect him."

Yes, Alek hated the gods, all right. Anubis had been on the receiving end of that hate often enough to know it wasn't fake. But he couldn't think of any god who would want the Nephilim interfering with their world either – Hel certainly wouldn't – let alone one who would confide in dryads, not even as pets. And yet, if not for the Suzerain, they would never have come to Niflheim. First the Merge, then Alek, and now Psyche had made an appearance as well. To Anubis' mind, this had all the markings of a trap. Only, who was the hunter? More to the point, who was the prey?

"Bugs! Look at these records." Namrive beckoned Anubis to the screen. He looked at the abstract characters moving across the glass panel. What the Nephilim called writing made no sense to his mind.

"What am I looking at?"

Namrive curled her lip at his ignorance. His kind had not been able to evolve from a writing system more complex than ideograms. "It appears the Suzerain has been experimenting with different genetic codes – I mean, look at this aberration!" She was pointing at images of a large creature with long arms, stocky legs and foliage sprouting from his head. To Anubis, it resembled a cross between a Jötunn and a tree. "He also built himself a new body every fifty days or so," she said.

"Why?"

"*How* is more important. We have safeguards against this sort of thing. Unbelievable! He synthesised hundreds of them! Where did he even find the resources? The cost in gold alone..."

"You mean there are hundreds of Suzerains out

there?" Anubis was still staring at the screen as if he could read the answer.

"No. Most appear to have been infused with the same toxin that killed the wolf."

"Your poisonous Ambrosia? I thought it was harmless to mortals."

"Not in these doses." She shook her head. "Why would Alek do this? He must have known the bodies wouldn't last."

"He must have considered the possibility of attack. The wolf did eat him, after all." Anubis grimaced at the thought. Loki's children were weird.

"Are you suggesting that poisoning himself was his way to avoid being taken by the gods?" Namrive asked cynically.

"Maybe he wanted to be taken and made himself bait."

"Bah," she scoffed. "So his plan was to poison every enemy god one by one by offering himself as their meal?"

No, Anubis conceded, that made little sense. Then again, Alek was a dryad. He had been fed upon before. Dryads had always been prey to other races and had no predatory instinct of their own. They survived by avoiding or deceiving their predators. Maybe this was indeed his way of eliminating his enemies.

"Besides," Namrive continued, "his consciousness is intact and stored. It's easy to take risks when you know you'll be fixed."

"Well, that depends," Anubis said.

"On what?"

"Us. Do you really want to bring him back?"

"Of course. He has a lot to answer for."

"His daughter disagrees. She's of the opinion we should not resurrect again him."

"Is she?" Namrive replayed the events before their arrival again. "Interesting."

"Care to share," Anubis said grudgingly. How he hated when she did that. Looking at things only she could see inside that maze of crystals and microchips she called a brain.

"She's lying about something. I could tell the moment I scanned her. Sadly, my senses only allow me to detect the lies, not what they are lying about or the motivation behind them. Personally, I believe her opposition is another excellent reason to bring Alek back. Not to mention that I for one would like to give him a piece of my mind regarding the abuse of power and wasting resources on family. If every Suzerain was allowed to reincarnate their family members, we'd run out of worlds to put them all in, never mind gods to sustain them."

On that, at least, Anubis agreed. Gods had become scarce in the last millennia. At first they had welcomed this, for every pantheon had undesirables, but now… it had gone too far. And he too would very much like to have a word with Alek regarding his outstanding success and the god who facilitated it. He nodded, realising Namrive was still waiting for his feedback.

"I've already started the procedure." Her eyes flickered unnaturally. The womb chamber at the end of the wall began to glow.

"What about the others? Anything worth sharing?" he asked her.

"The boy with the big blue eyes is harmless. He has the mental capacity of a five-year-old," she said as if it offended her.

"I guess that explains why he was never sent in Tribute," Anubis mused. "Why would Alek keep him?"

"You'll have to ask him that too. The damage to the boy's cortex was inflicted, not present at birth. I know the man didn't like to be around beings smarter than him, but what he did to the poor creature is cruel."

Anubis was surprised by the faint emotion in her tone. To hear Namrive, of all creatures, condemn cruelty was an unfamiliar experience for him. To her, dissecting a subject alive was only a necessary mess in the name of science, but apparently messing with a mind's ability to think and learn was an unforgivable crime.

"Can you reverse it?" he asked.

"No," she said morosely. "I can download his mind to a new brain, but the damage was done to the thought patterns themselves. His personally is set. He's useless and mightily annoying. It'll be better to just euthanize him. I will save his genetic code, though. It's quite unique." She peeled her eyes from the screens to stare back at Anubis. "Perhaps you should take the opportunity to study his body in detail? So it's not a total loss." This was not a suggestion.

"Sure," he said tiredly.

"Oric is an arrogant bleeder, but useful. I gave him permission to rebuild his arm," she said.

"Is he really worth the resources?"

"He's loyal, and we are short on faithful."

"How considerate of you," Anubis said sarcastically.

"And it's better to have him whole for the dissection."

"Am I to dissect him as well?" Cats, but he was as bored with dissections as with mummifications. "What is his flaw?"

"Not a flaw; quite the contrary. Oric is a natural hybrid, born of dryad and Dharkan."

Anubis' eyes went wide. "Truly?" Well, this made the prospect of dissection a lot more interesting.

"Mm-hmm, I figured you'd like that."

"Er… thank you," he said, not knowing what else to say to such uncharacteristic behaviour from her. "How do you know this?" It surprised him he hadn't noticed Oric's special trait himself, having known the man for years. His mind had been shielded against Reach, but flesh should hold no secrets to Anubis. He had to give it to the Suzerain, he sure had mastered the workings of both body and mind.

"I suspected something was off when I failed to gain access to his personal data. The information was carefully and suspiciously protected by a code – a code he had to input to initiate the rebuilding procedure," Namrive said, proud of herself.

"I see," Anubis said, understanding the motivation behind Namrive's generosity.

"The Suzerain had to harvest Dharkan genetic material for his experiments from somewhere," she said, squinting at a different screen. "Those two can wait, though. First, I still have endless data on his research to analyse. Not to mention I need to figure out this nonsense about time travel as well."

Anubis' breath caught. "I'm sorry, what?"

Namrive hesitated, surprised by his reaction. But

the truth was, she could not make heads or tails of the report, so she might as well share it with the god. "It says here the girl, Ileana, came from a different time in the future. And that time came back with her." She tutted. "I hate riddles."

"Oh, cats," Anubis breathed.

Namrive turned around and saw him covering his gaping mouth. He'd solved the riddle already. Of course he had; gods practically communicated through riddles. Her eyes narrowed. "Tell me what you know."

∞

"Are you telling me there's a god who controls time and trees able to transport creatures through time the same way World Trees take them to other worlds?" Namrive enunciated each word slowly, as if reciting the information in such a way would make it sound more plausible.

Anubis nodded reluctantly. "Not exactly in the same way, they are –"

Her gems flashed red. "How am I only learning of this now?"

He curled his lip. "Three reasons: One, I don't tell you anything unless I have to. Two, they were meant for living creatures, so they probably won't work on your kind without 'reconfiguration'. And three, Chronodéndrons are far more prickly than World Trees. They were supposed to have been destroyed long ago. Of course, if we were to find one, it would be in this forsaken world," he grumbled.

"Why would the gods destroy such a gift?" Namrive asked, aghast. Her kind had spent centuries trying to understand time, and apparently even trees had more insight into its workings than them. It was unacceptable.

Anubis laughed bitterly. "Chrono-travel is no gift. Chronos doesn't give gifts. If he has a hold in this world or if he's even remotely connected with the Suzerain, we need to leave immediately."

"Absolutely not. We won't go anywhere until Alek awakes. And if this Chronos is real, I must meet him."

Anubis winced. Stars, how was he going to explain the seriousness of the situation so she might understand. He took a deep breath to gather his thoughts.

"Namrive," he said, trying his best not to sound too patronising, "Chronos is not just a god. He is *The* God. He is to us what we are to mortals. His talent is time itself. Can you understand that? We don't meet with him, we do our best to avoid him, in fact. We ignore him and hope he returns the courtesy. Why do you think, despite all your knowledge, resources and experiments, you've never been able to control time?"

She considered this. So far, all the hypotheses presented by the experts to explain their failed experiments were pretty unsatisfactory and bordering on the fantastical, to the point where the existence of a God of Time deliberately thwarting their efforts made sense. This didn't intimidate Namrive; it excited her. She couldn't wait to meet this *god of gods*, master of Time and the Universe. If his power was half as great as Anubis claimed, he'd be worthy of a proper study, like a magnificent supermassive singularity or an aberrant celestial body able to escape its gravity. Time was not something the Nephilim were too concerned with, not on a personal level, anyway. But they'd always been curious about how it worked, and mastering time would surely open some interesting possibilities. The concept left her almost giddy! Yes, she would love to meet this God and see the look on his face when he realised he was nothing more than a curiosity to her kind. Better yet, if the other gods thought of him the way Anubis did, Chronos may well become an excellent ally to the Nephilim.

"Do not underestimate Chronos, Namrive. He cannot be captured, and he has no need for allies," Anubis warned.

The way he sometimes spoke as if he'd read her thoughts was the most eerie thing about the man. She had to remind herself again that the gods might be obsolete, but they'd been around for aeons. They had gathered more data and experience dealing with each other than the Nephilim had in centuries of self-analysis. It was too much information for their minds to process, of course, but to make up for that, they had evolved a way to use the excess information in the form of intuition – a trait her kind unfortunately still lacked. There had to be an equation or algorithm for such a thing, surely. They just hadn't come up with it yet.

"Are we clear?" Anubis insisted, proving that his insight was indeed limited. If he could actually read her thoughts, he wouldn't need to pester her with questions.

"Crystal," she lied.

Anubis drew a breath, held it in, then released it with a sigh. Gods only breathed when they were extremely agitated or angry. He seemed to be both.

"Good," he said, relieved. "Now, if you'll excuse me, I have a matter to attend to in Relicum."

It took him long enough, Namrive thought, aware he'd wanted to leave the Stump before their conversation even started. She wouldn't make it easy for him to get away, though. It would not do for him to suspect that she suspected misconduct.

"You can't. The synthesis –"

"I'll return before the synthesis is complete," Anubis added, pre-emptively addressing her objection. "Which won't be for another couple of days. And you said the dissections can wait too, so…" He fixed his gaze on her, and the image of a snarling jackal overlaid his face like a hologram. "I am free to leave, am I not?"

"Technically. If you have good reason," she said.

"I have a personal reason, actually. An old friend has taken up residence in the temple." He laughed at her sceptical frown. "Are you surprised I have friends?"

"No," she sneered. She was, of course. Anubis had never mentioned *friends*. Mostly she was surprised he hadn't lied about why he wanted to leave or where he was going. "This is a world dedicated to the dead. I assume you have many friends here," she said instead.

"That is the problem. Always remember where your allegiance lies and don't get too friendly with them. They are our enemies, after all."

"If you're thinking of Hades or Hel, they are not my friends. We avoid each other as much as possible, in fact. Even before you people came along."

Her eyes flashed with curiosity. "Why?"

"Underworld gods are like sun gods: too many

together can only cause trouble. Hades' and Hel's attraction already caused this mess. If I remain here too long, who knows what might happen to the different realms of this shattered world."

Namrive grimaced. She had not thought of that either. How she hated not having enough data on these matters to make her own conclusions. "Can you… er… feel Hades and Hel?" she asked.

"Not in here. Only a tingle, a frisson now and again. Once outside… well, I'll gladly keep you informed of my feelings if you like." He pointed at his forearm.

"Very well. Take the gifted shrine with you," she said. "And find out who his benefactor is," Namrive said, aware of his distrust of gifted mortals.

Anubis bristled. He wanted no witnesses or escorts, especially gifted ones. "Why, Namrive, you could always use someone of his aesthetic qualities," Anubis ventured, knowing it would be futile. Judoc might be the closest thing to male perfection he'd seen in a mortal, but that still put him orders of magnitude less than the perfection of the female form.

"I have more than enough information on metz specimens, thank you. Enjoy your day out," she said, feeling something suspiciously like jealousy. She never got to explore the worlds beyond their Stumps. The idea appealed to her, but to do it properly, first she would need to blend into the world's population, and that meant transferring her mind to a different body, a time-consuming and generally unpleasant experience. She dismissed it. "I'll be here going through the footage of the last several days… see what else I can find out."

"Ahh," Anubis said, glancing at the screen. "Looks like you found something already." He pointed at a screen replaying footage from the main portal, where a petite nymph sat dangling her bare legs over the edge. She appeared to be equally at ease with the Dharkan and the gods. How peculiar.

"I wasn't –" Namrive started, gems flashing.

"Don't deny it. I saw how you were looking at the nymph on that screen earlier." He leaned closer, further unnerving her. "I saw how your eyes flickered faster when her face was in full view. I even saw a glimpse of a smile on your face when she danced around the winged horse."

"I was smiling at the horse."

"Sure, sure." He laughed. "You should definitely take some personal time, Namrive. The Grove is only a short distance away. You might find something interesting there. Wouldn't you rather study your subjects in their natural environment?"

She was about to protest again, but Anubis had a point. Unfortunately, she couldn't rely on any observation where the observed was aware of the observer. Furthermore, she could not afford any distractions while on duty. Not in this place and company.

"Perhaps later," she said.

"Very well. Are you sure you'll be all right here alone?" he asked perfunctorily.

Her dark eyes flickered with amusement. "That almost sounded as if you care." Gods were known for being good liars. Not Anubis, though.

He laughed again. "Ah, Namrive, I *almost* do."

"Do not concern yourself with my well-being. We

still have a ship filled with faithful constructs, ready to annihilate any inconveniences."

And may they remain there, blissfully inactive, Anubis thought. "Very well," he said.

"You really believe the gods' absence is a trap?" she asked before he left.

"If it looks like a cat, and it hisses like a cat…" Anubis shrugged. To be honest, he wasn't sure anymore. This recent development with Chronos could mean the gods were simply too busy elsewhere. Besides, Namrive was practically invulnerable to physical or mental attacks. She would be all right – unfortunately. "Just don't do anything too harsh until I return."

She wasn't listening to him anymore, her mind lost in the virtual realm of the Nephilim.

CHAPTER 15

Ideth

Ideth held on to Xylo – it was easier to think of him by that name – while they glided across Aegea, and she was trying to figure out how the frost her life choices had led her to this moment. Sure, she'd been well aware of her debt to Chronos from the first time she prayed at the Chronodéndron, but riding behind the God of Time on one of the Suzerain's mechanical mounts was not how she'd imagined her fate at his mercy would be. Still, it could be worse, she supposed. After days cooped up inside the Stump, she was relishing the feel of her hair blowing in the wind and the sun on her skin. Enough to almost forget feeling guilty for leaving Oreth behind, locked up with Occa. Not that she'd had much choice, mind. Nor did she delude herself by thinking he would miss her or that it would be better for him out here with her and… Xylo. But mothers always feel guilty where their children's well-being is concerned. Gaea told Ideth she'd made it so on purpose, otherwise it would be too easy for mothers to forsake their children. As if! Then she had the nerve to lecture her on how to be a better mother.

What good are lessons on motherhood two decades after the fact? Oreth no longer had any need or desire for a mother now, and as for the guilt… Ideth had long learnt to live with it along with all the other emotional slush she'd accumulated over the years. One thing was certain, she would not have more children. The hate from one was enough.

He's safe, she told herself for the hundredth time. Safer than her, at least, gliding on a magical skiff with a flesh-and-wood hybrid construct combined by the Suzerain's sorcery and animated by the will of the most feared God in the Universe. She could well imagine what Chiron would say if he saw her now: *This is unwise, unbridled one, even for you.* Indeed… And where the frost was he? As if it wasn't enough to have lied to her all those years, he had to abandon her now as well? Pfah! Chiron probably knew Xylo's identity from the start, that was why he avoided landing on the Stump long enough to even change form, always ready and eager to fly off again. *Freezing horse*, she cursed, counting on the wind to dry the moisture gathering in her eyes. He could at least have warned her, or Hel, or Gaea even. Ideth had never seen a deity more discomfited than the Mother of Life when she found out Xylo's true identity. Ideth knew all gods feared Chronos, but what she'd sensed during their argument went beyond terror. It was an overwhelming sense of doom, not unlike what she'd experienced kissing Psyche. Fortunately – or unfortunately, she couldn't decide which – sensing it was as far as it went for her. The barrage of words shared between the two primordial deities made no sense to Ideth to the point she could have sworn there were three arguing instead of two. She wondered why they bothered to include her in the conversation in the first place. Freezing gods… they do love an audience for their dramas.

Xylo slowed upon reaching a thicket in order to navigate their way safely. Where were they going? She had asked, of course. And sure enough, she got no straight answer in reply. *It's a surprise,* was all Xylo had said. Ideth hated surprises. They never turned out well, in her experience.

She sighed as they passed a row of trees struck by lightning and tried not to think of how Aedan would react to her absence when he returned to the Stump. Would he come after her? Unlikely. She was not that important to the Wraith. Their relationship was one of obligation and responsibility, not actual friendship. Would he freeze Oreth in a fit of rage? Well, *that* was more than likely. Slush, she hoped the boy had the sense not to aggravate the Dharkan or the gods too much until her return. A dreadful thought entered her mind. She would return, wouldn't she?

They stopped at the edge of the forest, and Ideth didn't wait for a reason or permission to dismount. As fun as the ride had been, sitting for so long left her legs stiff and her bum numb. Dryads weren't made to sit still for long periods of time. To them, movement was life, and sitting down was as bad for their bodies as lack of sunlight was to their spirits. Once on her feet, she stretched herself back into shape while Xylo stared motionless at the skiff hovering two feet above the ground.

"Something's wrong?" Ideth asked.

Xylo turned his head slowly in her direction while keeping his eyes firmly fixated on the object of his contemplation.

"How is this… *thing* able to overcome gravity while I, in this body, cannot?" he mused, clearly still working on the problem.

Ideth crossed her arms. "You're asking *me*, mighty Chronos?" she teased, struggling to come to terms with the notion that this lump of wood was who he said he was.

He turned his mossy gaze on her, and any doubts about his identity crumbled under his stare. It was like staring at a great wave about to crash down on you. Better to trust her instinct than her senses, she decided, showing her most appeasing smile.

"I'm the God of Time, not gravity," he said.

"Is there a god of gravity?" she asked without thinking. Sometimes it was as if there was a disconnect between her brain and her tongue. No, not sometimes – at the worst possible times. When the most sensible option was to say nothing at all, in fact. She smiled again, batting her eyelashes for extra cuteness, fully aware that a pretty face could only go so far, and kept her mouth shut.

He shrugged and didn't seem to care for her face one way or the other. "I've never encountered one in this universe. It stands to reason there might have been such a god once, and this force pulling matter together is the remnant of his power. It never affected me like this before. Few things do." He sounded almost disappointed. "It does have a certain appeal: being grounded, connected to something. When you exist too long without limitations, it's easy to forget there are forces more powerful than gods. And more powerful gods in other universes," he added almost to himself.

Ideth guffawed.

"Do I amuse you?"

The eerie gaze fell on her again. This time she saw herself staring down a very deep well and having that well staring back at her.

She swallowed. "Oh, I'm not amused," she said truthfully, trying not to choke on her hopeless mirth. Chronos' idea of limitations was an insult to any mortal, and in her wretched state she could only giggle at the notion of even more powerful gods, never mind other universes.

Thankfully, he didn't pursue the matter. His attention was now focused on the woodland ahead.

"As mighty as this contraption is against the pull of gravity, it can't cut through trees. We must continue our journey on foot," he said and proceeded into the forest.

Our journey? She didn't like the sound of that. The temptation to run was strong in Ideth. She could do it. Encumbered by his vessel's weight and lack of mobility, Chronos would be no match for her swift legs. But run where? For how long? "Time always catches up with you," the old Aossi queen used to say. Never had the adage rung truer in Ideth's mind.

Frost.

She wondered again how her life had come to this and then, with a resigned sigh, walked into the forest after him.

∞

Ideth heard the tree snap in half and dodged just in time to avoid it falling on her.

"Watch it!" she yelped. It was a statement to the frayed state of her nerves that she'd raised her voice like a Narrum, heedless of who she was shouting at or of who else might be listening. "For frost's sake! It nearly hit me this time."

"It nearly hit you the last time too, and yet you keep walking ahead of me," Xylo replied unconcernedly.

She couldn't help it. It was dark now, they'd been waking all day. Ideth was eager to find shelter for the night, and for all his size, Xylo moved frustratingly slow, marching in a straight line, knocking down every tree in his path. Of course, keeping her distance from him seemed like a good idea also, even if she doubted any amount of distance would alter her fate. It was just that sometimes the illusion of safety was better than the certainty of danger.

"It's easier to go around the trees, you know," she suggested, trying not to sound too annoyed.

"I disagree. It takes more steps to go around a tree and therefore more effort."

"It causes less damage, then. And it's a great deal safer – for me, at least," she grumbled that last bit to herself.

"Darling Ideth, explain to me, why should I add more steps to my journey?" His tone remained calm, but there was an underlying sternness to the question.

Ideth gaped momentarily at the lumbering creature, not knowing where to begin. If the God applied a similar reasoning to everything, no wonder the others had so many issues with him.

"Having to walk is insult enough," he continued, knocking down another tree from his path.

Ideth took a deep breath. "I thought you liked gravity and the sensation of ground beneath your feet," she said, imitating his rumbling voice unconsciously, then bit her lip reminding herself, once again, that this was Chronos she was teasing, not Chiron. Fortunately, he didn't seem to be offended. Sarcasm often went over the old gods' heads. In Chronos' case, it went over the top of the trees themselves, apparently.

He grunted. "I did. The novelty wore off back at the slope. The constant downward pull is tiresome. I'm frustrated with it. This body is too heavy, too slow, and lacks the appropriate number of legs to be efficient in this terrain. Must I further demean myself by changing course every time I encounter a tree?"

"You don't need to change your course, just… adjust it. It's what we all do."

"But why would I?"

Another sapling fell at Ideth's feet.

"Because the trees were here before you came along!" she snapped. Few things upset a dryad more than the pointless destruction of trees.

"Were they?" Chronos' tone spoke volumes.

Ideth's stomach sank when she realised what she'd said. To whom she'd said it. *For frost' sake, Ideth!* No amount of smiling would get her out of this one. She had to stand her ground. No matter how dire the circumstances, her self-preservation instinct would never let her go down without a fight.

"Yes! It's all a matter of perspective. Your existence might have begun long before any tree, but these trees have been in Aegea longer than you. They are no threat to you or our destination, so yes, you should adjust your path to their presence. Not to mention you're signalling our position to the entire forest, knocking them down like this."

She kept walking, not daring to turn her head to see the effect her words might have had on him and bracing herself to dodge the next tree to fall. Eventually she ventured a glance over her shoulder and saw Xylo stepping around a young sequoia.

"You are correct, darling Ideth. Apologies."

Ideth stumbled and fell, disconcerted with his reply. She was still on her knees, mouth hanging open as he overtook her with a polite wink.

∞

They continued their walk side by side, making casual conversation, for it was preferable to eerie silence. Ideth still had no idea where they were going and could hardly see what was in front of her now. Chronos, on the other hand, seemed to be able to see clearly in the darkness. If this was an ability related to his body or his power, she couldn't say, nor did she care to ask. Other questions occupied her thoughts, and eventually she gathered enough courage to address the most prominent one.

"Why did you merge the worlds?"

"Because I wanted to."

She sighed. "All right. *Why* did you want to?"

"It suited my purposes."

Ideth shook her head, then tried a different approach.

"How did you do it?"

He was silent for a long moment. "I'd rather not answer your question."

"Why, is it a secret? I can keep a secret," she lied.

"No," he said hesitantly. "The process is laborious to explain, particularly to one who is not a god."

"Tsk. Chiron used to say the same thing, and yet mortality never stopped me from learning about the gods and their talented ways. Try me. If I don't understand, there's no harm done. And if I do understand, well, it's not like I can do anything about it anyway, is there?" she said cheerfully.

Xylo hummed. "I suppose not. Very well. Given a certain predisposition upon their creation, two worlds can potentially cross each other's path in the Cosmos and occupy the same location in space for a moment, millions of years apart. All I did was force that moment to happen without the devastating effects of an actual collision."

"Wow, that sounds… challenging." He was right. She did not understand how worlds could follow a path. It didn't matter, she still wanted to know more.

"It wasn't that difficult. After all, I control Time, and the realms of the Underworld don't quite follow the same rules of matter as those of regular worlds. They are not – how to put it – as substantial. Once free from Olympus, moving Hades' realm to Niflheim was easy enough. Had I tried this with a proper world…" He puffed out his cheeks and uttered a loud BOOM to the night sky. "That might still happen, actually. Matter doesn't like to be manipulated in such ways."

"Lovely. I'm so glad I asked."

"Do not concern yourself. It won't happen while I'm here."

"Great..." Ideth shook her head. His casual reassurance only made her feel worse. "No wonder you're the God all gods fear." Chiron had drilled that same fear into her before she travelled, but she had never been truly afraid of the God of Time until now. How can you fear something you can't see? Something that is always there, no matter what you do or where you go. Might as well fear the air you breathe or death itself. A waste of worry, in Ideth's opinion. But now... now, she could glimpse what the gods must see in him, and it wasn't pretty. Xylo's features took some getting used to, but he didn't look menacing the way most monsters do. Quite the contrary, her definition of *monster* featured creatures with longer claws and sharper teeth than his. It was the unlimited power wielded by the personality behind those features that was terrifying. And what was worse, everything would eventually end, except him. He was eternal, inexorable, unbeatable.

"Well, I am now," Xylo said, interrupting her thoughts. There was a cheerfulness to his tone. "The Merge did wonders for my reputation across the worlds. You see, the gods fear little and respect even less. They have a remarkable ability to avoid dealing with what they don't understand or can't control. So because of that, I received nothing but their indifference throughout the ages. To them I was little more than a redundant feature of the Universe: vast and yet as insignificant as space itself, worthy of little attention. All the while, I was paying attention to them." The playful way he said that made the hairs on Ideth's nape stand on end.

"Why?" she asked.

"They all owe their existence to me. I was curious about what they'd do with it. Now I know."

"All of them? Even Gaea?"

He grumbled something to himself, then said, "Unfortunately."

"But she's the Goddess of –"

He cut her off. "Gaea played a part in creation. That is all."

"What about Kali?"

"What about Kali?" he echoed ominously.

Ideth hesitated. "The gods don't fear her as much as they fear you, and yet isn't she the one able to end their lives?"

"She is."

"Does she take orders from you or something?"

His laugh rumbled through the forest like thunder.

"Kali takes orders from no one, darling Ideth."

Ideth's fear was turning into annoyance. "Where is she, anyway?"

"Why do you want to know? Are you so eager to end our acquaintance you wish to meet her?"

Ideth blinked. "No… no, of course not. I only ask because this is, after all, a world of the dead."

"A world of the dead, yes. Not of death. Dead and death are not the same thing, darling Ideth. And Kali is a very private entity. She only reveals herself to others when it's their time. Ahahah, I love that expression!"

Ideth wasn't laughing. "When she kills them, you mean."

He shook his head condescendingly, still chuckling to himself. "Death is sweeter when it's a surprise, darling Ideth. Besides, Kali doesn't kill as much as she halts one's journey through time, and just because you stop doesn't mean you're dead. Any god can testify to that. True death only happens when you're forgotten, and some creatures, gods in particular, are pretty hard to forget."

"Because they cause so much trouble..." Ideth grumbled.

His subsequent grunt sounded like agreement.

"What about mortals?" she asked. "It's pretty hard for a mortal to make a memorable impression when they have so little time to live."

"Ah, it may seem so from your perspective. Kali scythes the connection between time and life, but most life doesn't end with death either. Mortals keep finding ways to replicate, to pass on pieces of themselves generation after generation. In a way, their immortality surpasses those of gods, and they are nearly impossible to eradicate at this point. Besides, the spirits in the Underworlds are very much alive too, even if unaware of it. Mnemosyne thought it was best for them this way." He lowered his voice in amused conspiracy. "The truth is, her own memory can't cope with keeping track of both the living *and* the dead. There're too many of them. More and more with each passing moment... Even I struggle to keep track of them all! Still, spirits are not the problem, souls are. They never rest, never diminish, never really forget. Even without memory, they keep exerting their will. Born from darkness, they will not rest until the Universe is dark again," Chronos said, a rumble of resentful anger in his tone.

Souls. The things that make gods and humans special. This was all because of them. Souls and their devious goddess. Ideth decided it best to change the subject before she too got angrier.

"Er... can I ask you a question?" she said.

"You've been asking questions all evening without my permission."

"How does time work?" This question had been on her mind since she first considered chrono-travel. Chiron, if he knew, had never been able to explain it properly. But Chronos, of all creatures, should provide her with a satisfactory answer.

Xylo's features twisted into something like a smile. "Like walking: one step after another."

Ideth's eyes narrowed. "So how does one travel back and forwards through it?"

He fixed his gaze on her. She couldn't see it, though she sure felt it.

"You can walk backwards, can't you? Or leap forward, step sideways, go around in circles on the spot. Dance!" he roared. The sound resembled boulders tumbling down a hill.

Ideth eyed him askance, unable to relate to the apparent hilarity of the comparison. Dancing was fun. Chrono-travel wasn't.

He laughed again as if reading her mind, which he probably was. *Freezing gods.* Wyrds couldn't Reach for thoughts, only free gods could do it. She'd hoped Xylo hadn't been created with the ability.

"Reach is overrated, darling Ideth. Like every other sense, it has limitations. I don't need Reach to read your mind and learn your every thought and action. Besides, I'd rather listen to them."

Ideth closed her mouth, then cleared her throat. Well, if he'd been guessing her thoughts all day and she was still alive, she doubted anything she said would make things worse. She might as well get it all off her chest, then.

"Could you send me to a different time right now? Without the tree, I mean?"

"Of course. But I won't."

"Why not?" she asked petulantly.

"I prefer you right here and now with me."

He was smiling, but the words had a foreboding tone to them.

"What… er…" She had to clear her throat again before continuing. It was getting sore. "So what is the purpose of the Chronodéndron?"

"Chronodéndron are like legs. You need them for walking. They keep the traveller's body intact during the journey. You see, spirits and souls can move freely through time, but not flesh. Flesh is a weakness, a limitation. That was the agreement between Gaea and me."

"So… why…" She trailed off, testing just how accurate Chronos' prescience was.

"Why did I ask the Suzerain to make me this body?"

"Yes. I mean, did you ask him to look like *that*, or…"

Xylo was, for lack of a better term, hard on the eyes. Not that he was ugly; his features didn't fit any aesthetic definition she could think of. He was a puzzle. A poorly assembled one made with ill-fitting pieces of every race, and perhaps even a few types of trees jumbled together.

"He followed my instructions, yes. Why, you don't like it?" he asked, obviously aware of the answer.

"Just wondering what you really look like, is all."

He rumbled something akin to amusement. "Your mortal senses could never perceive my true form, let alone comprehend it."

"Pfah," she snorted. "You'd be surprised with the things I've perceived."

She expected her comment to elicit more derision from him; there was only silence. She ventured a glance up. Those eyes, darker than the surrounding darkness, bored into her appraisingly. She licked her lips, and memories of her travels made their way unbidden to a prominent place in her mind, adding more anxiety to her already anxious state.

"I am impressed and dare I say amazed by the things you can perceive, darling Ideth. And that is why I will teach you to understand them." He gave her a complicit smile.

Ideth paused. Somehow she knew he wasn't talking about her travels. "Do you know why I can taste souls?" A pointless question. The god seemed to know everything about her.

"I do."

She waited for more. He resumed walking.

"Well, are you going to tell me?" she asked, trailing after him when it became obvious he would not oblige her curiosity otherwise.

"When you're ready," he said.

She cursed. Gods apparently were born ready, but mortals had to wait. Quite the irony, since mortals were the ones with no time to waste. His tone and body language told her it was futile to insist, but then again, she had nothing better to do.

"Where do souls come from, and why is it that only gods and humans have them?"

"When I arrived in this universe, I had no –" He stopped walking to stare down at her with what looked like amazement. "Oh my, darling Ideth, how easily you make me talk. I've no doubt you'd have me blabbing like Gaea before the night's out."

Ideth was petrified when she saw his huge hand move towards her face. For a moment she thought he would crush her. A caress followed. Gentle, as gentle as being stroked by a tree branch can be. Then the hand moved away, pointing at the shadows ahead. "We've arrived at our destination."

Ideth's startled gaze followed the direction he was pointing. She squinted, trying to see past the shadows of the trees ahead.

"Oh, no…" She'd recognise that cabin anywhere.

"Come with me," he said.

With her heart still pounding against her chest, she tilted her face to the night sky, to the stars above the canopies, and prayed.

Orion, my love. I know you look after me. Please, if there's anything you can do, anything at all.

A few steps away, Chronos laughed. "Beware of prayers, darling Ideth. You never know who might be listening."

"Why are we here?" Ideth demanded sternly. "I thought we were going to the Chronodéndron."

"You were wrong," Chronos replied matter-of-factly.

At no point during their journey had he revealed their destination, true. But considering the direction they were travelling and her travel companion himself, she figured it a safe bet. She certainly had not expected they'd stop by the remnants of her old tree to socialise with the Narrum.

"This body needs rest and hydration," he said. "As does yours. I figured you'd be comfortable here. This is your tree, correct?"

"You know perfectly well it isn't Wyrae anymore," she hissed. "It hasn't been since the Narrum cut her down with their axes and…" She wrinkled her nose. "What is this smell?" Narrum were filthy, wasteful creatures. Every dwelling had a pile of digested and undigested waste accumulated close by. An enormous pile in this case, apparently.

"Come." The word was a boulder landing at Ideth's feet. A yellow light appeared behind Xylo's eyes to reinforce the command. She cursed, annoyed by its blinding glare. Gods were amoral. They would use any means at their disposal to get what they wanted.

Chiron had once told her that Bertho and Martha were good people. Well, time to put that statement to the test. She'd like to know what these *good people* would do when Xylo, the tree man, appeared shining on their doorstep. Although, she was less curious to find out what he would do to them.

As it turned out, there was nothing either could do.

"Frost," Ideth gasped when she saw the corpses.

"It's all right, Ideth. The dead can't harm you," Chronos said, not even slowing his pace to spare them a glance.

Ideth, on the other hand, could not peel her eyes from them. The woman, Martha, looked good for a corpse, she supposed, if not for the wide, empty eyes and lips pulled back in a rictus of terror. The child though... Ideth gagged. At first she thought it was an animal carcass the birds were pecking at: a piglet perhaps, except piglets don't wear clothes.

Oh, slush. Her gagging turned into a heave. She staggered away in the darkness until she found a tree and braced against it, retching. There was nothing but bile in her stomach, yet it wouldn't stop convulsing. Every time she closed her eyes, she saw the larvae squirming in the boy's empty eye sockets.

I will not cry for a Narrum, she repeated to herself between heaves. *I. Will. Not. Cry. For. A. Nar–*

"We'll shelter here tonight," Chronos said.

"What?!"

"It is decided. You need to sleep."

"Sleep?! Here! Now?" She'd wanted to sleep all right – two days ago. The word *tired* no longer defined how she felt, but after the horror she'd just seen, sleep was not what she needed. She needed to run, to put as much distance as possible between her, him and whatever horror had happened to those Narrum. How could she ever sleep there, inside the dead wood of her tree, with the rotting bodies and their stench? The God was insane!

"No," she said, cleaning spit from her chin. "I won't stay here. There's a crag with good shelter not far beyond those trees. We should –"

"Here is where we stay," Chronos thundered, marching in her direction.

Her legs began to shake. She told herself it was from shock and exhaustion. Terror, however, was closer to the truth.

With her sickness momentarily forgotten, she flattened herself against the bark, barely able to open her eyes to face the God, let alone do anything else.

Chronos' voice echoed through the clearing as he spoke. "We will stay here, and you will sleep. Now."

CHAPTER 16

Seshat

Being a god sucks, Seshat decided. Not godhood itself. She would not trade her divinity for anything in this Universe. It was standing around being worshipped that drained all her energy.

She'd been stuck at the temple playing Judoc since he and Oric left on what had probably turned out to be a suicide errand. She couldn't Reach either of them. She also didn't need to speak much beyond intoning the daily prayers, and even then, few cared about what she actually said. Their attention was focused on the speaker, not the speech. But having all those greedy eyes on her, longing, hoping, constantly following her every movement, it was like being on the exposed side of a planet tidally locked to a judgemental star. It burned her out.

Oh, sure, the experience had been an amusing one the first time, when she played the Suzerain. To be the centre of attention, to be heard and admired. It was exciting, even. But the elation experienced during the speech quickly turned to dread at the realisation that mortals, Narrum in particular, were too fickle with their favour. For them, admiration was always one breath away from jealousy and hate. Their contentment with the gods was ever short-lived, for the more you gave, the more they wanted, and their entitlement had no limits. Sooner or later they would end up disgruntled.

To make things worse, she could never do right by the creatures, no matter how hard she tried. For example, the previous day she'd abandoned her disguise to comfort a grieving mother who'd just lost her baby to a fever by offering to write an account of the child's brief life.

"I've heard about this writing," the woman said to her. "It is how the gods never forget."

"Correct," Seshat replied, pen ready in hand, papyrus under its tip. "So tell me about your child. Whatever I write will last forever." She even made sure she smiled as she spoke, the way she'd seen old nurses do to those dying under their care.

To her bewilderment, the woman cried even harder and screeched, "Witch! You want to take away the memory of my baby!"

"No, I want to preserve it, give it meaning," Seshat tried to explain. But it was of no use. Within moments dozens of other women gathered around them, spitting insults at her and posing suspicious enquires on the whereabouts of her own children. If only they knew how close they'd come to being incinerated.

Seshat puffed out a furious breath at the memory.

At least with gods she knew where she stood, as in, on very thin ice, constantly. But she could always rely on their selfish schemes and the certainty that if they came to her, it was because they wanted something from her or something they could not get by themselves. It was refreshing, really. The mortals' hypocrisy did not sit well with her being. It was also one of the reasons she rarely wrote about mortals. Not only were their actions insignificant, they were at odds with their assertions, much like their motivations were at odds with rationality. They were ignorant, short-sighted and incapable of adopting different perspectives, therefore their stories were short, dull and made little sense to a sensible, more evolved mind.

The sad fact was, she hadn't been able to write anything meaningful in days. Until now, that is. Now she was unable to write anything at all.

Perched atop the temple's dome, Seshat Reached over Aegea, and she really didn't like what she saw. The Boiling Lake boiled hotter than ever beneath the layers of rock and realm. There appeared to be some sort of anomalous gap in the forest and too many Dharkan gathered in Portum. And then there was, of course, the *Thing* – as she referred to the Nephilim's ship – looming over the land. Trepidation didn't quite explain what she felt whenever she sent her senses in *that* direction. It was a sense of imminent doom. It wasn't rational, it was detrimental to her work, and she had to get over it.

Easier thought than done…

Part of her unease came from the fact Anubis had arrived with them. She'd only sensed him briefly before the chariot landed, but it was long enough to be certain. And he'd sensed her too, she was sure. On one hand, she was glad that he was still alive; on the other, his presence jeopardised everything she'd set out to accomplish in Niflheim.

Hermes approached. She didn't need Reach to recognise the slight drag of his host's clubbed foot on the stone floor.

"Message delivered," he said.

She exhaled deeply. "Thank you."

"You're welcome. Does Toman have the girls ready?" he asked.

"Yes, five of them, as requested." Seshat raised her eyebrows. "Are you sure you are up for that many?" It wasn't him she was worried about, but his host.

"Always." He grinned, then proceeded to remove his clothes. "I'll need nourishment first, of course."

"Right..." Seshat came down from the dome, opened her cloak and let sunlight shine through her skin. In exchange for basking in her light, Hermes had been gathering and sharing sensible communication across Aegea while also performing the more hands-on duties of a shrine – rather enthusiastically, she might add. A beneficial agreement for them both, even if an unsustainable one. The temple needed a proper shrine. Iosh had many flaws, but he was good at what he did, and he had a singularity's appetite for adoration. If he did not return soon...

"Are the others still here?" Hermes asked. Together they'd rescued a handful of starving Wyrd from the settlement, who now huddled with the women at the temple, taking turns basking in her light – another thing that drained her. Seshat might be a goddess of light, but that was not her talent, and Niflheim had a way of snuffing energy from every god's soul, never mind the Wyrd's appetites.

"For now," she sighed tiredly, glancing at the Stump. "There's been talk of moving to the forest or even the Gharb. Perhaps we should go too."

"It won't be far enough," he said. "Besides, if they wanted us, they would have come for us already."

"What do you think they want then?"

He shrugged, a lopsided grin on his lips. "Chaos."

"Cats…" Seshat cursed.

Yes, she should have left the temple after the speech, yet she'd stayed for reasons she did not yet understand herself, and now she couldn't leave because the mortals needed a shrine and the Wyrd depended on her light. That's what she told herself, anyway. Without the blue sun, every god in Aegea was cursed, or as good as. Niflheim's natural sun was little more than an affectation in the sky to illuminate the land. It had no actual power. Even the plants had begun to wither. Hel did nothing about it. Some gods were not responsible enough to rule their own worlds. Then again… Niflheim was never supposed to host life in the first place. Why would Hel do anything out of her character to preserve it? *Why am I?* she asked herself. Seshat's main tenet was never to interfere, only record. And yet, here she was, interfering more than recording, exposing herself. Cats, she was being selfless!

"You are a goddess," Hermes said, kissing Seshat on the cheek once he felt replenished.

She brushed him away, pretending annoyance. "You always say that after basking."

He grinned. "Any other time would be redundant."

"Tsk."

But then there it was; the other side of her conflicted self. The pride, the sheer satisfaction she tried so hard to dismiss. Seshat might hate the mortals' attention, but not the gods'. The gods who never paid attention to her, who never cared about her work unless they were featured in it. The Wyrds, cursed and powerless, more miserable than she was. Deep down, she enjoyed being their star. What was happening to her?

She closed her robe and fetched her latest chronicles, then clicked her tongue. No wonder she couldn't write properly. It was against her nature to write about herself, even if she was pretending to be someone else. She'd hoped that taking a break to shine would improve her mindset, but looking at the page, she hated every word on it.

"Do me a favour and read this before you go." She shoved Hermes the pile of papyrus containing the speech she gave to the angry mob a few days back. "Tell me what you think."

He took the stack and looked up at her, a stupefied expression on his slack face. "All of it?"

She was about to hiss but remembered that the body of Hermes' host was rife with impairments. It actually surprised her how he managed to read at all in that poor vessel.

"Just the beginning, if you please."

Long moments passed.

Her mind drifted, the way minds do when they have nothing to anchor them, towards the story of an old man in ancient Midgard. He'd achieved near divine status by dedicating his life to preserving the planet's ecology, destroyed by overpopulation and greed, while claiming he'd done it for the sake of his twelve children and over one hundred grandchildren. When she pointed out the incongruity of his actions, he became hostile, claiming the problem was not his children, but everyone else's. He died, of course, so did his offspring and the rest of the planet. The only difference was that she remembered him. Not because he deserved to be remembered, not even because she wanted to, but because someone had to keep a record of the atrocities done by humankind. Some gods believed souls were what corrupted humans. Seshat wasn't so sure anymore. She'd lived aeons with a soul and it was only when she impersonated the metz that she felt corrupted.

"It reads fine," Hermes said, interrupting her thoughts.

"Did you notice anything odd?"

"No. It's exactly as I remember, word for word. Why?"

Seshat squinted at the page. "That is the problem. Those weren't my words. Yet I spoke them nonetheless."

"You were in character."

"It doesn't matter. Don't you see? This is as bad as answering a prayer."

Hermes snorted. "Don't be so dramatic. That little deception saved the settlement."

"For now, maybe," she said bitterly.

The speech, put together on the spot by the combined megalomaniac minds of the Suzerain's most dedicated followers, Oric and Judoc, had had the intended calming effect on the inflamed mob, but that had been then. Now, thanks to *the Thing*, they were again building up for another uproar. That's Narrum for you, always protesting, never helping, never thinking. Cats, no wonder the Suzerain chose not to mingle with them, not even to prevent their own self destruction. Alek understood that to the Narrum gods were only gods if they remained distant. He understood many things about mortals the gods themselves never did, and that was why he'd been so successful, so dangerous. And why she had been foolish. Cats, now she wished Oric had been right about him not being really dead and hoped that the thing over the Stump was his doing, for if she wasn't a suitable replacement for Judoc, she certainly wasn't capable of replacing the Suzerain. She had no talent or will to deal with mortals. And yet, she had to do something about them.

"Seshat, what is it?" Hermes asked, concerned. "You look about to combust."

She focused back on the page, unsure of how to explain the knot of conflicted realisations inside her mind. "It's just… I think I broke the narrative."

"Huh?"

"I record events. I'm not supposed to be part of them." She licked her lips. "Worse than that, whenever I write characters doing wrong things for good reasons, it never ends well. And now I'm one of those characters! I can't trust anything I write."

"Ah…" Hermes sighed, almost as if disappointed. She knew he'd done his share of wrong deeds for good reasons. That was how he ended up as a Wyrd in

Niflheim. "You did what you had to, Seshat. What we asked you to do. The deception bought us some time, and no one got harmed. Listen." He cupped a hand to his ear. "No more angry mobs. Besides, you enjoyed the attention, admit it." He elbowed her in the ribs as if that would instigate an admission. The sad thing was, she had enjoyed it: the power in her spoken words, so much greater and immediate than when they were written down. So much more destructive in the short term. So impossible to erase…

"Just because you enjoy something doesn't mean it's good for you," she said.

"Stars, you sound like a mortal at the end of their days. And I'm the Wyrd! Cheer up, Seshat. You don't have to play the Suzerain anymore."

She could slap him for the comment. "No, just his damned shrine."

"Only until the Nephilim come to check on their Tributes."

"Great. And then what?"

"Then worrying about how your character appears on the page won't matter. We'll have more important things to worry about." He grinned nonchalantly.

She glared at him. "My work is important. And how are you so calm about all this? Doesn't that *Thing* disturb you?"

His grin vanished. "A bit. But you know the best thing about being a Wyrd?"

"You have nothing left to lose?" she suggested.

He feigned surprise. "I have so much to lose! All those girls waiting for me inside, for example. No, being a Wyrd puts things in perspective. Life is not about mortality or punishment. It's about survival, and knowing that no matter how powerful you are, there's always someone or something more powerful."

"Tell that to Chronos," she said.

"I did. The point is: power itself is the enemy. No single entity can have it all, but they'll keep vying for it until it destroys them." He pointed at the Stump. "That's why I'm not too concerned about the Nephilim. They are doomed, just like their ancestors."

"You don't see what I see," Seshat whispered.

"Describe it to me, then."

"I don't know how…" Somehow Seshat lacked the words, and it scared her. "I've perceived many things: strange things, absurd things, ugly things. But I've never come across something I could not describe, even if poorly. That is one such thing. It is alive, Hermes. Not in the way gods and mortals understand life. It's… different. A life with no narrative, no story, only… data. We've always counted on the humans' ability to destroy themselves, from Midgard to New Omega, it always ended the same. But the Nephilim are different. They won't self-destruct easily."

Hermes stared at her with mismatched eyes, and for a moment she glimpsed the Olympian trickster behind them. Was that why she'd taken him under her protection? Because she had a fondness for tricksters? Cats, she had to find something else worth worrying about other than herself and her feelings.

"Well, if it's as bad as you say, then we are all doomed," he said. "I for one intend to make the most of my fated existence. You should do the same, Seshat. Don't further empower the Nephilim with your distress. They don't deserve it. And neither does Loki," he added meaningfully. "Now, five, you said?" Hermes rubbed his hands together and dashed down the stairs.

Interlude 2

Decisions

"Explain what you mean by 'she's alive'," I say with as much serenity as I can muster. If this is Psyche's idea of a jest, this time I will suck her Prana dry and burn the consequences.

Psyche adjusts the lily in her hair, as if consulting the flower before she answers. "I can't explain it. I just saw her through Mika's eyes. She was alive, by her father's side."

"Did the wolf eat her too?" Pan asks, highly entertained by the conversation.

"No!" she assures me, then ponders her reply. "He was going to…"

Ice spreads beneath our feet.

Psyche attempts an appeasing gesture. "But he didn't!"

"Are you sure it was her?" I ask.

"Yes."

"How is that possible?" Hel asks, struggling, as I am, to come to grips with the whole resurrection thing.

"I don't know," Psyche says exasperatedly. "How

is *that* possible?" She points at the Stump. "Or him?" She points at me. "How can a Dharkan wield a god's talent without his soul? I don't have all the answers. If I did, I wouldn't be here trying to answer them."

Hel purses her lips, not taking Psyche's bait. A pity, for I too would like to know how Zeus' lightning abilities were passed on to me. And I will, once I get to the bottom of this 'Ileana is alive' revelation. It can't be true. Can it? She can't be alive. I saw her die in my arms. I felt her last breath. Even Gaea declared she was not alive. Then again, I guess I'm not alive either, according to her definition of life. Can it be that Ileana turned into a Dharkan? I don't see how, nor do I care. The thought excites me. No. I can't let my mind meander like this. *Focus.*

"It's not that difficult to create a body," Hades says, pretending to ponder the issue. "The Nephilim are gods, after all. Or… something like it."

Hel gives him a baleful look. "I suppose. Still, it would not be her without her spirit. Are you certain it was Ileana?" she asks Psyche.

"Yes. At least she had her memories and personality. As to her spirit, Fenrir couldn't tell."

"Is she still inside the Stump?" I ask.

Psyche shrugs. "I guess."

Lightning strikes inches from her feet. "You need to do better than guess," I shout at her.

Her jaw tenses, her face contorts, and her dark brown eyes burn hotter than Hades' flaming ones as she fixes them on me. For someone with such comely features, she sure can make herself quite challenging to look upon. Maybe I pushed her too far.

"Fuck. You."

Yes, definitely too far.

"The inside of the Stump is beyond our Reach, Aedan," Hel explains.

"We still need to go back and save her!" If Ileana is alive, then burn everything else.

"She doesn't need saving," Psyche says.

I glare at her, then turn back to Hel. "Goddess, if Ileana is alive. I need to get her out of there."

"Yes, I agree. I can't abandon my brother either. If anything of him remains inside that place, we need to get him out."

Hel turns her gaze to Psyche. Hades, Pan, and I follow suit. Psyche glances at each of us in turn before narrowing her eyes back at the goddess of Niflheim.

"Hel, we had a deal. You promised you'd let me go."

"The deal is broken. They're here, and Hephaestus can't close the portal since he's dead. Burn you, Psyche. I asked you to intimidate the man, not fuck him."

I hear a loud slap. Psyche moved too fast for anyone to intervene. Hel's surprised face reddens from the impact, the imprint of Psyche's fingers starting to show on her white skin. No one moves, talks or even breathes for a long moment.

"It's the second time I've done your bidding, goddess of the dead. There won't be a third. I am leaving." Psyche walks up to Hel. I fear she might hit her again but can't bring myself to interfere. "Do not try to stop me. I will destroy you if you do. *That* is a promise." Psyche's crisp words ring truer than any she's said previously. She turns on her heel and walks away.

"Goddess of the soul!" Hel calls after her, bursting

with all sorts of emotions. Too intense and too many to keep track of.

Psyche whirls around. "You promised!" she shouts back, even more emotionally charged than Hel. Her hand lifts to the base of her neck, unconsciously clutching the absent pendant. She's crying again. It doesn't take much for the human goddess to shed tears. This time, though, they are not from anger or frustration. She's genuinely upset. Her grief is as raw and hot as my own was for Ileana.

"I had to," Hel admits with strain.

"To cover your own ass! No, Hel, I've done what you asked. It's not my fault I ended up here. You know that. And now I've done what you asked – *again!* Except you weren't the one asking, were you?" Psyche's voice breaks, the anger draining out of her. "Why, Hela?"

Hel squares her shoulders. Her lips press harder. Whatever her answer is, she says it through Reach.

Psyche shakes her head and lets out a heartbreaking sob, turns around again and resumes walking back into the forest.

Pan waves a finger at Hel, clicking his tongue reproachfully, then follows after the goddess of the soul. Hades is about to speak.

Hel silences him with a flick of her hand. "Let her go. It's better this way."

"No, it is not. We need her, Hel," Hades says, sounding genuinely worried.

"No, we don't. I need no one!"

Hel marches downhill in the opposite direction of

Psyche, towards the hunter's cabin. Hades and I follow her hesitantly.

"This is ridiculous, Hel. We can't save – I mean, exchange – the Titan's souls without her," Hades says. "Cerberus breath! What about the Nephilim and Fenrir? Hel!"

"We'll find another way," Hel says.

"There is no other way!"

"Gaea should be here soon. She'll fix Chiron, don't worry."

"You know about the horse?" Hades shakes his head. "Of course, you do. But you haven't seen Gaea's state back at the Stump, Hel. She looks like she's the one who needs fixing to me."

I have no idea what Hades is talking about, but the urgency in his tone sounds serious enough. Ulcan and Ulla come out of the cabin, running up the slope with sword and crossbow in hand.

"Freeze," Hel commands them.

"My lady, I beg you to reconsider," Hades insists, ignoring the stupefied couple.

I leave the gods behind, still arguing with each other, as I pass by the hunter and his strange friend on my way to the cabin to fetch Cornus' horn, and then find myself standing there, unable to decide what to do next. The animosity between Psyche and Hel stinks like a festering sore. Whatever the issue between the two goddesses is, it has nothing to do with the Stump, the wolf, Ileana or me. But clearly a line's been drawn, and I need to decide which side to stand on.

Hel is my goddess. My creator and the rightful

ruler of this world. I owe my allegiance to her. Her brother is inside that alien aberration with Ileana. I believe Hel wants to free him. Chances are she would free Ileana too, so I should do all I can to help her. Psyche doesn't really care for Ileana. She only has her memories and uses them as currency to get what she wants from me. She would never willingly help me or the gods free Ileana, for then she'd lose her leverage. She does seem to care for the wolf for whatever reason. Not enough to risk her freedom for his, though. And she hates me. She hates Hel and Hades. She seems to hate pretty much everyone. She's abrasive and difficult to deal with. She lies, cries, swears and screams frequently. I sigh. Burning light, she's also the only proper weapon we have against the Nephilim, and I bet my right hand she knows a lot more about them than she's led us to believe.

I make my decision.

"Aedan, where do you think you're going?" Hel demands to know the moment I walk past her towards the forest.

Where you can't go, goddess. You charged me with keeping an eye on Psyche. That is what I will do.

Relief and a sense of pride wash over me.

'*Thank you, Aedan.*'

CHAPTER 17

Ulcan

When Ulcan regained his senses, he wished he had died. His throat was raw inside and out, his body – the parts not numb with cold – ached from the Dharkan's beating, and his head throbbed like an anvil being used. He bit out a curse right before vomiting the fermented contents of his stomach on the grass, then lashed out at whoever was patting his back. "Get away from me!"

"It's me, you fool," Ulla said patiently.

"All the same. I'm not a pet nor a child to be coddled." He retched again, the sour sweetness of the mead making him sicker with each heave.

"What you are is a disgrace to your race," she said scornfully.

"Coming from you, that's high praise indeed, *dryad*." Ulcan spat, then wiped the slaver coating his lips with the back of his hand and squinted around. "Where did they go?"

"Over there, up the hill to get a better view."

"Of what?"

"Didn't you see the lights?"

He'd seen lights, all right. Some were still shining

behind his eyes, but he didn't think that was what Ulla meant. "What lights?"

"Something terrible happened at the Stump."

He wanted to laugh but croaked instead. His throat was too swollen and sore for laughter. "There's always something happening at the Stump, and it's never good," he said hoarsely.

"Not like this. The lights, the sound… It was like the grinding of a knife twisting inside the world's core. I think it happened again."

He blinked at her. "Huh?"

"The Fell," Ulla whispered.

He scoffed. That was ridiculous. You can't fell an already felled tree. Still, whatever happened had left the forest in an uproar and taken the edge off Ulla's nerve. She sounded as soft and helpless as a girl.

They couldn't see the enormous tree trunk from here, Ulcan had made sure of it when he built his cabin, but sadly you didn't have to go far to see it. It was, after all, the central point in Aegea. This meant the Wraith was close and might return any moment to finish his vengeful meal.

Ulcan laboured to his feet. "We must go, before they return."

Ulla waved a dismissive hand. "Relax. Psyche won't let the Wraith kill you."

"How can you be sure?" he asked. After all, she hadn't stopped him from trying.

"She's one of you, isn't she?" Ulla said.

"What?"

"Narrum."

He snorted. "And you're a nymph. Let's go."

They didn't go very far. Ulcan had just picked up Bertho's crossbow when he heard voices.

"Fuck. They're coming." He ran to the cabin, fetched the quiver and began nocking a bolt on the crossbow.

Ulla jogged after him. "What are you doing?"

"Preparing to defend myself, what does it look like? I won't die for a fucking horn." The crossbow was supposed to be enchanted. Bertho used to boast that every arrow shot from it always hit its target. Well, Aedan would be an ideal target to test the accuracy of the enchantment.

"Psyche won't let you kill the Wraith either," Ulla said patiently.

"We'll see about that." Ulcan scowled at her. "What's wrong with you? Not that long ago, all you wanted was to kill the fucker!"

Ulla assumed a confrontational stance: hand on hips, chin held high, the tip of a foot tapping the wooden floorboards. "I did. And I still do. I want to kill them all, but I can't, can I? Not by myself – as you kept pointing out before the freezing monster walked in." She sighed, lowering her head a fraction. The tapping ceased. "I think that maybe, under the circumstances, he might be better suited to help us kill the others." Beyond the cacophony of alarmed cries in the forest, the voices were getting louder. Ulla lowered hers and moved closer to his ear. "Maybe it's better to fight ice with ice, huh?"

Ulcan gaped. He knew pregnancy made women more irrational than usual, but this sudden change of heart had Psyche's name carved all over it. Most gods had the ability to meddle with your thoughts. This one seemed to be as skilled at cutting through minds with words as he was at cutting through skins with a flaying knife. Well, she would not be flaying his mind, that was for sure.

"I don't want to kill the others, only this one. Before he kills me."

Ulla touched his hand. "I know how you feel. Believe me, I do. But..." She winced as if she couldn't bring herself to say the next words, then puffed out a breath. "It's not worth it."

"Who are you and what did you do to Ulla while I was unconscious?"

She punched him on the shoulder. "I had a chance to think. Maybe the Dharkan are as much victims of their gods' schemes as we are."

"So? They're still our predators."

"True, but like you said, predators are not necessarily evil."

Ulcan spat. "So you're saying we should move the people out of Aegea and leave the gods with an empty battleground for their skirmishes, as Aedan suggested – right before he changed his mind and tried to kill me!"

"Not out of hunger."

"Oh, so I guess that makes it all right, then," he sneered. "I wish it had been hunger, Ulla. I understand hunger. I could forgive hunger. This is personal. I don't give a fuck about the gods, or whatever happened over at the Stump. We lived our entire lives under a tyrant's rule amidst the aftermath of the gods' quarrel. I don't care who's right or wrong, winning or losing. We survive by staying out of it and killing those who want to kill us first."

Ulcan finally managed to set the bolt on the bow and left the cabin, ready to shoot it.

He froze a few paces beyond the door. Instead of Aedan and Psyche, he caught sight of Iva, arguing with a creature of darkness and fire – no, that couldn't be right. This female Wraith's voice was crisper, more assertive than Iva's. To be fair, it was an easy mistake for Ulcan to make since all Dharkan looked alike. But the way she walked, as if crushing the world beneath her feet, and the outfit made of no fabric he'd ever seen in a hue not found in nature, tight as an extra layer of skin, told him she was no Dharkan either. Upon closer observation, he concluded she was to a Dharkan what Psyche was to a Narrum – a goddess.

"Shit," he cursed as all murderous intent drained out of him, replaced by an urge to run. His mother had always warned him not to evoke the world's gods in vain, for there was always a chance they might come, and he would bet his beard this Dharkan was none other than the goddess of the dead herself, Hel, mistress of Niflheim. Ulla whimpered behind him, probably reaching a similar conclusion and remembering to unsheathe her sword with unsteady hands, too late and too slow for the action to actually look convincing as a threat. Aedan marched behind them, alone and with purpose, making a beeline for the cabin. Ulcan took aim.

"Freeze," said the Dharkan goddess. The crossbow froze in his hand. She continued arguing with her companion, who sounded almost as frustrated as Ulcan felt. Aedan glowered at him as he walked by, leaving a trail of cold air in his wake.

"I don't see Psyche, nor the satyr," Ulla said, practically hiding behind him. She should know by now never to put her faith in gods. "What do we do?"

"Nothing." What else could they do? Attack the gods? Run blindly into the forest and hit a tree? He liked neither of those options. "For now," he added, for he wasn't too enthused about inertia either, but when surrounded by predators, any action could be your last. A smart prey knows it's best to remain calm and wait for an opportunity.

"My lady, I beg you to reconsider," Ulcan heard the shadowy creature plead with the goddess as they got closer.

To Ulcan's disbelieving eyes, her expression went from menace to grief. "There's nothing to reconsider, Hades. This is our world. She'll do what she must, and so shall we."

"Did she just say Hades?" Ulla whispered.

"Shhh."

Ulcan felt that cold breeze again as Aedan stomped his way back to the thicket of trees behind the cabin.

"Aedan, where do you think you're going?" the Dharkan goddess asked sternly. The Wraith didn't answer, didn't even bother to glance back at her. Well, at least he hadn't tried to kill him again, either.

Ulcan kept his attention on the one he believed to be Hel and re-evaluated his options. Perhaps making a run for the forest while she was distracted following Aedan with her gaze was not such a bad idea after all.

"Now, where do I know you from?" Two smouldering eyes framed by dark ebony skin and a fierce set of white teeth displayed in a wide grin suddenly appeared in his line of retreat.

Ulla screamed, and Ulcan shot a glance back at the one he thought was Hel, now alone, bobbing her head in Aedan's direction with a sad smile. He turned his attention back to the shadowy figure. "How the fuck did you –?" *He's a god, for fuck's sake*, Ulcan chided to himself.

"Nowhere," Ulcan stammered. He certainly had never met him. He'd remember.

The god's grin widened – a truly unsettling sight. "No. I've seen your likeness before." He sniffed at Ulcan. A predator assessing its prey. "At a smithy, perhaps?"

"Hades, stop harassing the mortals. We have work to do."

"These are not ordinary mortals, my lady." Hades smiled at Ulla with the familiarity of an old friend. "A pleasure to meet you, Ulla. Arianh thought often of you. Poor queen, she never realised how much she didn't know about the one she considered to be her best friend, tsk, tsk." His index finger tapped the tip of the sword in her hand. The runes glowed between her trembling fingers.

"Hel, do you mind translating this for me, please?"

"Hel!?" Ulla squeaked, dropping the sword in Hades' hand. He gave it to the icy goddess, and for an instant Ulcan thought she would use it on them. Instead, she simply stood there, shaking with rage, then to his eternal surprise, handed it back hilt first to the horrified dryad.

"You should use this well and use it often," she said, leaving Ulla dumbstruck enough to bow. Gods tend to have that effect on mortals.

"I have my eyes on you, dryad. You too, hunter," Hades said, gesturing at his own eyes and then back at Ulcan's.

Ulcan swallowed and took a step back, hitting something surprisingly soft.

Behind him was another woman: mature and well nourished with quite the expansive bosom, the sort of woman Ulcan would go for even without having to get drunk first. Of course, she too was no woman at all. He was learning to identify gods by the way they looked at you. As if you're just part of the scenery, like a rock or a tree. Insignificant at best; in their way at worst.

"Mother of Life! How kind of you to join us," Hades said sardonically.

Her eyebrows were tightly knitted together. Unfazed by Ulcan's impact, she redirected her vitriol at Hades.

"Why are you here?" She cast around, the frown deepening. "Where's Psyche?"

"Probably answering a call of nature," Hades replied.

"Very funny, Hades," Hel said dryly.

"I try, my lady."

"We had a disagreement," Hel said through clenched teeth. She took one step, freezing the vegetation under her feet, and loomed over the older Goddess. "You were supposed to guard the portal."

"They didn't use the portal, did they?" the older

Goddess said in a condescending tone, looking up. "Besides, we have something much worse than the Nephilim to deal with."

"Worse than *that*?" Hel pointed at the Stump. "My brother is still inside!"

Ulcan shivered at the sudden cold. Ulla huddled closer to him, her teeth rattling. He wanted to be anywhere else but there, yet he feared moving away. For now, the gods were focused on each other, so he thought it best to remain inconspicuous. *If I live through this, next time I see Pan again, I'll take his horns as a trophy,* Ulcan vowed.

'*I'll help,*' Hades said. Except he hadn't even opened his mouth to say it. Ulcan heard him loud and clear inside his head. So much for inconspicuousness.

'*Chill, mortal. And pay attention. This is about to get interesting.*'

"Damn it, Hel! You told me you found the cabin and that you would keep Psyche distracted until I arrived. We need her on our side," the older woman said.

"I *am* at the cabin!" Hel shouted, pointing at Ulcan's home. "Psyche's just having a strop. Aedan will bring her back around soon enough."

The matronly woman walked up to the Dharkan goddess. Her eyebrows knitted tighter as she placed her hands on her hips. A gesture, Ulcan realised, common to all females, deities and mortals alike.

Hades chuckled to himself, obviously still reading his thoughts. '*Good point, man.*'

The god had to be nuts to be this amused. Couldn't he see the goddesses were about to claw at each other's eyes and that he, as mate to at least one of them, would have to lick the wounds and take the blame for it afterwards?

"Do you see Xylo anywhere?" the older Goddess asked in a tone at odds with her demeanour.

"Well, no. What's he got to do with –"

"It's the wrong cabin!" she shrieked, then took a long-suffering breath. "And you, Hades. Shouldn't you be searching for your rebellious guest?"

He coughed, suddenly out of mirth. "I am. My lady and I were doing just that when the world almost ended thanks to your leaving the Stump unguarded!" His tone started soft and apologetic, then increased in volume and spite until it ended in a bellow.

The Goddess's heavy chest seemed to inflate to double its size with each of her outraged breaths, much to Ulcan's unwelcome delight.

She glared at him, also able to read his thoughts, of course. "Friend of yours?"

Hades placed a hand on Ulcan's shoulders. "He can be."

Ulcan swallowed. He had no intention of befriending the Underworld lord. Then again, the alternative had to be worse.

"We only just met," Ulcan said hopelessly. He'd rather fight Aedan again than be subject to this. And to think, all he'd wanted when he got home earlier was a quiet evening on his porch, playing with his new crossbow and thanking the forest for being alive. *Fucking gods…* he thought miserably, not caring if they listened.

"Mortal. I am Gaea. Show some respect."

"Fuck me, it's the Queen bitch of the pantheons…"

Ulcan said, then covered his mouth. "Did I say that out loud? I'm so sorry. I meant no offence."

"Gaea?" Ulla breathed the word. "You're the one responsible for this." She put her hand on her lower abdomen.

"No, mortal. You are," Gaea replied curtly.

Ulla advanced on her, sword in hand, runes glowing. "How dare you impose this curse on women!"

Ulcan stepped between the two on reflex. "Hormones," he said to Gaea apologetically.

Gaea glared at them. Ulcan saw her chest expand dramatically again and knew there would be no end to the barrage of words that were about to spew from her mouth.

"*Curse*, dryad? You dare to call it a curse? Being a woman is a privilege, and life is a gift!" She slapped her chest. "*My* gift to the Universe. It's how you cheat Time, you ungrateful creature. If you want to blame someone, or find help with your burden, turn to him." She pointed at Ulcan. "That's their purpose. Even if they often neglect it," she scoffed.

"Hey, I had nothing to do with this one!" Ulcan protested in vain.

"Shut up," both women barked in unison.

The three deities faced each other then, leaving him and Ulla out of their little circle. Their expressions ranged from scowls to raised eyebrows and, if he didn't know any better, anguish. Meanwhile, he and Ulla remained still, petrified prey doing their best not to draw more attention to themselves.

"Flaming sun," Hel said, mouth slightly agape, shooting daggers at Hades.

Hades grabbed a handful of his hair and winced. "I did not know, I swear!"

"I should have known…" Gaea said, deflating. To Ulcan's eyes, she seemed to have suddenly aged fifty years, and he tried really hard not to articulate the thought.

"All this time…" Hades cleared his throat. "Apologies, terrible choice of words." He rested a hand on Ulcan's shoulder again. "Well, that is unfortunate. I guess we'll have to continue our acquaintance in the Underworld."

Ulcan blinked and pointed the frozen crossbow at Hades. "I like it here." He would not go to the Underworld without a fight, even if the fight was with its lord himself.

"Boys, behave," Hel said tiredly. "And no, we will not start taking souls to the other side before their time or against their will."

"Why not? It's the only way to save them, right?" Hades said pointedly to Gaea. She scowled.

Hel stomped her foot, and the entire forest shook. "It's the easiest way, not the only way."

"Oh, come on, Hel. No matter what we do, between the faithless Dharkan, the Nephilim and what Gaea just told us, every mortal in Aegea has their moments counted. We're about to receive quite the influx of disgruntled guests. I'm just giving this one the opportunity to claim a cosy place for himself."

"I'm not interested." Ulcan, shaken as he was, accidentally pulled the trigger. The weapon shattered in his hands, but not before the bolt shot right through Hades' ear.

"OW!" he yelped. The damage was there and gone in a moment. Hades' grin vanished, then his eyes came aflame.

Ulla cursed. Ulcan was out of curses at this point. Hades lifted his hand.

"Wait!" Hel studied Ulcan up and down appreciatively, as if she'd just seen him. "This mortal has balls. He might be useful to us."

"He tried to ice me!" Hades protested, burning with outrage.

"Precisely." Hel pierced Ulcan with her icy gaze. "Do you have any idea how much trouble you're in now, hunter?"

Yes, he had a pretty good one. Still, Ulcan was a man too concerned with survival to waste time speculating on death. And taking into consideration he'd nearly died twice that day, being accosted by two deities from the Underworld seemed like a natural escalation of events.

"I'm always in trouble, goddess," Ulcan said.

Her lips twisted into a suppressed smile. "I have a task for you, then."

Ulcan was about to declare he did not take orders from gods, but the weight of Hades' hand on his shoulder silenced him.

"I want you to go to Relicum. There's a woman –" Hel hesitated, tapping her lips with her index finger. "Actually, she might be disguised as a man. Go to the temple and look for someone who doesn't quite fit in. Someone holding a pen or a stack of papyrus."

"Seshat?" interjected Ulla. She'd been talking in hushed tones with the Mother of Life and seemed in a much better mood suddenly. Ulcan shook his head. He would never understand women and their moods.

"Yes. You know her?" Hel asked, mildly surprised.

Ulla snorted, forgetting who she was talking to, apparently. "No one really knows Seshat."

"True…" Hel agreed. "Be that as it may, I need you to deliver a message to her. Tell her: the clock is ticking. She'll understand."

"Why don't you tell her that yourself?" Ulla said.

Hel blinked; ice formed on her cheeks. "Are you questioning my will, mortal?"

Ulla stared at the ice goddess eye to eye. "The Dharkan are your creation. They are feeding on the living again, and you're asking favours from us?"

Hel eyed Gaea askance, then sucked her teeth, pondering the two women. "Ah, I see. Ulla, is it? I don't have the *time* nor inclination to explain my actions or the workings of *my* world to anyone, and if you think the life growing inside you will deter me from extinguishing yours… Well, you are mistaken, so mind your attitude. I'll make it simple for you, *dryad*: do what I ask, and your kind won't ever need to fear the Dharkan again."

Hades' brows raised at her.

Ulla's sword flashed a couple times, but she did not touch it. "Give me your word, and we'll deliver the message."

"We?" Ulcan objected.

"Would you rather go to the Underworld?" Hades suggested sinisterly.

Ulcan removed the god's hand from his shoulder, stepping away from him. "No."

"I promise," Hel said.

Hades' brows raised higher this time.

Ulcan sighed longingly at the sight of his bed beyond the cabin's open door.

"You can sleep when you're dead," Hades whispered in his ear.

Somehow, he very much doubted it. "Well, if we're doing this, we better get going. Let me fetch my things."

"That won't be necessary," Hel said.

CHAPTER 18

Hades

"You lied to the pregnant dryad," Hades stated to Hel once Ulcan and Ulla had been reluctantly translocated to the outskirts of Relicum.

"Of course I did. What did you expect?"

"The truth."

"The truth wouldn't persuade her, now would it?"

"And here I was hoping Loki's ability to break promises was his alone." Gaea sighed.

"What can I say? I am his daughter."

Gaea's expression was an unreadable mixture of sorrow and concern, though Hades could swear he saw a touch of admiration in it as well.

"Seshat has her own agenda. She won't interfere."

"Did I ask for your opinion, Mother of Life?" Hel growled. "In my world I do things *my* way."

"Good luck, then," Gaea said before she vanished.

"Likewise!" Hel said crossly. Every god knew luck as a concept did not exist, it was merely the talent of a capricious goddess. And she was anything but good.

"I've never met a dryad with such short hair,"

Hades mused, lacing his fingers through his hazardous mane. "You think I should trim this?"

Hel glared at him.

"Fine. I won't." He exhaled and pulled her close to him so they could gaze into each other's eyes. "What was that all about with Psyche, Hel?"

"It's between Psyche and me," Hel replied in a tone that allowed no further questions.

Hades kissed her briefly and passionately, the way he knew she liked it. "And if only it stayed between you two. No, I don't want to know and I don't want to fight. Cerberus breath, I don't even care about your deal with Gaea, either. But why ask the mortals to go to Relicum? It's not like you can't deliver the message to Seshat yourself."

Hel puffed a lungful of icy air. "Seshat has the ability to block my Reach."

"Why? What did you do to her?"

The goddess narrowed her eyes to slits. "What did *you* do to her?"

"Nothing, I –" Hades tried to Reach Seshat and received the image of a hairless cat hissing at him. Claws followed. "I see…" he grumbled.

"Perhaps she's more inclined to act if the request comes from someone she doesn't feel threatened by," Hel said. "Besides, I'd rather not be anywhere near the Stump. And neither should you."

"You really think Seshat will help, considering how she obviously feels about us?"

Hel shrugged. "It's only a hunch. Her presence in this world made little sense until now. If I'm right, she will help us, or at least she'll be furious enough to do something that might end up being beneficial for us."

"I see…" Hades worried how much Hel was beginning to think like her father. "Well, and what shall we do in the meantime?"

"Look for the Hex, of course."

"How? We can't translocate there since we don't know where *there* is. I'm sure Hecate won't make it easy for us, and without Gaea, we'll be searching the forest looking for a tree, blind as Dharkan in daylight. We'll never find it."

Hel touched his cheek and leaned in for another kiss. "Never takes too long, lover," she said. "We better find it before sunrise."

CHAPTER 19

Ideth

Ideth woke up on a bed, of all places. A small and yet comfortable one, smelling heavily of feathers, stale sweat, mixed herbs and urine. Her mouth tasted funny: acrid, like she'd eaten too many sour apples, while her stomach ached almost as much as her feet and her legs.

"Ouch," she said, sitting up – her head definitely ached the worse. She massaged her temples to ease the throbbing pain behind her eyes while trying to discern her surroundings.

"Frost..." she moaned when it became clear she was inside her tree, Wyrae. Or more precisely, inside the box-shaped shelter the Narrum had built with its wood. And she was naked. Not an unusual state, to be fair, but she had no recollection of removing her clothes, or going to sleep for that matter.

She stood up slowly, blinking in the predawn light. She was alone – inside the cabin, at least. Outside, someone was singing in a deep baritone voice. *Slush.* She sat down again, not daring to go out in case the dead bodies were still lying there and Xylo – it was definitely easier to think of Chronos as Xylo – sang like a cock at sunrise.

This is *a nightmare*, Ideth assessed bitterly. Hiding inside the chopped remains of her tree, surrounded by corpses and guarded by the God of Time himself, was by far the prickliest, most disturbing situation she'd found herself in, and she had no idea how to get out of it. Sure, she'd dealt with gods before, and many other nasty creatures besides: Titans, satyrs, Dharkan, queens, Wyrds and hunters to name a few, but she was at a loss about how to deal with *Him*.

For frost's sake, Ideth, she chastised herself. How had she ever believed she could charm or outsmart Chronos? He knocked her unconscious with a word! What else could he do? She shivered at the possibilities.

One problem at a time is the key to solving all problems, she told herself, breathing hard. Lately it seemed she was accumulating problems faster than she solved them, but never mind that. This particular problem she would either solve or die trying. She pulled herself together and examined the room, looking for something she could use.

She'd never been inside a Narrum shelter before, and this was not how she imagined them to be. Their dwellings were never much to look at from the outside. Even the ones built with a stone foundation, like this one, looked as if they'd be blown away or drowned by the next storm. Still, Ideth had to appreciate the amount of care Martha – she assumed it had been her, since housekeeping, like most boring tasks, generally fell to women amongst the Narrum – clearly put into this one. Every surface was dusted and polished; every piece of cloth, clean and neatly folded. The floor was swept, the rugs beaten, and there were even curtains hanging in front of a glass-panelled window. These were not ordinary forest dwellers.

Receptacles and utensils for dealing with food were especially well taken care of and organised by shape and size. There was pride — dare she say, love — put into the small shelter. Even Ideth couldn't help feeling comfortable inside it, despite her circumstances.

Perhaps she should have listened to Chiron. How different things would have been had she come here with Psyche that first night instead of running back to the forest. Had she done that, Psyche would never have gone off on her own. Probably would never have met the Dharkan either, never entered Relicum or its temple. She would have gone straight to the Suzerain with his daughter, and Ideth would not have had to go with him to the caves after them, would not have had to beg Aedan to spare her life let alone protect her from Artemis, and she would never have gotten involved with the Underworld gods and their schemes.

Ideth shook her head ruefully. Hindsight was the most torturous sort of insight.

Of course, no matter what she'd done, Chronos would still have come for her, sooner or later, one way or another. Right now, *later* and *another*, seemed preferable to this, but she had to make do with her reality, the choices she'd made and the ones she still had left.

Ideth took a deep breath, then opened the large chest by the bed. It was full of clothes, more clothes than most dryads wore in a lifetime. And the Narrum woman had the nerve to give her grief over of a couple of rags? Apparently she'd underestimated how much value Narrum put on cloth. After all, walking around in the nude was considered barbaric and rude to them. Narrum were conscious of their bodies to a debilitating degree. Everything seemed to offend them: their size, shape, functions and especially the genitals – they were very self-conscious of *those*. It made absolutely no sense to Ideth. One would think that with so much fuss about their reproductive organs, the Narrum would be extinct. The reality was quite the opposite. Even with the Suzerain culling their numbers regularly, the world's ecosystem was failing. Of course, it was a tiny world and poorly designed to boot, since it was never meant for mortals of any kind. She closed the chest forcefully and moved to search the shelves above the work surface.

There she found a collection of jars, pots and flasks with the strangest of disgusting contents. The largest one was filled with chicken feet. Ideth's first thought was that this was perhaps some sort of delicacy for the Narrum. Then she saw the one next to it contained the beaks of several species of birds, judging by their colours and sizes. They couldn't eat those, could they? Taken by morbid curiosity, she kept rummaging through the shelves. One flask contained nothing but teeth. Another had eyes preserved in a murky liquid. She even found a badger foetus, if she was not mistaken.

"Ew…" Ideth said more than once. Narrum were sick creatures, she already knew that, but it never ceased to amaze her just how deep their sickness went.

One thing she had to admit, there was nothing easy about the way these people fed. From the time and effort spent preparing the carcass (not to mention hunting and killing the poor animal in the first place) to the cooking, cooling, carving and all that chewing! Ideth wondered how they found time for anything else.

With some effort, she ignored the jars and searched the wicker basket on the side table. There she found all sorts of tools for preparing meat, except a knife. The closest was a small pointy implement of a fathomless purpose, but it was sharp enough to pierce skin. She'd just tested this when a shadow moved across the wall.

"Good morning, darling Ideth."

She dropped her weapon with a curse.

Xylo's oblong bald head had sprouted branches and leaves as it did every dawn, and he looked particularly lush this morning. Ideth reckoned this meant he was either hungry or happy.

"Did you sleep well?" he asked.

She did not know. She clearly remembered being tired but not wanting to fall asleep. As to the quality of the sleep itself, her body felt rested enough, but there was something wrong with her head besides pain. Flashes of imagery she couldn't discern kept manifesting just out of sight of her mind's eye. And she remembered a familiar voice talking to her in her sleep. Yet she did not remember the words.

"How long was I asleep?"

Xylo gave her a condescending smile. "Long enough. Your body needed rest. Flesh: so versatile, yet so fragile."

Ideth didn't like his answer, nor the way he spoke, so she decided not to comment.

"Do you sleep?" she asked. After all, time never seemed to stop.

The simple question appeared to bewilder him. "Hmm. Yes. I suppose you could call it sleep. I sometimes ignore the Universe for a millennium or two."

"Luxury," Ideth thought bitterly and aloud.

He laughed, the sound rattling the cabin from its foundation to the thatched roof.

"Ah, darling Ideth. Keeping time flowing may require little conscious effort from me, much like breathing does for you, but you have no idea how frustrating it is to always be the one in the background, keeping all the pieces moving, just by existing. Never able to touch the pieces themselves," he said, touching her hand.

The roughness of his skin reminded Ideth of Yewlow's bark.

"Maybe it's for the best," she said, backing away and pulling the hand free to pick a random jar from the shelf. This one contained the hearts of small birds. Her own heart sank at the sight. She was trapped inside a cabin of pickled horrors by what looked like a tree conjured from a child's nightmare. Talk about rocks and hard places... Thinking of children made her cringe. At least inside the cabin she couldn't see the boy's corpse being devoured by larvae.

"Come with me." Xylo's arm was long enough to reach her across the small room and pull her outside.

She pulled back.

"I buried them," he said.

"You did?" Somehow the image of Xylo digging a grave and putting the toddler to rest didn't fit in

Ideth's mind. She poked her head out and saw no graves or disturbed soil. Still, there were no bodies or unpleasant smells either, so she took his word for it.

"Thank you," she said, stepping out of the cabin gingerly.

Things were different, though. There were more trees than she remembered. And something odd about the sunlight as well: it was brighter, more fulfilling, and it seemed to shine for her alone. Nonsense, of course. Her senses were all on edge, and she missed Orion terribly.

Xylo guided her to an open space where a tattered blanket lay spread over several inches of grass that definitely had not been there the night before. On top of it lay an assortment of fresh fruit neatly arranged around a bowl of crystal-clear water. She looked back at the cabin to make sure they hadn't moved while she slept. They had not. The cabin was the same old piece of Narrum architecture; everything else was different.

"Sit, if you please." Xylo sat himself on his ankles across from her, somehow graceful for someone as big and clunky as him, then smiled.

Ideth sat, hydrated, and picked a strawberry to nibble on so at least she didn't have to smile back. He remained silent, staring at her as she ate. By the fifth strawberry, Ideth decided she'd had enough of his attention.

"This is lovely, really. The fruit, the sun," she hesitated, "the company."

Xylo smirked at the flattering lie.

She carried on. "But I thought we were going to

meet the others. They must be worried. Have you spoken to them?"

Xylo waved his hand. "Do not concern yourself with their fate. They will come to us. In due time. Enjoy the moment. You won't have many of these in the future."

That did not sound good. Ideth crossed her arms, determined to find out what sort of problem she had on her hands. "Why did you bring me here? I want the truth. No more riddles. No more surprises."

He remained motionless, a slight twinkle deep in his eye sockets. Eventually he said, "I brought you here because I need your help."

Ideth blinked. Then laughed. Then frowned.

"Oh frost, you are serious. How can I ever help *you*?"

Xylo exhaled deeply and leaned against the tree behind him. She watched as his skin morphed to match the pattern of the bark and put some more berries in her mouth to keep it from hanging open.

"They call me Chronos, God of Time, because time is how gods and mortals are able to comprehend me. A more accurate appellation would be God of order, direction or *consequence*."

Ideth put a whole fig in her mouth this time.

"When I first arrived in this universe, there was nothing. No matter, no life, no sound, no energy. Not even light. It was a universe filled with possibility, or so I thought. My arrival set things in motion. No words will ever describe how beautiful it all was back then, back at the beginning of things. How happy, how proud I was to have finally found a place for myself. Before, I was just another concept in a universe of ideas; here, I ruled supreme over matter and energy." His dreamy expression darkened. "Then she ended my peace. I'm still not sure if she was already here and I inadvertently awakened her, or if she came from somewhere else, drawn to my presence. She never told me, and back then I was too nervous, too shy to ask."

Ideth frowned, sinking her teeth into the core of a peach, unable to imagine whatever made him nervous. "Kali?" she ventured while chewing.

"No. Kali came much later. Her name was Nyx." The word was uttered sombrely.

Ideth picked a bit of peach skin off her teeth, thinking. "Never heard of her."

"No mortal has. Until now. You are privileged."

Ideth could well do without the privilege. Knowing gods, nothing good would come from learning about this Nyx creature. Still, she had no choice but to listen, so she did her best to look interested. "Who was she? What did she do?"

Chronos narrowed his eyes at her sudden enthusiasm. Perhaps her best was a bit too much for the occasion.

"She was the darkness," he said. "And I unleashed it." He sounded regretful, mournful even.

"Well, it was hardly your fault," Ideth mumbled with her mouth full. "Darkness is all around us, but as the adage goes, you can't have light without it, so" – she faced the bright sun – "I, for one, am grateful for light."

He chuckled, a mirthless chuckle that sounded like a blunt woodpecker.

"Only you would see the bright side of this tale,

Ideth. Alas, you are correct. Light cannot exist without darkness, and so darkness is eternal." He shook his head. "I'm getting ahead of myself. Long before the first god was born, there was just us. It was bliss. I was young then, if you can imagine (she couldn't), and Nyx was unlike anything I'd come across, a force like no other, able to create and destroy on a whim. She was kind at first, demure and welcoming. She became my friend, then my lover. Then..." The leaves on his head withered. "It was aeons before I understood she was feeding off me. That the longer I stayed, the stronger she became. And when she thought she was strong enough, she challenged me for control." Chronos snorted. "Always so impatient, Nyx. Had she waited another age or two, she might have succeeded, but she could never match my patience. No other god can be as patient as I am. I refused to fight her at first. I loved her and I wanted things to continue as they were between us." His tone grew harsher. "But she had other plans. She made it clear that it was either her or me. There was no room in this universe for both of us." His eyes lost their shine. "Betrayal doesn't quite explain what I felt then."

"You don't say," Ideth said before she could help herself. She was well into the story now, popping grapes into her mouth one after the other, fascinated if slightly indignant at the size of the characters' egos that an entire universe was not big enough for them. "So you killed her, then?" More a statement than a question.

"Not exactly." He lowered his gaze. "Like me, she could not be killed."

That's good to know, Ideth thought sarcastically. "So what did you do?"

"My control over matter far outreached hers, and we fought every battle on my terms. But I could never win the war. What she lacked in raw power, she made up for with cunning. We fought and fought through the ages. Had she been more patient, perhaps she could have beaten me, expelled me from her domain by subterfuge – her favourite weapon. The stars know I fell for her tricks often enough... but eventually I grew tired of fighting. I realised that I could never change her will so I tried to expel her, as she had me. When that failed too, I finally lost my patience, and I... shattered her."

Ideth spat out a few grape seeds. "Shattered into what?" she asked, trying to get her head around the notion.

"Not what, darling Ideth – whom. Last night you asked where souls come from. Nyx, one might say, was the original soul."

Ideth whistled. No wonder she'd tasted so much darkness in Psyche.

"Once shattered," Chronos continued as if he were talking about a vase, "I was able to comprehend what she really was. And what I had done..." He sounded genuinely upset then.

"So by shattering this Nyx, you created souls?"

"Not exactly. I facilitated the manifestation of Gaea, the part of Nyx able to create life from matter and energy. She took most of her soul, and at first I thought it was an improvement, but... getting ahead of myself again." Xylo lowered his gaze, as if tired. Maybe he was, Ideth couldn't tell. "The side of her who wanted to kill me and take over the Universe took root in me, like a parasite," he said.

"How?" Ideth asked.

"She… wounded my mind – for lack of a better word – with a shard of her power, and it never fully healed. I've been carrying that part of her ever since."

Ideth blinked in expectation. "Are you trying to tell me you're dying?" she asked, trying not to sound too happy about it. A failed attempt.

Xylo's gaze bored deep into her, and Ideth had to fight the instinct to shriek.

"I'm trying to tell you I am death," he said.

Ideth wasn't sure of what to do with that information. It took her a few false starts before she could organise her thoughts into words. "You and Kali are the same God?"

"Call it an alter ego. The effect of her will on my mind is similar to what humans refer to as the subconscious. It influences me in ways I did not understand at first and still cannot fully explain or control. I had no proper soul until she *gave* me part of hers, and like a disease, it has been eating at me ever since. To put it simply, death nullifies time."

Ideth started chewing her lip, considering the implications. "So Gaea creates life, and Kali – or you – destroys it? What is the point?"

He looked at her the way Chiron did just before he declared she wouldn't understand something, which meant he'd rather not have to explain it. She doubted the mighty God of Time had had much experience conversing with mortals about personal matters, let alone giving them lessons on the intricate workings of the Universe. But he brought her here, forced her to listen to his story, so he better make an effort to elaborate on it.

"Kali doesn't destroy life, Ideth. She sends the departed to a realm where time – where *I* don't exist and therefore have no power over them."

"The Underworlds are Nyx's realms?"

"Not so much her realms as realms beyond my Reach. To be honest, I don't quite understand the reasons myself, just that they are anathema to my nature. Like the realms of dreams and illusions. They are chaotic, with no real substance, no order. Dark and mysterious, just like she was."

Ideth licked her lips. "All right... realms aside, you're saying the Three are actually only two, then?" That would explain why Gaea seemed so much less powerful and so terrified of Chronos.

"Yes and no. There is a third shard of Nyx. And it's by far the most dangerous one."

"If Gaea is the life-giving part of Nyx, and the death-giving part is within you..."

"Correct."

"What is left?"

"The troublesome part." The words rolled like thunder. "The part able to cross realms. Able to break the rules of the Universe – *my* rules." Chronos chewed on the words as if they were a bitter lime. "It has no substance, no beginning, no end. It's the spark that powers the gods' will and feeds the mortals' greed. It doesn't live and can't be killed. Like darkness, it can be everywhere, in anything. Mostly it thrives within the minds of sapient creatures. It gives them the ability to hold two separate, often opposite thoughts at once. It is anathema to logic and order and purpose – to sanity!"

"Souls…" Ideth breathed.

He nodded. "Now scattered across the Universe thanks to Gaea and her creations. Through life in its many forms, these slivers of Nyx's essence have the potential to become greater than she ever was whole. Left unchecked, they will eventually destroy everything, starting with every mind, dead or alive, until one day, every creature will think as she did. When that happens, she'll return to existence more powerful than ever, and then she'll finish what she started."

"Why didn't you stop Gaea from creating life in the first place?"

"Because I couldn't." The God's tone defined resentment. "Gaea is part of Nyx. I tried to guide her but she defied me from the very start, and Kali is the one who decides who lives or dies. In any case, Gaea is not the problem, she will perish soon enough. For every life she creates, she gives away a portion of herself. A fate shared by all mothers. At first I thought that was a good thing and even encouraged her to create, but once I understood Nyx's ultimate plan, it was in my best interest to keep Gaea and her creations alive, especially the earliest ones. The Ancient Ones and the Titans hold the largest, most powerful souls. Through the aeons, I was able to bend many to my will, but it's still not enough."

"I don't understand," Ideth murmured.

"You will," he said emphatically with a hint of

impatience. "When Gaea learnt of her own limitation, she created gods who are all but impervious to my influence, then they created mortals: disposable beings, bound to my power, whose very substance begins to decay the moment they come into existence." His tone deepened. "And they have the nerve to call *me* cruel." He paused as if straining with emotion. Which one, Ideth couldn't quite tell. "Over the aeons mortals have multiplied faster than Kali could kill them. But it wasn't until humans and their *souls* came along that the real problems began."

"Tell me about it," Ideth grumbled, surprised and slightly disconcerted that she could relate to the God in any way.

"I am telling you about it. Be patient," he snapped.

Ideth blinked at him a few times. *Wrath*, she decided, the strained emotion was definitely wrath.

"And then Gaea created Ambrosia. The final piece of Nyx's plan." He grunted. "That's when I took matters into my own hands. I can deal with gods, and I could deal with humans, but not if all of them become gods. Had I not experienced Psyche's apotheosis for myself, I'd never believe such a travesty. Talk about divine intervention." He snorted mirthlessly.

"You are lucky," Ideth said.

"What?"

"Mortals have to deal with the misfortunes of divine intervention all the time. It makes believers of us all."

"Humph. It embarrasses me to say it took me ages to understand the implications of life and death. Souls don't die, you see. Time puts an end to life, but souls are eternal. They gather beyond my influence. And when enough are gathered, Nyx will be reborn. I'm certain giving souls to humans was her idea, somehow presented to Prometheus as his own. Gods are too sensible to reproduce in great numbers – most of them, anyway."

Ideth thought she heard Xylo say "bloody Zeus" through clenched teeth.

"They are extremely hard to kill and dislike sharing their power. Their offspring often turn out to be their greatest rivals, after all. Humans, on the other hand, share the gods' ideals and ambition but have to breed if they want to have a legacy. I did my best to keep their numbers contained, but the gods *love* them. They protected them from me. Against their own nature. And when they die, the souls of both gods and humans go to the Underworlds, which are conveniently beyond my control. There, trillions have been gathering over the aeons, waiting for Nyx to become strong enough to claim them. And that is why I need your help."

"Er… I have it on good authority that I don't have a soul," Ideth said meekly. What did all this have to do with her? She wasn't a goddess and she certainly wasn't human!

Xylo grinned. "No, you have a powerful spirit, which is much better than a soul. You have a natural link to the Underworld and their souls, and you can channel Nyx's power without being bound to her will. You are perfect."

Ideth didn't like the sound of that. "Perfect for what?"

Chronos' grin crept wider. "To learn how to destroy them, of course."

"No. No, no, no." Slush, what had she gotten herself into? The old God had her confused with someone else, surely. "Psyche. She's the one you want. Destroying souls is her talent, not mine."

Xylo bristled. The branches on his head retreated inside his skull. "Psyche is Nyx's creature."

"One more reason to use her. Use the weapons of your enemies against them," she said, quoting the Aossi queen.

"I did. I used her to get myself here, and here she shall remain until this is over."

Ideth puffed out a mouthful of air, then fell back to her initial question. "If things are as you said, why did you Merge the worlds in the first place?"

"Ahh. You see, after a thorough analysis of the Universe's evolution and Gaea's preferences, I predicted Nyx would manifest either in the Olympian or the Aesir Underworlds. So I made sure I kept both under close observation," he answered patiently.

"But now there are more souls gathered in one place than ever before, wouldn't that speed up her rebirth?"

He sighed. "If left unchecked, yes. Perhaps I'm not as patient as I once was, darling Ideth. I admit I had hopes that maybe Hel and Hades would mutually destroy themselves and their realms. Instead, the opposite happened." He shook his head. "I have come to accept that I will never be rid of Nyx. Not completely. She's part of the fabric of this universe, after all. But at least this way, she'll never be strong enough to challenge me again."

Ideth had never found much comfort in the knowledge that her spirit would continue to exist in the Underworld after her death. It was the reason she linked to Wyrae in the first place. She knew that even with Ambrosia her life would be short compared with the seemingly eternal lives of gods, but now the idea of not having a place to go after it ended distressed her greatly. There had to be another way.

"Why not use the Suzerain's technology to create enough bodies to host the souls in the Underworlds so they can't gather? I'm sure many would jump at the opportunity to be alive again."

He gave her the flattest of looks. "For the same reason you can't create enough suns to banish all darkness from the Universe."

"I see…" Ideth's head throbbed, trying to make sense of it all, and she came to the conclusion that if this wasn't Psyche's problem, then it was Hades' or Hel's, definitely not hers.

"Listen, as fascinating as all this is," Ideth lied. In truth, she was appalled by these revelations. She'd known Niflheim was a freezing disaster, but she'd still held out hope for the Universe. Not anymore. "I don't have time to solve the Universe's problems, especially from here. Aedan will be furious to find me gone, and Oreth is still locked in a cell with no sunlight and little water. I need to go back."

Xylo gave her a condescending frown, his version of the smug 'all-knowing' gaze gods liked to display. On him it went beyond infuriating. It was terrifying.

"Darling Ideth," he said slowly, standing up. "You lost your son the moment you left him with Alek all those years ago. And as for time… You have all the time in the Universe at your disposal."

∞

Before Ideth could run through the implications of his statement, he pointed at something behind her.

"There is someone I'd like you to meet."

She got to her feet with a start and turned around. Someone stood there all right – well, kind of. The woman was tall and slender, with a pointy chin, pointy ears, pointy eyes, pointy breasts. Everything about her was pointy. She was not quite Narrum, not quite dryad, and most disturbingly, not quite there either. Ideth could see the forest right through her spectral form, which might explain why she hadn't heard the woman approach until she was right on top of her.

"Who the frost is this?" Ideth asked, taking a cautious step back.

The woman just smiled that patronising sort of smile gods often used to unnerve others. She had Dharkan white skin, like it'd never seen the sun or she'd been buried for a long time. Her hair was sleek, in a jarring shade of orange. Her pupils were vertical slits, like those of a snake. Ideth disliked her immediately on that ground. They shifted in colour between yellow, green and brown – if Ideth's own eyes weren't mistaken – and she held a flaming torch in each hand, which she planted on the ground beside them.

"Hello, Ideth," she said in a voice as disembodied as her form. It gave Ideth the creeps. Her head moved strangely in a blur, as if there were more than just the one atop her neck. Maybe it was because of the way the canopies' shadows rippled over her translucent face, but for a moment Ideth could swear she saw the woman looking simultaneously left, right and straight at her as she spoke.

"Hello," Ideth replied cautiously.

"Ideth, I present you Hecate, goddess of magic," Xylo said.

Ideth burst out laughing. That was an even worse title than 'god of gravity'.

The woman's eyes flared the way Hades' sometimes did when he was angry.

"Oh, frost. You are serious." Ideth moved further away from the strange creature.

"Deadly so," Hecate said in a tone to match the underlying threat. She knelt in silence between them with the subtlety of a deity, spread her long black dress neatly over her knees and beckoned. "Come, sit down, Ideth. We have much to discuss."

"Hecate is here to teach you," Xylo said, guessing her thoughts.

"Teach me what?"

"Sorcery. Specifically, how to cast curses," Hecate said.

Ideth guffawed. They weren't laughing. "You mistake me for a Narrum crone," she said, unamused.

"Do we?" All three of Hecate's faces turned in her direction.

Ideth swallowed. Frost this insanity. She tried to make a run for it and found herself rooted in place despite no visible restraints.

One of Hecate's spectral heads turned to Xylo, the

other remained facing Ideth. "You haven't told her everything yet. Have I come too early?"

"No," Xylo said. "Your affinity with time is impeccable, as always. It is I who forgot myself. Ideth has a way of making me talk far too long."

Ideth eyed him askance. "Yes, I can't shut him up, apparently."

Hecate laughed. The sound a disturbing combination of a coquettish giggle and an old woman's cackle. "I can see why you picked her, Chronos." All her faces turned to Ideth. "First lesson: show some respect to the old clock. He might look like a stunted tree, but we would not be here if not for him."

No kidding, Ideth thought, belligerently.

"Ideth, you've been chosen because your mind and spirit are unique," Xylo said.

Ideth didn't like where this was going. No conversation ever ended well when it began with the words 'you've been chosen'.

"I've searched for one such as you for aeons and may never have found you – let alone owned you – had you not used the Chronodéndron."

"How fortunate," Ideth said, eyes wide with unspoken protests.

"No, Tyche had nothing to do with it," he replied seriously. "I wasn't entirely honest with you earlier, darling Ideth. The Suzerain sent you to Yewlow – at my request."

Ideth's legs faltered. "You…" She trailed off, sitting down.

"I'm not usually aware of mortals; there are so many

of them and their lives are so fleeting, whenever I notice any of interest, Kali is already claiming them, but I was aware of your existence early on. Having dalliances with gods makes mortals susceptible to other gods' Reach – mine most of all. Sadly, I had no way to contact you in this world, no way to guide you to me. And you had no reason to pray to me either. Until he came along and told you to."

Ideth's heart sank at the idea she'd been deceived for so long. Could Chronos or the Suzerain have had something to do with Orion's demise as well? She tried to remain calm; her breathing betrayed her. She felt like a deer, ambushed and pushed into a trap.

"You have a talent, Ideth. If used correctly, it can rival a god's will. This talent is not linked to a soul but to the fabric of your being," Xylo said.

"I'm not a god. I have no talents," Ideth insisted, still trying in vain to escape her situation. This was definitely not what she had in mind when she imagined herself at Chronos' mercy.

"You have the power to combine elements to affect others, as I do," Hecate said.

"Pfah! Everyone has the power to affect others. If I were as talented as you say, I would not be your prisoner."

"You know nothing of imprisonment, mortal," Hecate said in a chilling tone.

Ideth turned to Xylo with a questioning, almost pleading look. She'd rather face him than her.

"Hecate was the first one to discover this power. And she paid the price for it. She's been Hades' guest for…" He trailed off.

"Too long," Hecate said, an almost imperceptible hint of bitterness and resentment in her tone.

Ideth turned to her. "Did Hades send you, then?"

"No. But he will come for me. So, despite having time on our side" – she glanced mischievously at Xylo – "we need to start your education immediately."

Education?! "I, I –" Ideth staggered, at a loss for words for once in her life.

"You are aware gods can't break each other's curses," Hecate said. Ideth nodded stiffly, able to do little else. "Sorcery has no such limitation."

"That sounds great," Ideth said, finding her voice again. "But I'm still waiting for you to tell me what exactly you want from me."

"We already told you. We want you to learn how to use this ability. It runs amongst most mortals, especially women. But you" – Hecate blew a mouthful of air – "you have the potential to become even better than I am."

Ideth took in the goddess's translucent, ever-changing form and very much doubted it. Actually, she dreaded it. "What if I don't wish to learn?"

The two deities exchanged amused glances. Obviously her wishes were not to be part of this arrangement.

Ideth inhaled deeply. "I appreciate the offer, really. I can think of a few creatures on whom I'd gladly cast a curse or two, but come on. You don't want to waste your" – she stopped just short of saying 'time' – "*teachings* on me. I'm sure there are other gods or Wyrds far more talented and willing to develop their talents." She turned to Xylo, running out of arguments. "Chronos, I have a son. He needs me, please. If you want me to learn this sorcery to help you defeat Nyx, at least bring him here." She used his actual name without realising, but once she did, she didn't break eye contact. There was no empathy in Chronos' gaze.

He stood up, towering over her. "Ideth, from this moment on, you will not use Oreth as an excuse for your choices or your failures again. Am I clear?"

Ideth gasped. "He is not –"

"He *is* an excuse. A powerful one, laden with guilt and obligation. But not love. No. Do not lie to me; do not lie to yourself. He's not the one you love. It was not for him you travelled."

Ideth bit her lip to stop it from trembling. She was crumbling under the weight of his stare and the truth in his words. Still, he could crush her, break her, but he would not bend her. "No," she said.

"No?" Xylo echoed ominously.

"No. I refuse to learn anything from this woman. I want no more part in any of the gods' schemes, especially yours. I want to go. You can let me, or you can kill me. Either way, I won't do what you want. You're right. I didn't travel for Oreth, and I know you won't give me Orion, so… no."

Xylo smiled. "Darling Ideth." He cupped her chin. Ideth expected to perish at any moment. "I cannot break the curse on your lover. But *you* can."

"Lies," Ideth drawled. "You gods are all the same. Always singing the same tunes: promises, conditions, deals. I don't believe you. And if it is true, then you're not half the God everyone believes you to be. The mighty Chronos wouldn't need to use me to achieve his goals. You are the God of Time, the God every other god and mortal fears, and you want *me* to help you do something because you cannot? Pfah." She freed her chin from his grip. "You can do anything. The truth is, you dare not. I bet there's a good reason for it. A price too high or too inconvenient to pay. Well, I won't be paying it for you either!"

His expression didn't change. "And how often mortals bid the gods to do their dirty work? When have mortals given us anything without expecting our favour in return, huh? If I brought Orion to you now, which yes, you're right, I can do. How would his presence here motivate you to learn and do what I need you to do? The distraction alone would prevent you from accomplishing anything. It's what love does. It distracts. Makes you obsess over one subject, forsaking all others. Many wars have been fought for it, worlds lost because of it. No, Ideth, I won't give you your lover back. Believe it or not, I respect you too much to do it." There was a hint of indignation in his tone when he first spoke; it turned closer to spite with each word.

"I am offering you the power to rescue your lover by yourself. The power of independence from the gods – all of them, even myself. Right now, you have nothing, which means you have everything to gain. If I bring him back, you risk losing him again forever. So tell me, how is it going to be, *darling* Ideth?"

Frost, she couldn't back down now. He was bluffing. He wasn't all powerful, otherwise he wouldn't need to wear Xylo's body. The problem was, she really had no idea what he was capable of or how far he would go to get what he wanted.

"Perhaps a little incentive is needed," Hecate suggested.

Xylo thrummed. "Very well. He's here. Let him in."

Hecate nodded. Standing up, she picked up one torch and drew a circle in the air in front of her. It shimmered as if being viewed from underwater. An opening like a hole burned in a piece of cloth appeared ahead of them. It was dark beyond that rip. The bright light above them did nothing to change that.

What the frost is happening now? Something approached. "Who's there?" Ideth asked, unsure of how much more she could take.

"Who do you wish it to be?" Chronos prompted.

Her first wish was for Orion, of course, but she knew it couldn't be him. Next she wished for Chiron, then Aedan for some reason. And only after guilt slapped her conscience did she wish for Oreth. She shut her eyes tight to hold back the tears. Chronos was right, she did not love her son, but the shame she felt because of it was nearly as strong.

When she opened her eyes, she saw Chiron gliding through the trees. He seemed to have appeared out of nowhere. The barrier parted at his approach, rippling wider to allow his large bulk to pass through. Ideth realised they were inside a bubble of sorts. The rest of the forest was not quite in the same realm as the immediate area around the cabin, yet this was no dream or illusion, she was certain of it. It didn't matter. Taken by overwhelming relief and joy, she ran to her friend.

"Chiron!" She hugged him tight. He felt wrong: thinner, feverish and – she wrinkled her nose – he stank.

"Unbridled one." He sighed with relief. "I'm so glad I found you. I'm so sorry, I should have been here sooner. I was blind without my Reach, and of all places, I didn't expect I would find you here!" He took a moment to catch his breath. "Are you all right?"

She could ask him the same. "Better than you, it seems," she said playfully. Then she saw his wounds. "Frost! Chiron, what happened?"

"There is no time to explain."

"Oh, there is, my friend. Rest assured, we are drowning in time," she said dramatically, her concern for his well-being increasing. His once lush mane was now thin and greasy. His eyes were rheumy and the skin around them creased with lines. He looked more human than ever, and a sick, old one at that.

Chiron stiffened. "Hecate! Stars, what are you doing here? Has Tartarus burned?"

"Not yet, Titan. I escaped."

Chiron looked further taken aback by that. "Hades. Is he…?"

"Pissed off, yes. Very much so. Still alive, though."

"Oh… Well, I guess it was just a matter of time before you and your curses found a way to… spread," he said sardonically.

She sneered. "Right back at you, Titan. I warned you; you can't cheat an oracle forever."

"Over an age," he replied proudly.

"Was it worth it?"

He looked at Ideth and smiled. "Yes."

Ideth was annoyed but not exactly surprised to

find they knew each other. Every god had a long and convoluted history. "What is the meaning of this?" she asked the goddess. "What is he doing here, in this state?"

"He," Xylo said, walking closer to the group, "is my gift to you, darling Ideth. To make sure you learn. Now, do not disappoint me." Something passed between him and Chiron. Chiron's jaw slackened. He glanced at Hecate. She grinned. A strangled sound escaped the centaur's throat, and he held Ideth tighter, protectively, possessively, desperately.

"You are free to leave whenever you want, Titan. But beware, outside this realm, time flows differently. You won't last long," Hecate said.

"Chiron…" Ideth whispered. "I'm so sorry." She hugged him again.

"Hush, it's not your fault."

She began to cry. For regardless of what he said, it felt like it was.

"It's all right." Chiron patted her hair soothingly as he spoke. "Do what he asks and it will be all right."

Chiron was a terrible liar.

INTERLUDE 3

Revelations

I finally catch up with Psyche far from the hunter's cabin, talking to a tree. I frown. No. Talking to someone *behind* the tree. It's probably Pan. She hasn't said how they met or what the nature of their friendship is, and frankly I've had too much on my mind to care before. But now I'm curious. They haven't noticed me yet, so I sneak closer, hoping to eavesdrop on something useful. Psyche lowers her head and nods morosely. That's... odd. A hand reaches out from the shadows, stops short of her face and retreats before she looks up again. Odder still. I creep closer, careful not to make a sound, and glimpse the hooded figure the hand belongs to.

"I wouldn't interrupt if I were you," Pan whispers behind my ear. I nearly jump out of my skin. Burn me! This one is even stealthier than Hades. I wonder if it's a satyr or an Olympian trait. Then wonder is replaced by a sense of foreboding. If he's here, who's behind the tree with Psyche?

"I advise you to give her a moment," he says.

I ignore him and move closer, determined to find out who she's talking to, or more accurately, arguing with. The woman seems incapable of having a sensible conversation. I'm nearly there when a twig cracks underfoot. Flaming sun, forests really are glorified traps. Psyche jerks her head up and sees me. Hiding is futile, so I abandon stealth and round the tree in a few strides.

"You?!"

"Hello, Aedan," Loki says as if he'd been expecting me. The tone is at odds with his demeanour, and his emotions match those of a thief caught in the act.

"Hel's been looking for you," I say to him.

"I am aware."

"Then why are you here, with *her*?" I don't know why this bothers me, but it does. "Are you two friends or something?"

"We are not friends," Psyche promptly states.

"Something," Loki sneers.

Lovers? I think with very mixed and very confused feelings.

Loki glares at me. He knows my thoughts as well as I know his emotions. "The goddess of the soul was just telling me of Fenrir's misfortune," he says by way of explanation.

"Humph," I reply. An awkward silence follows, and I know the two are still talking to each other telepathically.

"Well then. I'd better go check on Hel," Loki finally says. "Ow! Motherfucker!" A crossbow bolt just hit him in the chest.

I duck instinctively, casting in every direction, searching for the attacker. *Was the greedy hunter suicidal enough to follow me?* But there is no one but us and Pan in shooting distance.

Loki pulls the bolt out with a wince and a slew of mindless expletives. "Your doing?" he says to Psyche.

She bites her cheek, looking guilty and slightly amused. "Maybe..." she says sheepishly.

He stares at her a moment longer, his jaw muscles tensing furiously, then without another word, walks away, his long cloak getting caught on every other shrub. He pretends not to notice or be hindered by it, but I can sense his annoyance well enough. He nods politely at the satyr as he passes him. "Pan."

"Loki," the satyr mutters in reply, eyeing him askance as he chews on a reed, a knowing smirk on his lips. Eventually Loki turns into a moth and flutters away.

I narrow my eyes at Psyche, waiting for a proper explanation.

She opens her mouth to speak, then hesitates, purses her lips stubbornly and glares. "Did Hel send you to spy on me?"

"No. I sent myself to follow you. The spying was incidental."

"Tsk. Go back to your goddess, Aedan. Tell her she has nothing to worry about."

I fake a laugh. "Apart from the Nephilim, the Underworlds, the faithless Dharkan, Hades, Gaea, Iva and... ah yes, her brother?"

Psyche winces at the mention of Fenrir. "I stand

corrected. She has nothing *else* to worry about, least of all me."

"After your argument back there and what I just saw, I'm not so sure."

"And what exactly do you think you saw?"

I've learnt to recognise that tone well enough to know a slap or cringing insult usually follows. "I saw you being contrite and vulnerable for once," I say truthfully.

She blinks, the fury draining out of her like Prana from a cub.

"So tell me. What's the nature of your relationship with the Trickster?"

She laughs, too loud and too fake a sound to be convincing. "There is no relationship, only obligation. And it's none of your business!"

Psyche turns on her heel and walks away. Pan gives me a 'don't push it' look before walking after her. I send a prayer to Hel, updating her on the situation as I follow both.

"Obligation." I chuckle. "That is, by far, the least convincing lie you've ever told me, princess."

Psyche glares at me over her shoulder.

"I would not insist on the matter," Pan suggests.

"I did not ask for your opinion," I growl in reply.

"Shouldn't you be tracking Iva instead?" Psyche asks. "She's probably on her way to Portum by now. Wasn't saving the living the whole point of your speech? Please don't tell me you changed your mind already. Jonas needs your help to deal with her. The stars know that bloody hunter won't lift a finger to help anyone."

"Mmph." At least we both agree on that.

"Ulcan is a complicated man," Pan grumbles. "Still, it was worth the try."

"Hardly," I reply, still sizzling with offence. "It was a waste of time. I should have iced the piece of ash. At least Jonas will be ready with or without his help. And don't change the subject, Psyche." She always finds a way of redirecting the conversation whenever her or her actions are the topic. I won't let her get away with it this time.

Psyche eyes me askance. "Ready with what? The embers of his sanctuary are probably still smoking. The blue sun is gone. The dwellers of Portum can barely put up a defence against rain. *How* can he be ready?"

I clench my jaw before answering. "We made arrangements in case I wasn't able to persuade Iva – which I wasn't, burn her," I groan under my breath. "The foolish woman is hosting something vile."

Psyche stops walking to stare at me through slitted eyelids. "What sort of arrangements?" she asks dryly.

"The sort that will hopefully placate the faithless long enough for the gods to stop them reaching Relicum," I say, desperate to change the subject back to her and her *obligation* to the god of mischief.

"Aedan, *what* did you do?" Psyche persists, cocking an eyebrow.

Burning sun! It's like talking to a rock. I clench my jaw again and keep making eye contact, hoping she'll desist this line of interrogation. She doesn't. Her eyebrow just keeps rising. I hate staring matches.

"Tell me what your deal is with the Trickster first," I demand.

She chews on her cheek for a bit, eyebrow back to normal. "It's personal."

I freeze the vegetation at our feet. "We are way past personal, little princess." I try not to think about it, but by now, she probably knows me better than any other woman. And she clearly despises me for it.

Psyche lowers her eyes and takes a deep breath. "I... *owe* him," she says, still avoiding eye contact. Still, I can tell it's the truth and how much it costs her to admit it.

"Owe him what?"

She exaggerates her exhale and exchanges an anguished glance with Pan before answering. "My life. My godhood. My freedom." She snorts bitterly. "And the lack of it."

"Why –"

"No, Aedan. That is all I'll say on the matter. Now, explain how Jonas can be ready."

I grind my teeth. "The Dharkan's desires are simple..."

"Stars! Tell me you didn't." Psyche puts her hands on her hips. "So that's why you wanted to talk to him in private? First cattle, now bait? I can't believe I actually defended you to Ulla! Are the living meaningless to you people?"

"On the contrary! They are worth a lot to us. And so I'm confident the others will take the bait – the *opportunity*, I mean! Or you'd rather they went to the Grove first and found a few Wyrds to feed upon instead? As you keep reminding me, without the blue sun, that would be bad for them."

Psyche's scowl is one of pure disdain. Well, burn it! She knows what we are, there's no point in apologising for our nature.

"Personally, I think the gods' life force tastes much better than the common living, and I care a lot less for their well-being." I regret my words immediately, but I can't help it. That judgemental stare brings out the worst in me.

Psyche utters a series of words I do not recognise, none of them flattering, I am sure. "You know what," she says, throwing her arms in the air. "I don't give a fuck! Do whatever you want; feed on whoever you want. Just don't follow me!"

CHAPTER 20

Loki

Loki found Psyche in the forest, not far from the hunter's cabin where he'd last seen her, sat on a mossy tree trunk, her face buried in her hands, crying. For fuck's sake. How come she was always crying? And why did it always affect him so much?

"Psyche…" he whispered.

She inhaled sharply, then lashed at his mind. *'I told you to leave me alone!'*

"I'm afraid that's not possible," he said. He'd rather speak to her directly than think at her. It was safer that way. Besides, there was no one close enough to hear except Pan, and he knew better than to eavesdrop on their conversation.

She sniffed. "And yet it was so easy before."

It had never been easy, but there was no point in telling her that now. "I need to ask you something."

Psyche uttered a few choice words about his character, then lifted her tear-streaked face and looked up at him plaintively, her fingers interlocked under her chin as if she were praying – just as she'd been the first time they met. The sight hurt him as much then as it did now. "Well," she said waspishly, "ask."

"Did you know?"

"Know what? That you were playing with me. Or that you brought me here to buy your freedom with mine? Yes, I figured as much when you sent Fenrir to chase me into your nightmare," she said sourly.

Loki exhaled, disappointed but not surprised. "I wouldn't do that you," he said as sincerely as was possible for someone like him.

Psyche frowned, keeping one sceptical eyebrow raised. He'd always found that ability of hers highly attractive. "What are you saying?"

He crouched to her level. An excuse to be closer to her, to make himself appear more sincere. "I'm not the one responsible for your presence in Niflheim or your curse, Psyche. I actually thought you came of your own free will. I thought..."

Her expression hardened. "You thought what? That I was playing hard? Playing *you*?"

"Well... yes," he admitted. He'd obviously been wrong and, feeling like an idiot, had to hold on to his anger so he wouldn't break. "I did not expect you to simply forgive and forget but –"

"You thought that I *forgave* you?" By her tone he realised she hadn't, of course. "How could I forgive you when you obviously never forgave me?" she hissed.

He was taken aback by this. "That's not true. I never blamed you in the first place!"

"You used me and then left me there. You left me with *him*. If that wasn't a punishment, I don't know what is."

"I was angry," he admitted.

"You're always angry."

Ain't that the truth. "Not always…" He tried an appeasing smile. "Besides, it all worked out well for you in the end." The words sounded right in his mind and were out of his mouth before he could stop himself. Now that he heard them, though… He cringed.

"*Well?*" Her brown eyes were dark pools of rage. "I got lynched by an entire pantheon! Then you sent Hel to drive the final nail in my coffin. You weren't even man enough to tell me how you felt to my face."

"What are you talking about? I never sent Hel anywhere near you. Not before this, I mean."

Psyche's eyes narrowed. Her tone remained distrustful but less accusatory. "When I… *left* Olympus, I followed your soul straight to Asgard. You sent me away."

"I did no such thing!" Loki tried to remember the last time he'd even been in Asgard.

"A large gathering was taking place," Psyche continued, refreshing his memory. "Everywhere burst with activity, so I couldn't find you right away… There were so many souls… powerful souls. Very different from the Olympians. I'd never experienced anything like it, of course. New to godhood as I was. But for the first time in my life I didn't feel like a total outcast." She almost smiled in reverie, then sadness clouded her eyes. "They were troubled. One of their own had just passed away. I had little understanding of my talents back then, but instinct told me there was something I could do to bring him back. For once I had the power to make a difference." Her eyes came alive at the prospect. "I even convinced myself that fate had brought me there. That you'd known all along what would happen and it made it all worth it." Her expression soured. "But before I had a chance to find you or even present myself to the others and use my talent to bring the soul of their murdered god back from the Underworld, Hel found me first and stopped me from doing any of those things."

"Hel was there? In Asgard?" Realisation dawned on him. The last time his daughter been in Asgard was when she presented the Dharkan to the Aesir. When Baldur died and they punished Loki for it.

Psyche nodded. "She told me you left the moment I arrived. Told me that my talents were useless and you didn't want to see me again because I was not fun anymore and you would never forgive me."

"And you believed her…"

Psyche shook her head. "Not at first. I waited. Then I searched for you everywhere." She hesitated. "Well, almost everywhere. Obviously, I never went back to Olympus."

"Why would you?" He snorted rhetorically.

"Eventually I went to sleep. I slept until they forgot I ever existed. Until it no longer hurt."

"I see…"

His hand moved to touch her face, her hair, anything of hers, but closed into a fist instead, as it always did whenever she was close. He tried to speak, but no words would come after millennia of silence. They'd had thousands of talks in his illusions over of the ages. Lived so many lives together. Now the reality seemed both overwhelming and hollow. Loki didn't know what to say. Didn't know what to do. There was so much to explain, and yet, after so long, what would be the point? He looked into her eyes and saw proof that given enough time, whatever you believe becomes truth.

"So… you didn't send me away?" she asked, assessing her own deductions.

"No. I was accused of murder and taken away before I even knew you were there." He chuckled bitterly. "I spent the next thousand years waiting for you in the Olympian's Underworld, wondering why you weren't dead yet." He cringed again. "Not that I wanted you dead! I mean… I did, but… not for the reasons – oh, for fuck's sake. You know what I mean!" He punched the ground. "Fucking Odin! He knew. He knew about us all along."

Psyche, who listened to his outburst with a blank face, gave him a grieving smile. "I don't think he did, judging by how he reacted when we first met and his constant cursing of the Merge."

"Then who?"

Psyche shrugged. "Zeus."

Fuck. She was a probably right. And a great deal of nothing that was worth now.

Loki straightened himself up, and as he did so, the dagger fell from his belt. Such was his state of mind that instead of casting an illusion on it, he tried to hide it with his foot. It was too late, either way. She'd already picked it up, recognised it, and she sure knew what it meant.

"You son of a bitch." The scorn, the pain, the disappointment in her eyes. They were too much to bear.

"No! It's not what you think!" Oh, if Loki had a world for every time he'd said this…

"Don't you dare lie to me again." She stood up and pressed the dagger to his neck. "Give me a reason."

"I'm sorry." The words came out easily for a change. "I wish there'd been another way."

"There was!" she cried out, her lovely face contorted with the pain of disgust and betrayal. "You could have just asked!" She sounded so sincere, but Loki knew better.

"Could I?" He took the dagger from her. It was not like he was afraid of being cut or that she needed it to crush his soul. "You would have said no."

She did not contradict him. She just gave him the sort of look a monster like him deserved. "You used me, again and again…"

Loki refused to take all the blame. "Yes, I made a deal with Hephaestus, for the dagger and… yes, I told Hades to orchestrate you going there so he could take the sample of your talent, but I never intended… I didn't know he would –" He gripped the dagger harder. "I killed him, Psyche. I killed a god for you."

"Don't you dare," she snarled. "You did nothing *for* me. Ever!"

He did not contradict her. "You used me as much as I did you back then," Loki said, and could not regret it, for it was the truth.

"Fuck you…" She bit her cheek. "Had I known it was you pulling Hephaestus' strings, I'd have killed him myself."

"Who did you think it was, then?" he asked with indignation.

"Them!" She pointed in the Stump's general direction.

"What would they care? They want to capture gods' souls, not send them to the Underworld."

"He helped them build the vaults."

This gave him pause. "Oh, shit…"

"Exactly."

"Well, be that as it may, the Nephilim are the least of our problems right now."

"Tell that to Fenrir. He's still inside. Cut off from his own soul."

Loki blinked. His jaw tensed a few times before he was able to force the words out. "Are you sure?"

She glowered at him.

"Fuck!"

'Hel had the nerve to ask me to free him,' she said telepathically.

Loki made an effort to calm himself. *Will you?* he asked hopefully.

'Why should I?'

Because I'm asking you, he wanted to say. But words, even when spoken in thought, have a will of their own. Instead, he said: *He likes you, you know. Before you came along, I'd never seen Fenrir relate to anyone the way he did to you.*

'Are you actually trying to manipulate me again with guilt?'

No… just, I thought you should know. Whatever harm he did to you, he did at my request.

She scowled. *'Spare me your apologies, such as they are. I've already decided to free him — for his sake, not yours.*

Then we are even. You can let go of your anger and I my guilt. Deal?'

Psyche... This is not a good time to pick fights with the Nephilim. Something worse is happening. You're needed in –

'I don't give a fuck,' she snapped. *'Do we have a deal?'*

Loki winced. *Psyche, I really –*

"You?!" Aedan leaped from behind a tree. Distracted as Loki had been, he did not sense the Dharkan approach. His timing couldn't have been worse.

Loki spared him a glance, then took a long-lasting look at Psyche. *Deal,* he told her reluctantly, for she would not take any other answer.

Be careful, Butterfly.

'Goodbye, Trickster.'

INTERLUDE 4

Thresholds

"I told you not to follow me," I repeat, exasperated with the Dharkan's behaviour. *Personal,* indeed. After everything I've been through, I'll be damned if I'm letting another man dictate my fate.

"It's a free forest. I'll go wherever I want," Aedan says stubbornly. "It just happens we're going in the same direction."

Stars, give me patience. "Pan, you too. One shadow is enough. Besides, it's safer if you stay away from me. Go gather as many forest folk as you can and take them to safety. Things are about to get ugly for the living in Aegea."

"No can do, Butterfly," Pan says. "I'm not a shepherd."

"You're the god of shepherds!"

"I'm the god of the wild. Just because shepherds like to pray to me, it doesn't make me their god. And for now, I'll go wherever *he* goes; his stuff is better than the blue sun."

"Do not get too used to my Prana, Wyrd. It was a one-time perk."

Pan giggles. "That's what they all say."

A smile tugs at my lips, for I can imagine Aedan's reaction to this. Under different circumstances I'd welcome their company, for there's still a part of me who sometimes craves friendship and a sense of belonging, but I can't indulge or even allow any of those things right now. If there's one thing I've learnt from my conversation with Loki, it is that I don't have friends and I'll never belong with either gods or mortals.

"He's right," I say to Pan. "You'd better find some other source of nourishment. This one's too unreliable and costly. Life is only a currency to the Dharkan. Sooner or later you'll go broke."

Aedan huffs.

"I'm already broke," Pan says bleakly. "What other choice do I have? You won't put an end to my curse, and Loki hid the sun. I don't suppose you know where, do you?"

Damn it, Pan. You're not helping. "No," I reply curtly. "There's a scion of Ra in Relicum. Tell her who you are and she'll help you." Or at least I hope she will. Seshat's soul, like her character, was difficult to comprehend. But she's the only free deity in Aegea that I can think of with enough light to spare at the moment.

"As if I could get anywhere near Relicum without being flayed," Pan grumbles. "Even if I could, I hate Relicum. People are so easily offended there. Rotten to the core, the lot of them. They can't take a good prank, or any sort of prank for that matter. Always so serious, looking down on everyone, pampered by their privilege and greed, wrapped in self-righteousness and ignorance. That's what civilisation does to idiots. I'd rather take my chances with you two selfish savages."

"Well, I'm going to the Stump," I say, hoping to dissuade him from tagging along.

"Me too," Aedan says.

"Excellent! That is exactly where I want to go too," Pan says enthusiastically.

I stop and stare both men down. There could hardly be a set of more dissimilar features, and yet both wear a similar expression of smug innocence.

"I know why you want to go back there, Aedan. To save your precious Ileana."

The Dharkan figures he'll have a better chance of it with me than Hel. He's right. Hel has no defence against the Nephilim. This way he gets what he wants while remaining on good terms with his goddess by pretending to help me rescue Fenrir. Clever. Maybe some of Zeus' cunning has seeped through to the Dharkan's mind along with his talent.

"Obviously," he sneers. "Why are *you* going back there, little princess?" He puffs up his chest to make himself look bigger. *Infuriating man.*

"Because since Hel won't do it, the Nephilim are the only ones left who can get me off this forsaken world," I reply to his face, standing as tall as I can without cheating.

"You're lying." He sounds almost puzzled, which makes no sense, considering how often he accuses me of lying. "It's not a complete lie, but… still, a lie." He tilts his head like a confused puppy. "I wonder if you can tell the difference anymore."

"Oh, fuck off." I resume walking before he's able

to *read* anything else. The Dharkan's getting too good at discerning my behaviour. Damnation, this talent of his is getting out of control. It's one thing to watch my tongue, another to watch every single movement, expression and breath. He's right again, curse him. The Nephilim are not the only ones able to get me off this world. According to Odin, there is another way. Of course, there's a strong possibility the Allfather might have been lying too. I tried to pry the knowledge from Agnar when I healed him, but Odin was thorough. His host's mind is a maze of information organised without apparent logic or chronological order.

"I'd like to see them take your soul away or better yet, link it to one of their own," Aedan teases.

"I'd like to see them try," I tease back. "There is no one, nothing in the Universe able to take away my soul. Besides, they don't want my soul. They want me to capture other gods' souls for them. Which is exactly what Hades and Hel want me to do. It's what everyone wants from me," I say bitterly. "There's the truth for you, Dharkan." He doesn't dare to contradict me. I snort. "But since the gods have betrayed me – again – they've lost my trust. I'm tired of being used. Maybe the Nephilim will properly appreciate my talents for once."

"Psyche," Aedan says gravely. He rarely calls me by my actual name.

That gives me pause, and I glance up at him, searching for clues as to what he might say next.

He makes sure he has my full attention before he speaks. "Hel doesn't want to exploit you. She needs your help, and she's too proud to ask you for it herself.

And for all it's worth, she did not break her promise."

"Oh?" The nerve of the man. What does he know of my issues with Hel? I cross my arms, waiting for an elaboration.

"I was there," he says. "I heard what she said – what she *actually* said was that she would allow you leave Aegea and –"

"I know what she said!" I snap. "I don't mean the promise she made the other day at the Stump. I mean the one she made… oh, never mind. It doesn't matter anymore." The Dharkan knows nothing of our past, and I'd rather keep it that way.

"So you have met before," he says in a self-satisfied tone.

I glance over my shoulder. The bastard just played me, and I fell for it! Stars, what's wrong with me? This is not the time to go soft, or witless.

"Why did you call her Hela?" he asks.

I suppose I should tell him that much. "Everyone did, back then."

"Back when?"

Good point.

"You and Hel should sort yourselves out. You have more in common than you think," Pan chimes in.

I blow out an exhale. If only he knew how irreversible the animosity is, precisely because of what we have in common. "That is not an option. I'm sorry, Pan. You shouldn't have to listen to this shit. I've caused you too much pain already."

"What have you done to this one?" Aedan asks in all seriousness.

I wish the Dharkan had a soul so I could squeeze it

and wring it and twist it into the fabric of a less insufferable creature. *Breathe.*

Pan tuts. "You caused me nothing, Butterfly. I chose to help you, and in doing so, I chose this fate. I'm glad you did not take my soul as I asked earlier. I'd hate to have missed the events of this evening. And you two are quite entertaining, by the way."

"Olympians," Aedan growls to himself.

"What was the condition of the curse?" I ask Pan, ignoring the Dharkan. With everything that's happened, I haven't had a chance to ask this before. Knowing Pan has been fated because of me is bad enough, but perhaps there is something I can do to free him; something besides taking his soul, that is.

"Repentance," he says sheepishly.

I stare at him anxiously.

"Yeah, we both know that's not going to happen." He grins. "But I heard the Nephilim can break a Wyrd's curse. They did it for you, didn't they?"

"The Suzerain broke my curse, yes. But... Ileana's body died."

Pan hits his chest. "This one's been dead a long time now. How do you think I've made it look like the real me?"

"By owing a few favours to crafty gods?" I suggest, knowing fully well Hephaestus forged a lot more than weapons in Aegea.

Pan's impish face turns sombre while his ears move frantically in every direction. "We all do what we must to survive, Butterfly."

I nod dolefully.

"You told us Ileana is alive," Aedan says, a hint of a

threat in his tone. *Stars, the man has a one-track mind and one course of action when it comes to that dryad. Talk about curses...*

"She is alive, but her body is not the same one I was in," I reply cautiously.

"How can you tell?"

I do my best to sound patronising. "Hmmm... maybe because she *is* alive."

Aedan snarls.

"Shouldn't you be thanking the stars instead of attacking me with questions? I've already told you what – " I halt again. Then motion everyone else to stop as well. "What the fuck..." I murmur. There's a shimmering wall in front of us, too thin and almost too perfect to detect. Beyond it, my eyes see forest, while my Reach sees a tear in the fabric of reality.

"What is it?" Aedan asks, eyes glaring at the trees.

"I see nothing," Pan says, then turns to Aedan. "You?"

"Nothing. I mean... trees, what else is there to see?"

"They are not real," I whisper.

"The trees?" Aedan sounds alarmed. "Monstrous things with hundreds of leafy eyes staring critically at the world, biding their time, waiting for the right opportunity to either crush you with their branches or to swing them away and let the sunlight burn you. They seem real enough to me."

Pan and I exchange silent and slightly worried glances. I knew the Dharkan had issues with trees but never thought them to be this deep. Noticing our expressions, Aedan suddenly becomes extremely interested in the vegetation at his feet. "Just saying..."

"He's right... well, for the most part," Pan says mockingly. "Personally, I can't see anything wrong with these trees. Are you sure, Butterfly?"

I take another look, first with eyes opened, then closed. "Yes... Don't go any further!" I pull Aedan back from the anomaly just before he touches it. "Let me go in first."

"Why? I can handle whatever you can."

I raise a sceptical eyebrow at that.

"Perhaps if you can't see it, it can't harm you," he suggests.

"Because that is usually the case," I reply sarcastically.

"Every rule has exceptions, little goddess."

"Seriously, Aedan. You want to test your theory here, now?"

"Enough, you two," Pan says. "I think Psyche's right."

"Of course you do," Aedan scoffs.

Pan curses at the Dharkan. "Look, up there, the foliage on those branches. See how they ripple in the breeze, as if reflecting in a placid pool?"

Aedan squints at them, then blinks, not disagreeing with the satyr.

"It's a wall, a barrier of sorts. A cover over reality. The section of the forest ahead is in a different realm."

"I see it," Aedan admits. "Maybe it's an entrance to the Underworld or Helheim," he suggests, clearly unconvinced of it himself.

"They appear to our Reach. This does not," I say, then turn to Pan. "Morpheus?"

"Nah," Pan says. "He has no control while we're

awake." His ears shoot up. "Unless we are asleep. Have we fallen asleep without realising?"

I shake my head. Whatever else I may have doubts about, I can still tell the difference between being awake and asleep. This is no dream.

Pan glances in the Stump's direction. "Could *they* have done it?"

"The Nephilim?" I hesitate to dismiss the idea. "No," I say, hoping I'm not wrong. The truth is, I haven't the slightest notion of what they can or cannot do with their technology. I'm still pondering this hypothesis when Aedan simply walks through the barrier and disappears. Ahead of where he used to be, there are only trees, or the illusion of them. "You fucking –"

He runs back out, highly flushed, hands covering his eyes.

"Flaming sun!" he curses.

"What? There's a sun?" Pan asks and, not waiting for an answer, goes through.

Men…

"It's daylight! It's flaming daylight over there!" Aedan spits. "It's white light, but it burns worse than the blue sun." He pats his clothes and face, checking for burns. There are a few blisters on his nose and cheeks.

"What else did you see?"

He glares at me for a moment and then growls, "Daylight."

"Right… Stay here. I'm going in."

He stops fussing with his skin to put himself in my way. "You can't go in."

I roll my eyes. "No. *You* can't go in, apparently. I can, and I'm going to find out what the fuck is going on in there. Don't worry, I'll be fine. I am a goddess, after all."

"I don't like it. I won't allow it!" Poor Dharkan, he's visibly distressed by the experience.

Pan's head reappears, grinning through the illusion like the mad satyr he is. The rest of him is still invisible on the other side. The perceived effect of a bodiless head hovering in mid-air is disconcerting rather than funny.

"Psyche, you need to see this. It's like Elysium over here!" he says excitedly, then vanishes again.

"Like what?" Aedan asks.

"It's a good place," I explain.

"Psyche, don't." He places a trembling hand flat on my chest, holding me back. "Please."

I blink down at his hand. He seems infuriatingly unaware of the breast under it.

"I know you don't trust me, Aedan. But you can't stop me, and you can't follow me either, so you'll just have to deal with it. I very much doubt Ileana is in there, but if I find her, I promise to send her your way."

The Dharkan half shakes his head in protest, his hand moves up to my shoulder, gripping it possessively and, if I didn't know any better, anxiously. I figure this is a splendid opportunity to give him a hug. He stiffens, confused but to my surprise, he clumsily and half-heartedly returns the hug. I pat him on the back with similar gracelessness, smile as reassuringly as I can, turn around and enter another realm.

CHAPTER 21

Loki

Loki fluttered his way to Hel, who was wandering the forest in tears.

Oh, for fuck's sake. How come every woman he met today was crying? Even her! He'd never seen his daughter cry, not even as a child. He supposed he hadn't been around long enough back then to upset her. Now he saw Hel didn't actually shed tears but tiny ice crystals, each reflecting the starlight like diamonds. It was beautiful, so much it almost made him wish she cried more often. *Stars, I'm such a horrible father*, he thought. Then again, she hadn't been the best of daughters either, which probably said more about him than her.

"Daughter," he said loud enough to startle her.

"Burn you! Can't I have a moment to myself?"

"Not right now, no. I heard you were looking for me."

She pulled herself together. One moment she was an emotional young girl, the next an ice giantess, so much like her mother, Angrboda.

"I was," she said. "Where have you been? Do you know what's happening?"

"I know about Fenrir," he replied, ever bored with foolish questions.

Hel made a visible effort not to resume crying in front of him. "Silly pup, I shouldn't have left him there alone."

Loki agreed. "So why did you?"

Hel hesitated, visibly distressed and clearly not wanting to share the reasons behind her distress. "I had to go deal with the faithless, then Tartarus and Persephone and Medusa… Burn it, it's too much, Father!"

"Indeed, sounds like you and Hades have quite the imbroglio with the Olympians. I have no interest in any of that. I came to tell you one thing and ask you another. Fair warning, you won't like either."

Hel stilled her emotions and stared at him intently while he paced in front of her.

"I'll start with the question: Did you or did you not send Psyche away from Asgard?"

"Flaming sun, Father!"

"That's not an answer," he growled.

"Yes! I sent her away. You'd just been accused of murdering Baldur. She'd just turned a goddess – an Olympian goddess, no less. What do you think Odin and Thor would have done had they found her there? Had they known about your… *connection*? I saved her apotheosised ass!"

Loki shook with rage.

"I didn't know she meant that much to you back then…" Hel admitted.

"She could have brought Baldur's soul back and cleared up the whole mess," he said through clenched teeth.

Hel gave him a pitiful look. "And that would have made everything all right, you think? Odin would have freed you, apologised, and given you a prize, no doubt. Hey, I bet he would even have praised me for creating the Dharkan and hiding Apollo in one of them. And after he'd hosted a grand feast in our honour, he would have invited both Psyche and Apollo to be part of the pantheon!" Hel's expression turned bleak. "Seriously, Father. What has that woman done to you?"

A small part of his brain, still somewhat functioning despite the mindless anger, told him Hel was right, and yet it all felt so wrong, so pointless, so unfair he couldn't put it into thoughts, let alone words.

'What you deserve.' Perhaps the truth was what he deserved. Loki didn't dare to speak for fear of what he might say. Moisture began gathering at the corners of his eyes. He definitely wouldn't dare to blink either.

"Freya has taken up residence in one of my Dharkan, by the way. She's the one rallying the faithless," Hel said.

The information barely registered. Hel didn't seem to notice just how far gone his mind was, and so she kept talking. "She's trapped inside her host. Apparently Iva procured Ambrosia through the Cripple, believing she was dealing with the snake hunter. She wanted to be immortal, tsk. Well, I guess he did us a favour without realising and at least we don't have to worry about them for a while."

"Mmmm," Loki mumbled. He wanted to ask something, but the thought slipped away like a whisper amongst screams.

"The funny thing is," Hel continued, still oblivious to his mental state, "you were the only one who knew how Ambrosia affects the Dharkan. And Hephaestus, as talented as he was, had no knack for illusions."

"He learnt fast," Loki replied automatically.

"Burn it, Father, you don't even deny it."

His eyes were dry again. He blinked at her. "We are being truthful here, daughter, are we not?"

"You should have told me. All of it! I could have done things differently."

"Yes you *could* have, had you not been so selfish. And now you're so concerned with the Nephilim, you seem to forget who our real enemies are! Not to mention, your ambition may have cost us everything."

"Well, I guess it runs in the family. Honesty and humility are not our forte, and you, of all creatures, have no right to judge my decisions. You weren't here when the Nephilim felled the tree. And yes, I know now it wasn't your fault but I still had to learn to survive without your help. Isn't that what you wanted?"

"It was…" He squeezed his eyes shut. *What you deserve.* "Well, daughter, then you'd better stop crying and start cleaning up your mess. The Olympian twins won't remain in that room forever. My guess is they're probably negotiating their release as we speak."

Hel winced.

"Cerberus breath!" Hades appeared just inches away from them. He froze, realising his lapse. "Is that what you did to the twins? When you told me they were under your care, I thought you meant you sent them to Helheim or something."

Hel froze. "Hades, if you value any part of yourself, you'll forget everything you heard and vanish again!"

"You know what, Hel? Gladly!"

Loki thought he heard the dark god mumble 'like father, like daughter' under his breath before he vanished. He should have been proud. He was not. He'd always wanted more for Hel. Wanted her to be better that he was.

She sighed, as if coming to a similar conclusion.

"Father, I don't agree with your methods. Even less with your motives. And I know there is a lot you're not telling me yet. Wait, let me finish. Every god is entitled to their secrets, their quirks and petty deeds. And their desires, of course… but you never lost sight of what's important."

"Your point, daughter?"

She stepped closer and kissed him on the cheek. "Thank you. You've done a lot of wrong: to Mother especially, but you've never forsaken your children. Not willingly anyway," she added. "I've only recently learnt to appreciate just how much you did for us."

"Is that you asking me to rescue Fenrir?" he said.

"Maybe…" She smiled.

Like father, like daughter, indeed…

"It's already in motion," he admitted.

Hel's smile vanished. "Please don't tell me you asked Psyche."

"She volunteered."

"Burn it, father! I don't want to owe her."

"You won't. I'll pay the price."

Hel pressed her lips. "What was the other thing you came here to tell me?"

"Chronos is here."

She puffed out an icy breath. "Yes, I know. Gaea told us everything right before she left to confront him, leaving us behind, blind as mortals searching for a way in. Her moods are worse than yours."

He almost laughed at that. "Gaea has a plan. It's a bad one but it might work with your help. Psyche, despite her intentions, will not get to the Stump as quickly as she thinks," Loki said sheepishly. "If you want to find Chronos, I suggest you follow her. Oh, and bring your new Olympian girl*friend*."

Hel froze for a moment, then stomped her foot. "Fine. And what will you do?"

"I'll do what I can," he said, back to his usual mischievous tone. "And er… you might consider reaching out to your other brother in case things don't work out as planned."

Hel's eyes flashed in protest.

"It's an idea. I won't force either of you to reconcile, either way. You have my promise. See you soon, daughter."

"Where are you're going?" she asked.

Loki left without a reply.

CHAPTER 22

Jonas

Jonas rummaged through the ruins of his sanctuary. Around him, everyone else had already forgotten about the pile of charred wood in the middle of Portum's square. They ran past it – or over it sometimes – back and forth like headless chicken, their eyes darting beyond the settlement to the new feature dominating the Aegea landscape. As usual, the denizens of Portum were more interested in something they could do nothing about and probably didn't even concern them, rather than in fixing what used to be beneficial to their lives.

The object of their agitation had appeared during the unusually long night when a bright unnatural light followed by a deafening blare assaulted the land. Jonas had been awake for the whole thing and had not cared one bit. *The gods are at it again,* he'd reckoned, and he refused to pay them any attention. But the rest of the population, the Narrum in particular, reacted as if it was the end of the world. It wasn't. Jonas believed this world would never end, no matter what Judoc said. However, it did change drastically on occasion.

After the commotion subsided, dawn revealed quite the impressive sight, and not even he was indifferent to its sheer magnificence. It was as if the old World Tree trunk had suddenly grown a hood. That was the polite way to put it, of course. Every time Jonas looked at the thing, all he saw was the gods giving mortals the finger. He would laugh, were he less upset with his current situation.

From a distance, the material of this recent addition to the Stump resembled the one used on his fake leg: a glinting grey metal mixed with visible and unidentifiable streaks of black and silver. Perhaps he should be more concerned, for had the Blacksmith built it, such a craft would have cost its volume in blood. Gods did nothing for free, after all. Knowing what he knew of the Nephilim, perhaps that was what the Tributes had paid for – he truly hoped not. Regardless, he was not afraid. Surrounded by the ashes of everything he'd held dear and trying to come to terms with the fact that nothing could be salvaged from the fire, *annoyed* was as far as his emotions went. The monstrosity atop the Stump was just one more escalation in the gods' power games. It had nothing to do with him.

What is the point of gods, anyway? he wondered. He'd prayed to them while he watched his sanctuary burn, and there'd been no reply. There had never been a reply. A good thing Jonas had never needed a god's opinion to survive or to help him decide what to do. All he'd ever needed was a good night's sleep.

Jonas bent to pick up the scorched label of one of his best vintages and groaned in frustration at the waste. By the gods, he was tired. Tired of their games, of their displays of power, their disputes, their creations and interferences in his life. Tired of mortals too: of the Anann with their superiority complex and righteousness, of the Narrum and their small-mindedness and greed, of the Dharkan for… well, being Dharkan. Mostly he was tired of being awake. He always had the right ideas come to him in his sleep. Why couldn't he go back to sleep? Maybe he'd offended Morpheus.

He tutted to himself. Jonas was the one offended by the gods. He wondered if the fire had been a punishment for his deal with Aedan, then shook his head. Talk about self-importance, a trait from his dryad ancestry, no doubt. As if the gods cared about what he agreed with whom. Well, the Nephilim might, but the petty gods of Niflheim, he doubted. Besides, mortals had burned his sanctuary, not gods. All things considered, his guilt over any past or future offences to his own kind diminished substantially with this knowledge.

He froze as a new thought entered his mind. It was all that goddess's fault. She'd come to his establishment without a disguise. She must have done it on purpose, for that, more than anything else, was what caused the riot. Jonas hissed out a breath. Onanist, the insolent little cunt had called him. He'd bet his good leg she'd had something to do with the lightning storms, the fire, and that thing above the Stump as well. Women were devious creatures, and he'd never met a woman more woman than that one. What was Aedan doing with her, anyway? She must have had him under some sort of curse. That would explain how he behaved. The alternative was too bleak to consider.

Satisfied w ith h is c onclusions, J onas s pared one last glance at the Stump and plodded his way up the hill to the temple, staying out of anyone's path in order to avoid any sort of confrontation, or worse, a conversation. People always turned to him when they had questions or needed to talk. He had no issue with that, as long as he remained behind the safety of his counter and they paid him to lubricate their tongues. Being accosted on the street, however, was not something he could handle politely right now.

Once inside, free of the nagging populace, Jonas took a deep breath of relief. At least he still had the temple as shelter and some privacy in the back chamber, hidden away from the women and their children. Most were asleep now, judging by the snores. Morpheus always favoured the weak and the young, soothing their fears with beautiful dreams. He almost envied them.

The previous day had been long, the sort of day better left forgotten; except so much had happened, it made it impossible to forget. He'd lost a friend – maybe two – his sanctuary, all his possessions, or the ones that mattered, anyway. Who would have thought a day which started as any other day would end with his entire supply of spirits going up in flames? He groaned again at the thought. Gods, he could kill for a drink. His mind always worked better with it, but he had none at the temple for sensible reasons. Women could drink like horses given the chance, and there was nothing more annoying than a drunk female.

Jonas sighed, dropped the remains of his old life

on a table then curled himself on the pallet, tired of feeling sorry for himself. And he dreamt.

He woke up with an idea and the urge to draw. There was a piece of charcoal on the floor. He picked it up and began sketching plans for his new sanctuary on the wall. How had he not seen that the destruction of the sanctuary presented him with an opportunity to build something bigger and better than the shabby shelter down the hill had been? He would use the women to build it; the work should keep them busy. The children would help too, the ones who could walk and carry stuff, anyway. It was his firm belief that what all women in Aegea needed was an occupation, something to do besides pestering the men for trinkets and indulging in their breeding obsession. If they had to work all day, as he did, they wouldn't have the energy to waste on others.

Jonas would give them the opportunity to do something substantial, something that made a difference and lasted longer than their miserable lives, maybe then they'd not be so keen on motherhood in the first place. After all, having children was the only meaningful act they were allowed to perform.

Jonas would give them purpose.

His mind raced with possibilities as he drew. Instead of building a new watering hole, he'd expand the temple, taking advantage of its sturdy foundations and stone walls. It was much better to build with stone than wood. Harder to burn down, for one thing. Also harder to source, unfortunately. While wood was close and plentiful, good stone had to be quarried from the crags up on the way to the Gharb. He pursed his lips.

Women and children would be useless for such a task, and even if he used every able man in the area, such an enterprise could take years. That was too long. To build a stone structure properly and quickly, Jonas would need the help of the gods. He pondered this predicament, tapping his lips with the tip of the charcoal without realising the consequences. There had to be a better way. Bricks, maybe? Narrum had been experimenting with blocks of dried mud. Perhaps if they then piled them correctly, it would work.

Jonas kept drawing, his thoughts infused with inspiration and vigour until suddenly his mind stumbled on another problem. He'd need tools as well. And he'd rather not have to ask the Blacksmith for those. Being a god, he could probably build the whole temple all by himself, but… Jonas touched his leg. No. One favour was enough. To craft his leg, Hephaestus had demanded some of his seed and blood. He dreaded to think what he would want for a complete building. The fewer gods involved, the better. This would not be a temple for them, but for Jonas and any other man seeking refuge from the world's madness.

Delighted with his newfound skill – He could draw! Who knew? – Jonas continued drawing monochrome lines and gradients on the wall, ignoring the scrambling of feet, the snores of children and the mindless talk of their mothers, until suddenly all noise vanished. Deep in the haze of artistic creation, he did not notice this until he felt sure he was being watched. It was probably one of children, he thought. They liked to hide behind the curtains to glimpse the shrine whenever he was in the temple. Quite rude, really, but what could one expect from children? A distinct sound of boots on the marble floor behind him followed. Not a child then; they were all barefoot. Annoyed, Jonas pushed aside the curtain to the antechamber and saw death, smiling, almost flirting with him in broad daylight.

"Iva," he said curtly.

"Hello, Shrine. May I come in?"

"You already have."

For some irrational reason, Jonas had always imagined Dharkan would burst into flames inside the temple. Surely the gods could have warded their temples against the Wraiths in such a fashion. Sadly, there was not so much as a wisp as she walked under the skylight.

"I suppose I have." Iva kept walking in his direction, looking around, lips parted in awe or confusion, he couldn't tell. The Dharkan's facial expressions were always open to interpretation.

"Quite the talent you have here." Iva touched the wall with the tips of her fingers, and frost immediately spread over the stone. "It's been too long since we last spoke."

Not long enough, he thought.

"You looked better back then." She smirked.

"Likewise," he said, questioning the state of her attire. She wore a cloak as a cape over her shoulders and looked as if she'd crawled from the very muddy ashes of his sanctuary and then fought a gryphon on her way up to the temple. Aedan's work, Jonas figured. Except Iva was the one there, not him.

Her fingers caressed the marble wall. "Reminds

me of Asgard," she said absently and longingly. Her eyelids closed while she hummed something to herself.

Jonas frowned. There was something disturbingly different about Iva, besides her attire. She used to be abrupt in speech and manner. Now her demeanour was gentler, her voice more feminine, though somewhat bitter. "Are you... alone?" he asked.

"I'm never alone these days." She sighed.

She was hosting. Well, that explained why she was so comfortable in daylight. "Here, I mean," he added, hoping to learn more about her intentions.

She gave him a condescending smile.

No wonder the women had gone quiet.

"Is Aedan with you?" he ventured.

The room instantly turned cold. "No. Your friend is too busy to save you now."

Busy, not dead, Jonas thought. "That's a shame," he said.

"You know why I'm here, yes?" she asked.

"I have an idea." A pretty good one. How Jonas wished he had hidden some liquor in the temple.

"So how is it going to be?" Iva asked, grey eyes fixed menacingly on him.

"Are you giving me options?"

"For old time's sake." Somewhere from under the folds of her cloak, Iva produced a small flask and passed it to him. "Hey. I got you this as well."

Jonas' eyes widened in delight. "Where did you find it?"

"Does it matter?"

Jonas considered the question for a moment. "No."

He uncorked the bottle and drank the contents in deep, thirsty swallows. It was a poor vintage, amateurish. Likely made by one of the forest folk. "Much appreciated."

She walked to the fountain, filled a cup with water and raised it at him. "Cheers."

"What are we celebrating?"

"That depends," she said ominously.

He eyed her cup critically as she drank. "You know. I never understood why Dharkan only drink water."

Iva put down the empty cup, licking her lips. "Personally, I don't like the taste of alcoholic beverages, but I can hardly speak for my entire race." She paused, tilting her head. "Why do you drink? Dryads need constant hydration as I understand it; alcohol dehydrates you and makes you stupid to boot." She smiled to herself. "It is a trait common to gods and mortals alike, when you think about it. I know why gods drink; they enjoy numbing their brains and acting like fools, but mortals... Where does this proclivity to ruin your bodies come from? Defiance, maybe? Do you think that by tempting death, you have more control over your life?"

Jonas was beyond annoyed now. "I can't speak for all mortals. Personally, I just like the taste," he sneered, then swallowed the rest of the bottle's contents, hoping it was reason enough for her to find him unappetising.

She shook her head. "That's all right. You only need to speak for those inside this temple."

"Regarding what subject?"

"Their lives, of course. I'm here to offer you the

same deal I offered the shrine in Lagus: His life in exchange for the lives of his worshippers."

"How generous."

She shrugged. "It was wasted generosity, really. He hanged himself shortly after we left. I don't know why he bothered to make a deal."

"I suppose death was not what frightened him. Or maybe he wanted to keep his life for himself."

Iva raised her eyebrows. "Mightily selfish, I say. A waste of Prana."

"It was his Prana to waste."

She pursed her lips. "While we don't waste any. Dharkan *are* an honourable race, despite what everyone thinks. You, better than most people, know this."

"I do, but here's the thing. I too am an honourable man." Or he liked to think so.

"You were always fair to our people, yes," she conceded.

"Because I believed you weren't so bad once we got to know you. Was I wrong?"

Her voice changed again. "Is fire bad because it burns?"

"When it burns out of control, yes." His sanctuary was proof of it.

Her lips curved into a sly smile. "Dharkan are ironically like fire. We burn our way through life."

"And yet a Dharkan saved my life," Jonas said earnestly.

Iva raised her eyebrows. "So I heard. A manticore attack, was it?"

Jonas guffawed. "The last time I heard the story

being told, it was a chimera. People love to exaggerate. No, nothing so legendary, just a wild boar, I'm afraid. There used to be scores of them in the forest back in the day."

"How disappointing," she sighed. "But, easier to believe, I suppose. Even Aedan wouldn't dare freeze a manticore."

"Not back then," Jonas pointed out.

Iva sent him a withering glance, then nodded. "Not back then."

Silence fell. The bottle was empty, and he was still sober.

"The thing is, I have no authority to negotiate with you, Iva."

Her eyes narrowed. "Why not?"

"I owed Aedan. And recently he collected his debt."

"Did he," she said dryly.

"The women. They are all his, you see. Not mine. I'm not even a shrine anymore. I have no god to speak for since he slew the Suzerain."

"We have a new Suzerain by the looks of things." Iva tipped her head in the direction of the Stump.

Ah, she's hosting, and yet she doesn't know what landed on the Stump either. That's interesting.

"If we do, I've yet to meet him."

"Aedan has abandoned any claim to spoils, or our people. His property is mine," she said impatiently.

"Except it's not," he insisted matter-of-factly.

Iva stepped closer. Close enough for him to see through the ragged remains of fabric covering her chest. He disliked the way women used their breasts to make men uncomfortable, particularly when said women were taller than he was.

"Where's this honour you just mentioned, Jonas?"

Jonas looked up at her pallid face. He'd lost interest in breasts around the time he stopped sucking on his mother's. As to his honour…

"Most went up in flames with the rest of my possessions," he said. "The rest is mine to keep."

She bristled. Beads of sweat froze at the roots of her hair.

"But perhaps we can compromise," he interjected before she iced him.

"Compromise?" She laughed. "Jonas, come on, we're not gods."

"No. We are mortals." He hesitated, looking her up and down with disgust. "To some extent, anyway. Tell me, what happened to the women from Lagus after you took them?"

"My men were hungry. We travelled long under the sun."

"So you killed them."

"Not all at once, but… eventually, yes. We prefer not to, you know that. It just… happens sometimes. Had we a larger herd and a permanent settlement to feed upon, they would live much longer and the Dharkan wouldn't be as hungry. The gods knew what they were doing when they brought dryads to this world. It's a pity we can't make them see that."

Jonas felt no pity. He was, after all, half dryad. "Perhaps if you showed more restraint in your feeding. What will happen when you freeze all the living?"

She almost smiled. "We've found more nutritious prey."

"Is that so? More dangerous too, judging by your state. You really think this a good time to rally against the gods?"

She acted surprised. "It's the perfect time. Look outside. The gods have their hands full."

"I have a better suggestion."

"Oh?"

"Help us rebuild. Portum is a mud hole filled with women, children and old men with nothing to do, nowhere to go."

"Which is precisely why we are here."

He ignored her, pointing at the wall behind him. "I have a plan to turn this ruin into a settlement greater than Relicum. It's going to take time and manpower, so I could use good strong Dharkan for the task. And I bet the Dharkan could use Prana and companions. Even you can't be everything for them, Iva."

Her jaw tensed.

"Think about it. A permanent source of nourishment – *willing* nourishment. Isn't that what you wanted?"

Iva leaned against the opposite wall, staring him up and down. "It was. But I already told you. Things have changed. And you just told me the women weren't yours to give."

"I'm not giving them away, I'm just… lending their nutritional services for a while. Aedan imposed no such restrictions on that account. As long as everyone remains alive and well, what's the harm?" Gods, he couldn't believe he'd just said that, but he said it with a straight face and Iva seemed to be considering his words. A good thing gods can't Reach when being hosted by the Wraiths.

"How will you convince them to agree to such a deal?"

"I know how they think. Right now, they are more scared of the thing on the Stump than you. Help us rebuild, keep us safe and provide enough food for the children, and you'll find women, mothers in particular, can be quite… grateful." He waved a hand. "Sure, gods may be more fulfilling, but they are tougher prey. Do you really want a battle with them every time you need to feed?"

Iva looked at him quizzically. "Are you actually offering the women to my men?"

"*Lending*. And yes, not just the women, the men and children too. I offer you the whole settlement, if you refrain from overindulging, of course. This way, we'll both get what we want."

"For now." She then narrowed her eyes suspiciously. "Did Aedan put you up to this?"

Jonas didn't have to work himself up for this reply. "It's because of Aedan my sanctuary is destroyed," he said through gritted teeth. "The breeders and these plans" – he pointed at the wall – "are all I have left, so pardon me for trying to make the best out of the situation, without losing *all* my honour."

In fact, this had been Aedan's idea, forcibly imposed on him, Jonas might have added. It had seemed heartless at the time, but now, he finally understood the plan. Aedan must have considered the possibility Iva would not step down just because he asked her and had wanted to stall her incursion for as long as possible. He'd been in a darker mood than usual when they last talked, brooding with concern. Perhaps the annoying goddess was only partly to blame on that account, for something odd was definitely afoot in the world, and Iva seemed to be more victim than villain in the grand scheme of things.

Iva's guest wasn't convinced. "Is this a trick? Who gifted you, mortal?" She looked closer into his eyes and prepared to touch his face.

He slapped her hand away. "Hey! No touching. I'm off the feeding chart. It's part of the deal."

"Seems you're off character as well."

"It's what happens to character, given enough misfortune. And to be fair, you know I was always on *my* side, Iva. What did the Anann or Narrum ever do for me? What did the Suzerain? Or you or the gods? I've spent my entire life here, staying clear of conflicts. Picking up the pieces after each one. I'm sick of it."

"Still seems like an excessive amount of betrayal to live with."

"You'd be surprised with the things I have to live with." He touched his leg unconsciously.

Her eyelids fluttered for a moment, then she began talking to herself in an unfamiliar language. The argument was heated. Whoever the deity she hosted was, they didn't seem to like each other very much. How awful it must be to carry someone else's soul inside you.

He felt his skin prickle with impatience. The drawing on the wall, not yet finished, called for his attention.

"Stay," he said, hoping to force a favourable resolution to their argument. "Help me for a few days, at least until we know what's going on. I heard Relicum is building itself up for a fight."

"Against us?"

"Against anything. They just want to fight. And they have the numbers to win."

She snorted. "The people outside may not be as many, but they won't welcome us peacefully either, Jonas."

"Listen, of all the settlements in Aegea, Portum is the most forgiving of the Dharkan. Just… don't ice anyone, and they will tolerate you. They have more terrifying things to concern themselves with – no offence. I'll handle anyone who might have reservations about the arrangement. They always listen to me."

"I cannot fathom why," she said in the other voice.

He pretended not to have noticed the slip, as he did the previous times. Iva's mind had never been stable. Now it seemed to be going through a revolt. One more reason not to let her argue with herself for too long.

"Help me gather stone for the foundation at least. There's a good chance these Nephilim are as ruthless as everyone says. And if they contact me, wouldn't you rather look like you're on their side, helping their former shrine rebuild a temple in their honour?"

Iva sucked her teeth. Obviously this was far from what she had in mind when she arrived at the settlement. Still, her goddess appeared to be appeased by this argument.

"Very well." She pointed a finger at him. "But if anyone looks at us the wrong way, or tries anything against us, everyone dies."

∞

Everyone did not die. Though a few did.

Those who did not submit immediately were iced on the spot. And it only took a couple of demonstrations for the population to become subdued to the Dharkan's presence.

Soon, everyone in Portum forgot about the structure atop the Stump, the fire and the storm. No one was happy with their new masters, mind, but mortals are nothing if not adapted for survival. They will obey and even praise any lord: mortal, divine or dead alike, as long as they have something to gain, even if that something is just another moment alive.

By the evening, Jonas had completed the plans for his new sanctuary. It would be beautiful, much grander than the one in Relicum. And Portum would never be the same.

CHAPTER 23

Ideth

"So you're telling me this crap has power?" Ideth asked, examining the flasks in Martha's collection dubiously. The one in her hand contained what appeared to be blood. She pulled the cork out, and the pungent smell of vinegar filled her nostrils, bringing tears to her eyes. "Freezing goddess!" She stuck the cork back in.

Hecate snatched the flask from her hands and placed it back on the shelf. "Martha had the real power. This crap… well, it's mostly just crap, but when combined the right way by the right person…" She smiled at a rat's skull. "It's magic."

Ideth blinked at her. Clearly, the time spent in the Underworld had taken a toll on the goddess's sanity.

Apparently Martha had been an expert in healing potions, spells and deadly poisons thanks to Hecate, who had been teaching sorcery to the Narrum woman for years using a blood-based version of Reach able to penetrate realms.

"You talked through blood?" Ideth had asked incredulously. Considering all she'd learnt in the last few days, it was shocking how some things still challenged her comprehension.

"Few Narrum possess the ability," Hecate continued. "Let alone the desire to learn how to make use of what's available in nature. They rely on their senses too much. Worse, they think everything around them exists only to provide for their needs. Martha knew better. She could perceive the realms beyond her senses and she understood the power contained within herbs and bones and blood. I looked forward to meeting her in person. Her friendship was such a comfort, during my imprisonment." She sighed. "But every action requires a reaction. Balance must be maintained. Everything has a price, etcetera. The Underworld lost a soul, therefore another soul had to replace it, I suppose."

"With interest," Chiron piped up from outside the cabin, his tone thick with reproach.

"The child's soul was part of hers," Hecate pointed out.

"And the husband's?"

"He forfeited his life when he shot the Elysian horse."

"I wonder who gave him *that* idea."

"Artemis, most likely."

Chiron tutted. "She's insane and vicious, but she would never dare to take the life of an Elysian horse."

"No, she wouldn't; and he wouldn't do anything without her say-so. Don't you dare blame me for that tragedy, Titan. I'm not the one who encouraged her to hunt outside the forest, nor did I set the bounty for the horn."

"Are you implying that *I* am the one to blame for –"

He paused. "What did you say?" Chiron tried to drag himself closer to the entrance so he could look at them. It ripped Ideth's heart to see him in that state, but she refrained from going to his aid, knowing it would only make him feel weaker.

"Haven't you heard of Hephaestus' bounty?" Hecate replied, amused. "He badly wanted an Elysian horse's horn."

"Why would he…" Chiron trailed off, eyes growing wide.

"He was always searching for powerful items to embed in his crafts. Funny how Elysian horses are so dear to the gods, and yet there's fewer and fewer of them in their worlds," Hecate mused.

"Did he get it?" Chiron asked apprehensively. "Before he died, I mean."

"He's dead?" Hecate seemed pleasantly surprised by the news.

Chiron clicked his tongue, chastising himself for the slip. The Blacksmith's death obviously did not sit well with him, neither did the fact he was now the focus of Hecate's attention.

Ideth swallowed, her gaze bouncing between the two. She'd heard of this Hephaestus, of course. He'd been the one who gave her the Ambrosia. Well, he gave it to the Suzerain, and he then gave it to her.

"How did he die?" Hecate asked.

"I don't know the details, just that he is not in *our* Underworld," Chiron said. It must have been at least partly true, for the goddess did not press him for more.

"Oh well, good riddance." She shrugged and continued scrolling through Martha's ingredients.

Ideth, who had been hyper-cautious of her words since she realised the gravity of her predicament, wanted to ask Chiron for more information about this dead god or ask the goddess why she was so pleased with his death, but she took too long to decide which and so missed the opportunity for either.

"Ha, found it," Hecate said triumphantly, holding a clay pot. She stepped out of the cabin and showed it to the centaur.

He eyed the pot dubiously. "What's in it?"

Ideth supposed Reach was not available in his mortal state.

Hecate scrunched her face. "Better if you don't know. It will hurt like a manticore sting at first, but it will stop the rot from spreading."

When she opened the lid, he wrinkled his nose. His eyes widened, and he pulled back from it as far as he could. "Can't you just heal me like a normal deity?"

Hecate assumed a defensive stance. "You know very well my powers are linked to the moon."

"What is a moon?" Ideth asked.

"Precisely," Hecate replied dryly. Her snake eyes focused back on Chiron and the pot in her palm. "This is all I have to work with. Take it or leave it. Either way, he won't let you die, no matter how much you suffer." They glanced at Xylo, basking in the clearing with his eyes closed. He spent a lot of time immobile under the sun. "Listening," he'd explained to them. Ideth doubted many would pray to the Chronodéndrons. Whatever he was listening to, it probably wasn't meant for his ears, their conversations included.

Chiron looked sick in every sense of the word, but

reluctantly turned over, exposing the worst of his injuries to the goddess.

"Let me do it," Ideth said. "After all, aren't I supposed to learn how to use these ointments?"

"You're supposed to learn how to make them first," Hecate replied. "Not to mention it's grisly work for a nymph."

"This nymph is well used to grisliness."

Hecate's heads seemed to shake all at once, momentarily overlapping each other before she handed the small pot to Ideth. "Very well. It's your stomach. Make sure you cover every inch of the wounds. I'll gather the ingredients to prepare something more appropriate for a centaur's flesh."

Hecate moved away in Xylo's direction. "Chronos, are my herbs fully grown yet?"

Ideth stilled her stomach and got on with her task, taking the opportunity to talk to Chiron in private. Or under the illusion of privacy, at least.

"Why didn't you tell me, Chiron?"

He flinched both at the question and the stinky paste touching his flesh. "Do we have to do this now, unbridled one?"

"You promised me the next time we met you'd tell me about Orion." She wondered if gods remain bound to their promises when they become mortal. *They'd better.*

"There's not much to tell." Chiron sucked in a sharp breath as she continued her ministrations less gently. "Artemis couldn't have him, so she made sure no one could. I didn't want to upset you, unbridled one."

"You told me he would live again through me. You lied," she hissed.

"It was a metaphor – ow! You were so distraught. I had to tell you something to give you hope, to help you through motherhood. I promised him I would take care of you. His transformation was supposed to be temporary, just until Artemis' anger subsided. But then the Suzerain came and..."

"And he took my baby. And you, instead of acting like a god and taking him back, you let me fall prey to his schemes! Now I'm here, with *him*" – she pointed at Xylo – "instead of Orion, my son hates me, and you're dying!"

Chiron shrank away from her outburst. "Zeus assured me he had the Suzerain under control."

"Pfff," Ideth said. Everyone knew how well *that* turned out.

She took a moment to calm herself before speaking again. "I can feel him, you know. Looking after me, longing for me. Artemis is as good as iced. Why is Orion not back?"

"Artemis wasn't the one who cursed him, unbridled one. It was her brother, Apollo. And now, who knows what Loki did with the sun."

Ideth stared back at him, confused.

"Apollo used Orion to create the blue sun."

Her jaw slacked. Suddenly, the vision she'd had while kissing Psyche made sense. Orion wasn't amongst the stars, he *was* a star. The one responsible for life in Aegea; the one Loki had hid so Aedan could get to the Suzerain – *oh, no...*

"You can still feel him? Even after Loki hid the sun?" Chiron asked incredulously.

"I could. Not anymore. Not in here…" she whispered, still considering the implications.

"That's good, I think." By his tone, Chiron really wasn't sure. "If he still exists outside this realm, then the curse can be broken."

"Do you believe I have the power to do it?" she asked.

Chiron smiled. "If anyone can learn how to break a god's curse, it is you, unbridled one."

"Liar. You always said I couldn't be taught a thing."

He chuckled bitterly. "I may have been wrong."

She put on a brittle smile and focused on her task with diligence, determined to save him and Orion both.

"Ideth." His tone was serious. She lifted her gaze to meet his and stilled herself to hold it. "My wounds are not the result of a god's curse. You cannot save me. In a way, I died a long time ago. This life here in Aegea was only an extension. I always knew I'd have to face my fate, as Apollo prophesied. There is nothing you can do."

She was starting to hate this Apollo, more than she did his sister. Before she could say anything back, Chiron continued.

"Promise me that when the time comes, you won't interfere."

"I –"

"Promise."

She bit her lip. "I promise."

Hecate inspected Ideth's work when she returned and nodded her approval. "Not bad, not bad at all. Do you care to learn how to make it now?"

"Yes. Teach me everything," Ideth said.

CHAPTER 24

Seshat

"Lady Seshat? Er… I mean, sire?" Toman called.

"Up here," Seshat replied in Judoc's voice.

Toman's eyes followed the sound to the top of the domed roof. He knew what she was, of course. The boy wasn't the brightest of mortals, but since he did most of the work around the temple, she figured it was best to keep him in the loop of their current situation. He'd taken it surprisingly well. Perhaps due to ignorance or slow wit, the notion of shapeshifting deities did not perturb him as it would other Narrum.

He grimaced, muttering a few reproachful words to himself, then said, "My lady, I must advise against such reckless behaviour."

She glared at him. "I'd rather you didn't."

"But, my lady, someone might see you –" he insisted.

She slid down the stone tiles and landed on her feet, graceful as a cat. "I'm a goddess, not a lady." She let her eyes glint to reinforce the statement. This always seemed to make him uncomfortable and eager to get to his point.

"Yes, my – goddess," Toman murmured, staring down at his sandals.

Thin and insipid, the new temple attendant was the opposite of Fabrian in almost every way. Seshat supposed this was the main reason Iosh chose him, so he would not be reminded of his friend at every turn. To Seshat he had the opposite effect; she missed Fabrian dearly every time she had to deal with the creature.

"Well, why did you feel the need to come up here?" she asked patiently. "Any word from Iosh?"

"Er... no, lady goddess. But there's a man who wants to see you."

A man? Not another hormone driven woman demanding to be impregnated? That was refreshing. Even Hermes was having trouble keeping up with all of them. "Where is he?"

"Just outside."

Her Reach showed nothing. There was no light, no soul, no sound or smell behind the doorway. That was... wrong. Her wits might have temporarily abandoned her, but not her Reach.

"Have you spoken to him?"

"Yes, goddess."

"Who is he?"

"He didn't say. He only said he wanted to see you, and he knew you by name." He lowered his voice. "Your real name."

That didn't bode well. "Send him in," she said, for a god should never show weakness before a mortal.

Toman left to fetch the visitor, and Seshat checked her disguise. She wore an aspect identical to Judoc except around the eyes. She always liked to keep something of hers, and at least with this one she could wear kohl. Judoc never did, but no one questioned the new look either. If anything, it made his appearance even more appealing to the women.

A tall, slim figure with broad shoulders draped in a thick ebony cloak stepped onto the balcony. Two grey eyes shone underneath the hood.

Seshat took a step back. *Dharkan!* No wonder her Reach didn't work. She searched the area again, aware of what to look for.

"I'm alone," he said in a young man's voice as he pulled the hood back.

The youthful features matched the voice. He resembled Aedan. Then again, all Dharkan resembled Aedan to her eyes, but there was something about his nose and brow that made the resemblance closer than most.

"You have some nerve coming here in broad daylight, whoever you are. I advise you not to come any closer," she warned, preparing to burn him at the slightest threat.

"Is it courage when there's no danger?" He looked up, where only the weak white sun adorned the sky.

Seshat chuckled. "No danger? My boy, I can burn you to ashes."

He grinned. "Ah, that you could. It would be a shame to destroy this vessel, though."

Vessel? Cats, she should have guessed the boy was just a borrowed shell. "Who are you?"

"Has it been so long you no longer remember me, sunshine?"

"Apparently," she said dryly. The familiar nickname

wasn't enough to decipher who the god behind the Dharkan was. When you're a goddess of light, every other lover calls you sunshine. *Not Loki, though*, she mused, pushing him out of her mind. If not for him, she wouldn't be in this mess.

"We're both wearing strangers' faces, and yet I see you exactly as I remember," the young Dharkan said dreamily.

"And what, exactly, do you remember?" She sure did not remember him.

He smiled deviously. "I'd rather not make you blush wearing that boyish veneer."

She wasn't amused. "Who. Are. You."

"I am a friend."

"Not my friend."

"You don't remember me. I understand. I made it so, after all."

Seshat felt hollow... "Mnemosyne?" she whispered.

He laughed. "No. Although I am impressed with her work." He moved closer and touched her wrist before she regained enough sense to pull back. At his touch, her soul wrenched itself into a coiling mess of desire and revulsion. She felt what she'd often felt around Judoc: an unwelcomed burn of unjustified arousal, only tenfold. She jerked the hand away.

"Here. I have a gift for you." He pulled a small box from the folds of his cloak, black, with no ornamentation.

She stared at it, confused.

"Take it." He gestured.

Seshat hesitated, resisting the compulsion to do it.

"It won't bite." He smirked.

"What is it?" she croaked. The box, much like the thing over the Stump, did not appear in her Reach.

"A box," he said.

She narrowed her eyes at him, starlight about to burst through them.

"I want you to keep it safe until I tell you to use it," he said.

"I don't take orders from you!" The insolence of this creature.

"Yes, you do." There was that lewd smirk again, so at odds with the young Dharkan's innocent features. "Have you ever wondered why you go back to the Trickster again and again, Seshat?"

She blinked. "What?"

He gave her a wink. "Take it." As he handed her the box, his index finger touched hers, and a shiver ran down her spine. The sinking feeling began in her stomach, turned to longing when it reached her chest, to lust between her thighs, rage in her clenched jaw, revulsion at the back of her throat. All this she felt at once, and the one responsible for it was unmistakable.

"Oh, cats! It is you!" Eros, the Olympian god of love. Suddenly, Iosh, her feelings around him, her absent-mindedness, perhaps even her affair with Loki, everything made sense. Well, everything except the box.

"How…?" she mumbled. Gravity suddenly seemed stronger, and she absently searched for a wall to help her remain standing.

"Let's just say, sometimes I'm amazed by my own power." He kissed her on the mouth, biting her lower lip, dragging it slowly and painfully between his teeth.

She wanted to protest. Demand explanations. Scream. Burn him away. She did none of those things. Her will was his. So she remained silent and still.

He pressed the box into her hand when he was done. "Consider this my attempt to make amends – a peace offering. The closest thing you'll ever get to an apology. And you'll need it."

Seshat turned the box in her shaky hands.

"Don't open it," he warned mockingly. "Unless you intend to use it."

"What's inside?" she asked almost to herself.

"Blood of the Hydra."

Seshat dropped the box, flaring in fright.

Down at the forum, voices raised in alarm at the sudden glare.

He picked up the box and gave it back to her. "Calm yourself unless you intend to ignite the crowd. If I wanted you dead, you'd be so already."

"I'm not easy to kill," she hissed. The words, although true, sounded hollow in the presence of such a weapon.

"Neither are they." He pointed at the Stump.

She followed his gaze, absently gripping the box tighter.

"Why give me this?"

"For safekeeping. I'd rather give it to the shrine, but he's not available, sadly, and these vessels are too flammable to be trusted with valuables."

"You gifted Judoc..." It was not a question.

He clicked his tongue. "Obviously. If I hadn't, others would have. He's a metz. A spirit with enough soul mingled within to make the perfect puppet. Why possess his body if I can possess his mind easily instead? And I didn't even have to spend much talent on his looks or energy trying to convince him, either. He's a firm believer in love, ruled by desire. I could not have asked for a more dedicated subject. Judoc would burn for love!" He laughed. She could only scowl. "Oh, come on, Seshat. Each player has their pawns. I did nothing others weren't doing as well. Not all of us have the luxury to play out different characters, or to just stand back and watch the play."

She traced the edges of the box, torn between dread and the overwhelming desire to use it on him. It wouldn't work, though. Not while he was in that Dharkan's body.

"Is that why you're in disguise?" she asked. "You always looked down on gods who hide behind mortals. There are only two reasons for a disguise: survival and harmful intent."

"Aren't they basically the same reason?" he asked, amused. "One's survival often means harming another. Life is energy. The more you hoard it, the less is left for others. Gaea's rule, not mine. See how well it worked out for her." He laughed again.

Better than you'd think, Seshat thought. The sum is more than the parts. Gaea hadn't sacrificed her power; she invested it in every living creature in the Universe, weakening herself, true. But Life became something more powerful than any god.

"How can you trust me with this? I hate you," she said.

He shrugged. "Everyone does, it seems. Honestly,

people can't tell the difference between love and hate sometimes. But I know you. Better than you know yourself, chronicler. You don't take sides, you don't interfere... Well, not really." He smiled in a way that told her he knew all about the events that led her to her current disguise. "And I dare say you hate the Nephilim a great deal more than me."

At the moment, she wasn't too sure about that. "Everyone thought you were dead," she whispered, still trying to understand what it all meant in the grand scheme of things.

"Thought or wished?"

"Both," she admitted. "There's been no record of you since..." *Psyche's apotheosis,* she thought to herself.

Beads of ice appeared on the Dharkan's forehead. "I've been searching."

"For what?"

"*Her,*" he said with such loathing Seshat shivered. Cats, the world did not need his revenge right now, on top of everything else.

He pulled the hood of his cloak up. "I suggest you use your preaching privileges to convince the population that the Dharkan are not the enemy. You and the other real gods will need them if the Titan is set free."

"For what?"

"Survive. Their numbers are limited, though. There won't be enough for everyone." He laughed again, in earnest this time.

"You winged bastard." Seshat wanted to burn him to cinders.

"Ouch. Just because I don't know who my father is doesn't make me a bastard."

"He's not your mother's husband, so a bastard is exactly what it makes you."

He waved a finger at her. "You were always better at words than me, Seshat. I'd gladly stay here and lose every verbal battle with you. Alas, I have other battles to attend to. Time is not on our side."

"Neither is your host. Even without the sun, a Dharkan is a risky disguise, especially in settlements."

"Only until you deliver your next speech," he said. "Don't concern yourself with me, my host, or my reasons, sunshine. Just do what I told you. I'll know if you don't, and I will return for the box. So don't lose it."

There was no mirth in his voice, nor his gaze, when he said these words. He began walking backwards, whistling to himself and keeping her in his line of sight, or maybe not letting himself leave hers. He smirked one last time, hid his face beneath the hood and vanished down the stairs.

'Why are you still here, Seshat?' Loki had asked her.

She had no proper answer to give him then. She thought she had one now.

∞

Seshat ran her fingertips through endless sheets of papyrus, keeping her eyes on the black box resting on the marble floor next to her as if it were about to sprout needles. It might, for all she knew.

She'd been searching through everything she'd ever written, hunting for clues as to Eros' real reason for giving it to her. He said he'd made her forget. Forget what? She seemed to remember him in great detail now. However, something was missing, she was sure.

She always wrote down everything so she wouldn't forget even the most insignificant events in the lives of gods, but she hadn't written much about her own life events. She always trusted she would remember those, even after her disagreement with Mnemosyne, but now... now she wondered. The truth was, no matter how hard she tried to stay neutral, the speech she gave impersonating the Suzerain had not been the first time she'd inserted herself in a story. The narrator often leaves their mark on the narrative, after all. And there was something Eros had said or, more precisely, the way he'd said it, that set her mind on a quest to find out the truth behind the memory.

"Ah! Finally!"

Seshat pulled out a yellowed sheet from the pile in front of her. The title read: The Trial of Prometheus.

She chewed on the tip of her quill as she read.

It hadn't been her first visit to Midgard. She'd been there before, recording the atrocities of the Titanomachy, then later, when her pantheon's interest in the new race of mortals taking over the world had rekindled the conflict with the Olympians. A conflict so petty she had, at first, refused to keep it on record. But when Zeus accused Prometheus of crimes against the gods, she had no choice but to be there to record it.

The trial hadn't been triggered by a dispute or even a battle of wills between deities. This was a whole pantheon united to sentence a god to eternal suffering. More than a punishment, it was an act that bent all their rules and spoke more about the character flaws of the accusers than the crimes of the accused. For the first time in her long existence, she'd wished she could do more than just watch and record the atrocity, but record it she must. It was also the first time she'd met Loki. And the way Eros mentioned him – the very fact that he had – told her this might be important.

Loki had caught her eye early in the proceedings. He had a light of his own, different from any other she'd seen before or since. He'd disguised himself as a fly, eavesdropping on everyone before he'd settled on Prometheus' shoulder. The Titan's chains, dutifully crafted by the master crafter, Hephaestus, were made of a metal not found in any of the worlds she'd visited – and she'd visited many. They nullified the god's physical and telepathic powers. *Just like the vault*, she realised, and squirmed at the memory of her light being extinguished inside that cursed room. Nothing had ever extinguished her light. No Dharkan, no weapon, not even Chronos himself, only that cursed room. She clicked her tongue. Had she dared spend more time inside it, she might have come to this realisation sooner.

Back at the trial, the audacity of this strange god's intrusion – never mind his disguise – had been enough to earn her interest. She'd thought about warning the others, she probably should have, but back then she'd still been true to herself and so she hadn't interfered. Those present were not part of her pantheon and therefore not her responsibility. Besides, the trial was as close to a god's execution as it got, which was far more important than a rival interloper taking notes for himself.

She kept him in the corner or her awareness, curious to see what he would do. When the trial started, he, like her, had stood inconspicuously in the shadows a fair distance away. Except he hadn't been writing, he was just spying on the other gods, carefully studying their reactions to the accusations. Himself showing no reaction at all. Eventually her curiosity got the best of her. "Curiosity kills cats," Ra always said.

"You're not Olympian," she'd said to Loki as she 'accidentally' bumped into him. One of her cringiest lines ever; no wonder she'd forgotten this.

He'd smiled, as if being caught was a pleasant surprise. She'd been immediately drawn to that mischievous smile.

"Neither are you," he'd replied appraisingly.

"I have an invitation," she'd countered.

"I am a friend of the accused."

This had surprised her then. And it shocked her now. "Shouldn't you be over there, in that case? With him?"

"I fear my presence would only hinder his defence." Loki had sounded sincere, and when he lowered his eyes, she'd fallen for him.

"Ah," she'd said. She knew every word in every language, and that was the best she'd come up with? Looking back, she realised she never stood a chance against his charm. Except he wasn't being charming then. He wasn't even trying to seduce her. He was just... sad. She'd never found emotion to be attractive, quite the contrary, and yet in that moment, with him, it was worth an entire dissertation. And to think the reason she'd been far from the crowd with her senses on high alert was to avoid being seduced by another god. A god with whom, later that day, after Prometheus had been condemned to everlasting torment and Loki had left her without even a farewell, she would find solace.

Cats…

Eros had been pursuing her since the Titans' war. He was gorgeous, for sure, but he was also too smug and too attached to his mother for her tastes. Seshat wanted nothing to do with Aphrodite. The goddess of love always made her skin crawl: not Olympian, nor Titan. Not even that beautiful, just… alluring as a black hole. Any god who used lust as a weapon had Seshat's disdain. And still she'd ended up under Eros' thrall.

"Lady sire?" Toman's voice sounded as if he stood right on top of her.

"Not now," Seshat hissed from behind a pile of conjured manuscripts. He shuffled away. Funny, she hadn't heard him approach, so engrossed she was in her search. Regardless, whatever it was he wanted, it could wait until she found all her answers.

'What do you mean 'she's not available'? She's right there!' Ulla's voice echoed in Seshat's Reach.

'Are you sure he's a she?' an unfamiliar male slurred.

'Where did you find this?' Ulla's voice again.

"Pantry."

The sound of pottery shattering against stone followed.

'For frost's sake, this is important! Would it kill you not to be drunk for once?'

'Probably,' the man replied grudgingly. *'I promised myself I'd never set foot in one of these, and yet here I am. I'll be damned if I'm suffering this sober, on top of everything else!'*

"You *are* damned. For frost's sake! Get out of my

way. Seshat!" Ulla's boots hit the marble floor with purpose.

Seshat, her concentration long lost, lifted her head above the manuscripts to stare at the speaker.

The woman stomping the length of the balcony in her direction certainly looked, sounded, and for the most part thought like Arianh's escort. Still, Seshat wasn't trusting her senses with these things anymore. She could be another Wyrd, or worse...

"Ulla, what in the eye of Ra are you doing here? Arianh is at the Stump."

"I'm not looking for Arianh. I came to talk to you. It *is* you, right?" Ulla frowned from above Seshat's wall of manuscripts, taken aback by her appearance. She'd slipped into her true form after Eros left. Or she thought she did. Upon closer inspection, the goddess realised she was wearing a combination of hers and Judoc's aspects. She quickly composed herself.

"Yes. Why? And who's that?" Seshat squinted at the bulky, bearded, filthy to the bone and armed to the teeth Narrum male glaring down at her from behind the dryad. He looked drunk – he *was* drunk – and skittish as a cat in the rain. He spat on the floor, and Seshat flared unconsciously at the man.

"Hel sent us to deliver a message," Ulla said. And had she said the Suzerain had sent her instead, it would not have surprised Seshat half as much.

"What?" This narrative made no sense. For what possible reason would Hel have sent a dryad and a Narrum, of all creatures, to deliver a message to her? Couldn't she just have translocated there or sent a raven? If this was Hel's idea of payback for being blocked from her Reach, well… it worked. Seshat was dangerously close to annoyed.

The man walked closer, sure of himself but not his step, cleared his throat, spat again, leaned in, and with the complicit ceremony of someone who is about to share a worthy secret, said, "The cock is ticking."

"I will burn you from the inside out, mortal." Seshat glared.

"Clock! The *clock* is ticking, you idiot," Ulla said as she hit him across the back of his stubbly head.

Seshat dimmed.

"What the fuck is a clock?" the drunk man asked with indignation.

"I don't know! But what sort of message do you think we came here to deliver?" Ulla replied, massaging her bruised temple.

"Who am I to question the gods' messages. Have you looked at the Stump recently? As far as I know, it's open orgy in the pantheons!"

"Be quiet," Seshat hissed, her heartbeat drumming in her ears. "Are you sure that's what she said?"

They both nodded.

She swallowed. "The clock is ticking where?"

"Somewhere in the forest," Ulla said.

"Cats! And what I am supposed to do about it?"

"She said you'd know," the man said.

"Oh, she did, did she?" It made no sense. Unless… Seshat chewed the tip of her pen, inspecting the odd pair. "Did Eros put you up to this?"

"Who?" asked Ulla. The man just stared. Their minds seemed empty of any meaning associated with the name.

"How did you know I was here?" Seshat asked.

"Hel said you would be…" Ulla said.

"And when did you meet Hel?"

"She came by my shelter last night, with Hades and another one with big…" The man cupped his hands in front of his chest. "What was her name?"

Ulla hit him again. "Gaea. The Goddess's name is Gaea."

"I did not invite any of them," the man stated surlily.

Seshat blinked. They were telling the truth. A clear image of Hel and Hades in the forest appeared in Seshat's Reach from both of them, yet their next memory was of Relicum's gates. Nothing in between.

"And how did you get here?" she asked.

"We were dislocated," said the man.

Ulla glowered at him. "TRANSlocated."

"It felt like a dislocation to me…" he grumbled.

The two did look like they'd been through the eye of a tornado. It was not impossible to translocate mortals across relatively small distances within the same world, but it wasn't advisable either. Hel was either too busy to come here herself, or too desperate.

"I still can't feel my toes, or my fingers. Half my body is too cold, the other too hot. I feel sick, and you took away my medicine, bitch," he slurred at the dryad.

"Oh, stop complaining. You know nothing of sickness," Ulla replied, pressing her stomach.

Mortals… Seshat groaned inwardly. It was obvious these two were not Wyrds, or Nephilim, or anything beyond what they appeared to be. The question still remained, why were they here? And why now? She had enough on her mind to deal with as it was. And it was not like she owed Hel anything, or her treacherous father. But of course, this wasn't about debt. It was a courtesy disguised as a warning in the hope she would return the favour. Any other day, Seshat would summon her mount, Quetish, and ride to the forest in a heartbeat, but today… today her whole narrative was unravelling one chapter at a time.

With a sigh, she put away the cursed box and all her manuscripts. Then, to the man's great stupefaction, she conjured two large pillows, a pitcher filled with water, and three cups, then gestured for them to sit down. "You can go now, Toman," she said to her attendant, who was still half hiding behind the wall. Once she could no longer sense his presence, she turned to Ulla. "Very well, tell me everything you know."

∞

The boisterous Narrum fell asleep moments after Ulla began their tale. Seshat could have extracted the information directly from the dryad's mind, of course. It would have been faster, probably even more accurate that way, but it would have taken too much of Seshat's focus. She'd rather think while Ulla talked and, more importantly, keep her mind free to intercept what else might be of note. And sure enough, something was.

It was hidden inside the man's bloody satchel, out of sight but not of Reach. It cut through Seshat's senses like one of the Suzerain's wands.

Without asking permission, she opened the satchel and drew out a sunstone. Holding it was like holding a piece of Ra himself.

"Where did you get this, mortal?" she asked, caressing the smooth edges of the sunstone and relishing the feel of its essence, like the scent of a lost lover left behind on the bedsheets.

Ulcan stirred and blinked the sleepiness away, her compulsion overriding his exhaustion. "Payment," he murmured, not yet fully awake. "Is it worth good metal?"

Ulla fell silent, apparently in protest against Seshat's apparent lack of interest in her report. She *was* interested in her story, very much so, but this... this was far more interesting.

"Payment from whom?" she asked him. But she already knew the answer. She gripped the sunstone until her hands shook with strain.

She gazed across the land to the forest, then the Stump.

"Cats..." she cursed. "Ulla, listen up. We need to gather everyone and get as far away from the Stump as possible."

"Are we back to this again?" the man said.

"Why?" Ulla asked, obviously not too pleased with the idea herself.

"Remember the stories Judoc liked to tell us about the future?" Seshat said.

"Yes..."

"Well, the future is about to happen."

CHAPTER 25

Oric

Oric cursed the Suzerain's daughter for the umpteenth time as he picked up a foot and threw it in the incinerator. How in the shadow had she talked Namrive into giving him this task? Or maybe she hadn't. Maybe Alek was right, and Gaea naturally predisposed all females to conspire with each other against men. She would pay for this offence, he vowed to himself.

If there was one thing Oric hated more than wasting time, it was manual labour. He should have stayed at the Grove. He'd had this large tree hugger on his lap and was about to show her how a dryad uses a sword, when Judoc, who should have been halfway to the Stump by then, woke up the entire woods calling for him, his bracelet flashing alarmingly. Oric had known what it meant, of course. But for once, he'd been in no rush to answer his master's call. He'd rather finish what he started there first. No such luck, though. The birdbrained tree hugger, who at first had been captivated by Oric's talents, forgot all about him and his sword the moment the pretty shrine showed up.

Women, Oric mused resentfully, *so easily impressed*

by the wrong things. His evening thus ruined, he should have just returned to Relicum. Instead, he and the impatient Judoc made their way to the Stump and had just arrived when the Nephilim's ship appeared above it. Oric disliked ships. Something so large and heavy should not be able to fly. And the fact that the Nephilim had arrived in one instead of through the portal was not a good sign either. He told Judoc as much, and the shrine became almost hysterical at the suggestion they should wait outside to see what would happen. "Arianh is still in there!" the shrine shrieked, then all but bullied Oric with threats of unflattering reports to the Suzerain about his cowardice. Oric's instinct had been to stab the bloody man in the eye, but since his accident, he had had plenty of time to relive the circumstances leading to his misfortunes and had concluded that rashness had been the prime culprit. And so he took a deep breath and spared the life of the vain shrine. He figured that even if the gods were still inside the Tree, the Nephilim would have no problem dealing with them, and while they were busy fighting each other, and Judoc made a fool of himself in front of the Aossi queen, he would sneak into the labs and re-build his arm. This had seemed a reasonable plan, as most of his plans often did until something stupid ru-ined them. As Alek used to say: a man's plans are only as good as the men he relies on for their success.

"Bleurrgghh!" Oreth retching on his boots snapped him out of his reverie.

"Will you get a grip on yourself, boy!"

"I can't help it," Oreth bleated, tears in his eyes, bile on his lips.

Oric scowled at him. The boy gagged every time he picked up a body part. He knew it wasn't the boy's fault. Still, the urge to shove Oreth into the fire along with the dead was strong. Oreth and *her*, of course.

While they worked, Ileana stood by the corner with her ear pressed to the Suzerain's ring – the one that had allowed him to eavesdrop on anyone within the Stump. Oric still had trouble understanding how most of the Nephilim's gadgets worked. Regardless, he didn't need to understand them in order to use them. And apparently neither did she. He cursed her again. He had so many better things to do, like getting his body fixed (which would be a lot faster and a great deal less painful had he stayed in the lab), bringing Alek back to life (again! bloody man) and figuring out what exactly had happened in the Stump during his absence. What did the gods do to it? Where did they go? And why would they leave behind two Olympians prisoners alongside the dead Zeus? They looked suspiciously like bait. Bait that the Nephilim obviously didn't take. Still, Oric had expected the whole pantheon to come in force – why bring a ship otherwise? Instead, only two had arrived. Namrive alone was worth a pantheon, true, but Anubis? Oric didn't trust him. He didn't trust gods in general, apart from Seshat maybe, but Anubis had always looked at him the way a dog looks at a marrow bone. Bottom line, neither the gods' nor the Nephilim's behaviour made sense. Something was shady.

Oric often fancied himself the only sensible man in all the land, and he had good reason to. Most Narrum were slaves to their hunger and needs, barely more than animals, so basic and easy to control, they made excellent pests and pets. The Anann saw themselves as the perfect race, the chosen ones. Such arrogance. Just because they were amongst the first mortals created by the gods didn't make them divine. Besides, they'd created them as pleasure vessels, slaves to their creators' lusts and ultimately disposable to boot. Just a few days without sunlight – gods' light – and they withered like sapless trees. Oric wondered if they even understood how vulnerable they were. He grimaced. *We* are, he corrected himself, for he was Anann as well. Or a part of him was, at least. He might not need to bask as often, but he was not immortal. Not yet.

As for the Dharkan… Oric puffed out a mouthful of air. Another set of divine creations, as dissimilar to Narrum as they were to Annan. These gods didn't seem to agree about anything, especially where their creations were concerned. How could they? Gods were flawed, capricious and emotional, so any creation of theirs would also be flawed and predisposed to fight each other just because they were not alike.

Perhaps Alek was not that crazy after all, Oric thought, contemplating the intricacies of the exposed vertebrae he pulled from a corpse. Alek had been like a father to him, the only family he knew, and at least he had his priorities straight: rule a realm, find his mate and become a god – the only god. But as soon as Oric was old enough to think for himself, he realised the Suzerain was as delusional as the rest. Immortality was a good thing; godhood was not.

It's this place, he decided. Everybody in Aegea ended up crazy – except him, of course. Many had lost their sanity trying to make sense of reality, but Oric saw things as they were. He accepted them and he had no emotional attachments either. Those were too distracting, too hazardous to survival. The secret to sanity was selfishness.

"How much longer?" Ileana asked in the petulant voice of a young girl. He glared at her.

"It would go faster if you help us."

"I am helping," she said spitefully.

He didn't see how. All he'd seen her do was shake her head, pressing her ear harder against the ring, but he'd be damned if he was going to ask her what she was listening to.

The Suzerain had talked about his daughter often and at length. Oric had felt as if he'd known her. And yet the reality was not at all what he had imagined. Neither then nor now. She glanced at him, and he realised he had been staring at her for too long.

"What are you looking at?" Ileana demanded without breaking eye contact.

You, he mused spitefully. There was something about Ileana that had caught his attention when they'd first met in Portum, and that was the fact that nothing about her made sense, not even by tree hugger standards. He should have guessed she was a Wyrd, but now, even without the Wyrd in her, there was still something behind the girl's eyes that unnerved him.

"Just wondering why you didn't ask me to take you to your father that night in Portum," he said.

"I did not know the Suzerain was my father then, let alone that you worked for him."

"You must have seen the crest on our uniforms."

"I didn't."

He had indeed taken off his coat to dry by the fire. So had Isko, and Seshat never wore the uniform. Still…

"What about in Relicum? You ran away to the caves with the Wraith."

"I was possessed. Psyche had my body and mind at her disposal. There was nothing I could do."

"Must have been awful."

Her eye twitched. "I do not wish to talk about it."

"Tell me about this goddess, then. Seshat said she was brought here as a weapon to destroy the Suzerain. If that was her purpose and she was in control, she should have gone straight to the Stump."

"She got distracted by the Dharkan and his horse."

Oric considered this. The gods did have a bounty for the Elysium horse. It was plausible this Psyche wanted to distract the Dharkan so she could steal it. Except… no. He had been there. He'd seen her distress. She'd cared for the Dharkan. And he'd cared for her. Except gods don't care for mortals, and Dharkan only care for Prana. He smiled. Suddenly he knew exactly how he would make Ileana pay for all her offences. He would kill the scarred Dharkan. He would have to kill him anyway, Oric wasn't a man who liked to leave a task unfinished, but now there was yet another reason to do it besides following orders. Now it was personal. Not just for what he did to his arm, but so he could also teach that spoiled girl not to play with men.

He kept to his task and let the matter drop. Like her, he could play the fool, but he knew she was as selfish, ambitious and meticulously cold as her father.

CHAPTER 26

Iosh

To say Iosh was disappointed was an understatement. He had come to the Stump to give the Underworld gods a piece of his mind, then take Arianh and make her his wife in order to rule all the living in the land, as was his right. And once again, nothing had gone according to his expectations. The gods had already left. The Nephilim returned just as he arrived, preventing him from leaving, and instead of Arianh, he found Ileana. Not the woman hosting a Wyrd, the one he'd met at the temple, the one who died on ice a few days ago, but the girl he left behind when he'd travelled all those years ago. Gods! She looked and sounded exactly as he remembered. How was that possible? And... *why*? She was less beautiful this way, especially when angry. Anger gave her a petulant edge at this age, before time had transformed it into audacity. And there was something else lacking behind those eyes: a purpose, a fire he'd come to recognise as part of a memory or a dream. She lacked Psyche.

To make things worse, if Ileana was alive, then that meant Oric had been right about Alek's undying ability, which only complicated things further. According to Ileana, her father had already returned and died again. Regardless, this family's bizarre relation with mortality meant his chances of ever ruling Aegea were very much linked to them, and now that he'd set his mind on ruling both Aegea and the Gharb, he would not settle for less. Perhaps he could marry Ileana and Arianh both? There was no law against it. Every man could own as many women as he could afford to feed, and Iosh was wealthy enough to afford an entire tribe of Narrum breeders. Compared to them, dryads cost nothing. But of course, he'd have to find the queen first. He'd looked everywhere for her, including in the places he was not supposed to. She and the gods must have had warning of the Nephilim's arrival, for they were gone before he even arrived at the cursed Tree. Perhaps they just missed each other? He liked the idea of Arianh pining for him at the temple along with the other women, but that was of little comfort now. Try as he might, he could not leave the damned thing. The gods had locked the exits, rendering his bracelet useless. He could not leave until he was excused. Seshat would be furious... Well, as long as she kept impersonating him at the temple, she could be whatever she wanted. He would deal with her later.

This Namrive character, however, was a whole other matter, for he had to deal with her now.

He took a moment to soothe his frustration with a lengthy breath before he addressed the creature pointedly ignoring him.

"There was a woman here with the gods," he said

solemnly. "A dryad named Arianh. She has long azure hair, violet eyes… full lips."

There was no reply. Namrive just kept doing whatever it was she was doing, staring at the flat crystal panes. Alek used to spend days fixated on the things. He once told him they held the secrets of the Universe. All Iosh ever saw in them was gibberish. He reckoned those crystals had been responsible for the Suzerain's increased insanity over the last few years.

He tightened his fists, biting back a curse. He'd been so sure, so close to being the most important man in the land. And now, here he was subservient once again, waiting upon the attention of deities he did not care to worship.

"She might have been held here against her will," he added, hoping this would draw the woman's attention away from the crystal. Why would she insist on having him come to the control room to meet her if all she did was ignore his presence? She was obviously not interested in his counsel, nor his body – which was just as well – so what was the point? He wished he'd brought a blade. The more frustrated he got, the more he wanted to know the colour of the blood under her blue skin.

"The queen?" Namrive finally said, lifting her eyes from the crystal to look at him as if she'd been doing so the entire time.

"Yes! Have you found her?" After all, she had been looking for something in the crystal, that much he could tell.

"No. Only mentions of her."

Iosh waited for more.

She tilted her head slightly. "There was a female body amongst the faithful; it could have been hers."

Iosh's spirit sank. "What?" He'd seen the bodies, yet had paid little attention to them. Raw flesh made him hungry.

"Check the incinerator," Namrive said, turning her attention back to the crystal.

The incinerator was one of many contraptions in the Stump that defied Iosh's comprehension. If he didn't know any better, he'd say there was a fire god trapped inside it, burning on demand. That at least would have made sense, unlike Alek's explanation, which involved some sort of magic fume confined inside special tubes. The purpose of the woodless bonfire was to keep the inside of the Stump warm and eliminate any traces of the Suzerain's research – faithful, tributes and prisoners included.

He dashed to the ring, then remembered himself. "Do you, er… need me for anything?" She had demanded his presence after all.

"Yes, I almost forgot why you were here." She turned and moved across the room in one single motion to loom over him like a praying mantis. It was quite unsettling. Then she smiled as an afterthought, and it only made it worse. *Stars, this creature is crazier than a god*, he thought, looking up at her bug-eyed.

"I want you to escort Anubis to Relicum, observe and report his actions to me."

"Of course," he said. He had no intention of doing any of those things. Iosh wanted nothing to do with Anubis or reports, but he was good at saying whatever he must to get what *he* wanted.

"Show me your ear," she said, and before he could ask why, he was already turning his neck. Through the corner of his eye he glimpsed something like a thin caterpillar wiggling between Namrive's fingertips. Next he felt it twitching inside his skull.

"Aarrrh. What the frost!" he protested, trying to scratch inside his head unsuccessfully.

"You can go now," she said, back to standing in front of the crystal. "Anubis will summon you when he's ready to depart."

Confounded and torn between the urge to demand an explanation and to get as far away from Namrive as he could, Iosh eventually decided on the latter. Gods were strange; the Nephilim were even stranger, and this particular one was the strangest he'd ever encountered. He'd rather take his chances with Anubis. But first...

∞

Iosh blinked away the glare from the teleportation ring and cursed. A strong smell of roasted flesh reached his nostrils, and his stomach roared.

"Good grief," he whispered as he entered the incinerator room. Somehow there seemed to be more body parts than before, piled up in the small space. Where had all these faithful come from, anyway? They seemed to sprout from the Stump's rotting wood like mushrooms.

"Ah, there you are," Oric said a bit too loudly. "I thought you'd left." He had a contrivance attached to his shoulder and, if Iosh's eyes weren't deceived, the arm had grown a few inches since he'd last seen him.

"I will soon," he said. Or so he hoped. "I'm waiting for Anubis to" – he sighed through gritted teeth – "*summon* me."

"Good. Give us a hand, then," Oric said, pointedly throwing a dismembered hand into the roaring fire.

"I'd rather not," Iosh said, scratching his ear and successfully fishing out the remnants of the bug Namrive planted there. Gods, nothing about this excursion to the Stump had happened the way he wanted. Now, all he could hope for was to leave without further humiliation.

Oric didn't seem even a tiny bit concerned with his task or the latest turn of events. Iosh hated how jealous he felt of the man's ability to take everything in stride as if he didn't have a care or ambition in the world, and not for the first time since learning Oric was a metz, he wondered why he wasn't ruling his own temple. He certainly had the looks and charisma. He liked women well enough for the task, and he obviously had the Suzerain's trust in matters Iosh had been kept ignorant of. *But he's not gifted*, Iosh reassured himself. His gift was what set Iosh apart from the others. He'd been chosen; he was special. He was the most important man in the land.

"Did you find a woman amongst the remains?" he asked, almost forgetting what he'd come here to do.

"Huh-hum. I found part of one over there." Oric pointed to the pile furthest away from the fire. "I was saving it for last, actually."

Iosh spared him a confused glance before moving to inspect the gnawed torso. It was clearly female. "Gods," he breathed.

"Is that the queen?" Oric asked, now crouching at his side, contemplating the partial corpse.

Iosh shook his head. "Her sister, Occa."

"You recognise her from this?" Oric cupped a bloody breast. "I suppose they are more memorable than faces."

"You're disgusting," Ileana said, her upper lip curled up in a snarl. Iosh hadn't seen her there, sulking in the dark corner behind the furnace. She'd washed and changed into one of the Suzerain's dresses. They suited her, unlike her expression.

"Hush, girl. You're just jealous because you have nothing worth remembering," Oric said.

"How dare you!"

"Where's the rest of her?" Iosh shouted over them.

Oric shrugged, looking around at the corpses. "Frost knows."

"Already disposed of," said Oreth, clearly eager to get the task over with. "I hated her face, so I threw that in first," he explained.

"I agree. Her lips were too pouty. This was definitely her best feature," Oric said, still playing with her flesh.

"Would you stop that!" Iosh snapped, feeling flushed. "Show some respect, for frost's sake."

"What? You can gut a man in cold blood without flinching, but this bit of flesh perturbs you?" Oric replied.

"Yes!" Iosh averted his eyes.

Oric grinned mischievously and dragged the bloody corpse closer to him. "It arouses you, doesn't it? Come on, touch it, you know you want to. I bet it'll even feel better now with no face attached to it."

"Stop it!" Iosh kicked him away.

Oric fell to his side, laughing. Gods, the man was right, though. He was aroused. There was something wrong with his gift. There had to be. He scratched his ear again. And something was definitely still burrowed in there too!

Oric, still laughing at him, picked up the torso by the shoulder and tossed it into the flames as if it were a piece of firewood. He was the sick one, Iosh told himself, then glanced over to the corner, expecting another chastising comment from Ileana, but she'd stopped paying attention to them. She had her hand pressed against her ear and seemed to be listening to it intently, her facial expression caught between surprise and frustration.

"Hmm, I think you two should listen to this," she said.

CHAPTER 27

Ileana

"She thinks I'm arrogant?" Oric asked incredulously.

Iosh eyed him askance, an amused smile on his lips. "How dare she? You're a bundle of humility."

Ileana glared at both men. "Shhh!" she said, already regretting sharing the device with them.

The three huddled together over the communication gem. The device belonged to her father and therefore enabled them to eavesdrop everywhere in the Stump. She'd rather have been the only one listening to the Nephilim's conversation, but sadly she didn't quite understand half the things they were saying, and more to the point, every escape plan she'd come up with so far required the help of at least one man. Which one, though? She didn't trust either as far as she could throw them. Gods, it was like choosing between thirst and dehydration.

Oric tutted. "You people can't tell the difference between confidence and arrogance."

"Neither can the Nephilim, apparently," Iosh interjected sheepishly.

"Be quiet!" she snapped at the men. Honestly, this

was not the time or place for banter. This was serious. She'd learnt more about Psyche, the gods and her father in the last few minutes than in her entire lifetime, and the implications of this knowledge, combined with her own memories, disconcerted her.

"What does 'dissect' mean?" she asked.

"It's when they cut open a body to study it," Oreth replied grumpily. He hadn't been included in their inner circle and so sat sulking on a metal barrel some distance away, absently picking at the fabric of his ruined garment.

"Study a corpse?" she asked, appalled at the idea.

"Not necessarily. Father prefers to do it while the subjects are alive. He learns more from them that way."

She blinked at Oric for confirmation. He nodded.

"Can Anubis do it?" she asked.

"It's his talent," Oric said ruefully, walking away. Apparently he had heard enough. "Well, he won't be dissecting me, that's for sure." He reached the exit and, noticing no one was following, turned around. "Aren't you coming?"

Ileana, gemstone still pressed against her ear, couldn't believe what she'd just heard.

Iosh simply whistled. "Makes sense." He chuckled. He looked relieved, slightly vindicated even.

"What is it?" Oric asked.

"She said you're a metz," Ileana breathed unbelievingly. "A *Dharkan* metz. Is this true?"

Oric's eyes went wide in an expression that confirmed it more accurately than words. He crossed the room back to where they stood and snatched the device from her with ease. She was too stunned to react.

"How the frost does Namrive know this?" He pressed the gem to his ear, but it'd stopped working the moment it was no longer in contact with Ileana's skin.

"Freezing bitch! That's it. We need to leave immediately. I won't step foot inside this place again until Alek himself summons me." Oric tossed the device away.

Iosh caught it.

"Wait, put it on again. I want to hear more," he told Ileana.

"Why?" Oric asked impatiently.

"They were talking about chrono-travel."

Oric blew out a mouthful of air. "Who cares! Let's go. While they are still busy discussing the methods of our executions."

Everyone remained in place.

Ileana's body refused to move while her mind tried to process this new information. But in the end, only one thing really mattered to her. She shook herself out of her stupor.

"I can't stay here either," she whispered, still in a daze but confident in her decision. "The Nephilim woman knows I've lied. And if she resurrects Father... slush." It wasn't even worth considering the consequences.

"I may persuade her not to do it, or distract her until she forgets she ever wanted to," Judoc suggested brightly.

Ileana scowled. "She's a machine."

Iosh acted bemused. "My gift works on mortals and gods, why not machines?"

"Your gift won't work on that particular machine, trust me," Oric scoffed, one foot out of the room again. "Come on!"

"I've changed my mind," Iosh said, rubbing his ear. He'd been scratching at it almost incessantly. "I think I'd rather take my chances with Anubis after all."

"You're such a sycophant," Ileana said with visceral disdain.

"Funny, you never complained before, *Illy*." The way he said her name along with that boyish smile made her cheeks burn.

"Goddess," she whispered as she moved away from the shrine. "What happened to you, Iosh?" The boy she'd known would never be this cruel to her or any woman.

"I'm the same I've always been. I just don't feel guilty about it anymore. Thanks to you, actually."

"You mean *her*." She refused to say aloud the name of the Wyrd who'd taken her.

"Get a room and sort your issues," Oric said. "Just let me out of this accursed Tree first."

Ileana turned to him. "You want this?" She pointed at her bracelet.

"Girl, do not try my patience."

"You know, I'd love to see you dissected. Maybe I'll stay a little longer."

Oric marched over to her and yanked her hair. "I will drag you if I have to."

She protested, not because it hurt but because it messed it up, which made her hate him even more. That settled it, then. She would have to choose Oreth. He wasn't exactly a man, but considering her history with Iosh and her blinding hate for Oric, he would have to do.

She took the deathwand from the folds of her dress and pointed it at Oric's face.

His expression was priceless. "Where did you get *that*?"

"It was by my side when I woke up. A gift from Father," she lied.

"You can't use it," Oric said.

She fingered the trigger. "You have no idea the things I can do." Not a lie.

Oric took a good look at her and smiled smugly. "Yes, you do want to kill me – pretty badly," he purred in her face. "And because of that, you cannot use it. Go on, prove me wrong. Better to die quickly here than be dissected alive by that sadist."

She grimaced, determined, but try as she might she could not press the trigger because yes, unlike the many birds she'd killed in her youth, she truly wanted to kill this man, and as such, her nature forbade it. The gods were cruel indeed.

He let go of her hair and grabbed her wrist. Had she not been wearing the bracelet, he might have broken it and taken the wand from her. But with only one hand, all Oric accomplished was for her to recoil from him, accidentally triggering the thing. A deafening sound echoed inside the chamber.

"Hey!" Oreth protested, staring at his lower leg. He reached down to touch it on the side of the calf, and his fingers came up bloody. He stared at them, mouth agape, seemingly puzzled and annoyed but not particularly in pain. Behind the leg there was a hole in the metal barrel. It made a whistling sound like that of a window poorly sealed during a storm, and the smell of sulphur filled the air. Terrible comprehension dawned on Oreth's face. He tried to stand and fell with a yelp, the wound more grievous than it looked. Around them, the entire room began to vibrate. Oric cursed and, still gripping Ileana's wrist, dragged her with him down the corridor.

"Let go of me!" She tried to use the wand on him again with no success. Frost, but the man was strong. And fast! She could hardly keep up with his stride.

Ileana heard a dull whump sound just before the air seemed to ignite behind them. The fire spread across the walls, the ceiling, and even the floor! Looking over her shoulder, she thought she saw Oreth writhing in the flames, screaming his lungs out in agony.

"Look what you've done!" Oric shouted at her as they ran, not slowing down to look back at the blaze chasing them.

"What have I done..." she mumbled. *Oh goddess, what* have I done? Her legs faltered. She nearly collapsed, but Oric held her upright and dragged her ahead of the flames into the vault's antechamber, and only stopped once they were standing on the teleportation ring.

"Activate it!" he demanded.

"Let go!" she protested again.

Oreth still screamed, or was it Iosh? She couldn't tell. A buzz like a swarm of angry wasps distorted all other sounds. It didn't seem real. *This can't be happening,* she thought wistfully. Oric took the wand from her hand and used it to slap her across the cheek.

"Snap out of it! We'll burn alive."

She wasn't paying attention to him. Her eyes were still on the flames as they swept the room as if driven by a will of their own. Ileana followed their arc towards Apollo inside the vault. The door was still open. He had a wicked smile on his face.

"He's a sun god. He can control the fire," she said under her ragged breath, not exactly sure how she knew this, just sure it was true.

The sun god lashed the flames towards the units supporting his force field and within moments he was free. Landing on the floor with unnatural grace, he turned to his sister's power source.

"Illy!" Iosh's strained voice coming from down the corridor mixed with Apollo's triumphant laughter as he made the flames dance around him. He'd freed Artemis but left the other bodies to burn atop their plinths. Ileana watched her old self be consumed by the flames and felt… nothing.

Her dress caught fire; she stared at it as if it were happening to someone else until Oric patted it out and pulled her further away from the flames and closer to him, pressed together inside the ring.

"Get us out of here, please!" His voice nearly broke.

He was desperate and terrified. Why wasn't she?

A blackened hand jutted through the flames at ground level, gripping feebly at her ankle. She gasped.

"I'll take you with me, Illy!" She couldn't bring herself to touch it or look away, so she just put her weight on Oric and stomped on it with her other foot.

Around them the flames gathered into a stream,

flowing towards Apollo with a life of their own. It was horrendously beautiful.

"What did I tell you, sister," Apollo said.

"Well done, brother." The flames parted ahead of her as she drew closer to Apollo. They embraced.

The god gathered the flames into an incandescent ball between his hands. "It's your turn now, sister."

"My pleasure."

As one, the twins turned to their audience. Their eyes, Ileana thought absently, were the only physical feature the siblings had in common, but by the synchronised way they moved, it was as if they belonged to the same being.

"Ileana!" Oric urged in a hiss. He was holding her so tight she could barely breathe, never mind the smoke.

There was an explosion, and scorching heat hit them just moments before she finally activated the ring.

CHAPTER 28

Ideth

"Very good." Hecate smiled with approval at Ideth's work. She looked far less menacing and a lot more real when she smiled. Not that Ideth had grown fond of the goddess, for she had not, but she'd learned to interpret some of her facets, and this one was genuine.

It better be, Ideth grumbled to herself, since it was her third attempt at getting the mixture right. Hecate was a good teacher, even if a reluctant one, with very high standards. As a result, Ideth's education in the magical arts had not been easy, nor as fast as she'd hoped.

How long had passed since she'd been there? She didn't know. Hecate had created a barrier, a sort of bubble around the area, keeping the cabin detached not just from the rest of the forest but from Niflheim itself. There Chronos made time move at whatever speed suited their individual needs – useful for making medicinal herbs grow faster and Ideth's confinement potentially eternal. She couldn't get out of it. Others could get in, though. She'd seen animals come and go unhindered, and even a nymph basking the other day, but when she tried to talk to the girl, she'd screamed and run away as if she'd not recognised Ideth as one of her own. Perhaps she wasn't. Not anymore…

Chronos had told her – more like threatened her – that she had all the time in the Universe at her disposal. That might be so, but Chiron did not. At first, Hecate's medicine had improved his condition greatly. He had regained a healthy colour in his cheeks, even walked around the clearing without assistance for a while. But now he grew weaker each day. He could no longer stand on his own, nor had he the strength to drag his large body around. At first Ideth thought this was Chronos' way of motivating her to learn faster, but the more she learnt about how sorcery worked, the better she understood how the gods' talents worked as well, and she knew Chiron's condition was the result of a losing battle not just with the Hydra's poison but also between Chronos' and Kali's will. The mighty God of Time would never admit it, of course, but Ideth knew Kali's soul was his weakness, the wound that never healed. Ideth vowed to find a way to exploit it, to make it fester, until he was as weak as Chiron. That was why today, taking advantage of Hecate's good mood and positive feedback, she'd asked her about souls. After all, if Ideth was ever going to use her skills against the gods, she'd have to understand how they worked.

"The greatest difference between a god's soul and a human's is their resistance to change," Hecate explained while she skilfully and vigorously worked the mortar and pestle. "It's extremely difficult to change a god's will, and most gods are bigots, so there's hardly any point in trying by any conventional means. The older the god, the more dogmatic he gets."

You don't say, Ideth thought, crushing the pungent contents of her mortar with far less enthusiasm. Her eyes narrowed askance at Xylo some distance away, trying to catch a butterfly.

"Humans, on the other hand," Hecate continued, "seem to lack any opinion of their own. They agree with whoever shouts the loudest, shines the shiniest, or promises them the best reward. That's how they are able to worship anything as long as it suits their needs, even things like thunder, corpses and gold." She shook her head. "They are particularly devoted to those who make them look good and beautiful and powerful, for they are petty, angry, ugly creatures. So weak. So corruptible. So untrustworthy. So –" Hecate had ground the roots to a pulp, pressing the pestle mercilessly until it slipped, spilling the mortar's contents onto the grass. Her liminal features seemed to vibrate with poorly restrained fury.

"I agree," Ideth said coolly. She'd stopped feeling angry a long time ago. Anger was a god's prerogative. Mortals had no such luxury; they just had to do whatever they were told to by the angry gods.

"Ohh..." Xylo groaned, staring gloomily at his chunky fingers.

"Killed another one?" Ideth asked.

"Not yet." He clapped his hands, and fragments of delicate colourful wings fell from them.

"I keep telling you: a net is what you need," Ideth said patiently.

He uttered an unintelligible rumble and began

pursuing another butterfly.

Chiron tutted. He was patiently filling a flask with poppy seeds. "On behalf of all old gods, I apologise."

Ideth shifted her gaze to him. "Are you running a fever again?"

A ghost of a smile crossed his lips. "Since my… misfortune, I've become increasingly convinced every god should experience mortality as part of their education."

"Is that so?" she asked sceptically. They sat under the shade of an oak, as they often did, for the bright sun had become too much for the centaur's fair skin. He did not bask, and he did not eat, stuck in the limbo between mortality and divinity, but he did sunburn, apparently.

"Yes, unbridled one. Mortality provides perspective and enlightenment. While immortality foments carelessness and narrow-minded ambition," he warned her.

The centaur shuffled his weight on the skiff, skilfully adapted to accommodate his body and allow him the movement his legs no longer did. He looked uncomfortable. He probably was. His wounds had been cleaned, as they had to be each day, and the foul-smelling paste Hecate regularly applied to them seemed to ease his suffering. Still, his complexion was ghastly, with beads of sweat constantly dotting his forehead and his back legs had shrivelled in ways that pained Ideth to behold.

"Speak for yourself, Titan," Hecate said flatly. "I'd rather return to Tartarus for an eternity than spend a lifetime as a mortal."

"How did you end up there, anyway?" Ideth asked. She'd asked before, but the answer had always left her unsatisfied, so she repeated the question whenever the opportunity presented itself.

Hecate filled the mortar with fresh ingredients and began grinding them in a less violent manner. "I've done things other gods disapproved of," she said. The usual answer.

"They must have been really bad things for them to send you to the Underworld," Ideth insisted.

"Yes, some were quite shocking," Chiron chimed in.

Hecate's eyes flared at him; he rolled his at her. Ideth took it as progress.

"I was empowering women against their husbands," Hecate said.

Chiron faked a cough. "Sure you were."

"And the gods who might take advantage of them. Zeus especially, yes," Hecate admitted sharply.

"And you're surprised he punished you," he said sardonically.

"Yes. Surprised, disappointed, offended, furious!" A bit of pulp from Hecate's mixture landed on Ideth's hand. "He abused his power."

"He was taking no chances back then," Chiron said. "Can you blame him?"

"Yes! I blame him. If not for the apotheosised human, Zeus would not have felt threaten by my work. So I blame her too."

"Er," Ideth interjected. "You're talking about Psyche?" Chiron nodded. Ideth sighed, secretly pleased. "Continue."

"I met her, you know," Hecate said. "Not the goddess, but the mortal. Before the other gods even knew of her existence. I thought she had the talent."

"Had she?" Ideth asked.

Hecate shrugged. "Only a trickle."

"Tell me more about her," Ideth said casually. "Was she always cantankerous, or did that come upon apotheosis?"

Hecate snorted. "Always, I'd say. Although it's hard to blame her for that. She had the mind to accomplish great things, but all everyone saw was her beauty. Her family tried to make her the epitome of female perfection, virtue and obedience. They wanted her to be a goddess – a powerless goddess they could control and profit from. That would rankle me too."

"Indeed." Ideth sighed again.

"Every man wanted her, but none dared to court her. Every woman was jealous of her. They wanted to destroy her, but they feared the consequences from the men. Fear and worship always come hand in hand. And they often turn to hate. At first I felt sorry for the way they treated her. You won't believe how loud they cheered when the oracle declared she should be offered to a monster. She never flinched, though, not even once while she walked, head high, to her own funeral. I could feel how much she despised them all. She'd rather be free with a monster than bound to those people. I tried to offer her comfort, a potion to numb her senses when the time came. You know what she did? She spat at me and told me to shove the potion up my... Well, let's just say I stopped feeling sorry for her then. Stars, the woman had a mouth on her."

"Still does."

"Then when Zeus found out I had contacted her, he accused me of having something to do with Eros' infatuation and her impossible success during Aphrodite's trials."

"Did you?" Chiron asked.

"Of course not!" The indignation sounded true enough to Ideth.

"And he knew it! Zeus had been looking for an excuse to get rid of me for centuries. He saw my power as a threat to his rule and masculinity. It was my word against his. And since I had no friends amongst the Olympians, I lost. But I know who helped her," Hecate added in conspiratorial tones.

Chiron and Ideth eyed her intently.

"I'm not telling you," she teased.

"Why not? I bet *he* already knows." Ideth pointed at Xylo, who did not take the bait. He could look as passive as a tree when he chose to, but she knew he was listening to their conversation. He was always listening.

"Because I intend to poison my enemies with that information." She glanced apologetically at Chiron.

"Sounds like you and Psyche have a lot in common," Ideth said.

Hecate's heads shook in different directions. "Perhaps. But I believe Psyche and all human demigods who became gods should return to a mortal existence. A humble and limited existence as the Universe intended."

"I see," Ideth said, adding more herbs to her mixture. Then, taking advantage of Hecate's talkative mood, she continued. "You said they offered her to a monster. How did she escape? Did Eros rescue her?"

Hecate chortled. "No, silly. Eros was the monster."

Ideth's brow creased. "I though he was the god of love."

"Precisely. He's the greatest monster in the Universe."

Ideth stopped grinding. "For frost's sake. The gods' definition of monster is absurd."

Hecate smiled maliciously. "You have no idea."

Apparently not, and the goddess of magic was done elucidating her.

"Now, if you want to bring someone to Morpheus' attention, what do you use?" Hecate asked.

Ideth pursed her lips at the change of subject, then focused on the items on the table between them. "Chicken blood, a lock of hair or ideally a whole fingernail from the target and a generous amount of valerian root."

"Good. And if it's Kali who you want to pay attention to someone?"

Ideth looked over her shoulder, where Xylo was humming to a robin perched on his head. "Deadly nightshade."

"Very good." Hecate smiled in approval. She had a wicked smile. Whenever her images settled – which wasn't very often – she resembled what in Ideth's mind an Underworld nymph should look like.

"How are the lessons going?" Xylo asked.

"Very well. Ideth is a true daughter of the moon."

Ideth still didn't know what a moon was exactly. Hecate had tried to explain it to her, but as best she was able to understand from the goddess's explanation, a moon was a small world orbiting a bigger one and able to reflect sunlight during the night. It made little sense to Ideth. How could she be a daughter of such a thing? As most things the goddess said, she just took her word for it and moved on. She had to admit, though, it was empowering to have an ability able to match the gods' talents.

"Good, good," Xylo said appraisingly.

"Good enough for a day off?" Ideth ventured. She'd had few of those, and they were mostly for Hecate's sake, not hers. Ideth spent her free time with Chiron or, when he was too tired, studying subjects outside the goddess's teachings, such as how to render another sorcerer helpless.

"Not today, darling Ideth."

"Why not?" she pouted.

"Today you will be tested."

Interlude 5

Tricked

Psyche hugs me, then disappears into the forest's reflection.

I want to follow her. Not just because it feels too much like a goodbye and I don't believe her promises, but I also don't believe her belief that whatever is beyond the barrier is safe. It didn't feel safe, and not just because of the burning light. There was a wrongness about the place. An ill intent, if such a thing can be attributed to geography. Not even the Stump holds such a grudge to those inside it.

Many gods and mortals like to associate light with goodness and purity, while darkness is considered evil and tainted with shadowy creatures. They are wrong. Light burns and blinds. It exposes you to your enemies and leaves you helpless. Darkness is real. It takes you in. It keeps you honest, sharpens your senses and protects you from illusions. Only in darkness can one truly find oneself. The reason most people don't like the dark is because they don't like what they find.

Aegea's weak sun, rising on the horizon, only adds

to my misery. The forest does not improve in daylight; neither does frustration or despair.

I pray to Hel, tell her what has happened, more out of habit than anything else, and to my surprise, she promptly replies this time.

'*Good, you found it. Don't go anywhere. We're on our way.*' She sounds tired, almost breathless, as if she's been running, which is odd. Gods don't run. Well, Psyche does, but she doesn't count. Why would they run when they can teleport anywhere? Nah, she's probably humping Hades. Nothing like a good hump to forget your problems. At least in that regard, gods and Dharkan think alike.

I groan at the sight of the monstrosity atop the Stump. These Nephilim have a sick sense of aesthetics, and I can only hope they deal with their problems differently. The thought of Ileana in there, with them, freezes the vegetation at my feet. She's trapped inside their fortress, and I'm trapped outside of this sorcery. The frustration threatens to shatter me. I want to ice something.

I reach inside my coat to fetch the butterfly pendant. It's an ugly thing. Crude and artless, but I find it comforting to hold, to trace its edges with my fingers, follow the path of the tiny swirls within it. I freeze. It's not there. The pocket is empty. I check the other pocket. Not there either. I search the satchel. Cornus' horn is still there, buried under my books and statuettes. But no pendant. *How? When? That little cun–*

"We're here," Hel says, triumphantly stepping out of the foliage. She's flushed, her hair is a mess and her clothes muddied. Hades fights his way behind her.

His cloak is frayed at the hem, his hair is cropped short, and he seems genuinely offended with the world.

They look miserable, exhausted, and somehow less than themselves.

"Goddess, what happened to you?" I ask, momentarily forgetting my own problems. "Did you *walk* here?"

"Where is Psyche?" Hel asks curtly.

"In there." I point at the expanse of forest behind us.

"Ah, of course. I should have thought of it," Hades says, staring ahead. "It's the witch's hut."

"The what?" Hel asks, moving damp hair away from her eyes.

"The woman who lived there had something of a reputation in the forest. She was a sorceress. Her spirit rests in the Underworld now." His eyes flicker. "Funny, I have no idea where her husband's soul is."

"Burn you, Hades! How was I not informed there was a sorceress in my world?"

"I didn't think it was important!"

"We need to work on our communication."

"Speak for yourself!"

I roll my eyes to the sky, begging the Universe to make them stop their nonsense.

Hel touches the barrier. "Is this the work of your former captive?" she asks Hades.

"The barrier, yes. The rest..." He trails off.

"It's daylight in there," I say to them.

"It's daylight now," Hades replies.

"No. I mean, *bright* daylight. Like nothing I've ever seen."

Hel pokes her head through the illusion. "Remarkable," she says, pulling back out.

Hades tries to have a peek as well but his face hits the barrier.

"Cerberus breath!" he curses, massaging his nose. "I hate witchcraft."

"Goddess, what's inside that thing?" I ask.

Hades and Hel glance at each other. Their expressions suggest they'd rather enter the vault chamber than answer the question.

Hades sighs. "My boy, the question is not what, but who."

Hel puts a hand on my shoulder. "Aedan. This is between gods. There is nothing for you to do here. Go back to Portum. Tell the others I forgive them, and get them as far away from Aegea as possible."

Lightning cracks around us. "Goddess, with all due respect, they don't deserve your forgiveness, and I deserve more than that answer."

"Oh, for frost's sake, Hel. Just tell him," Hades says.

"We don't have time."

He snorts. "*Time*, exactly. That's what's in there, Aedan: Chronos."

"Huh?"

"Chronos is what's beyond the barrier," Hades repeats. "Can you do anything about that, Dharkan? I didn't think so. But, hey, now you know! Hel, let's get this over with."

"This is my fight, Hades," Hel says tiredly.

"The frost it is!"

"You can't get through," she points out.

"So help me find another way."

"What about the Nephilim?" I ask before Hades can protest further.

Hel scowls. "They are probably regretting ever having come here."

"Ileana and Fenrir?" I insist.

Her eyes flash blue for a moment, then avoid mine entirely. "I'm sorry, Aedan."

"Hel, you can't go in there alone," Hades says.

"I won't be alone. Psyche and Gaea are in there too."

Hades pulls at his hair. "Exactly!"

Hel walks closer to him. "Do you remember when you said I'd have to explain my family to you one day?"

"That was yesterday, so of course I remember."

Hel smiles and kisses him tenderly. "Find my brother," she whispers, then snatches his invisibility cloak and runs into the illusion.

"Hel! Gods damn it!" Hades kicks the frozen weeds around his feet to a pulp while spitting curses. I never thought I'd relate to the god, but I know precisely how he feels. Nothing I can say or do will make it better.

After a fair amount of stamping and cursing, he calms himself enough to address me. "Stay here. If you see anyone or anything but us, freeze them. Especially if it's Xylo or has orange hair. Got it? Oh, except if it's a beautiful woman with snakes on her head. If she shows up, do not engage her. Don't even look at her, understand? Good man." He taps me on the shoulder and vanishes again before I can say anything.

I curse. Once again left alone, empty-handed, more worried and frustrated than before. Personally, I'm not afraid of Chronos. Time has always meant little to the Dharkan. The light, though… I put one hand through and immediately feel the pain of it burning.

"Light's a bitch, ain't it?"

Loki stands just a few paces from me. Like Hel and Hades before him, he looks exhausted, yet still every bit the treacherous creature that he is. He holds a butterfly pendant in his hand.

"Looking for this?"

I don't make a move to retrieve it. Even from here I can tell it's not the real pendant, and I'll be burned if I'm going to humiliate myself by playing his games. Flaming sun, I'm really not in the mood to deal with him on top of everything else.

"What do you want, Trickster?"

He pretends to consider my question, dangling the pendant from his fingers. "I want to be appreciated for my talents, I want a galaxy of my own, I want my children to be safe, I want fame and glory and Odin's head on a spike. Not necessarily in that order, mind."

Lightning cracks between my blistered fingers. My patience is too thin for this ash.

"Oh, you mean right now?" Loki steps closer. "I want to get inside this private gathering, what the fuck do you think I want!" he snaps hysterically.

"Go ahead," I say.

"I wasn't invited." The moment he touches the barrier, a bolt of energy knocks him back. "I fucking hate sorcery," he growls. "As if I didn't have enough to worry about with *them*." He gesticulates in the Stump's general direction. "Now there's *this*!" He punches the barrier. The bolt hits him again. He's either a slow learner or he loves pain, I reckon.

"Tough. The Dharkan haven't been invited either," I say grudgingly.

Loki presses his lips into a thin line, clearly making an effort not to say something rude.

"It's sunny. Yes, I figured as much. Alone, neither of us will ever get inside, but together…"

"I swore I would not host you again."

"Now, that was a mistake," Loki says in a condescending tone. "One should never swear rashly. Fortunately, you're not a god, so you're not bound to that decision."

"The light in there makes the blue sun feel cool. You couldn't protect me from it; I doubt you're able to protect me from *that*."

"Couldn't, wouldn't, shouldn't… If I can hide a sun, I can hide you from it too, don't worry."

"So why didn't you before?"

"Because before it did not suit my needs," he replied truthfully.

Freezing gods. "What guarantee do I have that once you're inside, you'd not just let me burn?"

"It's a fair point. Under other circumstances and with any other Dharkan, that might be exactly what I would do. In this case, however, it is better if I remain inconspicuous."

"It often is with you," I sneer.

Loki exhales forcibly, his jaw muscles working harder than mine. "Aedan, I'm a little too pressed for time to stand here exchanging words with you. There's a lot to explain, which I will, as soon as you let me in. So shall we…?" He uses suggestively obscene gestures to complete the sentence.

I badly want to get inside this cursed realm, but I also meant my oath not to host him again. Loki has a way of getting under your skin, almost literally. Hosting him was like having Zeus' uncontrollable power burning through my mind, twisting my thoughts. And if I'm already this annoyed with his presence, imagine how much worse it will be with his soul in me.

"Give me the pendant," I demand to buy some time to think.

He tosses it over. I frown. It's definitely not the same pendant. This one has a chipped wing and no swirls inside the amber.

"Tell me why you have it, and I'll host you."

"I made it," he says.

"Really?" I reply in disbelief. The pendant is not particularly well crafted. "I always figured gods were more talented than this."

Loki seems offended. "I am talented." Suddenly the butterfly is the most exquisite piece of artistry I have ever seen. It almost looks alive, so much so I expect it to take flight at any moment. It even feels real to the touch, despite clearly being an illusion.

"I don't understand," I say. And I don't.

The pendant morphs back to a crude piece of poorly sculpted amber. Loki shrugs. "I'm not as talented with a chisel as I am with illusions."

"You sculpted this, for her? Why?"

He sighs. "I wanted it to be real, I suppose."

"So you were lovers…" I say more to myself than to him.

Loki snorts. "Did she tell you that?"

"She didn't have to."

"I doubt she ever will." He crosses his arms. "You see, *lovers* implies love. And all we ever had was a misunderstanding."

Now it's my turn to snort.

Loki grins. A sign he just had an idea I probably won't be able to counter. "My deal is simple. You get me through the barrier, and I'll protect you from the sun. We do what we need to do, and the moment, the very instant, we're out, I'll leave your body, never to return. I promise." He hesitates. "Except if I'm invited, of course. After all, we do make an excellent team, and you know that of all the Dharkan, you are my favourite." He grins again, eyes bright with mischief.

I stare at him unconvinced.

"Fuck me… Fine! I swear it on my daughter's life. Is that good enough for you?"

"You dare to jeopardise Hel's life for a lie?" I push him against the barrier. It ripples and cracks, but no matter how hard I push, it doesn't let him through.

"You're the one killing her!" he yells, his voice strained with agony. He doesn't fight me, though. Nor does he try to move away from the source of his pain. "Every moment you spend here arguing with me, she's in there, helpless."

"She has Gaea to help her."

"Aren't we all lucky, then!" His eyes glow, and his teeth rattle with strain. I let him go, mostly because his hair has started to burn and I dislike the stink. Loki collapses on the ground, groaning.

I toss him the pendant. "Keep your fake trinkets, Trickster. I don't need them, and I don't need you."

I can't host him. There has to be another way. Flaming sun, I'd rather take my chances with Psyche as a guest than him. *Forgive me, goddess.*

"I wish you hadn't said that." Loki's voice is an axe cutting through my senses. I shiver as if I'm cold, which is absurd, and yet that's how it feels.

Loki gets to his feet and walks in my direction, each step laden with menace. He doubles, triples in size right before my eyes. His face changes. Its expression goes from mischievous to villainous, and then it's no longer recognisable as a face as he's no longer himself. One moment Loki is a handsome Dharkan-looking man with sleek raven hair, the next he's a wolf, then a snake, a raven, an eight-legged horse, a ratton, a spider, a moth, a fly, that scion of Ra that nearly burned me to ash, Hel, Psyche, many others including myself! He settles back to his usual aspect as if nothing has happened. I take a step back, away from the monstrous god and his predatory grin.

"By the goddess, *what* are you?" I ask, horrified.

Something hits me seemingly from everywhere. One moment I'm standing, the next I'm lying on my back, blind with indescribable pain.

Loki looms above me. "New deal: Host me and live. Deny me and I will destroy you," he rasps.

The threat is real, unlike the rest of him. Whatever force knocked me down before hits me again and again. An enemy I cannot see, cannot defend against, cannot fight back.

"All right!" I shout moments before the power building in his hands burns me to ash. "But I want your promise."

"I already gave you one, you insolent creature," he growls.

"On Psyche, not Hel. I want you to swear on Psyche's life that you will protect us and leave me as soon as we're out of that thing."

Loki pauses, then smiles, then beams. And I know, somehow, I just made a big mistake.

CHAPTER 29

Gaea

Gaea stood outside the barrier, thinking about life and death. Lately she'd wanted nothing more than to sit under a tree and just stay there for eternity. Sadly, for her, true death would never be an option. She was the Goddess of Life, after all. She would eventually cease to exist, but she would never actually die.

Chronos liked to say souls were the gods' curse. Hers was life itself. Life and Chronos, of course. He was the curse of the entire Universe. She didn't know where he'd come from, only that he'd been there the moment she came into existence. From the very beginning he'd been a father, mentor and, most of all, oppressor.

For aeons he'd tried to control her, change her, smother her in unspeakable ways. But it was Gaea's nature to create, to expand and evolve, to give life to the Universe. More than a duty, it was a compulsion.

She created the Ancient Ones first, then the Elders, then the Titans. Most of these turned out to be disappointments, monstrous creatures, too primal to control their own powers. She was young then and had to learn how best to use her own talents. Mistakes were to be expected, and they cost her dearly since for every bit of life she gave, a little of herself was lost with it. Still, Gaea was resourceful. When she realised the extent of her limitation, she figured it was best to give a little rather than a lot, so she created gods. And eventually, after much trial and error, she found the perfect balance between soul and intellect. And most importantly, these new deities were as resilient to Chronos' interference as she was.

Gaea also learnt she did not always need to give up portions of her soul to create life. In fact, life was quite successful without souls, and soon the Universe was brimming with all sorts of creatures. There was a downside to this, of course: only a small portion of them had intelligence, and all of them were mortal. *Mortal...* the very word tasted rancid on her tongue, so she created Ambrosia, hoping to circumvent the problem – another mistake. Yes, she saw it now. Mortals don't have what it takes to live forever – not under Chronos' tyranny – they all end up insane, begging for Kali to take them. Oh, the irony...

Then along came humankind. They were so promising at first. Mortal beings with ambition and will to match the gods themselves. It was natural they would eventually try to imitate their creators, but instead of creating life, they created *things*. The Nephilim were proof humans could never be trusted as deities.

Loki appeared in her Reach. He was to gods what the Nephilim were to humans. She no longer remembered when they first met, exactly, only that he'd always been there, kinda like Chronos, testing her patience. This time was different, though. This time he actually cared, and for once, he was the one doing her bidding, not the other way around.

"I've done what you asked," he said flatly.

"Good. That wasn't so hard, was it?"

"Harder than you can possibly imagine..." He did look a bit frazzled.

Gaea tutted. *Loki, always so dramatic.* "You might be the one with the imagination, Trickster, but I've experienced things that would break your soul."

He ground his teeth audibly in disagreement.

"Will she come?" Gaea asked.

"She's on her way."

Gaea eyed him askance. "Burn it, Loki! You didn't tell her."

"I told her enough," he snapped. "Psyche's at her best when she acts on instinct, not command. Not to mention she has the habit of doing the exact opposite of what she's told."

"Good point," Gaea conceded. Still, that didn't bode well for her and her plan. Once in motion, there would be no time to persuade stubborn deities to do their bit.

"Hel has someone you can use if all else fails," Loki said, reading her thoughts.

Gaea's eyes widened when he told her about Hel's deal with Medusa. "The goddess of the dead has come a long way indeed to forge such an alliance."

"She is my daughter," Loki said proudly.

"Uh-huh."

"What now?" he asked.

"Well, I guess we'll go in and finish this," Gaea said.

"Just like that?"

She gave him a patronising smile. "See you on the other side."

Gaea took a deep breath, and stepped through.

Night became bright daylight. The perfect idyllic picture stretched before her eyes, and for a moment she felt proud, so proud of her accomplishments. Life – plant, animal and divine alike – was the most precious thing in the Universe, and it all existed because of her. A genuine smile tugged at her lips, and despite being at her weakest, she felt almost empowered by this, and when she stepped further into the clearing, she no longer needed to breathe.

No signs of Loki, though.

He probably can't get through. No surprise there. If Hecate was half as good a sorcerer as Zeus claimed, she would be able to tailor her barriers against undesirable trespassers, and none was more undesirable than him. The question was, had the Trickster been excluded by her or by Chronos? Gaea sighed. It didn't matter. One way or the other, she was alone for now. *Psyche better be here soon*, she thought.

She strode forward.

"Chronos? Show yourself! I know you're in here. It's not enough for you to change the very fabric of this world, do you have to further aggravate things with temporal nonsense? It ends now, do you hear me? Chronos!"

"Yes, Gaea, I hear you. Your voice never leaves me." Xylo stepped from behind a pine tree several paces away, a blackbird perched on one of his branches. "Be patient, dear. This vessel was not made for hurrying.

And you're the one we've been waiting for," he said, walking awkwardly slow in her direction.

Chronos' mocking tone crushed her serenity. No matter how hard or how long she prepared, the old God always had this effect on her. He looked ridiculous wearing that body, and yet she was the one who felt like a fool for not having seen through his disguise earlier. Who else would wear a Jötunn, even if a miniature one? She doubted any of her younger children had ever seen one of her earliest creations.

Gaea closed the rest of the distance between them. He feigned concern when he saw her up close.

"Oh dear, Mother of Life, you look awful," he said, visibly pleased with the fact.

"While you've never looked as good," she said spitefully, but it was the truth. Xylo, perturbing to the eye as he might be, was an improvement to any of Chronos' previous forms.

"Thank you for the compliment, dear. And how nice of you to finally join us. It took you long enough," he said ominously.

"What is the meaning of this place?" Gaea's tone was one of contempt and disbelief. She would not give him the satisfaction of seeing dread in her face or hearing hesitation in her voice.

The goddess Hecate appeared at his side, a wicked smile on her red lips.

Gaea frowned at the Olympian witch, curious as to what could possibly have possessed her to ally herself with a God who all but despised her kind.

"Sorcery, Chronos. Seriously? The lowest of the gods' talents – a *mortal's* talent. Talk about desperate times, *dear*. Was merging the worlds not enough?" Her words came out disdainful, just as she'd intended. Her mind was properly shielded. She didn't know the extent of Chronos' power while wearing Xylo's body, but she would not take any chances, especially in Reach of his witch.

He didn't seem offended or taken aback at all by her words. Then again, he never did.

"Desperate, indeed," he said gravely. "I was forced to suspend my prejudices and see the value in such trivialities since most of my talents are useless against the enemy *you* created."

"I –" *Breathe...* "had nothing to do with the Nephilim. And you seem to have made the most of their talents in any case." She scowled, shaking her head disapprovingly. Technology was not a talent, quite the opposite in fact. "How did you even manage to fit inside *that*?" The incredulity in her tone was neither forced nor faked. She'd studied his vessel from head to toe. Chronos should not be able to take form in any of the gods' realms, not even as a Wyrd, she'd made sure of that. He and Kali were forces in the Universe. Flesh was Gaea's gift and Gaea's gift alone.

"The Suzerain was kind enough to create this host especially for me as both an incentive and reward for my assistance in his quest for power," he said.

"I didn't know you took bribes, Chronos," Gaea replied, genuinely astonished by his answer.

He shrugged. "Neither did I. No one ever offered me anything before. The novelty excited me. The Suzerain is an extraordinary creature in his own way. The only mortal bold enough to come to my tree and demand to talk to me directly." He chuckled to himself. "He even had the courage to propose me a deal. I was so entertained with his audacity that I actually let him."

"A deal?!" Even Gaea had difficulty communicating with Chronos in his realm. That was the reason they created the Chronodéndrons in the first place. And prayers were not negotiations. They were demands, wishes, empty promises. A prayer offered nothing of use to the gods. She told him as much.

"Apart from themselves," Chronos pointed out.

"And what use do you have for their 'pathetic' existences as you like to call their lives? For their souls maybe, but Alek wasn't human and humans have long learnt not to pray to the Chronodéndrons."

"Yes, I wonder who put such aversion in them," he said, the words heavy with sarcasm. "Their entire race seems determined to fell every tree in every world just to be sure that doesn't happen."

Gaea held her breath, not taking the bait. "A dryad should have known better," she said instead.

"He did. And so he came to me. Of course, his deal was flawed. Alek couldn't see the big picture – only *I* can do that – so what he proposed was impossible nonsense. But then I saw something."

"What?"

"Opportunity, dear. For aeons, I found myself tormented by both life and death. One attacking from within, the other from everywhere else, threatening all that belongs to me." He spoke with flint in his tone and a twinkle in the dark green pits of his eyes. Gaea pretended not to see it.

The mortally wounded Titan and the nymph Ideth stepped into the clearing behind him. It made sense he would groom Ideth for his purpose. She was not only a terrible mother, she had one foot in the shadow as well. And Chiron... Gaea sighed. He was as good as there already.

No one uttered a word for a long moment.

"Ideth, darling. I believe the Goddess of Life turned shy and would prefer to talk to me in private. Could you give us a moment? You too, Hecate. Chiron's wounds need tending." He spoke casually, almost aloofly, but every word was a command and they knew it.

Gaea caught a glimpse of anguish in Ideth's eyes, once so bright and filled with wonder, now hard and wise and as discerning as a god's. She looked... not older, not exactly. Just less young. Burdened by years and maturity and... something heavier – *responsibility*. She nodded once and turned on her heel. Hecate took a little longer to abdicate her place at Chronos' side, but eventually sense took over and she did as she was told.

"Thank you, darling," Chronos said to Ideth, not Hecate, Gaea noticed.

"Why do you call her that?" Gaea asked after they left.

"Darling?" he smirked. "Are you jealous, *dear*?"

"No," she replied with indignation. "I'm concerned for the poor girl."

"Don't be," he said. "I call her darling because that's what she is. A darling. *My* darling. She will give me what you tried to take away."

Gaea guffawed, a mirthless, hopeless sound. Stars, she sure hoped he was wrong.

"Aren't you going to ask me why?" he asked.

"Why what? Why a dryad? Why her? Why now, why here, why like this? There're so many whys, I honestly don't care anymore. No Chronos, I've given up trying to understand why you do the things you do. I think, or at least I hope, they can't all be to aggravate me, but the result of the endless war raging inside your mind. I would like to know *how*, though. Something on this scale takes a lot more than a few spells and a god's whim."

He considered her for a moment, then looked up. "Do you remember when we first created the stars?"

"Yes," Gaea replied, confused as to what he was getting at now. She remembered feeling proud, amazed by their power. But also disappointed. They looked so lonely, and what a waste of energy they were without something to shine their light upon.

"You insisted we create planets to orbit them. To *worship* them, I believe was the word you used."

"Yes," she whispered again. It made sense.

"Yet you were not happy with those either. 'They lacked' you said and soon after began experimenting with your creations behind my back. Such an unruly child."

I was never a child, she thought, furious, but remained silent.

"I tried to help you. Remember?"

She did, although *help* was not how she would describe his influence. Together they created the first deities, monstrous forces of nature, larger than moons and barely sentient. Soon after they had to create singularities to bind them. Next they tried something completely different, smaller and already bound: Chronodéndrons, sentient trees linked to the very fabric of the Universe and all its realms. But the more they worked together, the more she learnt about herself, and the more she learnt, the better she understood he was not actually helping her. Quite the contrary.

"I really wish you'd stuck to trees, dear."

Gaea winced at the way he spoke.

"You'll never rest until you're alone in the Universe, will you, Chronos?" she said, fearing it was the truth.

"Not alone. I just want it less crowded. I long for quality company, not quantity. You spread yourself too thin, dear. Some of these creatures are not worth the air they breathe."

She had no argument there. Sure, as a mother, she would defend her creations until her last breath, but if she was ever honest with herself, she had to agree with him. There were indeed more than a few runts in her litter.

"All they do is spoil, cheat and eat each other. They blame us for their miserable existences, and rightly so. I don't know about you, but I'm tired of listening to their endless complaints. Enough is enough," he said, the words cast like runes.

Gaea let them wash over her. If all Chronos wanted was to destroy life, he could have unleashed Kali from anywhere in the Universe. There were far more populated worlds out there, with far more destructive and unworthy creatures than gods or Narrum. Why come to the one world where he was not welcome, a world he had so little power in. Why put himself through the trouble of even talking to a mortal in the first place? The God of Time didn't see himself fit to talk to other gods, and suddenly he was friends with dryads? Something did not add up.

"In that case, shouldn't you have stayed at the Stump with your lifeless minions?" she asked.

He gave her a condescending smirk. "You would like that, wouldn't you?"

Stars! He knows about the Tree! No, how can he? It's not possible! Gaea, pull yourself together!

She smiled back with a motherly, condescending smile of her own. "This is pointless, Chronos. You control the Universe no matter what I do. The only thing you can't control is me. Must we keep having this argument again and again, in different worlds, different forms, through the ages until both my life and your time run out?"

"We both know that's not true, dear. I only control the space between life and death. A narrow existence for a God like me."

"But what Kali doesn't take, you will. Time outlasts everything, even memory or death. You'll get what you want not matter what any of us do. You'll always win!"

His expression darkened. "It doesn't feel like winning."

Gaea sighed. She could well relate to the feeling. Maybe that was the fate of every god, no matter how powerful. "Well, you'll be the last one to lose, then."

He shook his head. "It's not good enough, dear.

Besides, there are so many battles yet to fight and so much to gain before losing it all."

Gaea was about to ask him to elaborate on this last piece of intelligence when a satyr came galloping through the trees whooping like an idiot. She recognised the fated Pan immediately, of course. Definitely not one of her proudest creations. The timing of his appearance could not have been worse, though. She was sure Chronos would use him as an example to reinforce his argument. *Damnation.*

"Ah! There she is," the God of Time said with audible vindication.

Gaea turned. Chronos was paying no attention to Pan, who was now spinning in place with Hecate in his arms. His eyes were set on another deity, treading gingerly through the grass. *Psyche.*

INTERLUDE 6

Truth or Dare

I recognise this place, I realise the moment I step through the barrier. The experience itself perturbs me, for I felt nothing. If not for the dramatic change in scenery, I wouldn't know I stepped into a different realm. Not even Loki is this skilled. His illusions are just that, illusions created in the mind of his victims. This, whatever it is, is real. Ahead of me is another barrier of sorts. This one is visibly marked by a shimmer, like the mist above the Boiling Lake, a representation of the immense heat underground, except in this case it's not the heat I'm worried about.

I am at the Narrum's dwelling from where Ideth stole clothes that first night in Aegea's forest. Only a handful of days have passed since then, yet the cabin looks years older. The trees are taller; the grass is greener. There's a shed built next to it that looks new, or at least newer, but no animals or Narrum to be seen.

"Woohhooo!" Pan cheers as he jumps around in the sunlit clearing. "This is pure energy! Can you feel it?"

I can. Whatever is shining above us has been

created specifically for gods. And sure enough, we are not the only ones here.

I sense Gaea's presence first, or at least I think it's her. Her soul appears diluted, for lack of a better term, but at least it's not muffled like Chiron's. I'd have a hard time recognising the Titan under different circumstances. I also sense the uncanny power of an Olympian I don't quite recognise, and the lively spirit of a nymph I know all too well.

"Finally," Ideth says.

I turn to face her. She looks older and, for lack of a better word, wiser. Still fairly young-looking, her large owl-like eyes, always so clever and perceptive, now hold the bottomless depths of wisdom as well. Her hair is shorter and tamed into a ponytail.

Chiron stands at her side on his front legs. The rest of his equine body is supported by one of the Suzerain's gliders, strapped to his waist. His hind legs are limp, their muscles atrophied. Chiron himself has aged drastically. His hair is thin and streaked with grey. He has a beard now, which does not improve his fine features, and he bears the marks of pain and anguish carved deep in his face. "We've been waiting for you, friend," he says. His voice is unchanged.

I take a moment to reconsider the possibility this might be a dream. The alternative is too dreadful to contemplate, for it's only been a couple of days since I last saw them, which means this realm is not only segregated from reality, it's also set in a different time. Only one God has the power to do such a thing. Aedan was right. I should not have entered here alone.

Overconfidence is a god's curse, optimism a mortal's, and I seemed to have been afflicted by both.

I need to get out of here.

"Goddess of the soul. How nice of you join us," says a woman's voice. The tone, akin to a spider greeting the fly in her web, has a ghostly ring to it.

"Hecate!" Pan yelps in delight. "You sorceress, I should have known this was your doing."

Hecate… yes, I remember you. To the naked eye, she's a beautiful woman. As pale as a Dharkan, with blood-red lips, orange hair and snake eyes. She wears a pitch-black dress, clinging to her body as if it's wet, and to my perception, she has three distinct faces. One face remains serious, eyes set on mine, another beams at Pan as he takes her in a heartfelt embrace. The third turns to look in the cabin's direction, where Gaea and Xylo are slowly making their way towards us.

I'm pleasantly surprised and relieved to see the Suzerain's gentle hybrid creature safe and away from the Stump. As always, he appears in my Reach as an absence rather than a presence, but he looks well and at home amongst the trees. I don't see or sense Oreth, though, but I'm glad he's no longer tied to him, at least.

"Did Hades let you out?" Pan asks Hecate.

"I let myself out."

He laughs. "Good for you! Can you do something about my fate?"

"Perhaps." She winks.

Pan whoops again, picks up Hecate and takes her for a spin. "This is the best day ever!"

I met Hecate back when I was still human. She offered to 'numb my pain' after I'd been condemned by the people. Even then, unable to Reach her soul, I'd sensed a disconnect between her words and her intentions. Now I see her soul clearly, and it all makes sense. I doubt there's any good reason for her to be here, using her talents like this.

"Welcome, Psyche," Xylo says, polite as always. "I did not expect to find you here." He spares a glance at the two rowdy Olympians.

I summon a smile. "Hi, Xylo. It's nice to –"

He puts a finger to his lips – such as they are – and takes my hand. I feel a tickle, then a jolt. I try to free myself from his grip. He doesn't let me and pulls me closer instead. He leans down to fix his empty gaze on mine, and immediately I realise three things: First, this is Chronos, the God of Time himself. His cosmic soul is tucked away inside Xylo's artificial body like Pan's is in the satyr's. Second, now that I perceive his soul, I realise it was not Chronos I met after the confrontation with the Suzerain atop the Stump. And third, he absolutely loathes me.

The bitter taste of betrayal mixes with the bile at the back of my throat.

"Fuck."

CHAPTER 30

Gaea

Psyche frowned. Not the sort of frown pre-emptive of a protest, but the far more dangerous reflexive frown of someone who just added a bunch of numbers together and found someone had cheated the result.

"Fuck…" she grumbled when she realised who Xylo really was. Her mind was well guarded, but not her face. A part of Gaea still hoped Psyche had been cunning enough to see Chronos through Xylo's disguise. Then again, she hadn't, so perhaps her expectations had been slightly high regarding the talents of the goddess of the soul. She was supposed to have been Gaea's greatest success, divine proof of the power of Ambrosia. So far, she turned out to be her greatest disappointment.

"You really didn't know?" Gaea said to her. "Seems you're far less clever than you think, girl."

"And far more troublesome." Chronos cupped her chin, his eyes two bottomless pools of contempt. "Is godhood everything you hoped for?"

"Yes," she hissed defiantly.

Xylo snorted.

"Gaea, do you ever wonder why gods felt compelled to create mortals?" he asked, keeping his eyes on Psyche.

Gaea didn't answer. The truth was, she wasn't entirely sure. She gave her creations free will, so when they tried to imitate her, the act, more annoying than flattering, wasn't entirely a surprise.

"They are flawed," he answered. "*You* gave them that flaw."

"Which flaw are you referring to, Chronos? The will or the ability to create?" she replied contemptuously.

"Both. Gods have immense power, and yet their powers cancel each other. It's not an accident, but a necessity to maintain order in the Universe. *My* order. To cope with their frustration, they need constant validation. Of course, being gods, they can't worship anyone but themselves, so they had to create something more predisposed to the task. Mortals have no power, but they were made to believe that if they worship us hard enough, we will gift them scraps of ours." He considered Psyche again with scorn. "I suppose some do. But scraps will never be enough for those cursed with souls. They'll always want more. The evolution of mortals back to gods was inevitable, with or without Ambrosia. Although, without would have been preferable." Xylo's mossy eyes slitted in Gaea's direction. "I saw it coming. From the moment you started down this path. That is why I forbade you to waste your talent, *dear*. Not out of spite or fear or jealousy. I was trying to save you and the Universe from yourself." He shook his head. "And now, look where you brought us. There's no deity with a talent to cancel hers. I wonder why that is." His gaze locked back on Psyche and hers on him. Gaea had to give it to the apotheosized goddess. She had nerves of tungsten.

"I earned my power," Psyche said.

"Is that so?" he said stiffly.

"Yes."

The way he stared at her then made Gaea feel sick. But Psyche, her expression now as blank as her mind, didn't even blink.

"You are wrong," he thundered. "You're an accident, a mistake, an anomaly born of chaos and disobedience." He glowered at Gaea again, then at Hecate. "How did she get in?"

"I-I don't know, Chronos, apologies. It's difficult to tailor a curse for a god you've never met," Hecate said. "I only had the memory of her mortal soul. She's changed."

The witch lies, Gaea noticed.

Psyche bit her cheek. "Well then, since I have no interest in being part of this… cult, or whatever the fuck this is, I'll see myself out." She turned to leave.

"Wait," Chronos commanded.

Psyche obeyed.

"Since you *are* here, you might make yourself useful – set him free," Chronos said.

Psyche turned around and adjusted the lily in her hair. "Who?"

The sun seemed to dim around them. A rumble of irritation rolled in Xylo's throat before he spoke. "You forget yourself, goddess of the soul. Worse, you forget who *I* am. I was there, by your side, when you did it. You cannot hide your actions from me, even in this form, not when I'm that close."

"I don't know what you're talking about."

She's a better liar than Hecate, but still a liar, Gaea mused, intrigued.

There was a long pause.

Xylo stepped closer to the goddess of the soul. "Set. Him. Free."

Psyche breathed heavily with barely contained anger, or perhaps fear, it was hard to tell now. She bit her cheek a few more times, then her lips. Her eyes darted in every direction, searching for an escape, a solution, anything.

'Gaea,' Psyche said straight to her mind. '*I could use your help.*'

I don't know what he wants! Gaea protested. *Whatever it is, you'd better give it to him.*

With one heavy pull, Xylo ripped Psyche's dress to shreds.

"Pick it up," he said.

It took Gaea a moment to understand he was not talking about the ruined dress but something concealed within it.

Psyche, chest heaving, eyes wide, jaw tensed, bent to pick up a pendant shaped like a butterfly. Gaea had seen it before. First around Ileana's neck, then Aedan's. She hadn't understood its significance. After all, trinkets were not her speciality. But now... now she did.

Oh, Psyche. What have you done?

INTERLUDE 7

Out of control

I let Loki in. Not only would he kill me otherwise but I have no choice if I want to survive on the other side of this barrier. I immediately regret it, of course. Loki's anger is a barrier in itself; it overwhelms the senses and hinders the mind. I push through it while he's still distracted trying to get his bearings within my own being, and again, I wish I hadn't. Behind the anger there's so much longing and sadness and pain, it's maddening. Flaming sun, I'd rather deal with the anger. I suppose he does too.

'*Ready?*' he asks inside my mind.

Yes, I reply. Although, *resigned* is a more accurate answer. We step through.

The light is blinding and the temperature just short of unbearable, but I'm not burning. Not yet, anyway. I wait for my eyes to adjust. There's a cabin not far ahead, similar to Ulcan's but larger, maybe older, and a shed annexed to it. I hear voices in the clearing: Psyche, Gaea, Ideth (how did she get here?) and another woman I don't recognise. She's quite unusual-looking: White as snow with flaming hair, long limbs and sharp curves, a bit like Ileana, but unlike Ileana she moves gracefully, like a spirit in the Underworld.

Who's that? I ask Loki.

'*Hecate. The Olympian goddess of magic. It's her will holding the barrier.*'

I have to give it to the Olympians. Their pantheon has a god for everything.

They are not alone: Chiron is here too, by Ideth's side as usual, although he's no longer winged or even able to stand, apparently. Xylo – of all creatures – stands next to Gaea, looming over Psyche.

Are they… is this real? I ask Loki. Of all creatures, he should know the difference.

'*Unfortunately,*' he says.

Where is Hel?

'*Hiding, if she knows what's good for her. This way,*' Loki says, forcing me to sneak around the cabin. I hate it when the gods do that. Technically, they should not be able to make a Dharkan do something they don't want to do. A rule easily circumvented if the action is simple enough. After all, we do let them take control of our bodies, and the more a god gets familiar with their host, the easier it is for them to control it.

Now what? I ask him, crouched behind a shrub, feeling like a nimrod.

There is no immediate reply, just a change in position to get a better view of the group.

'*Now, Aedan, we wait,*' Loki says.

I assumed you had a plan.

'*Such changeable things, plans,*' Loki muses, straining to eavesdrop on the conversation. '*You rely on one plan too much and you risk missing out on the best opportunities.*'

"So that's it? We wait. For what?" I grumble in a whisper.

'*The right moment. Be patient. And quiet,*' he adds with impatience.

I don't like waiting. Never did, and I doubt I ever will. I'm not sure why. After all, for most Dharkan, waiting is not much different from simply being. We even use the same word for both. My father once told me restlessness would be my downfall. It was one of the last things he said to me. Perhaps he was right. Perhaps Loki is too.

I focus my attention back on the group. Psyche is cursing; nothing unusual there. The hostility carried along the conversation between her, Gaea, and Xylo escalates. Xylo talks the loudest, silencing the women, and I can feel their apprehension from here. I never trusted the creature. Not just because he's the Suzerain's creation, but I'd never trust anything that is part tree. He's even more creepy talking than he is silent. *Burning light, imagine if trees could talk.*

Loki chuckles at my thoughts and lets me know with absolute certainty that some trees *can* talk, the knowledge shared as an image of himself talking to one and it talking back. Flaming sun. This will give me nightmares for sure.

I cast my gaze around the clearing. *Where is this Chronos, anyway?* I ask to take my mind off talking trees. By the way the gods refer to the God of Time, I've always imagined him as a Kraken. We are in a forest, though, so maybe a Wyvern would be more likely.

'*Right next to her,*' Loki sighs.

I blink. *Xylo?*

I can't tell if I'm more concerned or annoyed by this. On one hand, there's no point trying to take his Prana. Like the Suzerain, the creature is empty of it, but he was not immune to Zeus' lightning bolts.

'*No,*' Loki warns, reading my thoughts.

Why not?

'*It would give away our location, and besides, it's not enough.*'

Loki shakes my head. '*Oh, Psyche, I wish you hadn't done that,*' he thinks morosely. Not in disappointment, not exactly. The feeling is closer to sadness or sympathy.

What did she do?

Xylo rips off her clothes in one blunt motion.

"What in the light?" I try to intervene. Loki doesn't let me.

She can take it, he says.

She bends to pick up something from the fabric: the butterfly necklace.

Psyche closes her fist around the pendant, hands shaking, lips tight, brows furrowed. She spares a glance at Gaea and the others watching her, then tilts her head down and lets out a defeated breath.

A darkness, deeper than anything I've ever seen, appears between her and Xylo. It expands and moves like mist, buzzing like a swarm of locusts as it takes shape. The shape of a man: Bearded, ageless, lean and handsome in an effigy sort of way. I recognise him – *Zeus.* Psyche lifts her face and opens her hand. The necklace is black as onyx again.

"Huh," I say, slightly numbed by what I'm witnessing. "I guess she wasn't lying about that, after all."

'*Fuck. Fuck, fuck, fuck. Do you have any weapons with you, Aedan?*' Loki is rummaging inside my satchel even before he finishes asking the question.

"No," I say bleakly.

Loki freezes. '*But you brought this.*'

Something changes in his emotions. They go from dread to a sort of elation, excitement even. I feel a grin tugging at my lips as he holds the horn in my hand, and I'm not amused.

"It's not a weapon," I say.

'*This is the ultimate weapon, Aedan. An Elysian horse's horn can cancel a god's design. Any god, even Chronos.*'

"Humph." *No wonder the gods were after it.* A thought occurs to me. *It was you! You broke the shelf.*

Genuine surprise radiates through our bond. '*Aren't you a clever boy.*'

Psyche is cursing at Xylo again, while Gaea is doing something to the apparition between them. Zeus looks solid now, real. He collapses on the ground, unmoving.

'*Listen to me very carefully, Aedan,*' Loki says, holding Cornus' horn in one hand and a dagger I don't recognise in the other. '*I need you not to fight me on this.*'

On what?

The pendant in Psyche's hand begins to glow. Xylo hits her hard enough to force her to join the King of Olympus on the ground. She doesn't stay down, though. She gets up and spits a mouthful of blood at the tree man. The pendant glows brighter. Xylo lifts his hand again, and I'm sure this time he's going to crush her.

Loki can see it too. *'I have a plan, Aedan. But you need to do* exactly *what I want.'*

INTERLUDE 8

Price or Prize

"He's going to need a body," I say to Gaea.

She looks more distressed than Odin had under Fenrir's predatory scrutiny. "Psyche, you should have told me."

"So you'd be the one bullying me into giving up my prize instead of him?" I nod at Xylo, who still glowers at me. "Besides, I told you many times that I did not kill Zeus. You just chose not to believe me."

Gaea's about to say something but has enough sense to save her energy and get to work on Zeus' new body.

I grip the now empty pendant in my hand. I didn't realise it was a Soulstone until it began to change, and even then I had no control over it, locked in Ileana's body. The realisation that the butterfly was never meant to protect me from the God of Time was a bitter one, but I thought it was Loki's soul or Prometheus himself, the one I carried into this world, not Chronos. Then again, Chronos' actual soul would never fit inside the stone. I just brought enough of his will to animate Xylo and cause all this trouble. He would never have been able to interfere in Niflheim beyond the Chronodéndron otherwise. Once the Soulstone was empty, its purpose should have ended there. But how could I let something so precious go to waste?

I tighten my fist around it and curse. Gaea, Chiron, Ideth, Xylo, Hecate… they all have their eyes on me. Some with understanding, most with confusion. I've only ever done this twice before, but the action comes as easily as breathing. Same as it did the second time, in the split second I had to decide whether to let Aedan take Zeus' soul or not.

Xylo's wooden features contort into a cruel smirk. "What do you think you are you doing, Butterfly?" he asks, taunting. "Trying to take my soul?"

"Not *your* soul," I say, struggling to understand what I'm dealing with.

Xylo falters, and his mossy eyes narrow, no longer gleaming with amusement. "Stop it." There is no mirth or taunt in his tone now.

He hits me hard across the cheek. The blow knocks me to the ground. My mouth fills with blood. A tooth comes loose. Still holding the pendant, I stand up and spit both blood and tooth in his face.

He's still for a moment, resisting my will, then punches me square in the chest. The blow sends me flying backwards across the clearing, sternum, ribs and spine crushed by the impact. I grind my teeth, unable to breathe or overcome the blinding pain, trying desperately to keep holding onto the soul in my grip, willing it inside the Soulstone.

"I said, stop!" Xylo charges in my direction, and I know if he touches me, I'm doomed. It was foolish to try to take back his soul by force, but then again, I wouldn't be me if I hadn't tried.

Someone cuts across his path at great speed, knocking him sideways on the grass before he has a chance to reach me.

Aedan? I see the Dharkan through the pain-induced haze. He's not burning. And he's holding a dagger. I recognise it. *It won't work,* I think. But of course, he can't hear my thoughts. With a guttural growl, he stabs Xylo in the head. Nothing happens. Except now the God of Time is no longer intent on murdering me, but him. And then I see it. In his other hand, concealed behind his back, Aedan holds Cornus' horn, and in one swift motion plunges it in Xylo's eye.

The tree man falters, falling over, momentarily stunned, then he pulls the horn out and shatters it to dust before Aedan's disbelieving eyes. I can't tell if the horn affected the God of Time or his host in any way, but it did unfortunately sever my grip on his soul.

"No..." I moan, releasing the pendant, and focus all my energy into fixing my broken body.

"Everyone avert your eyes now." Hel's voice comes from right behind me. She's been there a while, concealed beneath Hades' cloak, witnessing all and putting a lot of effort into not freezing everything and everyone around her. And she's not alone.

I've never met Medusa but I'd recognise her mutated soul anywhere. Cursed before my time, she's exactly as I imagined her. Her soul as coiled as the snakes in her hair, her power something most gods would envy. Not exactly a goddess and clearly not a mortal, Medusa is a creature unlike any other. She runs in Xylo's direction, snakes hissing, ready to strike.

I roll over and do as Hel says. Hecate advances in my direction, holding a whirlwind of energy between her hands. Chronos' soul might be hard to handle, but hers is not. I can send it straight to the Underworld with one thought.

Hecate, don't make me do it.

"Get out of the way!" she shouts. Not at me, but Aedan, who is about to stab Xylo again with the dagger. I will not let her hurt the Dharkan, either. Fortunately, he obeys just as she flings the ball of energy in his direction. Too late Xylo understands her intention and, still stunned by either the dagger or the horn's effects, fails to defend himself.

Hecate's hex wraps him like a membrane, binding him in place. It stretches but does not tear. He roars and curses in vain. Medusa, now standing in front of him, removes her goggles.

He stares at her and laughs. "Insolent creature. You have no power over this flesh. It is not alive."

"No. But close enough." She bores her gaze into his.

"You'll pay for this," he says to Hecate as he struggles with the cursed veil.

"I already have," she says, shielding her gaze.

"I freed you!" he insists, so far not one bit affected by Medusa's stare.

"Only when it suited you," Hecate replies vengefully.

He laughs harder. A terrifying sound. "So be it."

The world begins to shake.

The barrier around us collapses. Chiron cries out and falls from the glider.

"Chiron!" Ideth's kneels by his side, a white light glowing between him and her palms. I'm impressed with the devious nymph. I always knew she had power, just didn't understand how much until now. Sadly, it won't be enough to save the centaur. His fate became legend a long time ago.

My grandmother once told me a story about the kind and wise Titan, Chiron, tutor of heroes and half brother of Zeus, who when shot by a poisoned arrow, unable to heal or to die, gave up his soul to free Prometheus.

'*Psyche, you have my permission. You know what to do. Do it,*' he prays to me.

I wish my grandmother had told me about my part in his sacrifice. Then again… she too died long before I was born.

The sound of green wood crackling in a fire fills the clearing. Xylo blinks and stares at his hands. "No… it's not possible." He turns to me. Then Gaea. "What did you do?"

"I gave Xylo life." She exhales despondently. Stars, she looks ancient and barely alive herself.

"No!" Chronos roars. "Zeus! Do something."

The king of Olympus doesn't reply, still pretending to be unconscious on the ground.

Lying a few feet away with a clear line of sight to his face, I'm probably the only one who sees his triumphant sneer.

EPILOGUE

Agnar waits by the Chronodéndron.

It's been days since Arianh disappeared through the tree after fighting the mortally wounded Chiron for the Ambrosia buried there. Days since Hades, Lord of the Underworld, came for the wounded Titan. Days since the Nephilim arrived from the sky and landed on the Stump, marking the beginning of an end he now remembers so well.

Agnar is used to waiting. After all, his entire life has been about waiting. He had to wait to grow up and become a man so he could leave the fated settlement in the Gharb. After that, he'd waited years in the caves, studying the past, the gods, other races and other worlds. Then he waited for an opportunity to be free of Alek's shadow and then to be free of Odin's soul. Many years he'd waited, dormant within himself, dreaming of the day when he would not need to wait any longer.

He waits alone, but he's not lonely, nor is he idle: he thinks, he remembers, he understands what he's learnt. Odin left him all the information he needs to change things and plenty more besides. It's stagger-ing the amount of knowledge a deity can gather over the aeons. Alek always said knowledge is power, and by that measure, Agnar figures he's the most powerful mortal in Aegea, and it is all because he waited.

He wishes he had not brought Arianh to Yewlow, knowing what she would do. Wishes he had stopped her from digging up the resin and eating it. He wishes he hadn't lied to her. But how is one supposed to change events if there's always the same characters in play, performing the same actions?

He hopes he said enough to prepare her. He wonders if she's made it, if she's all right, if she remembers him as well as he remembers her. He waits, he wishes, he hopes, and he wonders. And now, after days of waiting, he fears.

It should not have taken her this long.

He asks Yewlow for information, for a glimpse of Arianh's fate. The tree ignores him.

Exhausted, Agnar sleeps. And he dreams. He always loved to dream.

The entire world trembles, and he's awake. The tree shimmers, the spirals in the bark turn into swirls, the spearhead-shaped leaves vibrate on their branches. The sound of wood straining under the pressure of centuries fills his ears, and then there she is: her face is different, her body is older, curvier, riper, but it's her all right. Beautiful as always, Agnar would recognise the queen anywhere in any time, even when she no longer recognises herself.

He smiles. "Welcome back, *Ann*."

She returns the smile.

ACKNOWLEDGEMENTS

I'd like to thank my husband Dave for his constant support and encouragement throughout this project, and my friends, especially Callum, Cris and Maria, for continuing to read the series.

A huge thank you to everyone who pledged in the Kickstarter campaign to help finance The Dharkan and Nephilim's Hex audiobooks.

I'd like to once again thank my editor, Lisa Gilliam, for her patience and professionalism. My mother, for learning English so she could read my books, Locke for always being there, and myself for not giving up after many disappointments, months of lockdown and years of depressing weather.

9 781916 140271